The Queen's Intelligencer

The Shadow of the Axe: Book One
A Robert Poley Novel

PETER TONKIN

For: Cham, Guy, Cat, Mark and Lana

As always.

CONTENTS

Chapters 1 – 11
Afterward

'The Earl of Essex was fetched off by a trick.'

Sir Walter Raleigh, confessing to Robert Tounson, Dean of Westminster, on the eve of his execution, Wednesday, October 28th 1618 (Julian calendar).

1

The seven horsemen rode at a fast canter southward along the mud-covered Roman road. It was just after nine on a stormy autumn morning and their cloaks flapped behind them like soggy banners. The fact that they were not at full gallop belied the urgency of their mission. That was caused by bad luck and bad planning; a familiar combination, given the identity of their leader. Their horses were a job-lot obtained at hap and hazard from the stables closest to the ferry-landing in Lambeth on the South Bank of the Thames. They were by no means the quality of mounts that the impatient riders were used to. But, as had been observed in a recent popular play, 'needs must when the Devil drives…'

The seven of them had set out at full gallop as soon as they were in the saddle. But had been forced to slow before they reached the broad common at Clapham, their horses winded and threatening to fall lame. Every man paced his own ride as best he could therefore. Each trying to keep up with the rest while their commander pushed on relentlessly. Normal rules of precedence perforce gave way to necessity as first one took the lead and then another. Whoever was riding to the rear was showered in splashes of filthy water and clods of mud kicked up by the hooves in front, no matter how elevated his social station.

1

Now, however, as they swung to their right, they were forced into single file. The ground beneath their horses' hooves became, briefly, less muddy as soil was replaced by stone. One after the other, they thundered over Wandle Bridge. The river ran lively and in spate close below, brimming its banks after two soaking months at the end of an unseasonably saturated summer. A water mill, turned by its torrential force, splashed and groaned nearby upstream. No sooner had they crossed the bridge than they were forced to follow another twist in the otherwise deserted road, but at least they could ride in a group once more, each taking courage from the closeness of his companions. The highway turned westwards to skirt the remains of what once had been a great park. The estate's boundary walls, like the buildings just visible at its heart, were overgrown ruins now.

As they passed this, Henry Cuffe wiped a hand down his streaming face and mud-clotted beard. Then he shouted over the noise of the wind and the water, the hoof-beats and the jangle of tack, 'That is Merton Priory. Or so it was when it stood. Famed because Archbishop Saint Thomas Becket studied there, and Nicholas Breakspear who later became Pope Adrian IV. Both under King Henry II.' Even at full bellow, Cuffe's cultured tones betrayed him to be highly educated. Just as the fact that he was the only one not wearing a sword showed him to be a secretary not a soldier. He was a Fellow of Trinity College by the time he was fifteen; a tutor and Master at Merton College soon after, which explained his knowledge of the ruined Priory which shared its name; a lecturer in antique languages at

Queen's and Regius Professor of Greek to the university. All of which he had been before he quit Oxford in his early thirties five years ago. He had headed for London in search of more lucrative and powerful positions. Such as the one he held now – ignorant though he currently was of the deadly dangers that could accompany it. His learned observation, however, was designed to take his mind off the enterprise they were engaged on and the incredible risks resulting from its likely outcome. And, in truth, to take it off the weather as well. This was the kind of relentless downpour he had hoped to leave behind in Ireland when he and his companions came east to England four short days ago.

'Merton Priory indeed. Famed these days for its utter destruction under Her Majesty's father, King Henry VIII and his creature Thomas Cromwell,' grunted Gelly Meyrick, his cynical words made to sing by his Welsh accent, his voice trembling with tension too. A swashbuckler, soldier and swordsman of many years' standing, he paid no notice to the filth on his face and his hooded cloak; but he was not immune to the relentlessly mounting pressure they were all feeling as they got nearer and nearer to their dangerous objective. Every now and then he would ride with his reins in his right fist while his left rested on the hilt of the rapier at his hip.

'Much to the injury of the local peasantry, no doubt' observed the Irish lord Christopher St. Lawrence, shaking his red head sadly despite the danger into which it put his saturated hat with its bedraggled feather. 'Many of whom lost employment at the priory thereby and any chance of help or relief of their poverty at the same time. At least so it is at home.' The tenth Baron Howth was a new addition to their leader's closest companions. He had joined the army only a few months ago and the inner circle more recently still. Now he pulled his Irish green plaid cloak tighter about his shoulders and shivered. Cuffe wondered whether the fiery baron with his notoriously short temper was beginning to regret his association with the rest of them. And with their charismatic leader.

'It rests in her Majesty's hands to take care of her poor now not only as sovereign but as the defender of the faith in all her realms,' added Thomas Gerard, with a shrug. 'Now that the old church and its institutions are no more.'

'In the hands of Cecil and the Privy Council more like,' sneered Gelly Meyrick, no friend to either the Secretary or the Council. 'Each one more grasping than the last.'

In almost any other company this would have been a dangerous conversation; one leading to the Fleet prison or the Tower; perhaps even to Tyburn and the gallows there. But in this company such treasonous blasphemy could pass for everyday banter.

'But her Majesty has lately instituted laws for the succour of the poor,' said their leader, Robert Devereux, the Earl of Essex; who was almost impossible to pick out of the crowd for he was as wet and dirty as the rest. And he was content to be so – a soldier among soldiers - in spite of his importance at court and his favour in Her Majesty's eyes. Importance and favour he was carrying southward along the road the Romans called Stane Street in hopes that they would stand the test in spite of the fact that he was in disobedience of his Sovereign's explicit commands. And by no means for the first time. 'Don't forget that,' he insisted. 'Her Majesty can be generous, when her mood and disposition are aligned. And let us pray that they are so this morning.' He kicked his mount fiercely in the ribs, raking its flanks with his spurs and it leaped into a grudging gallop once more.

Essex's tone as well as his words and action ended the brief discussion. But Henry Cuffe suspected that he was by no means alone in wondering distractedly whether Her Majesty's Council would ever release sufficient funds to make Her Majesty's Poor Laws actually bring relief to those who needed it most. In the absence, as St. Lawrence had observed, of the Old Church and its charitable institutions. Independently of the alignment of Her Majesty's mood and disposition.

They hadn't lingered in London for long, but he had seen at first glance how the streets were littered with the starving poor hopelessly begging from near-destitute citizens, a situation that had worsened during the months since he followed the Earl across the Irish Sea to war. And recent experience with Essex's forces in Ireland suggested that support and finance were likely to be insufficient rather than generous or, indeed, adequate. Even when the support was needed for an army which was in the field. Fighting to control a country risen in revolution. A near-universal uprising led by Catholic traitors supported by the Spanish and Italians at the behest of the Pope, so that the security of the realm stood in deadly danger.

A fact that lay at the root of their mission this stormy

morning of Michaelmas Eve, Friday, 28th of September in this last year of the century. A time when change was in the air and the promise of it on almost every tongue. Except one: for Her Majesty had made time appear to stand still, certainly in the way she presented her own apparently ageless person. And by making any plans for her death and talk of succession close to a capital offence.

*

At the end of the ruined estate, the road turned south once more. It re-joined the ancient highway which stretched before them, straight as the flight of an arrow. Cuffe spurred his mount back into a reluctant gallop in pursuit of his master and the others. He steadied its head to face along the way towards the distant port the Romans called Noviomagus Reginorum, named as Chichester since the Norman Doomsday Book. He was the last of the group once more so he lowered his head, as his wise mount was doing, rounded his shoulders and tried to calculate how best to maintain close contact with his companions without being showered by yet more of their filth.

'You there!' called an imperious voice from behind him. 'Make way!'

Cuffe turned to look over his shoulder and there, close behind, was another wayfarer wrapped in a cloak, astride a horse that looked to have all the fleetness of foot and depth of wind that Cuffe's mount lacked. The hood of the cloak held the stranger's hat firmly in place and a strip of cloth covered his mouth and nose, protecting it from the mud and the rain as surely as it concealed his identity. Even so, Cuffe found the voice and the half-hidden face vaguely familiar.

'Make way,' the stranger called again. 'Make way all of you! I am on the Queen's business and you must let me pass!'

Cuffe amenably slowed his horse, pulling out of the way and the stranger galloped past, then began to push through the rest of the group. They each pulled aside on his bellowed command, gathering together once again in his wake. 'Did you recognise him?' Gelly Meyrick asked the group in general.

It was Essex who replied, 'That was Thomas Grey. I'd lay my life on it.'

'Grey is no friend of ours,' said Meyrick at once. 'Not since the Earl of Southampton put him in charge of the marshal for leading a mounted attack against the Irish rebels without his orders as General of Horse. A humiliation I doubt Grey will ever forget or forgive.'

Sir Thomas Gerrard turned to Essex and said at once, 'Let me go after him and talk to him. He has declared himself Cecil's man and is likely about Cecil's business more than the Queen's. But it may be that I can at least convince him to talk to you directly. I'm sure if he will do so, he will agree to give you precedence, my Lord, and hold back so you can reach Her Majesty first. And unannounced, as you had planned.'

He spurred after Lord Grey before Essex could reply and caught up with him after a few moments.

Grey reined to a halt and turned. He pulled down the covering and revealed his familiar face to his erstwhile companion in Essex's Irish army. 'Well?' he demanded.

7

'My Lord, I beg you will speak with the Earl,' said
Gerard.

'No!' snapped Grey. 'I have important business at court.
I have said.'

'Then I pray you to let my Lord of Essex ride before so
that he may bring first news of his return himself,' said
Gerard, his tone making clear that he saw Grey as a junior
officer if not of lower social rank; that he was unused to
begging favours of underlings in this manner.

'Does he *desire* it?' asked Grey, his own tone little better
than a sneer at the thought that the great Earl of Essex, who
had seen him humiliated in front of the entire army at the
hand of his acolyte Southampton, should be begging for
favours now.

'No,' answered Sir Thomas, understanding Grey's tone
only too well. 'Nor, I think, will he ever desire anything at
your hands.'

'Then I have business at court,' said Grey. He pulled up
his scarf, turned his horse and spurred on.

Gerard also turned and trotted back to the rest with the
news of his conversation – though the fact that Grey was
galloping into the distance spoke volumes for itself.

'God's death!' St. Lawrence shouted, instantly enraged
at Gerard's report. He dragged his rapier half out of its
scabbard. 'Let me go after the preening popinjay! I will
kill him where he sits. And, after him that foul and twisted
toad his master, Secretary Cecil!'

Essex was tempted to let his hot-headed companion
loose. He took a moment to think. But eventually he
decided, 'No Christopher. I will have no violence done to

Her Majesty's servants or her servants' servants. Especially not in her palace. Particularly not on the day of my return.'

And so the bedraggled group rode on along the ancient Roman road toward the great palace of Nonsuch. And towards the Queen who was not yet awake or preparing to dress, don her wig and apply the layers of paint and powder she needed in order to face yet another weary day as the ageless Gloriana.

*

Sir Thomas Grey, 15th Baron Grey de Wilton, dismounted at the Court Gate Post, handed the reins of his winded horse to a waiting stable lad and strode into Nonsuch. It was soon after half past nine in the morning and almost all of the vast palace was up and a-bustle. He knew the intricacies of the place's labyrinthine layout and where his objective was to be found: Robert Cecil, Secretary of State and Lord Privy Seal, successor alike to his father Lord Burghley in power and the late Sir Francis Walsingham in spycraft. Not only did he control the Council, he also sat at the centre of a web of agents, couriers and intelligencers stretching from north of Edinburgh to east of the Ottoman Empire, from Cambridge to Cadiz.

Now Grey found him sitting warming his feet by the fire in the private chamber normally assigned to him when he was attending Her Majesty at Nonsuch. On a table beside him sat a bowl of milk which was steaming gently and some crusts of bread. 'Welcome, Thomas,' said Cecil as a servant held the door open for Grey. 'What news?'

Cecil was in his thirty third year, which was young to be already the most powerful man in the land; one of the most powerful in Europe, even though he was his father's second son and his elder brother now bore the title 2nd Baron Burghley. His slim figure with its slight hunch was clad as usual in black. Only the thin ruff was white. His long face was pallid, its colour, or lack thereof, emphasised by his dark brown hair and thin, pointed beard. The agonies of his childhood – from being overlooked and patronised as second son to the ministrations of a series of physicians employed by an upright, athletic, deeply disappointed father to straighten his back and make his dwarfish figure stand tall – had forged some kind of iron in his will. His time at St John's College Cambridge and studying Disputation at the Sorbonne polished his intelligence and his purpose. Honed his ruthless streak to razor-sharpness.

'Essex is just behind me, riding with half a dozen of his closest companions.' Grey shrugged off his wet, mud-spattered cloak and draped it over a chair near the fire. He put his hat and scarf on top of it. His eyes never left Cecil's long, pale face.

There was an instant of silence. 'A small group? Not his Irish army or a regiment from it?' Cecil's slightly bulbous brown eyes rested on him, their gaze almost luminous, at its most piercing.

'Not with him now. Not yet. He has left more men under the command of Southampton in London. How many more I can't say. But he's in too great a hurry to wait for a larger force to be organised. And of course a regiment would have to march here in any case.'

'Not a regiment of horse. But it would be slow work bringing so many horses across the river – either by the Bridge or the Horse Ferry.'

'He came over by ferry himself - from Westminster to Lambeth. Hired horses there and came galloping south as though the Devil was at his heels. I dogged his footsteps on a faster horse; unsuspected until I overtook him on the road.'

'We need to know how many are under Southampton in London. Especially as he is General of Horse.' Cecil reached across the table. Beside the steaming bowl was a small bell. He lifted it and rang. 'How many more may be following on behind. And what Essex in fact purposes by this.'

'He says he wishes to talk with Her Majesty,' continued Grey. 'His man Thomas Gerard asked me to yield the road to him so he could come to her unannounced.'

'Did he so?' Cecil fell into a calculating silence.

The door to the room whispered open. A servant stood awaiting his command.

'Bring me…' said Cecil, then he paused. Took a moment more, his mind clearly racing. Came to a decision. 'Bring me Robert Poley,' he commanded. The servant turned to go. 'Wait,' ordered Cecil. The man froze as though the quiet word had been one of the Queen's shrillest commands. 'Thomas, have you broken your fast? Do you require anything?'

'No, thank you,' answered Grey.

'Very well.' Cecil turned back to the servant. 'You may

go. And fetch me Robert Poley.'

The servant bowed and disappeared.

Grey shifted his steaming cloak to one side and, at a nod from Cecil, he sat. '*Go fetch Robert Poley*?' he asked. 'Not, *Go warn the Queen that the Earl of Essex is on the way*?'

'I thought you said,' mused Cecil, his voice little more than a whisper, 'that My Lord of Essex wishes to come upon Her Majesty unannounced.'

'That's what Gerard told me.' Grey paused, frowning. 'Do you mean to permit such a thing?'

Cecil's lips stretched into the ghost of a smile; an expression without the slightest hint of humour. 'Just because the Earl has been so precipitate in leaping into action does not mean that we should be equally hasty in countering him.'

Grey opened his mouth to ask for a further explanation when the door opened and Robert Poley stepped into the private room. Grey looked at the man. He had heard whispers about Poley and the uses he had been put to in the relentless defence of the Realm. Even nowadays he could be found in the Clink Prison as readily as Constantinople or King James' Scottish court. Depending on whether he was acting as agent provocateur or courier, informer or intelligencer. But this was the first time he had knowingly seen him, and it seemed to the young baron an ideal time to take the measure of the man about whom he knew at once so much and so little.

*

Poley was 44 years old. He had been working in the

English intelligence service since his days as a lowly sizar at Clare College, Cambridge, the better part of thirty years ago. He was that·strange but priceless chameleon, a Catholic and a patriot willing to put his sovereign above his soul. An unrivalled asset to the first Lord Burghley and to Sir Francis Walsingham; and, one generation later, to the men who replaced them: Cecil and Sir Thomas Walsingham. He was of middle height, though also of erect carriage. His build was slight but looked strong enough, perhaps athletic. His eyes and his hands were large. His hair and beard were russet. He might have been accounted handsome. Other than that there was little striking or memorable about him. Which qualities seemed to Grey to be perfect in an intelligencer.

Poley paused. The door whispered shut behind him. He glanced from one man to the other. His gaze was piercing. Intelligent, thought Grey. 'He's on his way?' he asked, his voice as soft as Cecil's.

'He will be here within the half-hour,' confirmed Cecil.

'So soon?' asked Poley.

'Indeed.' Cecil nodded.

'Is he alone?' wondered Poley, cutting straight to the heart of the matter, thought Grey – just as Cecil had.

'He has some half a dozen riding with him,' shrugged Cecil. 'On hired horses, apparently.'

'Anyone of account?' Poley's steady gaze rested on Grey.

'Swordsmen and swashbucklers for the most part,' Grey answered. 'They all rode well armed. His secretary Cuffe is there.'

'And his steward Gelly Meyrick I would guess.' Poley nodded. 'A swashbuckler born and bred.'

'Apart from them, Thomas Gerard and the new man Christopher St Lawrence,' said Grey. 'That's all I recognised.'

'Not Southampton, then,' said Poley. 'If he's not on the way here with Essex, he'll be in London with whoever else Essex brought across from Ireland. Cavalry I would hazard as Southampton is General of Horse. Such horses as they have winded and rendered useless after their ride to the city from the west coast. Hence the hired horses. It's certain that he would never have come with only half a dozen to watch his back and I would suppose we may expect the others to follow soon enough, as soon as their horses are rested.' He paused. His gaze grew distant as he became lost thought. 'But not his Irish army. Not yet, at least. An army is a slow and unwieldy thing. And the Earl is in a hurry, you say?' He paused as Grey nodded his confirmation. Then he said, quietly, as though the words were treasonous, 'My Lord of Essex could be Bolingbroke reborn as it said in the book *A Conference about the Succession* that was dedicated to him. And in Haywood's *Life of King Henry IV*, also dedicated to him. But do we really believe he wishes to play Bolingbroke's part in truth and take the throne for himself as Bolingbroke took Richard II's? All because a book examining the matter of the succession was dedicated to him – likely without his knowledge – and another purporting to tell a true history of the same events?'

'The *Conference* was dedicated to him and banned at

once,' said Grey. 'As is all conversation about the succession.'

'It was not banned swiftly enough even so,' said Cecil. 'And the succession is a matter that simply cannot be ignored, especially if My Lord of Essex has decided to take an active part in the debate.'

Poley nodded once and continued, 'And we can ask Master Heywood yet again what he meant by his *Henry IV*, for he is still in the Tower. But more than Bolingbroke, the Earl is seen in some quarters even as Her Majesty's grandfather the Earl of Richmond coming out of Wales to snatch her throne as though she were Richard III as well as Richard II.' He paused and Grey marvelled at the man's adroitness. All the world called Richard III 'Crouchback'. But not Poley; especially not when talking to Robert Cecil, who had a crouchback of his own. But the intelligencer continued smoothly, 'He may have half a dozen with him now and half a hundred waiting in London, but he has an army across the water and he has paid for it out of his own purse and knighted everyone he plans to count upon. He must mean to push the matter forward, albeit slowly if he plans to bring the whole force home behind him. But still, we must prepare as though he designs to use it.'

'But what does he mean in the meantime? That's the question,' whispered Cecil. 'What does he mean this morning?'

'To talk with Her Majesty,' said Grey.

'He will have to come upon her unannounced, then,' said Poley. 'Given any warning of his arrival or intentions, Her Majesty will prevent him. She will wall herself around with her soldiers led by Sir Walter Raleigh as Captain of the Guard, then deploy the entire Council against him – as many as are in attendance here. He is returning from abject failure after all, and without royal permission. Indeed, in direct contravention of Her Majesty's most specific orders.'

'And yet…' said Cecil. 'And yet…'

Poley glanced at Grey, then back at Cecil. 'And yet, each time he has thrown himself upon her mercy, Her Majesty has forgiven him everything,' he observed. 'He will be let through Raleigh's guards. The wisdom of the Council will stand as nothing against him. When all is said and done, he is like the lost son from Our Lord's parable returning to his rejoicing father and Her Majesty will kill the fatted calf for him. Again.'

'Unless we can assist Her Majesty in understanding how dangerous Essex might actually be. Unless he is reined in and confined,' said Cecil.

'But how will you do such a thing?' demanded Grey. 'Surely Her Majesty has been warned against him by every voice on the Council time and time again.'

Cecil did not answer directly. Instead he looked at Poley.

'Perhaps,' said Poley, speaking slowly as his thoughts formed into a plan; an image, perhaps, of what Cecil already had in mind. 'Perhaps we should let the Earl take her that warning. Himself. In person. Unannounced.' He paused for a heartbeat and then continued. 'So we had better clear the way for him. From the Court Gate Post to the private bed-chamber door.' He paused again. Lowered his voice. 'Allow him such swift and untrammelled access as could only be explained if he had in fact brought his army home. As if his soldiers already surrounded Nonsuch and held the palace itself. As if, no matter what he says, he has really solved the matter of the succession by preparing to take the throne for himself; and all he truly wishes to discuss with the Queen is whether she abdicates or dies.'

*

Robert Devereux, 2nd Earl of Essex, swung himself a little stiffly out of the saddle and stepped down into the courtyard beside the Court Gate Post. It was almost 10 o'clock. The rain was easing. Which was a reflection of his most recent experiences, he thought. When he was out there riding through it, the weather was foul. The instant he arrived at his destination with the promise of warmth and shelter, it improved, as though it mocked him. He glanced up and caught the eye of his secretary Henry Cuffe who seemed to see into his very thoughts.

'It's as though even the gods of the weather are sporting with us,' said Cuff. 'Notus the storm-bringer of Greek legend at least. Unless there is some Irish weather-god who has taken a strong dislike to us and managed to follow us out of the bogs.'

Cuffe began to dismount, as did the others. Essex paused for a moment, thinking: *There's more than weather gods that stand against us. And in more places than here in Surrey.* 'Find warmth,' he ordered. 'Get clean and dry Demand food and drink. I will come to you after I have talked with the Queen.' He turned, settling the hilt of his rapier comfortably against his hip, strode past the stable lads and ran into the palace. His heart was beating unusually fast, but he hardly noticed. As soon as he moved, he became more preoccupied, for a moment at least, with the stiffness in his shoulders and a cramp in his thighs. *God's blood*, he thought, I am yet a month and some days away from my thirty-fifth birthday and yet I seem to have the body of an old man! It is this cursed dampness that has crept into me! Unless, as Henry Cuffe suggests, the foul Irish weather has followed me here.

Absolutely unaware of his surroundings other than the familiarity of the passages he was following, too preoccupied to register that they were unusually quiet and empty, he worked his arms and shoulders as though wrestling an invisible opponent. As he did so, his thoughts returned to the matter that had occupied them to the exclusion of almost everything else for the last week and more. The cramp in his thighs eased and his impatient pace accelerated. He began to mentally rehearse the conversation he was just about to have with the Queen.

She would be standing – she liked to stand; it made her seem taller than she really was. She would be wearing the shoes with the thick soles and high heels that made her stand taller still and the bright curls of her hair would be piled high. She would be resplendent in her court dress, threaded with gold and studded with pearls. The high lace ruff would frame those vivid red-gold tresses. Her face would be set in that beautiful white mask; lips red, cheeks perhaps a little rouged, eyes wide and dark. Fathomless. Only rarely betraying what she was really thinking. He would throw himself down on his knees in front of her, pressing kisses to the backs of her heavily beringed hands.

He would tell her what he had come to tell her. And she would forgive him as always. And all would be well.

As he mentally rehearsed the words he planned to use, so his lips began to move and he started to speak aloud. 'Yes, you sent me to Ireland with the greatest army you have ever assembled,' he mumbled. 'But even its size was a weakness, trapping me to the south behind the Pale in Dublin. All in a massive camp raised on fields knee-deep in mud where the rain never eased. No sooner did we arrive than my men started falling sick. It was as if the Plague itself was visiting us. The soldiers started rotting before my very eyes, consumed with foul rheums, agues, the bloody flux. I had no alternative but to leave the camp myself and take up residence in Dublin Castle in the very rooms where my father the first Earl died, also fighting to quieten the place, poisoned at dinner by his enemies. Enemies perhaps in Ireland. But also, perhaps, nearer home. He had jealous enemies here at Court, as do I, who would not hesitate with hemlock.

'Furthermore, the men who built your army, the recruiting captains like Sir Thomas North, whose *Plutarch* you so admire, charged your purse for strong, well-trained, well-fitted soldiers and yet they supplied the sweepings of taverns and brothels, the halt and the lame, dressed in rags and armed with little more than antique toys so they could slip the difference onto their purses and grow fat on it. Then when I turned to Muster Master General Lane seeking more men and supplies, I found him to be one of Raleigh's followers who had no intention of helping me. Even so, I took my army, such as it was, into the field as you ordered. But the Irish would never stand and fight. It was all ambush and retreat, skirmish and run. I needed more supplies, more men, more arms. Appeals to the Council and to yourself were useless. I soon suspected that my messengers have been stopped or suborned so that my letters either failed to arrive or else have been read and even rewritten by my enemies. Majesty, you are ill informed, and ill-advised how best to answer such requests as have been allowed to reach you. I have begun to pay the troops out of my own purse to stop them selling their arms to the Irish and deserting in droves. I have been forced to grant knighthoods to the commanders who were becoming unwilling to continue the war without recompense or honour. Both actions that I know have been turned against me by venomous tongues here at court. Tongues which tell you I have passed out money and honours so that the army will be mine instead of yours to command. Which is a lie – and even were it true it is no matter, for *I* am yours to command. And will be until I die.

*

Still muttering to himself, quite carried away by the power of his own eloquence, Essex arrived at the door of the Presence Chamber. It was guarded, as always, and the Earl hesitated for an instant distracted by several things. He noticed for the first time how quiet everything was; how deserted the corridors and stairwells had been. He seemed to catch a glimpse of someone watching him from the shadows between two tall casements, a figure there becoming nothing more than a black silhouette, turning silently away. And out of nowhere it suddenly struck him just how wet and filthy he was. But the instant he hesitated, the door was thrown open for him and he entered the Presence Chamber. Everything other than this enormous gamble driven from his mind.

Robert Poley paused, relying on the light behind him to lend him anonymity, and watched the Earl of Essex passing in through the door. The thing that struck him most forcefully was how dirty the Earl was. His hair, face, beard and clothes were covered in mud. The fact that the Earl did not appear to have realised this – nor the inappropriateness of presenting himself to Her Majesty in such a state – seemed to symbolise the man's greatest weaknesses. His pride. His arrogance. His inability to see himself as others, and especially his Queen, might see him. And yet, thought the intelligencer, turning away as Essex vanished, there was about him a magnetism, a magnificence. *Were I not sworn to the service of Secretary Cecil*, he thought, *I could follow a man such as that.*

The great Presence Camber was unusually empty, thought Essex as the door closed behind him. Not absolutely empty of course, for there were always men whose calling brought them here for one reason or another. Men with messages, suits, pleas that only access to Her Majesty – torturously and expensively achieved – could answer. But the throne on its raised dais remained empty for the moment, though the regal magnificence of the room itself made waiting almost seem a privilege. He had never really paid attention to these lesser mortals. Nor did he now. His gaze raked over the cringing crowd of them. He saw no-one he recognised. No-one worthy of his attention.

Certainly no-one of equivalent rank or power. He strode on, therefore, like a great galleon surging through a fleet of skiffs, cogs and ferryboats, until he faced the guards at the door to the Privy Chamber. He thought for an uplifting moment how these commoners left bobbing and bowing in his wake must regard him with awe and jealousy as he made a gesture and the doors were opened before him at once. Access to Her Majesty like this was a privilege beyond price.

The Privy Chamber was smaller than the Presence Chamber with its dais, throne, priceless carpets, silken hangings and crowd of cringing supplicants. It was, as its name suggested, private. Here everything was on a smaller, more intimate scale. There were chairs, not thrones; tables for writing on, not for displaying gifts from other sovereigns and wealthy courtiers culled from near and far. It was a place for men and women to meet, rather than kings and queens. There was a fire spreading homely warmth and a flickering golden glow. And, straight ahead yet another pair of doors. These were smaller and unguarded, as the Privy Chamber was, as yet, untenanted. Neither the Queen nor her closest councillors had arrived for their morning conference. Propelled by the momentum of his eager rush to get here as much as by anything else, and certainly before he allowed himself an instant of reflection, he reached forward, took hold of the handles, twisted them and opened the door to Her Majesty's bedroom.

The impetus of Essex's journey up from the Court Gate Post pushed him on for a few more steps before he stopped. He looked around, frowning with confusion. The Queen was nowhere to be seen. There was no one in front of him but a crowd of women he did not immediately recognise. All of various ages, all with their faces frozen in a range of expressions, mostly of disbelief and shock. And in the midst of them, the only one seated, was an ancient, twisted crone in a linen nightgown; and not a very clean one at that. His glance passed over the ancient hag without pausing. Then it returned, registering almost in spite of itself, her balding head; a kind of tonsure ringed with straggling stands of hair as thin and white as spiders' webs. A flat chest, withered dugs ill-concealed by the gaping linen. Wattled neck, red and hanging like a fighting cock's. Slack mouth half open to reveal uneven stubs of occasional black teeth. Raddled, pocked and wrinkled cheeks. Dark eyes, round with disbelief and horror. No eyebrows at all.

Then his Queen's all-too familiar voice demanded, 'My Lord of Essex. What make you here?'

He looked around, shocked to hear that accustomed voice, still unable to see Her Majesty anywhere nearby.

*

When the door to her bedroom opened, Elizabeth looked up expecting to see one of her familiar women. Lady Audrey Walsingham had been away for several days, perhaps this was her returning. Instead, a strange man strode into the holy of holies. For an instant she simply could not believe what she was seeing. The interloper was tall, broad-shouldered. Armed, though his rapier hung untouched at his side. Or so it did at the moment. Julius

Caesar leaped into her mind unbidden, for she had just been perfecting Thomas North's translation from *Plutarch* of his life. And his death. The skin on her shoulders and back rose in goosebumps. The stranger bore himself with an air of command. But he was impossible to identify because from head to foot he was spattered in mud. Mud so thick in his lank hair and full beard that he seemed like one of the savages Raleigh described as inhabiting the New Found Land of America. Not only that, but he stank like some unwashed aboriginal. Stank of mud, leather and horses. Then breath-taking shock struck her a body-blow with the realisation that a strange man could only reach her bed chamber if he came sufficiently supported with soldiers to have cleared his way through Raleigh, the Captain of the Guard and his men. Would only dare to enter here if he had an army surrounding Nonsuch and probably another occupying London.

For a moment Elizabeth knew indeed what Richard II must have felt like, confronted by Bolingbroke and the end of his reign. And in two weeks' time it would be three hundred years since Bolingbroke's coronation as Henry IV. Dethronement suddenly seemed more than probable. It seemed imminent. A simply terrifying prospect; more so even than death.

But then, a blessed light of recognition caused the scales of fear to fall from her eyes as though she were St Paul on the road to Damascus. She drew breath to call the interloper by name, for beneath the filth she thought she could still see the wilful boy she had spoiled and indulged ever since he first came to court and refused to take his hat off to her. But immediately Cecil and the Council's warnings stopped her. Robert Devereux was supposed to be in Ireland, not in Nonsuch. And if he was here, could he have brought that enormous army with him? The Council had half convinced her that Essex was impatient enough, arrogant enough, ambitious enough to reach for the throne himself. Was there in fact an Irish army surrounding the palace? Were Southampton's troops occupying London? Was Captain of the Guard Raleigh dead or imprisoned and the Council slaughtered or helpless? Were her protectors, friends and advisors lost? Was she, too, after all, lost?

There was only one way to find out. She sat up straighter. Squared her shoulders. 'My Lord of Essex,' she said, pleased to find that her voice was steady and her tone as commanding as ever. 'What make you here?'

The stupid, filthy boy gaped around the room as though this were some play of tragedy and revenge and he was being addressed by a spectre rather than his sovereign. The Queen pulled herself onto her feet and one of her quicker-thinking handmaidens draped a robe over her shoulders. Her movement caught his eye and the robe seemed to be a revelation to him. 'Majesty!' he said, his voice full of wonder. He fell to his knees in front of her, only thinking to swing the long blade of his rapier back at the last moment. He tore off his gauntlets. Dropped them on the floor. 'Majesty.'

Without thinking she extended her hand to him. He had grasped it in both of his and begun to kiss it before she realised how much like a raven's claw it looked without

25

its usual shield of jewel-encrusted rings. And that realisation brought home to her with stunning force, the fact that the rest of her was equally unmasked. Effectively naked. Only the most loyal of her handmaidens, Ladies of the Bedchamber like Audrey Walsingham, had seen her in this state for years past – as she stood now, unclothed, unadorned. Her face was still bare of its layers of paint and powder and her precious wig lay elsewhere. Even if Essex had come about some other business than her immediate removal from the throne, he must be thinking about the succession most urgently now - confronted as he was with her frailty and all-too obvious mortality.

But then she drew herself up, thinking, as she had said eleven years ago at Tilbury with the first Armada bearing down upon her ill-prepared country, that if her body was weak, as it most assuredly had become, she nevertheless still possessed the heart and stomach of a king.

'You, sirrah, should be in Ireland,' she snapped. 'With your huge and ruinously expensive army. From whence you were most strictly forbidden to return until our business there was well and truly done. Have you brought me the Earl of Tyrone's head? Or have you come hither that I might box your ears again?'

'Majesty,' he said once more, and launched into some self-serving gibberish about how he had achieved great victory in Ireland by simply talking to the traitorous rebel Earl of Tyrone. A meeting she already knew about – Cecil had informed her as his spies had informed him. But she let Essex run on while her own mind raced. However he had managed to reach her bedroom unannounced, his behaviour and his garbled words made it obvious to her that he came as supplicant not would-be successor. Her next move seemed quite clear. She had to get him out of here while she got dressed and prepared to face him as a queen. Ideally in company with her Council, preferably also under the protection of Raleigh and his guards. She began to berate herself for her initial fears. Every report that had reached her from Ireland via Cecil and his network of intelligencers, made it clear that, despite his one great success at Cadiz three years ago, Essex could hardly have organised a successful masque let alone an effective coup.

'Of course, My Lord,' she said softly, placatingly. 'We will discuss all this at length and in detail. But not here. Not now. Let me complete my preparations for the day and we will discuss your concerns with my Council and you may have every hope that we will listen indulgently and act supportively. Take the opportunity to wash and change, to break your fast, perhaps, and we will meet again by noon, I promise.'

*

Cecil's occasional eyes and ears in the Queen's most private chambers belonged to Lady Jane Percy, granddaughter of Anne Boleyn's first suitor the Earl of Northumberland and his wife Lady Mary, daughter to the Earl of Shrewsbury; both long-deceased. The current Earl maintained the family tradition of constant plotting against the powers in the south. At the moment, the main focus of the Percys' mistrust was the Earl of Essex, because, on the one hand, they inclined towards Hugh O'Neill the Earl of

Tyrone's militant Catholicism, as many of the older families did, for their religion like their land-holdings, went back to the days of the Conqueror. And on the other hand they were concerned that Robert Devereux was plotting either to take the throne into his own fiercely Protestant grasp or facilitating King James of Scotland's equally Protestant pretentions toward the succession. The second was a more worrying prospect, given James' oft-proclaimed plans to clear all the most troublesome families out of the Scottish Borders – dangerous enough in a king of Scotland but potentially fatal in a king who ruled both Scotland and England and could therefore clear troublemakers out of both sides of the border. But all of this was balanced by one simple fact. The Earl of Northumberland was married to Essex's sister Dorothy Devereux.

Lady Jane, known to one and all as 'Janet' as a result of her slight figure and gentle disposition, had arrived in the court as a hostage to keep her wild northern relatives in order, but had stayed because the Queen took a liking to her sweet, open, eternally cheerful disposition. Which suited Janet very well, as she secretly maintained her family's fierce northern loyalties and was happy, therefore to pass secrets occasionally to Cecil – usually, as now, via his chief intelligencer Robert Poley, for whom she was developing a decided weakness. One which – although she did not know it – he was beginning to reciprocate.

'He strode into the bedroom as though he were king already,' Lady Janet was saying, he tones ringing with outrage. 'Covered in filth and still bearing arms! How in the name of all that's holy did Sir Walter let him pass?'

'A terrible oversight, Lady Janet. I'm sure Master Secretary will take it up with the Captain of the Guard; though Nonsuch is not so heavily manned as the other palaces. Even so, such dereliction cannot pass unnoticed.' Poley was the very essence of courteous concern. 'But My Lord of Essex burst in all filthy and still armed, you say?'

'Aye,' said Lady Janet. 'And he's been Esquire of the Body Extraordinary into the bargain. He should never...'

'But if we may proceed, Lady Janet. My Lord of Essex entered the Royal Presence. What then?'

Janet Percy described the horrific details of the incredible encounter and Poley noted them in his capacious memory, all the while maintaining his façade of shock. 'But then,' he prompted after a while, 'After the Earl retired from the Royal Presence. What thoughts did Her Majesty voice that you might properly recount to me for the notice of Master Secretary and, mayhap, the Council?'

'She sent word to Master Secretary and to the Captain of the Guard and received replies almost at once – that the Earl was attended by no more than half a dozen men; that there was no army at the gate, that there was less than a regiment with Southampton in London. That there was nothing immediate to fear.' Lady Janet paused.

'And then, my lady?' prompted Poley gently.

'And then her disposition moved as you might expect, from disquiet to outrage. "I will find a way to box his ears for this," she said. "He will find he is not so easily forgiven this time." Just as any woman might who had been so

29

abused. To be revealed in her shift. In her *shift*. To a man who is neither husband or lover! And she a queen to be treated like some drudge or slattern, visited will-she or nill-she. She will never forgive him such a slight. She will punish him, oh she will punish him I swear it.'

'And this rage, the outrage, does it surpass the measure? Will she lose her composure when she sees him? I understand they are to meet soon, more properly and formally. Will she really box his ears again?'

'I think not,' said Lady Janet. 'But with Her Majesty you can never be quite certain...'

*

Henry Cuffe stood stripped to the waist, in a room full of filthy, stinking, half-naked men. He did not find the experience entirely unpleasant. The rest were all soldiers and used to this kind of thing. He, as an austere academic, was not, but he felt the manly comradeship it could engender. And he approved it, even though this was not a large room and seven men almost crowded it, especially given that palace servants were bustling to and fro bringing more hot water from the kitchens and cloths to wipe away the mud as well as thicker cloths to wipe the clean skin and hair dry.

The Earl had arrived last having come from his conference with the queen, and was most fully attended. As well as a bevy of palace servants, he brought some Castile soap, which he swore he had taken in the sack of Cadiz, and he used the fragrant white bar to cleanse his hair and beard. Fresh clothes were being laid out for him in the room he usually slept in when attending the Queen here with the rest of the Council, though his companions would have to fend for themselves. But Essex was the sort of leader who was happy to muck in with his men. Though, Cuffe noted, none of the others got offered any soap, nor private rooms or new raiment.

But it was hard to be vexed with the Earl. He was at his most cheerful and charming, bubbling with the heady excitement that comes with deeply-felt relief. It was almost as though he had cheated death in some great battle. Cuffe had not seen him so ebullient in many a long day. 'She forgave my intrusion at once,' Essex was saying to anyone who wanted to listen – though Cuffe calculated he was really talking to himself – to reassure himself. 'She was most gracious and loving,' Essex continued blithely, his face white with lather. 'I said I had suffered much hardship and storms abroad but now I have found myself in safe haven. At which she was very kind and said I had come to safety at last indeed. Concerned that I had got begrimed on my journey hither, *Through these hardships and storms* as she said, she bade me wash and change! As though she would be mother to me. She has most courteously agreed to see me in her Privy Chamber when we are both properly attired but I am certain she means no harm to me or to my suit!'

'But what of the Council?' asked Gelly Martin guardedly, lowering his voice, even though the last of the palace servants had left them all alone, their absence freeing his tongue. 'What of Raleigh and Cecil? They do not wish to mother you, my Lord. They wish to break your influence and see you thrown down. Remember, they are each most anxious to ensure they remain in power whoever succeeds to the throne in due time. And they understand all too well that if it is you who holds supremacy, then it certainly will not be them.'

'I do not fear them!' said Essex. 'Let Cecil send his slavish messages to King James in Edinburgh, either under his own seal or that of Thomas Walsingham his acolyte. Who sends his wife the Lady Audrey as his spy and courier I hear! But His Majesty King James is a man who regards men. He does not wish to consort with women or grovelling, twisted toad-eaters. Especially not like Cecil the Toad who also courts the Infanta and is in the pay of Spain. Oh, I have the measure of the Scottish king. He had his tutor George Buchanan, the greatest mind in Scotland, who died seventeen years ago this very day, to teach him love of learning which he has never yet forgot. And I have my Henry Cuffe do I not? A mind to match Buchanan's and entertain the king with the most abstruse of arguments! The way to King James's heart is not through the back door of secret spycraft but in the open, matching his passions man to man. And as for Raleigh, he stands torn between his whores Arabella Stuart and the Spanish Infanta. They will never get the strength to succeed! In any case we are done with women on the throne. Whereas I have…'

Essex stopped mid-sentence, his face folding into a frown. Cuffe turned, abruptly aware of a subtle change in the room. A sudden chill. He followed his master's gaze and there in the doorway stood a familiar figure, framed against the shadows of the corridor behind him.

'Grey!' said Essex as though spitting something foul out of his mouth. 'What does your twisted master want of me?'

'Not Master Secretary, my Lord, but my Queen. She has honoured me with a message to be carried to you.'

'And that message is? The burden, quickly man! I grow cold here!'

'That Her Majesty confirms will see you at noon, my Lord. Alone. She will await you in the Privy Chamber. At noon.' Grey paused, his cold gaze sweeping over his erstwhile companions. Then he turned and was gone.

*

'She will see him at noon,' said Cecil to Raleigh. 'In the Privy Chamber. Alone.'

Raleigh was far too quick-thinking to echo that most dangerous word *alone*. 'Then I will have the Presence Chamber cleared of suitors and pack it with my guards.'

'No. I think your men would be better employed following my men up to London. Some of your men at least. Following some of my men. We need to achieve several things before dinner at three. We need to have summoned several more members of the Privy Council. An invitation I fear they will only answer if they believe they may come to Nonsuch in safety. Therefore we need to know with some exactness how many of Essex's men are with Southampton in the City, whether more men have been summoned from the Earl's Irish army and if so how many and when they might be expected. All the while making sure that nothing occurs here to disturb the Earl's apparent cheerful certainty that all is well and he stands already forgiven.'

'He believes that, does he?' Raleigh's eyebrows rose up his high forehead. 'How do you know?' The quick, intelligent blue eyes gleamed in that long, weathered face. Raleigh threw his head back in a characteristic gesture that emphasised at once his height, impatience and arrogance. His beard gleaned with golden threads in the sunlight and seemed to curl as though it had life of its own.

Cecil inclined his head towards the third man sitting silently in the room. 'Ah,' said Raleigh. 'I might have known. How do *you* know, Poley?'

'The Earl rarely lowers his voice,' answered the intelligencer quietly. 'Especially when he is surrounded by his close companions and particularly when he is cheery or excited. He was both when he came down from Her Majesty's bedchamber and joined his men in the wash-room. I caused the servants to be obvious when making their exit and waited just outside the door. He was extremely cheerful, even when my Lord Grey was kind enough to pass Master Secretary's message to him. As I lingered in the shadows without. Unobserved.'

'He'll be cheery because he was still able to walk, I should imagine,' said Raleigh shortly. 'Not having been arrested, chained, crippled or killed outright by my guards. Very well.' He turned back to Cecil. 'So I must choose my most reliable men and put them astride the swiftest horses available then send them to discover the size of Southampton's force and so-forth as you describe. I will also summon my guards from the Palace of Whitehall to make assurance double-sure. And in the mean time?'

'I will advise Her Majesty that the surest way forward at the moment is for her to continue to placate the Earl in their noon-day meeting. My men will ensure nothing untoward occurs…' he glanced at Poley then turned back to the Captain of the Guard. 'Then, when the wisest heads in the Council have been assembled, we will allow the tone of the encounter to change during the evening. To become, shall we say, more realistic, given the nature of the Earl's failures and offences. But even so, I think a summons to the guards at Whitehall is taking things a little far. Essex only has six companions after all.'

Walter Raleigh stood. He was tall, lean, still strong after an active life of forty-five years so far, handsome and possessed of that magnetism which the Earl of Essex shared in some measure. The exact opposite of Robert Cecil. The way he looked down at the Secretary emphasised all of this. That gleaming, fashionably heavy, beard almost concealed the slightest of sneers. 'You may feel responsible for the protection of Her Majesty's realms,' he said. 'But it is I who must guard Her Majesty's person.'

He stalked out of the room, his footsteps ringing in the passageway outside. After a moment, Cecil glanced towards Poley once more. The intelligencer stood up and walked silently to the door. His shadow loomed out into the passage moments before he reached the doorway. Suddenly more, quieter, footsteps could be heard walking rapidly away. Poley reached the doorway and glanced out. Sir Walter vanished into a side-corridor. Other than that, the passage was empty. 'Do you think we should close it,

Poley?' asked Cecil quietly.

'No, My Lord. If you wish to discuss anything sensitive it would be better if we were sure whether or not there was anyone out there. The only way to be more certain is to have a musician play such instruments as drown out the human voice, such as are used in this and many other courts where secrets are exchanged by word-of-mouth.'

'Well, today has been quite busy enough without summoning a consort of viols into the bargain. I am minded to destroy both of those men.'

Poley waited silently, coming to terms with the abrupt change of subject. Then he queried, 'Destroy them both, my Lord?'

'Both. Eventually. But we will begin with the Earl of Essex.'

2

Robert Poley watched Joan Yeomans as she washed. She stood facing away from him beside the ewer of warm water Bess the servant girl had brought, lazily rinsing herself. He could never quite get over Joan's lack of modesty and he found it both unsettling and exciting. His wife Anne would never go naked, as Joan was now, not even in front of him. Anne always wore a loose shift if she was forced to wash in his presence on his rare visits to his home in the country, and changed it modestly in darkness – often while he slept. Most of all, she kept it on during the increasingly occasional times they came together as husband to wife, pulling its hem up just enough for him to exercise his marital rights and duties. Lying like the carving on top of a tomb as he did so; dry as a desert. Joan Yeomans was another case entirely. But then, he thought idly, perhaps Joan kept her shift on at all times when she was with Master Yeomans the silversmith and cutler, her wittol husband and Poley's landlord.

Perhaps the activities that they so pleasantly explored together freed something in Joan that lying with her staid, long-suffering Puritan spouse did not; especially when – as today – they were enjoyed in the brightness of early afternoon. He wondered idly whether his eye should have offended him with its vision of forbidden pulchritude; whether he should be plucking it out as the Book of Matthew directed. He closed his right eye and left his left eye wide as he began to enumerate the sins and commandments he had just been breaking with Joan's willing help. Lust, gluttony, greed, envy and sloth amongst the cardinal sins. He was even now spending a slothful afternoon in her company instead of going about Master Secretary Cecil's work as he should have been doing. Robert Devereux was out of the Queen's favour and caged with Lord Keeper Edgerton in York House; not that he was well enough to go abroad in any case – even as far as Essex House to see his wife and new-born daughter. But the sickly Essex was confined, not broken. There was still work to be done on that score. But, thought the slothful intelligencer, returning to the tempting figure displayed before him, whether Joan kept on her shift with Master Yeomans or not, he envied him everything except his cuckold's horns. He wondered also whether there was another sin which covered the fact that even when Joan and he were at their most sportive, Lady Janet Percy had a habit of creeping into his mind. As different again to the woman he had married and the woman he was bedding. What was it the poet soldier Philip Sidney had written before his death in battle? Lady Janet was Stella to his Astrophel: a distant star to his ardent stargazer.

Then, his thoughts ran on, as for the ten commandments: he had come dangerously close to worshipping that soft, warm, pink and alabaster body, with which he regularly committed adultery, which swept him back to the heart of the world of lies he inhabited and sharpened his envy of Master Yeomans even further. Five cardinal sins and four commandments not so much broken as shattered into atomies. It was probably just as well he had been bound for the everlasting bonfire these twenty years and more, he thought ruefully. And for sins far more serious than those he had broken today. None of which, despite the religion he had been raised to believe in, he had ever confessed away or atoned for with any penance whatsoever.

Joan swung round to face him and he caught his breath, wide eyed at the sight of her, so wantonly displayed. 'Come, Master Poley,' she said brusquely, well aware of the effect her nudity was having upon him. 'Stir yourself. I am off to dress and you need to do the same. Was it not the Cross Keys you promised after an afternoon of delight?'

'It was,' he agreed, 'with its ordinary of boiled beef and snippets, together with sweet wine and sugar. And whatever else your fond heart desires.' *That I can afford*, he added silently. He swung his legs out of the tumbled bed and stood. He bent to retrieve his clothing and by the time he had straightened once more she was gone, calling for Bess to attend her as she headed for her own room. He used her cooling water to rinse himself then dressed quickly, lacing his old-fashioned codpiece uncomfortably tightly. Perhaps there was a kind of penance there after all, he thought.

The late afternoon was clement for the season and promised to stay dry. They wandered apparently aimlessly out into the street, side by side, with Bess close behind as the lady's chaperone. First they meandered east along Hog Lane, where the Yeomans lived, until they came to the

Bishops' Gate. Then they turned right, passed under the gate's stone arch and joined the bustle on Bishopsgate Street. They followed the thoroughfare south through the city until it became Gracechurch Street at the crossroads with Leadenhall and Cornhill. The Cross Keys stood a little further south, on the very last quiet section before the clamour of Leadenhall Market began, opposite the house belonging to Thomas Smythe, one of London's leading sheriffs. It was a big, bustling tavern, a cut above most. In terms of facilities, food, drink and clientele if nothing else, thought Poley. Certainly above the brothels of the South Bank he was used to. Where others of his shadowy profession, perennially in debt, foregathered, plotted and planned.

What went on at the Cross Keys might not be much more honest, he thought, but at least it was a cut above the Southwark alehouses and indeed more local hostelries like the Bell away on the south side of the market, whose proprietoress had been carted as a bawd not long ago. The food was certainly better; the patrons richer – or more confident in their debt-management. And none of the drink was watered.

*

Both Poley and Joan Yeomans were regular customers. This was not only a pleasant place to pass the time, but also an easy walk from Master Yeomans' shop – so, should occasion call Poley to leave unexpectedly, Joan could call on her husband easily enough and he would take her home. As Poley led the women through the tavern's main room, he automatically scanned the other clientele crouched secretively over tables under clouds of tobacco smoke. He registered and dismissed the carefully manipulated games of chance, cards or dice, the purse-cutting and the pocket-picking. None of it was his concern. He paid closer attention to the more familiar faces – minor hangers-on at court or at the great houses that lined the Strand, standing between Whitehall Palace and Bridewell, fronting onto the thoroughfare but backing onto the River.

There were actors between assignments or out of work with their theatres closed by the Chancellor, though not, this season, by the plague. Playwrights who honed their wits against each-other across the tables with raucous verbal sallies then put their sharpest witticisms into the actors' mouths. Words which could lead those that spoke them as well as those that wrote them to the Clink, the Marshalsea or the Fleet prisons, depending on which of the powers that ruled their lives and their city was most offended. The pamphleteers whose printed work was for sale in the precinct of St Pauls and who ran the risk of the Fleet or even of the Tower if what they wrote caused offence in the wrong quarter. But most of all, Poley was keeping an eye out for others of his own shady profession who might have come north of the river today. Men like that might well come hunting him.

For an unsettling moment he thought he caught sight of Richard Baines, with whom he had worked in the low countries ten years since. The sight disturbed him because he had watched Baines being hanged at Tyburn six years ago. Baines' neck had been thick, the drop short and spy had lacked sufficient merciful friends to pull his heels and break his neck. It had taken a long time for Baines to strangle as the noose tightened slowly despite his wildly jerking dance. The Tyburn Jig they called it, danced beneath the Three-legged Mare of the gallows there.

But then Poley saw Richard Paradine and at least he was certain Paradine was still alive. Nodding to his fellow intelligencer, he settled Joan and Bess at a table near the door where the breeze kept the tobacco fumes at bay. He pulled his sword and scabbard from his belt and laid them across the table, then called for sweet wine and sugar as one of the servers came over. The sweet wine was an indulgence which Joan had more than earned, even though Poley was very well-aware that by buying her a bottle he was putting money into Essex's purse, for the Earl owned the license to import sweet wines at Her Majesty's gift. Master Secretary Cecil would not approve, should he ever find out. He ordered a flagon of Malaga sack for himself, righting the balance a little on the assumption that part of the payment would be bound for Spain. Perhaps, he thought wryly, he should also order uskebeaghe and send some revenue north to Scotland. Cover all ends that way. For the succession to Gloriana's throne seemed to hang between Essex, the Spanish Infanta Isabella, Lady Arabella Stuart or King James. But when the server came back with their order, Poley put all such idle thoughts aside and demanded food for them all – beef boiled with herbs, lovage and spinach in a thick savoury sauce with peas on snippets of fried bread. There would be sweetmeats in due course as well – Joan shared her sovereign's taste for all things saccharine. But then, so did most of the women in

Elizabeth's wide realm, he thought.

They had no sooner settled with their drinks than there was a stirring at the door. Poley glanced up. Nicholas Skeres came shouldering ill-temperdly into the place followed by John Wolfall. Skeres was retired from intelligence gathering. He was Essex's man these days and, like most of the Earl's hangers-on, he was short of cash. As was the sickly, incarcerated Earl himself of course – his profits from the sweet wine trade long lost in paying his Irish army and likely to be confiscated in any case at his angry monarch's whim. Skeres had probably borrowed some cash from Wolfall, a notorious money-lender, who was dunning him for repayment now by the look of things. Though the moneylender would need to be careful how he went about it. Skeres was solidly built. His neck was almost as thick as Baines' had been. As for the size and power of his limbs – the only man of Poley's acquaintance who exceeded them was the murderous Ingram Frizer. Both Frizer and Skeres had dangerously short tempers and had relied more than once on their powerful masters to save them from accusations of murder. Skeres and Poley exchanged glances. Poley shrugged, hoping to convey sympathy, understanding and inability to help.

Even if Skeres understood the full complexity of Poley's gesture, he chose to disregard it. Instead, he came pushing through the bodies and weaving between the tables like a bear escaped from the Baiting Pit with Wolfall dogging his heels like a starving cur.

*

'Poley!' bellowed Skeres. The unsteadiness of his gait and the volume of his voice explaining why he appeared to have no ready money long before the stench of Canary wine on his breath confirmed the matter. 'Robert Poley! Well met!'

Joan Yeomans stirred unhappily at Poley's side. 'What is this?' she wondered.

'I don't know,' he answered. 'Yet.'

Poley weighed the alternatives, which were admittedly few in number. Skeres and he had worked together in the past, together with Ingram Frizer who was now Sir Thomas Walsingham's man. Bonds stronger than friendship lay between them. The fact that they had been commissioned to murder the playwright, poet, spy, smuggler atheist and trickster Christopher Marlowe major among them. Skeres had a claim on him that could not be dismissed too lightly therefore. Any attempt to do so, indeed, might well lead to violence. And there were always watch-officers hanging round the edges of the market ready to arrest rufflers too ready with their swords, daggers or fists and throw them in the nearest jail.

'I have given succour to the Earl of Essex already,' said Poley easily, nodding at the bottle of sweet wine. Then he looked past Skeres to Wolfall. 'How much more coin to give some relief to the Earl's man here?'

'He owes me sixty pounds!' snarled Wolfall.

'Does he?' Poley glanced at Skeres, who was hanging his head now. He glanced back at Joan who was frowning, clearly and wisely wanting the matter settled as quickly and quietly as possible. 'And how much will satisfy you this afternoon?' he asked.

Wolfall hesitated, his mouth working as he tried to calculate a meaningful sum.

'No more than a shilling,' suggested Joan.

'A shilling,' agreed Poley. He looked up at Wolfall and Skeres. 'It will be a shilling or nothing and both of you can go hang.' He reached into his purse and produced the coin. An old silver shilling minted for use in Ireland; probably worth about ninepence, he thought. But it would do. He tossed it onto the table beside his flagon of sack and his sword. 'Here,' he said. 'Though God's my witness I can ill-afford the sum.'

Skeres made a grab for it but Wolfall was quicker. He snatched the money and was gone. 'There,' said Poley. 'Now you have an afternoon of quiet at least, Nick. Spend it wisely. And spend it elsewhere.'

Skeres snarled inarticulately and ungratefully but he turned and began to push his way towards the bar.

'Was that wise?' wondered Joan. 'Should we have sent him off with nothing but a boxed ear?'

'Probably,' answered Poley. He reached for his glass. 'But your suggestion was charitable. And I have several very pleasurable sins to atone for this afternoon.'

Joan Yeomans chuckled – a most unladylike sound.

Before Skeres even reached the bar, there was another stirring at the door. Wolfall was back and once more he was not alone. Poley frowned as he recognised the money-lender's new companion. It was another old friend from Francis Walsingham and William Cecil's superannuated secret service. The very man he had just been thinking about. It was coincidence almost stretched into witchcraft. The professional murderer Ingram Frizer paused in the doorway. Frizer still worked for Francis Walsingham's nephew, and successor as spymaster, Sir Thomas. Try as he might to forget it, every time he encountered Frizer, Poley saw Christopher Marlowe's stricken face as Frizer's cheap dagger went into his forehead, just above his eye. Poley had seen his fair share of death, but he had never seen anyone die as quickly as Marlowe died with Frizer's blade stuck inches deep in his brain. He would never forget the way the life in those quick and clever eyes went out. No lingering. No last thoughts. No time even for surprise.

Like two bright candles snuffed by one icy breath.

'Not another one!' said Joan Yeomans as Wolfall led Frizer across the room. 'This looks less like coincidence and more like a stratagem.'

Poley said nothing. He nodded his agreement as he watched them coming. Frizer was as drunk as Skeres but he went quiet where his ex-colleague got loud. Mean and deadly where Skeres was all puff and bluster.

'Frizer here owes me one hundred pounds,' said Wolfall.

'That should be worth two shillings,' said Frizer. 'I'm worth twice what Skeres is worth in any case.'

It was at this point that Poley found himself fully in agreement with Joan's assessment. He was caught in the middle of a dangerous and carefully prepared trap.

*

Poley sat silently, looking up at the two men. Then his gaze flicked over to the service counter. Skeres was standing with his back to the board, elbows up on the edge, his expression somewhere between a grin and a sneer. Poley's primary objective – other than ensuring he came out of this alive – was to keep Joan and Bess clear of the violence whose threat hung in the air like the tobacco smoke. Like thunder. 'Not today, Ingram,' he said quietly, shifting his attention back to the money-lender and the murderer.

Frizer's hand dropped to the hilt of his sword. 'D'you tell me I'm worth less of your charity than Skeres?' he demanded, his eyes two venomous slits. 'Or is it that you hold my master Sir Thomas lower than the Earl of Essex? Is that it?' He leaned forward but raised his voice. 'Do you secretly consort with the Earl of Essex?'

'*Consort*? What are you thinking, Ingram?' asked Poley mildly. 'You would make the matter of a shilling or two into a matter of lies and loyalties?'

'Of treachery and double-dealing!' sneered Frizer.

Poley's eyes narrowed to match his accuser's. They were sailing desperately close to the wind here. Thomas Walsingham's man accusing him of being a secret supporter of Essex could not be too loudly rebutted or Skeres – as someone who genuinely worked for the Earl – would wade in. Which at the very least would put Joan and Bess in danger of wildly wielded blades. Unless he could find some way to defuse the situation, it promised to run all too swiftly out of control. 'Two shillings it is, then,' he acquiesced. And knew at once that he had made a mistake. Skeres shrugged himself off the bar and started shoving his way back across the room. 'Two shillings for Walsingham's man and but one for the Earl's?' he bellowed.

Poley grabbed his sheathed sword and heaved himself to his feet. 'Outside,' he snarled, pushing past Frizer and Wolfall, leaving Joan and Bess safely at the table. The two spies fell in behind him and Skeres fell in behind them. Poley could feel his self-control beginning to slip away as he became more and more certain that this was a trap. Skeres and Frizer, with the help of Wolfall, were up to some game to snare him like the most gullible coney being gulled in a Southwark alehouse brothel. By the time he attained the street, he had talked himself into a rage. 'So!' he growled, swinging round. 'Who dies first in the matter of an Irish shilling?'

At the sound of his voice, the passers-by fell back but a good number of them stopped, a makeshift audience to a promising drama, their numbers soon augmented by a crowd of idlers tempted up from the nearby market.

Frizer answered at once by tearing his rapier from its sheath. Poley did the same, throwing the empty scabbard aside. He fell into his preferred posture, side-on, feet spread, fist in the basket hilt low, point held high and steady; his gaze flickering to the surface of the road which was their makeshift piste, registering the slope to the kennel or gutter in the centre of the street on his right. Then up to Frizer's sneering face. He would have liked to be certain of Wolfall's whereabouts – and Skeres' for that matter – but Frizer looked too serious to take for granted. Especially as he threw himself into the attack at once.

Poley had on occasion taken lessons with a master of defence and was quite capable of applying the lethal theories propounded by Maestro Capo Ferro of Siena but two circumstances stopped him. The first was the simple wildness of Frizer's attack and the second was that he did not wish to kill the man, though the temptation to do so was strong. He collected Frizer's blade in an enveloping riposte, therefore and guided its point over his shoulder as he stepped in almost breast to breast. Had he been holding his dagger, Frizer would have died then with the blade deep between his ribs. But Poley was not, so he stepped back and fell into *terza*, the third defensive position; the only true defensive position according to Capo Ferro. Side-on, leading foot forward and pointing towards his opponent; rear foot crossways, anchoring him firmly should he wish to step forward into attack or backward in riposte. His hilt was near his leading knee and his point was angled upwards once more, blade ready to meet anything Frizer did.

Frizer was clearly beyond calculation or strategy. He might as well have been wielding a club. He brought his blade down from a position that was so high it didn't have either a name or a designation in the books of fencing. The force of the move made him grunt with effort and threw him off balance. Poley stepped aside and let the steel whisper past his shoulder. Then he resumed his original position in *terza*. Because Poley's hilt was low, his blade rising almost from knee-height, Frizer came in high again – this time with a little more finesse. The murderous bully had obviously realised Poley had no intention of killing him. So he could more or less do what he liked without fear of reprisal.

A miscalculation, as things turned out.

*

This time Poley's reply was more than defensive, his whirling blade dismissed his opponent's in riposte, and the deadly point returned to the line of attack with dazzling speed, striking for his opponent's face. Frizer jerked his head aside with such force that his upper body followed it, throwing him entirely off-balance once more. He staggered down the slope, fighting to stay on his feet. Poley changed the angle of his thrust and struck at once, throwing himself forward into a lunge. The point of his rapier pierced Frizer's leather breeches and disappeared into the outer curve of his right buttock. Poley jerked it back, even as Frizer fell to his knees, dropping his weapon and clutching at his wounded backside with a howl compounded of agony and outrage.

'Let that be a lesson…' said Poley.

He would have added more but a blow across the back of his head felled him face down in the kennel. The gutter ran down the centre of the street. It was a couple of feet wide and maybe six inches deep. It was full of the effluent created by the occupants of the houses on either side. Luckily, at this time of day the nightsoil from numberless chamber-pots that filled it in the morning was diluted by water from the various commercial and domestic buildings nearby. Water from washing people, clothing, shops, houses and animals. Still, there was enough of it to drown in, had Poley just been left lying face-down there for long enough. But he wasn't.

Even before he took his first water-filled breath, Poley

was distantly aware of strong fists closing on his arms and pulling him erect. He seemed to hang there, strangely suspended. He thought once more of Baines dangling as he slowly strangled at Tyburn. Distant voices held a bellowed conversation. One voice close to his ear clearly belonged to the leader of the men holding him. The watch, as likely as not; and their leader the local constable. He heard the questions, but was far more interested in the answers, many of which came as a revelation to him. And proof-positive that he was caught in a trap after all.

Yes, he was known to the vociferous witnesses: as Poley, a notorious trouble-maker.

A Catholic recusant and whoremonger at the least.

Yes, indeed, his near-fatal attack on the wounded innocent Ingram Frizer was unprovoked – except that he announced his hatred for Frizer's master Sir Thomas Walsingham and for Master Secretary Cecil, Walsingham's friend and colleague.

And, by the same token, they said, he had voiced his support for the Earl of Essex and his faction. He might even have been overheard to say on more than one occasion, that the Earl was fitter to be seated on the throne than was Her Majesty.

Nobody offered a word of contradiction to any of these lies and slanders. Not even Poley himself who was so far removed from the reality of what was going on that he could not even make his mouth work

It was enough for the constable. Poley distantly felt himself to be in motion.

'It is sedition at the very least. Perhaps treason,' the

enforcer of the law decided. 'You witnesses follow along. We'll go to the Justices first. I wouldn't be surprised if this situation ends up in the Fleet, the Tower or even Tyburn.'

But first it went to Newgate.

Newgate was not the nearest prison, but it was the most convenient for several reasons, Poley reasoned, as the power of thought began to pierce the haze of agony pulsing out of the wound at the back of his head. Particularly if the entire incident had been as well-planned as it now appeared to have been. The principal benefit would be that Justice Hall was in session and his case could be presented to the Justices of the Peace at once, with the testimony of the witnesses immediately available. Furthermore, he thought, as waves of nausea began to sweep over him as a result of the attack, the face-down visit to the gutter and the way he was being handled now, he was in no condition to mount any kind of defence – and would not be so for some considerable time. His silence would no doubt allow the witnesses' accusations to stand. Nevertheless, he found himself imagining the conversations he might have with judges of varying standing, persuasion and readiness to condemn those before them to the mercies of Rackmaster Topcliffe, chief interrogator at the Tower, or the Three-legged Mare at Tyburn.

*

These thoughts occupied the time it took them to drag him along Cornhill into Poultry, then down Cheapside through yet another market, into Newgate Street and along it to the corner of Old Bailey, where the 'gate' itself stood; or rather the towers that had flanked it, extended now with cells and courtrooms, the major of which was Justice Hall. But the gate was hardly 'new' it had existed as an opening in London Wall since Roman times and had functioned as a court and prison since Henry II had been king. Its cells would no doubt be packed today with those passing through Justice Hall, but Poley was spared any wait – or any incarceration therefore. For the time-being at least.

Poley, the constable, his watchmen and the throng around them pushed through into the Hall itself. The first thing Poley saw clearly in an uncounted time of sickening pain and flashing lights was a bench of Justices frowning down on him. The first words that made any clear sense since the answers to the constable's original enquiries were those of the constable himself as he recited the accusations: brawling in a public place, attempted murder, sedition against Her Majesty overheard by witnesses here present, public contempt against Her Majesty's councillors most especially Master Secretary Cecil; hardly surprising in a recusant whoremonger such as the prisoner Poley was widely known to be.

The Justices hardly needed to bother with examination of the witnesses, or hearing any plea from the concussed and still-inarticulate accused, before finding him guilty on all counts and sending him down to the cells to await transfer to Westminster and further examination and sentencing by the senior and much more powerful judges who sat in Her Majesty's Court of Star Chamber.

Poley endeared himself to none of the other occupants of the long holding cell by vomiting onto the rancid straw flooring as soon as he was chained in place. He might have requested access to the filthy bucket which passed for a chamber pot before emptying his belly but he knew the rules. Access to the bucket came at the whim of the guards who had to loosen the leg irons to allow it. And they did that only once or twice in a day unless there was coin available to bribe them with. Poley was wide enough awake to know he would have more urgent need of the guards' indulgence in due course. And to note the fact that, as with his sword, his purse had gone missing somewhere along the way. With a little care he could shuffle the stinking straw away from himself without pushing it too close to his nearest neighbour. He managed to do this, then he simply curled up on the filthy, stone-cold floor and passed out.

As things transpired, he need not have been so careful. After what appeared to be a couple of moments of deep unconsciousness, he was woken by the guard as he loosened the leg irons. 'Up,' he ordered. 'They're here for you.'

Still dazed, Poley pulled himself unsteadily to his feet and allowed himself to be guided out of the cells to a reception area. He saw at once that a good deal of time must have passed, for Justice Hall was empty and the sky outside the windows was dark. He also noted that while he had been asleep he had somehow managed to roll into his own vomit. And the unusual weight of his ice-cold codpiece warned him he had also wet himself.

The men who had come for him were wrapped in cloaks, their hats pulled low over their eyes. One of them closed a pair of gyves joined by a short chain round his wrists, then they lead him out of the prison and into Old Bailey. They hurried him through the icy, clear-skied night down Old Bailey past Lud Gate and Black Friars into Water Lane which led down to a set of steps set into the north bank of the Thames. At the Water Lane steps they called, '*Westward ho!*' and bundled him into the skiff that answered their hail.

Beneath the chilly magnificence of the night, Poley's faculties were beginning to return, but they were of little use to him. He could see the star-filled sky high above with the promise of a rising moon but he could make more sense of the distant constellations than he could of his current situation. An icy easterly breeze swept up-river from the Bridge towards the twin palaces of Whitehall and Lambeth standing brightly on each bank ahead. He shivered convulsively, his mind clearing a little further. This was not the first time he had been struck on the cranium and he recognised the results of yet another blow. He reached back as best he could, given his chained wrists and felt the back of his skull. His hair was thick and set solid with dried blood. Gentle probing revealed that there was swelling beneath the carapace, but no softness. That fact alone seemed to help him start to organise his thoughts. That, and a burgeoning anger at himself that he had managed to get himself into this situation. And at the fact he was being so slow to make a full assessment of what was actually happening here and why.

He was clearly bound for the Court of Star Chamber as the magistrates in Justice Hall had said. Which meant the next set of judges he would likely face would be members of Her Majesty's Privy Council. With any luck Master Secretary Cecil would be presiding – and in that possibility lay some hope of an explanation if of nothing more. 'Nothing more' seemed the most likely outcome – certainly not a declaration of his innocence and an honourable discharge. This had all been too carefully planned. Her Majesty's senior advisers sitting in her most powerful court would have a purpose in all of this. And that purpose would be fulfilled whether he understood what it was or not.

*

The skiff slowed to a stop alongside the Westminster Stairs and Poley was hurried ashore. With one guard at each shoulder, he stumbled up the steps into New Palace Yard past the fountain, before he was guided roughly to his left. The door into the Great Hall stood on his right hand, closed and guarded. The smaller door into the Star Chamber gaped on his left and he was thrust through this almost brutally. There were passages and stairs leading upwards before at last the door to the Chamber itself was opened before him.

The Star Chamber, named for the design of its ceiling painted like the firmament he had just been gazing up at, was unlike any other court Poley had ever been in. He knew the place, of course, for his work as an intelligencer had brought him here as witness and informer on more than one occasion in the past. But now he stood as the accused, and was forced to take a whole new perspective on the place. It was more than the fact that the great room was lit by candles and lamps now. It was the fact that he had come through the door that the accused entered by whereas he had only ever entered through the door used by witnesses and officers of the court. There was no bench such as there was in Justice Hall – it was replaced by a table behind which those members of Her Majesty's Council sat. Or a representative sample of them did – nine of the nineteen who could serve as Her Majesty's Privy – private - Councillors.

Poley looked along the length of the Chamber towards the central chair, the position of ultimate power where Master Secretary Cecil habitually positioned himself. Cecil was not there. The Lord Keeper of the Great Seal and Chancellor Sir Thomas Edgerton was in his place, with Lord High Admiral Howard of Effingham on his right and the Lord Chamberlain, young Lord Hunsdon on his left. There were others there, of course, six of them, but Poley hardly registered their presence. Hunsdon and Effingham would have been here no matter what was going on, Poley thought. But the Lord Keeper was in charge of keeping the Earl of Essex safely confined in York House. Why had he come away from that duty to replace Master Secretary Cecil now? And why had Cecil needed replacing – or wanted to be replaced?

Fighting to maintain some kind of dignity in spite of his battered head, his filthy, stinking clothes and his chained wrists, Poley drew himself up, squared his shoulders and stood tall. Edgerton, Howard and Hunsdon looked at him coldly, unimpressed. He knew them all; had worked for them all as a courier if as nothing more, and yet he could have been some random stranger plucked at hazard from the lowest trugging house and thrust into the dock before them.

'Call the witness,' ordered Lord Keeper Edgerton.

One witness, thought Poley. Someone who could distil all the accusations that had brought him here so far. Who on earth...

A door half way down the length of the chamber opened and a slight man of middle years with short-cropped dark hair and a clean-shaven chin stepped in. Poley recognised him at once, but the surprise of seeing him there was so great that he wondered for a heartbeat whether he was dreaming.

Until Lord Keeper Edgerton spoke. 'You are Master Cutler and Silversmith John Yeomans?'

'I am My Lord,' nodded Joan's husband.

'You own an establishment in Gracechurch Street?'

'And a house on Hog Lane, yes My Lord.'

'And you recognise this man, the accused?'

Yeomans' narrow brown eyes swept over Poley, taking in the bruises, the filth, the manacles. Poley had never before noticed how small those eyes were. How mean. 'I do My Lord. It is Robert Poley who lodges with my wife and myself at our house in Hog Lane. He has done so for some good long time. Since a year or two after Armada year.'

'And what have you learned about him in that time?'

Yeomans glanced back at Poley, smirking with ill-concealed triumph. He's not going to tell them I cuckold him weekly, thought Poley in a kind of Pyrrhic victory.

'He is a recusant,' Yeomans began, 'though he plays the

game of obeying the laws so as to escape too heavy a fine for his Romish inclinations. He consorts with others of like-minded Catholic beliefs. I have heard him speak against the Council on many occasions. Against Master Secretary Cecil in particular. Just as he conceals his true beliefs, he conceals his liking for the Earl of Essex. I have recently heard him discuss how the Earl has a better claim to the throne than does Her Majesty. That a young, powerful monarch such as he would make, could be another Bolingbroke, destined to rule in her place.

'As though Her Majesty were Richard II. Indeed. I have heard as much said in secret treason,' said Lord Hunsdon.

*

'I have heard him share the Earl's calumny that her Majesty is 'as crooked in her disposition as in her carcase' begging your indulgence for repeating it myself, My Lord. It was said, I believe in reply to a just and well-earned punishment served out by Her Majesty when she boxed the Earl's ears.' Yeomans persisted, bowing and smirking; the very personification of oily duplicity. Given a crouch back, thought Poley, he would make a creditable Richard III on stage at the Globe. What did the malformed monarch say in the play that bore his name? *For I can smile and murder as I smile*. It was John Yeomans to the life.

'You have our indulgence for quoting another man's treason in order to trip him,' said Lord Admiral Effingham. 'I was myself present during much of the incident you refer to.'

There was a debate, Poley knew, as to whether it was Lord Admiral Howard's hand that had stopped Essex drawing his sword against the Queen when she boxed his ears or Captain of the Guard Raleigh's. No matter which it was, they both earned the Earl's undying hatred. 'You have done well to alert the Council to this sedition,' the Lord Admiral broke into Poley's thoughts. 'But what proof can you offer beyond your word under sworn oath?'

'This, My Lord.' Yeomans produced a tatty, oft-fingered volume and passed it to the nearest guard as though ridding himself of some unholy, poisonous thing. 'He keeps it close by him at home. He has a secret cavity in his bed.'

'The only secret cavity I have in my bed belongs to his wife!' shouted Poley as he realised what Yeomans had handed over – though only Heaven above knew where he had got it from. 'These are the lies of a cuckold set on revenge! Do not believe a word, My Lords.'

A moment of silence settled on the Star Chamber. It was as though Poley had never spoken. Edgerton looked up from the book Yeomans had caused to be passed to them. 'It is the banned book *A Conference on the Succession,*' he said, glancing at the others. 'We need no further proof of guilt. We will discuss his fate at full council, having referred the matter to Master Secretary Cecil and Her Majesty. In the meantime, take him to The Fleet.'

Whitehall led into The Strand at Charing Cross; The Strand led into Fleet Street. The Street led to the Fleet Bridge and the Lud Gate beyond it, then a sharp left turn a little way down Ludgate Hill, between the bridge and the gate itself, took them into a narrow alley leading to Belsavage Yard and the prison. It was by no means a long walk but it gave time for Poley's head to clear further. The temptation was just to give up and let whatever was happening simply wash over him. But so much careful planning had gone into getting him here that he could not resist trying to work out what the scheme was likely to be and his probable place within it. But before he had leisure to do that, he had the immediate situation to take care of. And to do that he was going to need either coin or credit. Credit – because his purse like his sword had vanished.

Poley knew every gaol in London and a number close-to in the nearby countryside. They were all run for profit and the Fleet was no different. Whether Warden Tyrell was presently within the walls or not, the men to whom he had sold the list of gaolers' rights would be. It would cost Poley a sum to be welcomed into the place. His ability to pay would govern the assignation of his cell, the availability of comforts like a chamber pot, water and a cloth; access via friends – when they came aware of his predicament – to clean clothing; to warm clothing. And – tomorrow – food. He would have to pay to have his leg irons put on unless he wanted them so tight he risked losing his feet. He would have to pay to have them taken off or foul himself further with the bucket out of reach.

But Belsavage Yard was a busy commercial hub. Prisoners who could afford it were permitted to have rooms outside the main prison building, mostly on the far side of the Yard which therefore teemed with men and women keen to supply their wants. The place was noisy with the shouts of costermongers selling hot food and good ale, girls selling cherries and Seville oranges, and women selling themselves. The air was heavy with the aromas generated by all of this together with clouds of tobacco smoke and – occasionally – the eyewatering stench of sewage blown in from the Fleet River. For those less fortunate, less financially secure – like those reliant on the Earl of Essex's bounty, for instance – there were plenty of brokers waiting for those willing to pawn their possessions for ready money. And, of course, there were the outright moneylenders. The first of these that Poley spotted as he was escorted into the Yard was John Wolfall.

It was almost as though the loan shark had been waiting for Poley to arrive. No sooner was the prisoner pushed into the Yard than Wolfall was at his side. 'You'll need ready money,' he said, paying no attention to the prisoner's taciturn escort. 'I can offer a line of credit may make things easier for you within, Master Poley.' He held up a purse that looked suspiciously like Poley's missing one. 'Two pounds to start with. Forty silver shillings. What say you? At a bargain for an old friend, costing only one pound extra.' He jingled the purse once more. 'Three pounds signed for and they're yours Master Poley.' The purse vanished and a paper contract appeared together with an inked quill to sign it with. Poley paused and the escorts let him. He took the agreement and signed it, all too well aware that he had no alternative. Wolfall waved the ink dry as he followed Poley towards the prison's main entrance and he handed the purse over at the last possible moment. At least the weight felt right, thought Poley as he climbed the broad steps and was ushered through the great door into the cavernous reception hall, for there was of course no time – and this was no place – to count it.

*

His cloak-wrapped escorts stood one at each shoulder as Poley paused at the table to be signed in. The book-keeper was one of the few within these walls who could read and write, thought Poley as he answered the gruff questions then watched his name and address in Hog Lane being recorded. The page of the leger in front of him was marked with five columns, each with a clear purpose in the keeping of records – personal and financial. The information he had just given went into the first two; the date and time of his arrival were recorded in the third column beside name and address. In the fourth would be recorded the date and time of departure and on occasion, the nature of that departure. More than one entry in this column was marked D for 'deceased'. Others were marked religiously, with any outstanding sum owed. Too great a sum outstanding, of course, meant simple movement from the criminal and political section of the prison to the debtors' section. The great, long room where those without friends or finances were held. A room which stood beneath a grille looking out onto the street through which the destitute could beg. Then there was a final column where the level of accommodation would be noted as defined by its daily rate.

Poley had no idea how long he was likely to be here but he was confident that if his funds ran low he could call on Wolfall for more. For a shilling, 12 pence, a day he could share a fairly clean cell with three others, one bucket and light leg irons. For two groats or eight pence, it would be with seven others and the straw would not be so clean, the irons would be heavier and the bucket further away but no bigger. Below sixpence and below a fourpenny groat, things began to get really grim. As the clerk's quill hovered enquiringly over the last column, therefore, Poley said, 'A shilling.' His fingers slipped into the purse Wolfall had passed to him and he pulled out a silver coin. The clerk took it, glanced at it and bit it. 'That's an Irish shilling,' he said, with a sneer that seemed to say *you can't hoodwink me, cully.* 'You'll be lucky to get more than a couple of groats for those in here. Turnkey! Here's another guest needs leading to his bed. The two groat cell it is!'

As the turnkey led him down towards the cells, lantern held high and bunch of iron keys in a great ring jangling at his hip, Poley was distracted from any thoughts of the wider situation by simple outrage at the manner in which Wolfall had gulled him – as though he was the most innocent virgin coney fresh up from the country. Not only had he been fooled into paying three pounds for two pounds in silver shillings, he now discovered that the shillings themselves were worth two groats – eight pence – instead of twelve. He had promised to pay back three pounds or sixty shillings. And for that promised outlay he had actually received forty Irish shillings, worth less than half of what he had paid out instead of the two-thirds value he had been promised. He was still planning his revenge on the devious moneylender when the turnkey stopped at the door of a cell. 'Here you are,' he said. 'The two groat. You look like a cove who can write.'

'I can write,' confirmed Poley.

The turnkey reached up and removed a writing tablet

such as a schoolboy might use. It was backed with wood and faced with wax on which a series of marks had been inscribed. 'Here,' said the turnkey, handing the writing tablet and a metal stylus to Poley. 'Write the first letter of you name and your number alongside of it.'

'P' said Poley, showing the letter to the turnkey. 'And my number?'

'Six. You'll be P6 as long as you're here and I'll keep a tally of petty charges until they adds up to some coin worth having. Then you pays up or you goes on my debtors list. And I strongly recommend you stays off of my debtors list.' He replaced the tablet on the wall and sorted through the keys as he continued to speak. 'You're late. So no victuals tonight nor drink. If you need the bucket be quick about it and then I'll bed you down. You'll learn the routines and the charges fast enough in the morning. At least you can sleep sound. Your cell's not too crowded and none of the others can reach you. Chains is too short, see?'

The door creaked open and Poley followed the lantern into the cavernous darkness.

In spite of the turnkey's cheery assurances, he did not think he was going to sleep soundly at all. But as things turned out, he was wrong. Use of the bucket relieved a good deal of personal pressure. The gyves round his ankle were not too tight and, as the turnkey had promised, there was an empty space between himself and his nearest companion. The aching in his head and the nausea which had accompanied it eased. The straw was cleaner and thicker than he had feared it would be. His situation was nothing like comfortable and the cell was nowhere near warm. But as he lay on his back with extra straw piled to support his damaged cranium as best as could be, he was able to see through the slits in the walls – the closest they had to windows. There was a full moon hanging low in a jewelled sky and he was staring mindlessly at this when exhaustion finally claimed him.

*

Poley was awakened next morning not only by the sunshine streaming through the slit of the window but also by the arrival of a new companion. The turnkey led a frightened, confused-looking man to the empty space beside the battered intelligencer. Like Poley, the new man showed every sign of having been held for some time elsewhere and in accommodation even less salubrious than this. 'You're C5,' the turnkey was informing the new arrival as he settled him into his place and put the hoop of iron round his ankle, chaining him to the wall. 'Your tab stands at two groats owed already. A bad start. You should have accepted what the money lenders offered out in Belsavage Yard. Just to tide you over 'til your family and friends can organise some aid. Always assuming you have either and if you do, that whatever they send makes it past them out at the front whose task it is to read letters and open parcels and so-forth.' The new prisoner gaped up at him, clearly overwhelmed by what was happening. Blissfully unaware, the turnkey continued, 'There's a limit, you realise, on how large I let the tab run up before I either ask to have you transferred or simply stop being of service to you'.

'Transferred?' quavered the newcomer, clearly far

beyond any concept of how terrible his existence would become if the turnkey simply left him to rot alive untended. 'Whither?'

'Down to a cell as seems more suited to your circumstances. Or over to the debtors' cell. Then you can beg through the grill and hope for the charity of passing strangers. Though in my experience such charity runs pretty thin, even on the Sabbath.'

He straightened, looked around. 'Now,' he said, broadening his remarks to his captive audience of eight chained men. 'The first charge in the morning usually concerns the bucket. Who'll be the first to spend a penny?'

He stepped out through the cell door and retrieved his record tablets, then he organised the prisoners by letter and number into the order they would be unshackled for a penny, use the bucket at yet more charge and be shackled back in place, gratis. As he did this, Poley noted that the key-ring on one hip, a lethal enough weapon in itself, was balanced by a sizeable club on the other. He also noted that his companions in misery spoke only to the gaoler. Not to each other. Not to each other yet, perhaps. But then, looking around the cell rather than at the latest man labouring over the bucket, Poley noted the air of tense suspicion. None of the others, it seemed, trusted any of the men they were surrounded by. Probably with good reason. There were *agents provocateur*, as the French had it, everywhere. Which, thought the battered intelligencer, was interesting. Because he thought he recognised his new companion in misery. Knew the face; certainly felt he recognised the voice. The accent. The tone. But he just couldn't quite put his finger on the man's identity.

'Now,' announced the turnkey, distractingly, when the last man was back in place. 'The next order of business concerns victuals. Nothing fancy,' he said pointedly to C5. 'Simple bread and ale. Part of a loaf fresh from the bakery outside and some ale from the barrel men in Belsavage Yard. One loaf. One flagon. Shared by those as can pay. And in the matter of consumables, the custom of the country is money up front.' He looked directly at Poley, then at his new companion. 'And any overpayment set against the next meal, for those rich in shillings but poor in groats and pence.'

The other six inmates wearily reached into purses and wallets. Poley did the same. His belly was rumbling. It was a full day since he had eaten and what little had been left in his lean belly was in the straw on the floor of the Newgate cell. Bread and ale sounded like manna from on high to him. But then his attention was attracted by his companion once again.

'Have mercy!' cried C5. 'I have no coin nor access to any as yet. I have been held for more than a day before my arrival here. And my belly is as empty as my purse!' Seven pairs of eyes regarded him with no sympathy whatsoever.

'No coin, no victuals,' said the turnkey. 'Now who's got a groat for their breakfast?'

Everyone had, with only that one exception. But as the turnkey came to collect Poley's Irish shilling, the intelligencer said, quietly, 'Feed one more at my charge. For today at least.'

The turnkey stopped and looked askance at him. 'You're

not some Jesuit balancing charitable works with plans to kill the Queen, Heaven defend her, are you?'

'No,' said Poley. 'I'm no Jesuit. But I'll not see a man go hungry if I can help it.'

'Only until my friends find out what has happened to me,' said C5 gratefully. 'They will see me out of here in no time I am certain. And pay for my welfare in the interim. And they will repay you, I promise. Who may I name as my kind friend and benefactor?'

'Robert Poley,' said Poley.

'Well met, Master Poley,' said C5. 'I am Henry Cuffe, Secretary to the Earl of Essex.'

'Ah,' said Poley softly, as the light of understanding began to dawn.

3

Sharing his Irish shillings with Henry Cuffe meant that Poley's funds began to run low on the morning of the third day. It also seemingly made him a friend for life. He and Cuffe were chained side by side at the end of the cell near the slit-window. They were as far from their companions in misfortune as the size of the place allowed. And they were further isolated by the positioning of the slop-bucket, which hid them – at least partially – from the others sitting on the straw-strewn stone-slab floor. Every afternoon, one of the prisoners was unshackled and made to carry the reeking vessel out to be emptied into the Fleet river which flowed by the prison. When they returned it, empty, it was always to the same place. So Cuffe and Poley found it easy enough to exchange whispered conversations without being overheard.

They talked incessantly during the waking hours when they were together, except only for those periods at dawn and dusk which they filled with silent reflection and prayer. During those times, Poley would slip a rosary out of the breast of his doublet and finger it as surreptitiously as possible. This covert activity was something Cuffe pretended not to notice as he too muttered his prayers, hands clasped reverently in front of him. At all other times, Cuffe was by far the more voluble, probably as a result of finding himself utterly out of his depth in a nightmare he had never dreamed he would have to suffer. His situation, as described to Poley, seemed to be compounded by the fact that he had no idea what he had done to warrant being taken up by the constable as he visited the bookstalls in St Paul's churchyard. Or why he had been hauled before Justice Hall, unable to defend himself against a charge he did not understand. How in the name of Heaven he had been convicted out of hand, then sentenced without being able to alert his friends. And, finally, why he had been condemned to spend some unspecified time in the Fleet with no-one apparently any the wiser. Though, thought Poley feelingly, Cuffe's unfettered volubility might also have been designed to distract him from the pain in his backside from sitting on a cold stone floor hour after hour. The intelligencer was fortunate in that both his doublet and breeches were well padded, even though parts of them were soiled and still damp.

Poley observed all this from a mental distance, as coldly and purposefully as the manner in which he had fingered the rosary, reading much into the fact that Cuffe made no remark and no report that he had done so. Cuffe's failure to react to the rosary and his all-too anxious conversation were traits he had seen before, and made good use of, when the situation dictated. At almost any time during the last ten years or more, Poley could have been found in one of London's jails, chained beside men suspected of holding treasonable views, showing them his rosary, holding calculatedly treasonous conversations with them, listening as they unconsciously confessed, unaware that every word was going to be reported to the Council. That each guilty syllable was carrying them closer to Rackmaster Topcliffe at the Tower or the Three Legged Mare at Tyburn. The simple fact which ruled Poley's world and actions was that men like these had planned in the past - and would in the future as the Council feared – to remove the occupant of the English throne by fair means or foul. Given liberty to do so thirty years earlier by Pope Pius V's *Regnans in Excelsis* bull which excommunicated the young queen and promised absolution to anyone who murdered her. Absolution and a place in heaven, in fact. As long as such men continued with their lethal plots, the Queen's life was in danger; and only men like Poley stood to guard her. In ways that even the Captain of the Queen's Guard could not conceive of.

Automatically, almost unconsciously, the intelligencer now replied to Cuffe's loquacious confusion with ready sympathy, as convincing as it was shallow. He answered Cuffe's questions with vague revelations about his own background and beliefs which were close enough to the truth to be plausible and to elicit further revelations from his companion. Consequently, Cuffe duly revealed all about his childhood in Somerset; his preferment by various noble families near his childhood home; his years at Oxford and his work with the Earl of Essex. He chatted about his experiences in Ireland, in the field with the army, in Dublin Castle and in Essex House with the Earl. About the Earl's current household and the important figures within it.

'I have often wondered,' lied Poley on the morning of the second day, 'how great houses such as those you are familiar with, Master Cuffe, are organised. I have sometimes seen great lords and ladies at a distance and thought to myself I'm sure I could find employment in their establishments if only I knew how such things were organised, for I am not without some talents.'

'Well,' Cuffe answered eagerly enough, 'I cannot speak for the generality of great houses, but I know the Earl of Essex's well enough...'

'Anything you could tell me would be most welcome! As welcome, I dare say, as that breakfast bread must be to your empty belly...'

'Of course.' Cuffe chewed ruminatively as he took Poley's point. It was Poley who had paid for the bread. A little information seemed a fair recompense

*

'Lady Frances oversees the day-to day domestic matters in Essex House, the cooks, servants and so forth with the help of Fitzherbert the major domo and the housekeeper his wife and his son Tom who is the Earl's page. Fitzherbert is the man to approach if your ambitions lie in those areas, because Lady Frances was recently delivered of a baby girl and is busy with the child. She remains fiercely loyal to my Lord of Essex, of course, despite the fact he has not yet even seen the child. Furthermore, her loyalty to her Lord has led Lady Frances to attend court almost daily, usually dressed in mourning, as she pleads the case of her husband as though he is dead to the world as well as to his Queen. Often carrying the babe into the bargain. During Lady Frances' confinement and occasional absences, the Earl's mother, Lady Lettice, Countess of Leicester, takes charge - as well she might as wife to Sir Christopher Blount who, with Sir Gelly Meyrick, stands in charge of the wider household in any case. To be fair, though,' admitted Cuffe, 'Lady Frances or Lady Lettice would have been in charge of domestic elements even had the Earl been at home instead of incarcerated with Lord Keeper Edgerton in York House.'

Poley was silent for a moment, apparently digesting all this information. But he was actually thinking about Sir Christopher Blount. They had briefly worked together some years ago, employed by Sir Francis Walsingham, the Queen's long-dead spymaster. Would Sir Christopher be friend or foe? He wondered. But then he asked, 'So it would be to these high-born ladies or their immediate underlings such as this man Fitzherbert and his wife that I might apply in the matter of employment,' mused Poley. 'But you mentioned other elements in Essex House,' he prompted. 'I see myself as something more active than a mere servant.'

And in all innocence, Cuffe prattled on. 'Indeed. And with my support, I think you would do better to consider the first of these. As assistant secretary perhaps. Can you write and cypher?'

'I was at Clare College, Cambridge,' answered Poley, truthfully, 'though there was some confusion over the matter of my graduation.' Just the way he phrased it so calculatedly made his position as a recusant as clear as praying over his rosary had done. Catholic students were forbidden graduation in almost all cases; Protestants rarely were.

'Well! There you are then!' Cuffe took this on board, becoming more confident and expansive still, though keeping his voice low: Essex House had a welcome for

Catholic malcontents along with almost every other kind, he inferred without using the dangerous language too clearly. There were great hopes that whoever succeeded Elizabeth would look kindly on the Catholic cause.

'But we digress,' he concluded. 'These more masculine elements, if I may so phrase it, are split into two sections overseen by other important individuals, who would be directed by the Earl when he is there, of course. But they fight to follow what they believe his orders would have been had he been present to issue them.' Cuffe washed the last mouthful of breakfast bread down with a draught of small beer emptying the flagon Poley had purchased for them both.

'There is the martial, almost military, element,' he continued, after wiping his mouth with the back of his hand. 'It is led by the Earl's Welsh steward Sir Gelly Meyrick. It is made up of soldiers, many from the Irish army, many also knighted by the Earl himself. All of them preferring to remain with him rather than to follow the orders of Lord Mountjoy, who has been named as his Irish replacement, in spite of the fact that he and my Lord of Essex are close friends. Mountjoy is also related to the Earl's step-father Sir Christopher Blount; and family ties are very important, of course. Most of these men seem to be in debt and desperate. They see the Earl as their last hope of solvency, let alone of standing and respect. Sir Christopher Blount and Lady Leicester, for instance, are even today fighting to pay off the late Earl of Leicester's debts, and are ever more desperate to do so. They and their household are currently resident in Essex House, having closed their main residence in Drayton Basset and their London house in Wanstead. Sir Christopher is Sir Gelly's equal in authority, being of course, the Earl's equivalent in power at Wanstead House.'

*

Cuffe at least had the good sense to lower his voice to little more than a whisper as he continued, 'Whatever the Earl's position after the succession, they all fervently believe it will be one of influence and power – no matter who sits on the throne. And they will all rise with him, as he has promised they would. Have you served as a soldier?'

'No, friend Cuffe. My service has been little more than secretarial, and to no-one of any standing or nobility. But the Earl's men are the men headed by this Welshman, you say?'

'Indeed. The steward Sir Gelly Meyrick, a Welsh soldier – and aptly enough, for many of the men in this section are Welsh too. Meyrick is supported by petty aristocrats like Sir Thomas Gerard and the Irish lord Sir Christopher St. Lawrence while more substantial friends such as Henry Wriothesley, the Earl of Southampton, Henry Percy and his cousin Thomas the Catholic Earl of Northumberland, married to Dorothy Devereux, one of the Earl's sisters, stand ready to throw their weight behind the Earl's cause if called upon. But in my opinion it is Sir Christopher Blount rather than Gelly Meyrick, even, who currently holds sway over them all. Especially while Lady Lettice and the Leicester household are in residence with us.'

Cuffe fell silent but Poley allowed his own thoughts to

run on, rehearsing a recent discussion he had held with Master Secretary Cecil. While the Queen remained immoveable and Essex stayed out of her favour, the Essex House contingent existed as a constant bodyguard for the ailing Earl; desperate to a man. That most dangerous and combustible of problems – a command of soldiers, armed and ready for battle, being held back with nothing to do. Always, therefore, on the edge of explosive violence. They saw themselves as protecting their master, when he was at home or away from home, from the kind of evils that had poisoned his father in Ireland and would literally stab him in the back in London given half a chance. Especially now, as the Earl lay far beyond their protection though less than a mile down the road. Suffering by all accounts, from the bloody flux – the same illness that had killed his father - an illness widely rumoured to have been caused by poisoning his food in Dublin Castle. The Leicester household, as Cuffe called them, were hopefully something of a balance to the more desperately warlike elements within Sir Gelly Meyrick's command, even though Lady Lettice had been a loving wife to the murdered First Earl and remained as loyal as Lady Frances to the second Earl, her son.

'But you said there were two sections, Master Cuffe,' prompted Poley after a while. 'Might there not be a place for me in the second one?'

'I think not, for you are too simple, kindly and open-handed, friend Poley. This is the intelligence section, if I may so describe it. Sir Anthony Bacon heads a web of spies and agents, even though he is bedridden and possibly near death. He is still powerful and supported by his brother Sir Francis who is much more mobile in every sense – not only moving in and out of Essex House but also from one camp to the other, so to speak; with the ear of the Queen herself as her newly-appointed Queen's Counsel Extraordinary. At the very least he is a useful go-between; perhaps a vital spy, if a gentleman can be said to lower himself to such a profession. The Bacon brothers are motivated on the one hand by the Earl's certainty that his enemies at court - Cecil, Raleigh, Walsingham and the rest - are working tirelessly to accomplish his downfall by any means they can manage. On the other hand, they are working to forge links with all of the Queen's likely successors. Bonds that are stronger than those created by Cecil, Raleigh and Walsingham. And, now I think of it, there might be employment for you as a scribe in this section, for we send out letters all over Europe in a range of languages including French, Spanish, German, Dutch, Italian, Latin and occasionally Greek – hence my association with Anthony Bacon, as well as wielding the pen on behalf of the Earl himself of course,' explained Cuffe earnestly. 'But Bacon's letters have contents that sometimes go beyond the social and academic; that are occasionally set to ensure as far as possible, that whoever ascends the throne – as someone must do soon – all of their fortunes will be mended while their enemies will fall from grace like Icarus of legend flying too near the sun with his waxen wings.'

Poley's self-effacing approach worked well enough to begin with but by the afternoon of the second day, the intelligencer discovered that gossip throughout the prison had overtaken his modest plan; had made him a celebrity among the prisoners, and something of a hero to some of them, including Cuffe. 'Is it true what they are saying?' demanded the secretary, wide-eyed, as he returned from pouring the morning's excrement onto the Fleet River and placed the empty slop-bucket precisely on the spot he had lifted it from some time earlier then wiped his hands on the thick woollen hose clothing his thighs and sat to have his ankle shackled again.

'What are they saying?' Poley genuinely didn't know.

*

'Why,' hissed Cuffe as soon as the turnkey had left the cell, 'that you have been arrested and condemned to be shackled here on the direct orders of Secretary Cecil, whom people call 'The Toad'. Orders that you be arrested and imprisoned because you wounded his man by running him through the arse in defence of the Earl's man Nick Skeres.'

'It may be…' Poley weighed the impact of Cuffe's revelations. The common people hated Cecil The Toad. The insulting nickname had even been scrawled on the door of Salisbury House, his London residence: *here lives The Toad.* Essex, on the other hand, was still the people's favourite. The hero of Cadiz and the Azores campaign, nearly ruined in Ireland by the secret machinations of The Toad and his foul cohorts. 'It may be…'

'Hush!' commanded Cuffe, too little too late. 'There are ears everywhere…'

But the situation Poley found himself in the midst of was

simply a reflection of wider problems, he admitted to himself. Problems that reflected on Master Secretary and the wayward Earl alike. Harvests had been bad of late; the last few summers and autumns cold and wet, winters harsh and spring-times non-existent; the weather out of joint. People were starving. Even those with work and food were growing desperate. Poverty-stricken families from the countryside were leaving their ruined farms and desolated small-holdings to come crawling up, begging in the London streets, selling their sons and daughters into the brothels on the South Bank, desperate for succour that never appeared. In the absence of any real replacement for the Old Church's charitable institutions, the destitute were simply starving to death in front of anyone who cared to look. But the only people who did look nowadays were the sextons' men with their death carts who collected the corpses and piled them in anonymous mass graves as though they were victims of the plague.

No-one dreamed of blaming the Queen who was constant in her protestations that she loved her people. That she was, indeed, wedded to them as her single, virginal, life proved all too clearly. So the situation must be blamed on her minsters, chief among them Cecil The Toad, whose occasional attempts to fashion a 'Poor Law' were always too little, too late. On the other hand, the dashing Essex was blameless in this catastrophe. He was almost worshipped. He was famous both for his heroic bravery and his open-handed generosity – which was why so many desperate men clung to him.

Like leeches thought Poley but he was careful to keep his

own counsel. Wary of finding himself in another trap, Poley neither confirmed or denied anything about the events which brought him here. The rumours persisted, however, and even the turnkey began to treat him with a little respect. Unfortunately, that respect did not stretch to delivering services without payment. Poley was distractedly beginning to calculate how he could get to Wolfall for further funds or cut his overpoweringly talkative and grateful companion loose, when events took another turn in the mid-morning of the third day.

The turnkey shuffled in at an hour when he was usually elsewhere. And, for the first time, he was not alone. The big, shambling tatterdemalion was followed by its exact opposite – a slim, neat, precise man of middle years. His cuffs and ruff were pristine, his cloak looked expensive, warm and new, his freshly-brushed hat sat at a precise angle, its feather on the sober side of stylish. Not a hair on his head, moustache or beard appeared to be out of place. Poley knew him at once. This was Francis Bacon who, together with his brother Antony, was in charge of the Earl of Essex's spy network, as Cuffe had already described. He was also, perhaps more relevantly in the current circumstances, as the Queen's Counsel Extraordinary, a leading member of the Bar; one of the most powerful lawyers in the country.

'Master Cuffe!' said Sir Francis, his face a mask of shock and horror, 'Even though I was alerted to the fact, I hardly believed I would find a scholar and gentleman such as yourself here!'

Poley was certain at once that Bacon was play-acting. Sir

Francis himself had occupied the debtor's cell not far from this one quite recently, Counsellor to the Queen or not. Debt was common fate among Essex's followers; and, indeed, among some of those reliant on the Royal Purse as well. The poet and politician Edmund Spenser had been found stone cold at his lodgings in King Street not long ago; starved to death by all accounts while waiting for the exchequer to disburse a grant of £50 promised by the Queen herself.

'We must secure your liberty at once,' Bacon continued. 'Wait there! I will return as quickly as I can.' He turned to leave, gesturing imperiously to the turnkey.

Poley laughed inwardly at the lawyer's thoughtless words. As though Cuffe had any choice but to *wait there*. He was chained to the wall. But then the voluble academic surprised the cynical intelligencer. 'Sir Francis!' he called. The lawyer turned back. 'This man beside me has been my friend and saviour. Can you not secure his liberty as well?'

*

Bacon's cold gaze rested on Poley for a heartbeat. 'But that is Robert Poley,' he said. 'He is Master Secretary Cecil's man. A courier and an intelligencer to the Council.'

'Not so,' said Cuffe fervently. 'Or if he was once, he is no longer. Master Secretary has cut him off. Disowned him utterly. He is here for aiding the Earl of Essex's man Nicholas Skeres, who is well known to both of us, I think. And for speaking in defence of the Earl, against Master Secretary.' The academic lowered his voice. 'I have heard that he stands accused of possessing *A Conference on the*

Succession which, as you know, is banned; and saying in public that the Queen is best succeeded by the Earl, and that as soon as possible!'

Bacon paused for a heart-beat longer, his speculative gaze still resting on Poley. 'Turned from Master Secretary to The Earl, has he? Well, he wouldn't be the first to do that.'

Poley said nothing but he met that insightful gaze as though it were a rapier blade, steadily.

'His misfortunes started when he sought to help Skeres, giving him monies because he serves the Earl, and was forced to wound Ingram Frizer, Secretary Cecil's creature, who challenged him in consequence,' persisted Cuffe anxiously. 'Furthermore, I am certain that he would be welcomed in Essex House for the services he has rendered to me if for no other reason!'

'Very well,' decided Bacon after a moment more. 'I will see what can be done.'

Poley had no idea what magic Francis Bacon used, but Cuffe and he were free by noon. The lawyer was nowhere to be seen, so they walked shoulder by shoulder through Belsavage Yard and out onto Ludgate Hill, Cuffe chattering excitedly about the welcome they would both receive in Essex House when they got there. No-one in the Yard disturbed them. Partly because Wolfall was not there, reckoned Poley. And partly because men walking *out of* the prison were nowhere near as interesting to the businessmen and women thronging the place as men being escorted *into* the prison. The sky was clouding over and a wet afternoon was in prospect so they hurried up Ludgate

Hill, across the Fleet Bridge into Fleet Street, then straight on until they reached the Temple Bar, beyond which Fleet Street became The Strand. From there it was no distance to hurry past the Middle Temple grounds to the church of St Clement Danes. Ahead of them, the Wych Street led up towards Holborn while the hill at their feet led down into The Strand which ran straight on to Charing Cross and York House where the ailing Essex lay imprisoned.

Essex House, however, stood immediately across the road on their left, the first house on The Strand. It could almost have been the last on Fleet Street but Robert Dudley, Earl of Leicester, who had caused it to be built, planned that it should be the first house on The Strand, confided Cuffe, rendered even more voluble by relief at his release. And the Earl of Essex insisted on the same thing now that the house was his. 'No-one wishing to shine at court would wish to be domiciled on Fleet Street, associated as it is with the filth of the open sewer the river has become,' said Cuffe cheerily.

Or with the prison from which we have just been released, thought Poley. He paused there, aware of the enormity of the step he would be taking if he accepted Cuffe's repeated assurance that there would be welcome and shelter for him at Essex House. But then, to be honest with himself, he had no practical alternatives. The Yeomans' house was clearly closed to him. He had no money to finance a trip to his wife in the country – nor any hope of employment there if he managed the journey somehow. The hovel Mistress Poley currently resided in belonged to her sour-faced parents in any case and he would risk anything rather than go crawling back there. But the fact clearly seemed to be that he now found himself in a place and situation which forces far beyond his control had put him in. And there was, realistically, only one path forward. He would have to take it, no matter what dangers lay in ambuscade along it.

Chattering on excitedly and hurrying as the first drops of rain began to fall, Cuffe led the way across the busy road to hammer on the great gate that led into the courtyard which fronted the main entrance to the house itself. The small postern in the great gate was opened at Cuffe's knock, and the pair stepped through into the flagged courtyard, standing between Essex House and The Strand as the gardens behind stood between it and the River. The yard was wider than the house-front which stood high and imposing. It loomed intimidatingly in solid red brick, reaching four stories before it attained the roof-leads that bounded the roof itself. The red clay roof-tiles sloped up in a hill behind them, broken by a series of dormer windows, and a low wall stood knee-high in front of them, square holes in which were releasing runoff from the rain already.

*

The roof-leads would make a good defensive position, thought Poley, his mind still running along martial lines, for they looked over the top of the solid outer wall and commanded a wide view of The Strand and Fleet Street. Take a few snaphaunce or firelock muskets up onto the leads or the dormers and there would be slaughter amongst any force trapped against the great outer gate. Or, indeed, one breaking into the courtyard and finding they had nowhere to go. Furthermore, at each corner of the broad frontage stood a turret that must offer even greater defensive potential. Back at ground-level, there were stables on the right opposite a smithy on the left – which Poley reckoned would make a tidy armoury if needed. The Earl's blacksmith could sharpen swords as easily as he could fashion horseshoes, cast bullets as well as nails. Beyond the stable and the smithy, paths led down the sides of the house towards the gardens at the rear and the River beyond.

But the pair did not linger. As the rain intensified, Cuffe led the way across to the steps that mounted up to the main door. He bounded up these with scarce-contained excitement and hammered once again. Poley followed more circumspectly, but even so he had reached Cuffe's shoulder before the door was opened. 'Master Cuffe,' said the servant who let them in. 'Welcome back, sir!' Then he saw that Cuffe was not alone and the welcome seemed to cool.

'This is my friend Robert Poley,' said Cuffe. 'He wishes to become the Earl's man. That is, he already is of the Earl's faction but he wishes to be recognised as such.'

'Master Poley,' said the servant. 'Your fame precedes you, sir. The moment you arrived I was to conduct you to Master Bacon.'

'Oh, has Sir Francis preceded us?' asked Cuffe.

'He has sir. It was Sir Francis who warned us you were coming. But I am to conduct you to his brother. Sir Anthony.'

No sooner had the servant said this than a loud voice spoke over him. Poley knew at once by the accent whose voice it was. 'You need not bother,' said Gelly Meyrick. 'I'll take Master Poley to Sir Anthony myself.'

'I shall accompany you,' said Cuffe. 'I can explain the situation to Sir Anthony.'

'No,' said Meyrick. 'Sir Francis has explained everything. Sir Antony wishes to see Master Poley alone.'

Cuffe opened his mouth, almost certainly to argue, thought Poley, but Meyrick simply turned and began to stride decisively away. Poley met Cuffe's outraged gaze and shrugged, then he turned to follow the Welsh steward. Meyrick had broad shoulders and a slim waist, thick thighs and muscular calves, his legs being well matched by his arms. He was dressed in a dull brown padded doublet and breeches, canions and hose. Shoulder-length hair fell past his slim white ruff. He was neatly turned out, as one might expect from a gentleman soldier. As he was in the house, he did not carry a rapier but there was a long dagger thrust through the back of his belt to lie across the top of his buttocks.

Poley followed Meyrick silently, keeping firm control of his imagination. Speculation could do nothing other than create fear that might prove to be groundless but would certainly prove to be distracting and dangerous. Better to stay calm and await events, thought the spy. But it seemed he could do nothing about the speed at which his heart was beating; a situation made worse by Meyrick's icy silence. This meeting would be the first test of many if he followed what was apparently firming up into a clear mission –

namely to stay undercover in Essex's household and do his best to follow Secretary Cecil's desire for the Earl's total destruction. Destruction in a manner that could not possibly lead back to Cecil or the Council and arouse the anger of the still-indulgent Queen. Or, come to that, the outrage of the hero-worshipping populace, who, it was feared, might even rise in revolt if their hero was brought down by The Toad.

Certainly, in the short term at least, he should stay here, where he had been so carefully placed, and discover the lie of the land. Cecil had other spies working undercover here, he knew – he just did not know who they were, yet. But the fact that he himself was known to be – or to have been – one of Cecil's chief intelligencers might put him in a good place to become a contact if he played his cards right - as well as in a good place to get his throat cut if he put a foot wrong. Sending him alone into the enemy camp without disguise or defence was an interesting tactic, however. But, knowing Master Secretary there would be a reason for this seemingly suicidal approach; if Poley was to be Daniel in this lions' den then there would, somewhere, be an angel to seal the lions' mouths.

*

Poley soon found himself distracted, however, by his unexpected surroundings. He knew the basic layout of Essex House, as it shared its architecture – internal and external – with York House and Durham House both of which he knew well. In the most general terms, the formal and family rooms upstairs, mostly to the front but also overlooking the gardens and the River to the rear; below stairs and to the rear with little if any view were only the servants' quarters – though some servants also slept in tiny garrets high up in the eaves. Space was likely to be at a premium. Not only were the Earl's numerous hangers-on to be accommodated here along with his household and servants, by the sound of things Lady Leicester and Sir Christopher had brought a number of their household from their great houses. The Bacon brothers would be housed with one or other of these contingents, he thought. But Meyrick passed the stairs' foot and led him into the rabbit-warren usually only occupied by retainers of one sort or another, the store rooms and the kitchens. Silently but unhesitatingly, Meyrick plunged on through the corridors past rooms of varying size, function and heat – from carpentries and cold storage rooms to oven-warmed bakeries and kitchens. The further they went, the narrower and darker the passageways seemed to become.

At last, Meyrick's purposeful footsteps slowed and Poley found himself confronted by a kind of partition that seemed designed to wall off a considerable area at the very back of the house. Meyrick opened a door in this and stepped forward into a disorientating brightness. Poley followed him, eyes narrow against the glare, every nerve alert against the possibility that this was a trap. So that, confusingly, the first thing that struck him was the smell. The whole place stank of sickness and damp. Stenches powerful enough to overcome the ripeness of any odours clinging to Poley himself and his soiled clothing. He froze, blinking away tears, vaguely aware that Meyrick had stepped behind him and closed the door. There was a moment of silence, then Francis Bacon's familiar voice said, 'Welcome, Master Poley.'

As his eyes cleared, Poley stepped forward. 'Sir Francis,' he answered guardedly as he made his formal bow. 'Sir Anthony.' The brothers could hardly have been more different. Sir Francis sat on a high-backed wooden chair beside a small table piled with documents, precisely as neat and tidy as he had appeared that morning in the Fleet. His brother lay propped against a pile of pillows in a tumbled bed within reach of that same table. His face was thin and sallow, all cheekbone and straggly beard. Hooded, intelligent eyes stared unwaveringly from the dark depths of sunken sockets. Poley had heard they suffered from occasional bouts of blindness but they looked clear-sighted now. The bedding covering his body could not conceal the bloated belly and the swollen, thick-bandaged, gout-stricken legs.

Sir Anthony explained the odour of sickness. The rest of the room explained the odour of dampness. A pair of store rooms had been knocked together into a makeshift bedroom with a third enclosed by the partition to make a dressing room cum hospital. The outer walls in all three rooms were floury with damp that seemed to be rising through the very brickwork. Sizeable windows looked out along the garden down to the River and the Essex House steps where a skiff was currently moored. By Poley's reckoning, they looked a little east of south but they still let in the last light of the low sun before it was doomed to be swallowed by the clouds already raining here. There was a rainbow over the Paris Garden on the south bank opposite.

'Thank you, Sir Gelly,' said Anthony. Even his voice was sickly and old. But he must only be in his early forties, thought Poley; the same age as he was himself and a couple of years older than his brother Francis. But, sickly or not, there was no doubting the tone of command. Apparently without another thought Meyrick turned and left the room. As the door closed behind the Welsh steward, Sir Anthony said, quietly, 'Well, Master Poley. And what are we to make of you?'

'Cuffe says he is turned,' said Sir Francis. 'Certainly, rumour has him cut off by Cecil on some whim or other and resentful. Possibly seeking redress. Mayhap revenge.'

'Cuffe does not lack learning,' nodded Sir Antony. 'But as sure as there is a Heaven above, the man lacks insight. He is an innocent, scarcely more than a babe-in-arms for all his Latin and Greek.'

'Is he such a bad judge of men?' wondered Sir Francis.

'Is he?' wondered Sir Anthony. 'What say you Master Poley?'

*

'I say, Sir Anthony, that what Master Cuffe reported to Sir Francis is the simple truth. It required understanding but no insight. I was in all innocence passing the time of day in a tavern near my lodgings when Master Secretary's creatures descended upon me. Wolfall, his moneylender and Frizer his roaring boy. Their excuse being that I had advanced some coin to Nick Skeres, who is the Earl's man. Frizer the bully challenged me over the matter and when I answered him in the street outside, I was beaten unconscious and shoved into the kennel where I near drowned. Robbed of my purse and my rapier, I was dragged before Justice Hall and thrown in the Fleet. What I have done in offence, I know not; certainly I have done nothing that I stand accused of except wounding Frizer. But I have clearly angered the Council in some manner so that they now seek to destroy me through false accusations and summary arrest. If you can discern any friendship towards me from Master Secretary Cecil in all of this then you can see a great deal more than I can. I have been done down by him and his creatures, robbed of property, reputation, comfort and lodging and I find myself saved only by Nick Skeres' friends and allies, to wit Master Cuffe and Sir Francis. If this does not show you my new situation and reason for being here as plain as day, then the problem is yours, not mine.'

'And if I decide you are a liar, that this sad story heard by my brother has no more substance than a performance at the Globe or Blackfriars; and that Master Cuffe, for all his vast learning, has been all-too easily deceived?'

'Then you must fear that I am in truth still working for Master Secretary Cecil despite all the evidence to the contrary. And, if that were the case, you would need to decide how you should react to this suspicion.'

'And if I wish to react by slitting your throat and leaving your body outside Cecil's front door at Salisbury House beneath the writing that labels him *The Toad*?'

'I suggest that it would be unwise to do so – or even to have me disappear, in fact,' answered Poley, his tone reflecting a calm he did not feel. 'For you know that

Master Secretary has eyes and ears here in Essex House that will report matters to him. Especially were I still his man in truth. Anything out of the ordinary, particularly of a fatal nature, might stir him and the Council into retaliation. Which might prove dangerous while the Earl your master is caged in York House and so near death with the bloody flux. There is, as you of all people must understand, a danger in even the slightest hesitation in his treatment. Her Majesty, I understand, has sent no fewer than eight doctors to examine him. Eight doctors and her special soup.'

'Her soup!' Sir Francis almost scoffed.

'Perhaps it would be as well, Sir Francis,' observed Poley quietly, 'to remember that the last great favourite to whom she sent her special soup was the Earl's step-father Robert Dudley, Earl of Leicester, as he rode north in Armada Year, growing ever sicker as he did so. The outcome, as I'm sure you know, was fatal.'

'A threat?' whispered Sir Anthony.

'A consideration. Against which letting me run free to convince you and the highly suspicious household of my good intentions towards the Earl must carry some weight.'

'At least it would give us time to devise a fate for you that causes no alarm to the Secretary or the Council,' said Sir Francis.

'Or one we can explain away,' added Sir Anthony, 'as the death of Christopher Marlowe was explained away seven years ago. Of course, the middle route – and one which might serve us well,' he mused after a moment more, 'is to let Sir Gelly and Sir Christopher Lawrence have their way with you. They have questions they wish to have answered. And, though they might lack the equipment or expertise of Rackmaster Topcliffe in the Tower, they are sure that you would tell them everything they want to know after a while.'

'I can see two possible problems with that notion, Sir Anthony.' Poley held up a finger. '*Imprimis*, that approach would be bound to lead me to a fate similar to Marlowe's, with the concomitant dangers to the Earl we have just discussed' He held up another. '*Secundum*, it would in any case be a waste of their time. If they simply ask what they want to know, I shall answer as truthfully as I am able without any pressure being applied.'

The brothers exchanged a glance that seemed to establish some kind of agreement. 'I'm satisfied,' said Sir Francis.

'As am I,' said Sir Anthony. 'For the time-being.'

*

'I will send to Hog Lane for Master Poley's possessions, clothing and other necessaries,' said Sir Francis. 'Then we must see to the matter of tending that headwound, bathing, and dressing in clean raiment.'

Sir Anthony reached across to the table and lifted a bell which the pile of documents had concealed. He rang this, and almost immediately there was a soft knocking at the door.

'Come!' called Sir Anthony, and a slight young man entered. Poley did not have any particular knowledge about Sir Anthony's household – as he did about the Earl's, for instance. But the moment the newcomer spoke, Poley knew him.

'Oui, Monseigneur?' This was Sir Anthony's servant Jacques Petit who had served him during his years in France and followed him to England on his return.

'Jacques, conduct Master Poley to Fitzherbert and ask him to arrange ablutions and accommodation. Master Poley's necessaries will be arriving in due course.'

'Of course, Monseigneur. Master Poley, if you will follow me…'

As Poley obediently followed the Frenchman out through the maze of corridors, he allowed his mind freer rein than he had permitted on his way in. Sir Anthony clearly and understandably remained suspicious. But Poley could now add Sir Francis to Henry Cuffe on the growing list of his friends in Essex House. That was a list which would require careful nurturing if he was to survive – let alone do any real service to Master Secretary. Should his first moves be defensive – keeping his head low, making himself as nearly invisible as possible? Or should he be more active, seeking out Cecil's other spies in the household and challenging any suspicions voiced against him? As he followed Jacques Petit into Fitzherbert's office, he decided that circumstances far beyond his control were likely to decide the matter for him.

'You present me with a conundrum, Master Poley,' said Lady Frances' major domo. 'Of course, I am happy to accommodate you at Sir Antony's command given only the agreement of Lady Frances and Lady Lettice. But where shall I put you? The household as it currently stands has been organised in sections for simplicity and efficiency. So where would you best be placed? In the

Secretariat, alongside Master Cuffe and Sir Henry Wotton
who is in charge of it? Or rather in the Martial section with
Sir Gelly Meyrick, Sir Christopher St Lawrence, Sir
Ferdinando Gorges and the rest? Or, again, with what we
might term the Leicester household with Sir Christopher,
Lady Lettice and the others?'

Gelly Meyrick and Christopher St Lawrence interrupted
the major domo's thoughts by shouldering in through the
door one after the other. 'No need to trouble yourself,
Fitzherbert,' growled Meyrick. 'We'll take care of Poley.'

The major domo said nothing but his lips thinned and his
eyes narrowed in a frown. Jacques Petit was not so quiet.
'You'll do well to calculate how far you can go in causing
affront to Sir Anthony, monsieur,' he warned. 'He has
given orders that Master Poley be housed, not harmed.
Also Sir Francis and, I believe, Master Cuffe will stand for
him.'

The two soldiers hesitated but Poley was pretty sure they
were not unduly discomfited by the list of men they might
offend by damaging their unexpected guest. The hesitation
was enough, however, to let another player join the game.
Lady Leicester's husband, Sir Christopher Blount entered
the crowded little room. It was immediately obvious that
his presence and importance were at least equal to Gelly
Meyrick's. The Welshman and the Irishman both stepped
back. Christopher Blount was a tall, slim man whose long
limbs looked every bit as powerful as Meyrick's. His
clothing was richer and more ornate. His hair and beard
were trimmed as precisely as Francis Bacon's. He had
piercing blue eyes which not only betrayed a decisive,

intelligent character but also explained why the Earl of Leicester's widow had fallen so completely in love with him mere months after her second husband's death. And he returned her affection by all accounts, even though she was nearly ten years older than he was. He also had the military swagger that made it no surprise to realise that he had been a colonel with a heroic reputation in Essex's famously successful attack on Cadiz and his expedition to The Azores.

'Well, Fitzherbert,' he barked. 'Have you housed Master Poley yet?'

'We were just debating the matter Sir Christopher...'

'Well don't bother. He'll come with me into the Leicester household.' Sir Christopher Blount turned to the intelligencer as though there was no-one else in the little room. 'We are old friends. More than that, I haven't worked out the precise degree of our relationship, but my mother was a Poley. Lady Margery Poley of Badley, some sort of cousin of your father's, I believe. It is a relationship I mean to stand by.' He turned back to Fitzherbert and continued, still paying no attention whatsoever to Meyrick and St Lawrence. 'He comes with me. He stays with me. And anyone wishing him ill or doing him harm will answer to me!'

*

'Even were we not already acquainted,' said Sir Christopher, 'blood is thicker than water.'

'So they say,' agreed Poley as he followed the decisive commander out of the servants' areas and into the great house's public domains. 'And I am most grateful that you believe in the saying.'

'My belief will only take us so far,' warned Sir Christopher.

'How far is that?' wondered Poley

'To Lady Lettice's chamber. As Thomas a Kempis observed, *Man proposes, God disposes*. In our household it is Lady Lettice who wields that authority. Indeed, there are times here in Essex House when even Lady Frances defers to her. And Lady Frances as you must know, was a Walsingham.'

'The only daughter of the late Sir Francis and widow of Sir Philip Sidney the poet, courtier and hero of Zutphen,' Poley nodded. It was common knowledge after all. 'But Lady Lettice was not only a Knollys born and bred, she was a Devereux by marriage and the Earl's mother, before the First Earl died in Ireland and she attracted the attention of the Earl of Leicester.'

'Indeed. I am third in the line of her husbands and thoroughly content to be so. The Earl her son is a good friend to me rather than a step-son. I believe you wish to be of service to him. I wish to help you in that endeavour. Especially as, as you well know, I too have turned my coat and changed camps from the Council to the Earl.'

This conversation took the two men to a large, bright room on the first floor which shared the view with Anthony Bacon's sickroom below but from a superior aspect. And there was no sign or smell of the dampness. Sir Christopher opened the door himself and the two men stepped through side by side. As they did so, they fell under the scrutiny of a lady seated comfortably, apparently enjoying the sight of the clouds snuffing out the last of the sun. Sufficient brightness lingered above the Paris Garden, the Thames and the gardens of Essex House to show her profile, which appeared to Poley to be that of a woman a good ten years younger than he knew Lady Lettice to be. Like the door, the lady was unattended. A situation that Poley supposed to be unusual. And the only reason he could think of to explain it was that the lady, like Sir Anthony Bacon, had been expecting him and wished to hold a private conversation with him.

The youthful profile was presented only for a moment before the Countess of Leicester swung right round. As she did so, she revealed a high, pale forehead that remained unlined despite her years. Green cat's eyes. A long, straight nose, a firm mouth and a determined chin. Her hair was piled in fashionable ringlets and was the same flame red as the Queen's, and indeed, that of the Queen's mother Queen Anne Boleyn, who had been Lady Lettice's great aunt. Royal blood *was* clearly thicker than water, thought Poley as he, like his companion, gave the formal bow her years and standing required.

'So this is him?' demanded the countess as the two men straightened to stand shoulder to shoulder before her.

'It is,' answered her husband.

'You need not have confirmed it, Sir Christopher. The man could be your brother, almost your twin. You are alike in age, I hazard. Certainly similar in build. And – save for some circumstance of beard, hair and cleanliness - your faces are alike. Your eyes, in particular, are much alike.' She paused, lowered her head in a slow motion of courteous welcome. 'We shall be pleased to see you joining our household Master Poley. And more pleased still to see you after you have bathed and changed. Sir Christopher, tell Sir Anthony's physician to see to the wound in your cousin's head.'

'I believe he has been instructed to do so already, My Lady. He awaits only the arrival of a bath, which in turn only awaits the arrival of Master Poley's necessaries from his lodgings.'

'Very well. And has your cousin been assigned quarters?'

'Not as yet My Lady.'

'As close to ours as can be managed, Sir Christopher. He is, after all, family.'

Fitzherbert found Poley a good-sized corner room at the end of the corridor occupied by Sir Christopher and the Countess. The windows on one wall looked out over the smithy and Fleet Street, and on the other looked over the stables and The Strand. Such rooms being notoriously draughty, the bed was a heavily curtained four-poster and a lusty fire blazed in the grate. Poley had done little more than glance around when a gentle scratching at the door announced Jacques Petit and the modest boxes of Poley's possessions from the Yeomans' house in Hog Lane. The young Frenchman showed a small team of servants into the room and, as his clothes and books were unpacked and stored, Petit led him down to a warm room between the kitchens and Sir Antony's sick-room where he discovered a steaming bath, a pile of towels, a warm robe and a doctor.

4

Poley lay back in the steaming water and let his mind drift while Anthony Bacon's doctor, Dr Wendy, attended to his head. The bath was a traditional design, fashioned from half of a large barrel. It stood upright beside the drain that would guide the water out into the garden when the bung at the bottom was removed, in a room close to the kitchens to make it easy to fill with tureens of water hot from the cooking fires. It had been just possible for Poley to step over the high side into it and sit down on the submerged stool provided for the purpose, though he suspected some shorter occupants would need a stepping stool to get in and some help to get out again. He was the first to use the facility today, though he had been warned there was a queue. There would be bodies to wash though mostly without soap, one after another, until the water grew cold and the bung was pulled at last. He tried for a moment to remember the last time he had been immersed in water this hot and this clean. *Never*, he thought. The edge of the barrel, lined with cloths, came up to his shoulder-blades at the back but its circumference was not large enough for his knees to be under the surface in front; they stuck up like white islands. The water was as hot as he could bear and there was castile soap available but Poley could do nothing until Dr Wendy was finished. So, as gentle fingers cleaned away the dried blood and began to probe the damage beneath it, he allowed his thoughts to wander.

What had at first glance seemed to be a dangerously ill-thought-out plan was beginning to show more promise. He had been sent into Essex House as himself, with no disguise or cover that he understood or had helped to plan. But this appeared to be a surprisingly effective strategy rather than a dangerous gamble. Too many of the Earl's family and followers knew who he was in any case and would recognise him no matter what. Most of those who knew him had good reason to wish him ill and perhaps to do him harm. Those facts alone gave unexpected weight to the deception because unless Poley was telling the truth about turning from Cecil to Essex, he was plainly committing suicide in coming here. Furthermore, there was no alternative to revealing his true identity. There was no make-up or wig that would disguise his appearance as they did actors on the stage. Or as, it was said, these things served to disguise the Queen's true age and appearance at court. The discovery of which, of course, was what had put the Earl of Essex where he was – both physically and politically. But it appeared that Poley's true identity had elements that might help rather than hinder him in this still dangerous situation. Those he might look to for support now apparently included the Earl's mother, her husband, Poley's distant cousin who had briefly worked for Sir Francis Walsingham in the past and then, as he said himself, become a turncoat. To them, add Francis Bacon and Robert Cuffe. The main problem, as far as he could see, lay in the differing beliefs and expectations of these apparently willing supporters.

Cuffe, of course, was motivated by gratitude and by a naturally open heart – arising from a situation that had been as carefully constructed as any performance at the Globe. Sir Francis Bacon appeared to have been swayed by Cuffe's belief in Poley's story. Furthermore, Poley had no doubt that Lady Lettice wished to accept him into the Leicester household because he appeared to her to be a potential asset in her fight to restore her son to the power and position he had lost so disastrously in Ireland and at Nonsuch. Sir Christopher was willing to stretch the outer limits of his familial relationships at her behest because, like her, he believed Poley could be manipulated into helping Essex's cause, even if he was lying when he said he wished to do so now. Sir Christopher Blount had worked for Walsingham in the past. He would be well aware of Poley's continued employment by Cecil up to the present. Or, rather, *almost* up to the present – until the falling-out, the arrest and the sojourn in the Fleet. But Sir Christopher himself had changed sides from the Council to the Earl and he seemed have some understanding, therefore, when Poley protested that he had done the same. Understandably so. Either way, Poley had little doubt that Lady Lettice and her husband hoped he would prove an undercover equivalent to Francis Bacon, able to carry messages and maybe more between Essex House and Salisbury House; eventually perhaps between Essex and Cecil themselves. And that Cecil might even have placed him here with that very purpose in mind. There was, it seemed, sufficient self-delusion hereabouts to encompass that strange notion with ease.

*

Was it possible Sir Francis and his ailing brother saw him in the same light as the Leicesters? He doubted it very much. He doubted in fact that Francis and Anthony actually both saw him in the same way. He got the feeling that Francis might support him – perhaps even more effectively than Cuffe. Anthony on the other hand didn't trust him at all, despite the case Poley had made in the stinking sickroom. But then, Essex's spymaster might well see him as a potential pawn to be used will-nilly in the larger game of thrones and successions he was playing. Only time would tell.

But Cuffe's suggestion, thrown away without a second thought, had merit. With luck, it would give Poley a reason for staying as part of the combined household; one strong enough to explain his continued presence. A positive purpose rather than the simple negative of hiding from the Council and their sinister acolytes out to destroy him. One that would also allow him to test what each of the Bacon brothers truly thought. How far even Anthony might trust a Robert Poley avowedly at war with Master Secretary; and what use he might wish to put such a creature to. A bitter turncoat keen to avenge the damage done to his person, possessions and profession by thwarting the Council's plans for the future would certainly be a useful weapon in the elder Bacon's armoury. Especially if Poley, with the Bacon brothers' assistance, could exercise his revenge by raising Essex, the hated Council's greatest foe, high above them in the end. Poley's mind was made up. He would see about joining Cuffe and the others in the

Secretariat, therefore, writing letters on behalf of the Earl at first; but later, perhaps, on behalf of Sir Anthony the spymaster.

Poley considered himself well qualified. He had a fair round hand. Courtesy of his frequent travels through Europe on behalf of the Council, his grasp of a series of North European languages almost matched the Latin and Greek which he had learned on his way to Clare College, Cambridge. He also understood French, Spanish and Italian. Like Raleigh, Essex had an enquiring mind, fascinated by the seemingly limitless possibilities of the world around him and the Heavens above it. He was, Poley knew, in correspondence with scholars and philosophers as well as with sailors, soldiers and courtiers all over Europe. His correspondents, via his Secretariat, apparently included, among others, Jacobus Arminus the Dutch philosopher, the Italians Tomaso Campanella the Jesuit, Cesare Cremonini and Galileo Galilei; the German Nicolaus Torellus, and the precocious young anatomist Caspar Bartholin of Copenhagen. Much of the correspondence would be in Classical Latin and Greek, of course, but there must be men in the Secretariat who spoke and wrote the recipients' native languages as well.

Essex was not alone in this breadth of correspondence. Sir Anthony had begun to correspond with the philosopher Michel de Montaigne during his years in France. Before French correspondent had died and Anthony's letters had turned, it was said, towards the Spanish court and the Scottish court amongst other places. Dealing less in in matters of natural philosophy and more in those of the

Queen's succession. At which point they had passed from good, clear English or Spanish into all-but impenetrable cyphers. So Poley's first order of business must be to discover which of Cuffe's colleagues fulfilled what part of the Earl's wide-ranging correspondence. Then look for an opening he could fill.

Or create one.

'I have cleaned the wound,' the doctor interrupted Poley's thoughts. 'It has stopped bleeding and will not need stitching or bandaging. There is swelling but no softness. There is a contusion therefore but your skull seems whole. Send word to me however, if you experience any powerful headaches or dizziness.'

Poley nodded, thanked the man, reached for the soap and began to wash.

Poley and Cuffe had missed dinner at mid-day but there was a formal supper held in the great hall just after sunset. Poley, wrapped in towels beneath the voluminous robe and smelling of lemons courtesy of the castile soap, retired to his room as soon as his ablutions were complete. He was guided this time by young Tom Fitzherbert, Essex's page. 'Fear not, Master Poley,' Tom assured him, 'you will soon be as familiar with the house and the household. I must observe, though, that you are fortunate in your accommodation. Essex House is badly overcrowded and more men seem to arrive each day, all desperate and many half-starved. But Lady Frances, on the Earl's behalf, will never turn any away. And they are not only to be accommodated but fed and watered into the bargain. My Father says much more like this and we will have to hire

more cooks and set up as many tents in the gardens as were
erected in Ireland to house the army there!'

*

A clean and freshly-dressed Poley joined the Leicester
household as they descended in formal ranks and in
anticipation of the meal. Apart from Lady Lettice and Sir
Christopher, he knew none of his new associates. But, he
reasoned, he would have plenty of time to learn who they
were and whether they might have any importance in any
plans he was able to formulate. They were easy enough to
identify. All the members of the Lady's household wore
the Leicester coat of arms – even Sir Christopher. But
more importantly still, he wished to examine the Essex
household, equally clearly identified by the Earl's coat of
arms, except for his friends and associates of independent
wealth and power who were visitors rather than members
of the household. All of whom he recognised in any case.
He needed to see who else was there who might know him
– which recent experience suggested could be a help as
much as a hindrance.

As Poley entered the great hall just behind Lady Lettice
and Sir Christopher – family taking pride of place – he
caught the eye of Cuffe. The innocent academic gave a
friendly wave. Cuffe was amongst the Secretariat, all
wearing Essex badges. They were led by Sir Henry
Wotton, as scribe in chief, rather than by Sir Anthony
Bacon who no doubt remained in bed. Sir Francis Bacon
was also notable by his absence. Wotton and Poley were
old acquaintances but by no means close ones – they
exchanged no greeting when their eyes met. The familiar

figure of Gelly Meyrick swaggered in with St Lawrence at one shoulder and Ferdinando Gorges, Governor of Plymouth wearing that city's coat of arms, at the other. They too failed to greet the newcomer in the Leicester household. The men who had accompanied Essex to Nonsuch were familiar faces ranked behind them and, further back still Nick Skeres, who graced Poley with a curt nod.

But Poley's attention was soon distracted. His gaze was focused on the leaders of the Essex contingent, not their followers. In front of them all were two ladies. A tall woman in her early thirties dressed in black led the Essex House dependents with a shorter lady of more advanced years at her side. The taller of the two was Frances, Lady Essex. Poley had known her from childhood when she had been plain Frances Walsingham and he had worked for Master Secretary Cecil's predecessor as Her Majesty's spymaster, Sir Francis Walsingham. Time out of mind over the years he had visited The Papey, Walsingham's London home hard up against the City Wall opposite St Mary Axe, where Camomile Street became Bevis Marks. Or, later, at the Walsinghams' house south of the River at Barn Elms. He vaguely remembered first seeing her as a four-year-old when he, recently down from Cambridge and just starting out in the service, had been involved in the outer edges of what became The Ridolfi Plot. The Ridolfi Plot had been one of the earliest serious attempts to assassinate Queen Elizabeth and replace her with a Catholic monarch – preferably the Queen of Scots - unless the entire country could be pulled under the rule of the late

Queen Mary Tudor's Catholic husband, King Philip of
Spain. Who, as Bloody Mary's widower, was seen by
some as having a powerful right to succeed her to the
English throne.

As time went on and Poley gained experience and
seniority through his work on other plots centred around
conspirators like Sir Francis Throckmorton and his wife
Bess, Anthony Babington and John Ballard, he saw her
grow to womanhood and be wedded first to Philip Sidney
and then, after Sidney's heroic death at the Battle of
Zutphen, to Robert Devereux. Their glances met and he
knew at once she recognised him, which was no surprise.
But, he wondered, did she count him as friend or foe; and
which of those two opposites might he rely on her to be?

Lady Frances turned away and spoke to her companion
who, judging from her formal dress, had accompanied
Essex's wife directly from the court. At no time during all
this had anyone stopped moving. Chance brought Poley
quite close to the two women heading the Essex
household, therefore, as he was – at least for the time-
being- amongst those heading the Leicester household. So,
as the diners were guided to their seats by the Fitzherberts
and the house servants, Poley came face to face with Lady
Essex's companion and he recognised her as clearly as he
had recognised Lady Frances. He caught his breath as his
heart thumped unaccustomedly loudly and quickly in his
breast. It was Lady Janet Percy, Cecil's most reliable
informant amongst the Queen's handmaidens. Whom he
had last seen this close-to in the flesh when she fed back
to him the details of what had happened when the Earl of

Essex burst uninvited into the Queen's most private chamber at Nonsuch. But who had occupied his mind and imagination spectrally much more recently still.

*

Supper came and went in a series of removes which Poley ate but hardly tasted and had he been asked later what he actually consumed, he would have had almost no idea. Conversation swirled around him but he heard little and spoke less. He had acquaintances who indulged in new-fangled ideas from Italy, such as forks. But Poley was staunchly traditional in this as in much else. Dagger and digits were good enough as mealtime tools for him, with sauces and gravies sopped up by the trenchers of bread on which the courses were served; finger bowls and napkins as required to keep hands, faces, beards and clothing clean. Such was his preoccupation, however, that he was lucky he didn't find himself consuming morsels of his own fingers. Especially as the dagger, borrowed from Cuffe, had a blade as sharp as a razor.

Called out of his brown study by the noise of bagpipes, he looked up to see that the evening's entertainment had begun. Two of St Lawrence's Irish followers were performing a sword dance with crossed blades unsheathed and gleaming wickedly on the floor while their flashing feet were bare and their toes at serious risk. It was the sound, however, more than the vision which recalled him to himself.

To discover that the companion on his left hand was deep in an earnest conversation he could not remember starting or participating in. 'Therefore I owe Master Cuffe almost as much in goodwill as Master Cuffe vows that he owes to you…' The conversant's voice just rose above the tortured-cat screaming of the Irish pipes.

'Master Cuffe is too kind,' said Poley automatically. 'He owes me nothing.'

'I believe he would beg to differ…'

'Well, well, let it rest.' Poley abruptly realised he was probably talking to a member of the Secretariat that he planned on joining. The man was wearing Essex's crest and was clearly a friend of Cuffe's. His interest stirred. 'Tell me, what is your function within the household?'

'Why, I am one of the Earl's secretaries,' his companion confirmed.

Poley's neighbour was younger than Cuffe by a couple years and seemed almost equally as innocent, judging by his wide eyes and open expression. 'So you work for Sir Henry Wotton? Or is it Sir Anthony Bacon? Or, perhaps, both?'

'Each, I would say. *Both* might lead one to infer that they share their responsibilities. But in fact, each is fiercely independent of the other and there is, as they say, *no love lost* between them.'

'But they each make similar demands, Master… I'm sorry, I didn't catch your name amongst the skirling of the pipes.'

'I am Thomas Legge. As I was saying, I was at one time a student of Master Cuffe's at Oxford, and he has done me the good office of recommending me to the Earl for employment here, even though our ways have been parted for ten years and more. So, to answer your question straight: we members of the Secretariat each have our particular areas of expertise.'

'I see. And are you all the Earl's men – as your badges would suggest – or might someone from the Leicester household gain employment alongside you?'

'That would require some negotiation, I suppose. But I believe, if the speciality was seen as sufficiently vital, exceptions could be made. We are all on the same side, after all.'

'So, Master Legge, may one enquire, what is your speciality? I would guess an Oxford man and student of Master Cuffe's must be involved in communications written in Latin or Greek.'

'Not so! I handle much of the communications with Denmark. I have visited Copenhagen, Aarhus, Skanedebourg; and Elsinore, the court of the late King Frederick who died in Armada Year.'

'An unusual experience.' Poley was genuinely surprised. He had taken messages to Elsinore and Copenhagen himself and supposed his involvements there must be rare, perhaps unique. 'May one ask how you achieved it?'

'I am related to George Bryan, Groom to the Chamber,' Legge explained, 'who was at one time a player with the Lord Chamberlain's Men.'

'He did well to leave them. Acting is a corrupt and sinful profession. But I do not see the relevance…'

'It has its uses, I believe. It plays games with truth and reality, does it not? Such games can be of vital moment given the right situation. However, my cousin George Bryan and I accompanied Will Kempe the famous clown soon after I came down from Oxford. We two, Will Kempe and Thomas Pope who has remained an actor, all travelled together when Kempe toured the Low Countries and Denmark in the two years before Armada Year. I was little more than travelling companion and auditor; holding the prompt book as occasion dictated. But I became fluent in the Danish tongue and…' Legge's voice tailed off, as though he was suddenly worried that he might be giving too much away.

'… and conversant with the Danish court perhaps,' Poley prompted. 'At Elsinore. In the year before the princess, Anne of Denmark, became wife to King James and thus the Queen of Scotland.' He lowered his voice although well aware that the bagpipes made it near inaudible in any case. 'And, some might wish, Queen of England in reality and in due course.'

*

'Indeed.' Legge blinked rapidly as though Poley had slapped his face. He paused for a moment, frowning. Then he continued, 'I was fortunate in getting to know Prince Christian who was a lad of some ten years old in those days. And by chance also I came to know Jorgen Rozenkrantz who was among the Regent Council that held power on the Prince's behalf, after his father King Frederick died, until he was old enough to assume the throne himself.'

'An almost miraculous turn of fortune, friend Legge. To know old King Frederick, father to the Scottish Queen, and her young brother, now King Christian - as well as the most important member of the Regency Council - who remains, I believe, a power in the land! But still, I have heard of this man Kempe and his mission to the court at Elsinore. There are those who believe he was employed by Sir Francis Walsingham as a spy, which might explain the breadth and depth of your own acquaintance amongst such important personages.'

'Cousin George and I knew nothing about such things...' Legge's frown deepened.

'However you came by the knowledge, you learned the language and the names of men and women at the court,' Poley persisted smoothly. 'Yes. I can see how such acquaintance would prove useful to the Earl; perhaps even vital under some circumstances. No-matter how innocently it was obtained.'

The pipes fell silent and the men who had performed the sword-dance retired to count their toes amid generous applause loud enough to stop Legge giving any reply. Gelly Meyrick rose. He signalled to Thomas Gerrard who also rose. Both men walked round to the clear space in front of the tables that had just been vacated by the sword-dancers. The manner in which they were easing their shoulders warned Poley that they were about to fight an exhibition bout. Their doublets were removed. Four line-judges took up positions at the corners of the makeshift piste. The director of the bout brought their rapiers in. Each man took his weapon and extended the loosening of his shoulders by wielding the lengthy blades. They each started stepping forward and back to ease the muscles of their thighs and calves. Then, at a word from the director they stopped.

Both men formally saluted each other. They turned to the three ladies and bowed once to each. They turned back and fell into their preferred positions as the director called 'En garde!' All conversation stilled and an atmosphere of tension settled on the room. As had been the case with the swords for dancing, both of these blades were naked. The director called 'Engage!'

At the first bell-like ringing as the blades crossed each other, Poley sat back, frowning. Meyrick had bowed to Lady Frances, Lady Lettice and Lady Janet. But his threatening gaze had been unwaveringly fixed on him.

This was not an exhibition bout at all. It was a threat.

Although the fire had burned low, Poley's room was still hot when he reached it an hour later. Even so, his preparations for the night involved only the removal of his doublet, but not his belt or shoes. When he pulled the curtains surrounding his bed back, he was still holding his borrowed dagger and regretting the disappearance of his sword. Only when he was satisfied that he was alone and slid the bolt securing the door home did he wash his face and hands in the ewer of water by the bed, make use of the chamber pot, snuff the candles and the lamps – all except one which he left burning on his bedside table beside his naked dagger. Then he made sure that the bed-curtains were tied back as tightly as possible, lay down on the coverlet and stayed awake for a while, watching the red shadows begin to gather like congealing blood as the light from the fire died, all his attention focussed on the door.

It was the gentle tapping that awoke him. Gentle tapping rather than the full-scale assault from Gelly Meyrick and his cohorts he had been expecting. Nevertheless, as he swung his legs off the bed, he caught up his dagger as well as the low-burning candle. He crossed to the door as swiftly and silently as creaking floorboards allowed, still half convinced this was some kind of trick. 'Yes?'

'Master Poley?' A woman's voice. To set him at ease before Meyrick's trap was sprung?

'Yes. And you are?' He whispered in return.

'Agnes Alnwick. My mistress wishes conference with you.'

'Your mistress?'

'Lady Janet Percy.'

*

Poley's door was secured by a simple bolt which he slid back without difficulty using his dagger-hand. The door whispered open an inch or two and there, standing alone in the corridor outside was a young woman. The candle she was holding showed an anxious expression. So, thought Poley, maybe I'm not the only one at risk here. He pulled the door wider with his foot, stepped out, glancing up and down the corridor to satisfy himself that it was empty, slipped the dagger into his belt and pulled the door to. 'Lead on, Agnes,' he whispered.

The route between the two rooms was lengthy, the corridors and stairwells dark and silent except for their shielded candle-flames and hushed footsteps. It was also direct and easy to remember. At last Agnes stopped at a door and tapped it just as she had tapped at his. 'Come!' came a quiet order. Agnes pushed the door and the pair of them stepped in.

Poley found himself in a room that was at once larger and warmer than his but was a reception room rather than a bedchamber. There were candles on every surface. The fire had not been allowed to die down. Lady Janet sat at the outer edge of the flickering light and stultifying heat. She was ready for bed, dressed in modest night attire, several layers deep. Which was a relief to Poley who had, for a moment imagined he might discover her as Essex had discovered the Queen; or – worse – in the state in which he had last seen Joan Yeomans in private. In which state she had filled his imagination more than once of late.

Another case of self-delusion, he thought as he paused inside the door and made his bow, holding the candle well clear. Nevertheless, his heart was pounding and his mouth was dry.

'May I entertain you, sir?' Lady Janet asked, nodding towards a table that contained a bottle and two glasses as he straightened.'

'If you please, Lady Janet.'

Lady Janet gestured to Agnes who put down her candle and poured two substantial measures from the bottle. She passed one glass to Poley who also put his candle down and took it. She passed the other to her mistress, who sipped appreciatively at once.

Poley did the same and was lucky not to choke.

'It is a particularly potent uskebeagh from Scotland, a little north of my own home on the Borders,' Lady Janet explained, amused at the sight of his streaming eyes. 'You had best be seated before the full impact hits you.' As Poley obeyed, she continued, 'Leave us, Agnes.'

'You wished to see me, Lady Janet,' said Poley as Agnes hurried obediently out of the room and he regained the power of speech.

'That I do, Master Poley. But we had better not linger, I think. My reputation is likely suffering more damage that it can readily bear every second that you remain in my private chamber. You a notable *swordsmith*, according to Master Yeomans at least. And myself unchaperoned.' Lady Janet sounded not in the least worried by her position or Poley's reputation. She appeared to be amused, if anything, he thought. She sipped once more.

'You have a message for me, My Lady?'

'Not a message. Not as such.'

'Then what?' Poley snapped; only to realise as he spoke that it was he, not she, who was feeling the pressure here. And the impact of the uskebeagh. So he modified the rudeness of his sharp riposte by adding, 'By your leave…'

Lady Janet inclined her head in mute forgiveness of the solecism.

'What is your purpose in calling me here?' he continued. 'Damage to your reputation or no. Have you a message to give me?' He sipped the fiery liquid again as she considered her reply.

'You stand in no need of any obvious intercourse from me, Master Poley. And in truth, I have little to give you that is clear.'

'Then what, my Lady?'

'A moment's reflection must show you that I have knowledge which could only have come from one source…'

'Master Yeomans' testimony before the Star Chamber…'

'And that fact alone should make plain to you that my presence here is not without purpose. That what is happening has been caused to happen. And if that is so, then it has been caused in the expectation of an outcome. One dictated by the originator of the circumstances in which you currently find yourself. But then, by extension, the possibility that this originator must at all costs remain demonstrably unattached and innocent of any outcomes which might follow any action you might choose to take.'

Poley remained silent. His mind turned Lady Janet's wilfully obscure statements over and over. She might suppose that what she said and how she said it went some way to ensuring secrecy but in truth everything seemed as light as day. Poley was caught in a web of Master Secretary's weaving. On the one hand, Cecil required Essex be destroyed. On the other, Poley had to engineer matters in such a way that Cecil was demonstrably innocent of any involvement whatsoever. And the word 'engineer' was the right one. For on the battlefield it was the engineers' duty to tunnel in secret beneath the enemy's lines and plant there petards that would blow their foemen all to atomies.

*

Poley stayed with Lady Janet until they had both finished their drinks but their conversation did not get any clearer. He had been on the point of telling her what he planned as his next step but even that simple revelation felt almost like a betrayal and so he revealed nothing. Not even when she asked him about the young man he had been in such animated conversation with over supper. Telling her a little about Master Legge's adventures with Kempe the clown and the Danish court at Elsinore came as something of a relief. At least it had no obvious hidden meanings and did not tax his wits with a kind of spoken cypher. Especially as the Lady's Scottish liquor was having an increasingly potent effect. And so, indeed, was her presence.

Not, he thought, as he returned towards his room later, his way lit by one of Lady Janet's brightest candles, that he was left in any doubt as to her message for him. The two central points of the mission he was apparently embarked upon were simple. Master Secretary wished him to hasten Essex's downfall and now more than ever. But at the same time Cecil must remain so far distanced from the outcome that no shadow of suspicion could ever touch him. To such an extent, indeed, that his messenger Lady Janet Percy, was only allowed to speak in riddles so torturous they might almost pass for code. And with good reason. The Queen remained as changeable as ever. There was no saying whether or when she would forgive Essex everything and destroy anyone who she could prove had been working against him. Eight doctors sent to tend his illness and a ninth bearing her special soup did not bode well for his continued disgrace, nomatter what it seemed to promise for his speedy recovery.

Further, even if the Queen refused to relent, it was only a question of time before Nature took its course and she was succeeded on the throne. Cecil knew all too well that her most likely heir was James of Scotland and it was rumoured that Essex kept in a securely locked box, letters from James thanking the Earl for his support in the matter of the English throne and promising that he would do well under his rule when he succeeded. Inevitably, therefore, anyone His Majesty King James the First believed to have been working against such a valued ally would, again, face destruction. Hence the lack of disguise, the lack of cover, the lack of detailed briefing or organised support. If anything at all went wrong, he was most definitely on his own; eminently deniable.

And yet, despite the secrecy and prevarication - the simple bloody obfuscation – Poley felt as though he was a central cog at the heart of a vast machine being turned like some massive waterwheel by the unstoppable flood of events. Cecil needed to be able to deny him if he failed. But he also wanted to give him the tools he needed to succeed.

Poley had reached this point in his reasoning when he was stopped by sounds up ahead. Shielding the candle flame even more carefully, he crept forward. The sinister sounds were augmented almost at once by flickering light. Poley tip-toed silently up the last staircase separating him from the corridor that led to his room. Crouching down so that nothing more than his head would be visible, and that only to someone looking down at the passage floor, he peeped round the corner. He saw at a glance that his bedroom door was wide. Men were coming and going through it, their whispers echoing with near-hysterical excitement. The excitement he was used to hearing at the

Bull-baiting, the Bear-baiting and the Cockpit. Men lusting to see blood spilled by the bucketful. He did not need to see more than their outlines and their shadows to know them. Gelly Meyrick and his acolytes, come to question the interloper. Making up in enthusiasm any finesse or technique of Rackmaster Topcliffe that they lacked.

Poley eased himself into a seated position that allowed him to continue watching. The excitement around his room slowly died as his would-be assailants realised he was not there and showed no immediate sign of returning. After a while, a few of them began to drift away, then a few more. At last their leader emerged, the candle he held illuminating his glowering face as he looked left and right before heading off down the corridor, thankfully away from the stairwell Poley was hiding in. When everything was dark and silent again, Poley stood stiffly and crept forward, his candle still shaded in case Meyrick was more cunning than he looked and was waiting to spring his trap anew. But no. He clearly was just as brutish as he appeared to be.

Poley crept into his room, and looked around. His clothes and possessions lay scattered hither and yon but thankfully as the result of a wild search rather than a desire for destruction. Whoever had searched for him had obviously just thrown everything he might be hidden behind out of the way. And, on failing to find him, had kicked his necessaries into a pile in a gesture of childish frustration. Poley decided he would tidy in the morning, closed the door and bolted it, thanking Heaven he had left it unlocked so the bolt remained intact. Finally he crossed to his bed. Only to pause before he lay down once more. Paused and reached down to pull free the long dagger that had been plunged through the counterpane and deep into the mattress where his heart would have been had he been lying there asleep.

He straightened, holding the would-be murder weapon, wondering whether or not it was a lucky coincidence that his long and obscure meeting with Lady Janet had ensured he was well away from his room when Gelly Meyrick led his lethal attack on it.

*

'I appreciate the offer of your skills, which I'm sure are manifold,' said Sir Henry Wotton. 'But I fear that they would be surplus to requirements, at least for the moment.' He gestured around the room which housed the industrious Secretariat. Cuffe, Legge and their companions were all busily transcribing or translating whatever was written on sheets of paper beside their elbows and producing letters in clear, perfectly-formed handwriting on the superior sheets of parchment or vellum in front of them. '*Si linguis hominum tu loqueris et angelorum…* "Though you speak in the tongues of men and of angels" as the Bible has it, we still have no employment for you. Perhaps you should enquire whether Sir Anthony has need of an extra amanuensis.'

Poley was still debating whether he was more irritated by Wotton's curt refusal or his patronising translation of his misquote from the Roman Vulgate as he strode past the stair's foot and into the servants' quarters, heading for

Anthony Bacon's sickroom. His preoccupation was nearly the undoing of him. Oblivious to his surroundings, he suddenly found himself surrounded by half a dozen of Gelly Meyrick's murderous swashbucklers. He glanced around, noting their faces. St Lawrence, Gorges, Gerrard… Robbed of their fun in his room last night, they clearly planned to make up for their disappointment now. Poley gave himself a mental kicking. He had been careful to avoid the bullies all day so far, though every now and then he had felt certain he was being watched. To have walked straight into the pack of them now was the sort of thing an amateur might do. And in Poley's profession, amateurs did not last long. As Kit Marlowe had proved all too clearly.

'Ah…' Meyrick's greeting lingered. 'Master Poley, well met…'

Poley knew better than to answer. Anything he said now was likely to make matters worse. Though there were few things worse than a dagger in the ribs, he had to admit. But none of them could be done outside Rackmaster Topcliffe's domain or, indeed, in a passage leading to the servants' areas in Essex House.

'… we sought you last night but you were absent from your room...'

Poley still stayed silent.

'… mayhap you had divined our intent and scurried off to hide somewhere. But it makes no matter, for we have you now.'

A hand behind Poley's shoulder pushed him forcefully forward so that he staggered into his tormentor. He glanced over his shoulder. It was Gorges who had pushed him.

'What is this?' demanded Meyrick, outraged. 'You think to assault me sirrah?'

Poley stepped back. But the strong hand pushed him forward once again. This time Meyrick staggered backward when their bodies crashed together. Poley, winded, gave a guttural gasp. 'A challenge!' called St Lawrence at once. 'He challenged you, Gelly. I heard him.'

'I accept the challenge. And, as the injured party the choice of weapons is mine and I chose rapiers. Let us settle the matter now.'

'I'll stand as Poley's second,' snapped Gerrard. 'Let St Lawrence stand as yours.'

Poley was swept along the corridor towards Anthony Bacon's sickroom but before they got there, Gelly Meyrick led the group off to the left. A moment or two later they stepped out through a wide doorway into the garden behind Essex House. The rear wall, pocked with windows from the ground floor on upward, towered immediately behind them. In front of them, the formal gardens swept down to the Essex House steps and the River. Grass paths and private areas wound or stood between walls of pollarded trees and square-cut hedges, brightened by flower-beds. The grass, trees and hedges were vivid green with early-season growth but there was little in the flower beds besides semi-liquid mud.

Between the back wall and the first lawn there was an area of flagstones that was both wide and deep. Tables and chairs had been cleared off this and stood in covered piles waiting for the Summer. Other than the tight group of bullies and their victim, the place was deserted. 'This will do,' said Meyrick. 'Someone go and get the swords.'

St Lawrence vanished back through the door they had just come out of. Gerrard and Gorges held Poley's arms. The intelligencer did not resist or speak. Wriggling and threatening would be a waste of time and would do nothing other than to give Meyrick more license to hurl insults. And any show of weakness would simply diminish Poley in his own eyes. Bargaining and begging were both alike out of the question. Instead he catalogued the faces of Meyrick's cohorts in the hope that he would get a chance of revenge. If he was allowed a fair fight, he stood a chance. He had been instructed in the finer points of rapier play by a Master of Defence. As Ingram Frizer's backside had discovered the hard way, he had mastered much of Ridolfo Capo Fero's technique. He had seen Meyrick in action which was a considerable advantage. In the unlikely event that he was given the chance to use it.

*

St Lawrence returned with a pair of weapons. He offered them to Meyrick first, who took one without hesitation and began to exercise his shoulder and arm just as he did last evening. St Lawrence gave the second one to Poley. 'I understand your rapier was lost during your most recent arrest,' said the red-headed Irishman, his green eyes glittering as hard as agates. 'Here's one we found to replace it.'

The moment Poley took it, he knew at least part of their

plan. The blade on this rapier had been snapped off a yard from the guard, no doubt by some officious lawkeeper keen to enforce the local statute about blade-length. Meyrick's came to a point at least a foot longer. The edges of Poley's truncated blade were chipped and dull with rust. Meyrick's gleamed wickedly – clearly brought almost immediately from the blacksmith's whetstone. Poley himself stood tall. His arms and legs were long. Now as he also eased his shoulders he fought to recall those sections of the fencing lessons he had skipped over. Those which contained advice for men with shorter arms and legs. Or shorter swords. How a duellist with a limited reach could nevertheless bring a taller opponent – or one with a longer blade – into his own short measure, where the thrust is the most efficient attack. With his sword's greater reach, Meyrick could use the lighting-quick thrust to kill his man without even moving his feet. Given the state of his blade, Poley would have to rely on the slower and much less certain lunge, which required that he step forward to complete it. Meyrick had not removed his doublet, which was obviously well padded and Poley's broken weapon had no point. To be certain of victory, he would have to lunge at once, before Meyrick could divine his purpose. And aim for the most difficult of all targets – the face.

Blissfully unaware of his opponent's lethal plan, Meyrick gave the briefest salute in form, which Poley did not return, and settled into his position as St Lawrence called 'En garde.' The Welshman stood not quite sideways on, his blade in the second guard, wrist high and point low.

During the next heartbeat, Poley fell into his own

favoured guard, the third. His wrist was low and steady, the broken stub-end of his blade high. There was no chance for deception. He would just have to rely on Meyrick's arrogant assumption that the better man in the better position with the better blade could not be bested. That he had the means and the time, indeed, to humiliate his opponent before despatching him.

'Engage!' said St Lawrence.

Poley lunged with all his speed and might, hurling his blade's broken end into Meyrick's sneering countenance. But as he did so, Gerrard kicked his ankle and he tumbled forward onto his hands and knees as his blade skittered and rattled across the flags.

'For once,' said a precise voice that carried over everything else, 'Fortune does not favour the brave. Bad luck Master Poley. And you, Sir Gelly, must needs thank both Goddesses of chance Tyche and Fortuna that the flagstones were still slippery after the rain.'

Poley picked himself up and saw that the window to Sir Anthony Bacon's sick room stood wide. Sir Francis was leaning out of it, conversing calmly as though what he had just witnessed was no more than a sporting contest.

'As chance would have it,' Francis Bacon continued urbanely, 'I was requested to ask that you attend Sir Christopher and Lady Lettice, Master Poley. A matter, I believe, of supplying you with the Leicester coat of arms. And I understand Sir Christopher has expressed a wish to purchase a decent blade to replace the one stolen from you. I'm afraid the one you have just this moment dropped reflects very poorly on the Leicester Household and the

Blount family's honour, especially in the hands of a close and valued relative.'

As the pair of them strolled towards Lady Lettice's chambers, Sir Francis said, 'I must apologise if you felt I overstated the closeness of your familial relationship with Sir Christopher, but it seemed the best way to ensure that Meyrick would think twice about assaulting you again.'

'Not at all,' said Poley, who was still fighting to catch his breath. 'Your intervention was most welcome. Does Sir Christopher in fact wish to see me?'

'He does. And for the reasons I stated. It was the exhibition duello at supper, I believe, which put the idea of the sword in his mind. His family's honour is precious to him and now that he has publicly admitted his relationship to you, your situation, possessions and actions reflect upon that honour. And, of course Lady Leicester's.'

The two men were welcomed into Lady Leicester's rooms by Lady Lettice and Sir Christopher. Lady Lettice held a short discussion on the matter of a light tabard with the complicated but beautiful Leicester coat of arms on the shoulder, all azure, or, gules, and white with leopards and lions rampant. As soon as Poley declared how honoured he would be to wear it on formal occasions, Sir Christopher took over. 'Now that *that* is agreed, we must find you a blade worthy to be worn alongside it. We will go to the Steelyard straight away.'

When Sir Francis accompanied them, Sir Christopher didn't raise an eyebrow. But apparently word of their mission and destination had somehow got out. Amongst the younger, poorer members of both households as well as the guests from far afield, a visit to the Steelyard was an adventure in itself. And a visit in pursuit of a first-quality blade made the expedition more exciting than a visit to the Globe or the Bear-baiting pit.

*

Sir Christopher led Poley and Bacon down to the foot of the stairs then back into the servants' areas and along the route Poley had been shoved by Mayrick's bullies, and out onto the flagged terrace and the gardens. As they crossed the terrace, Cuffe and Legge appeared with, of all people, Nick Skeres keeping them company.

'Is it true you're bound for the Steelyard?' asked Legge a little breathlessly.

'We are,' answered Poley because the question had been addressed to him.

'May we accompany you?'

Sir Christopher heard the request and shrugged amenably. He didn't even seem unduly put out when the Irish baron St Lawrence also joined them. Fortunately no-one else did, for they were taking a ferry from the Essex House steps to the Steelyard steps and there were seven of them already, eight including the ferryman – a heavy load for a Thames wherry. But the river was running smooth and still on the back of a falling tide. Shooting the Bridge would have been a dangerous undertaking but they were not bound quite that far downriver.

So, once they were gathered on the steps, Sir Christopher caught the eye of a ferryman sitting at liberty. 'Eastward Ho!' he bellowed and a few moments later they were off. As the great houses and their landings, stairs or steps sped by on their left, from the Temple Stairs past Whitefriars and Bridewell on down to Broken Wharf and Queenshythe, Legge and Cuffe chattered excitedly and St Lawrence pretended not to be listening to them. 'It must be two years and more that Her Majesty withdrew her warrants to the Steelyard,' said Legge.

'But before that it had been, more or less, a liberty for the German merchants of the Hansa, as I understand it. Since the reign of King Edward Longshanks,' Cuffe the ex-Oxford professor informed him.

'For all things German, from cloth to cheese, from schnapps to steel,' supplied Sir Francis. 'And although the Royal charters and warrants have been withdrawn, the merchants are still there. Some of them. If you know where to look.'

As they passed Three Carters Wharf and were rowed into the Dowgate ward, the ferryman began to pull in towards the north bank and a few moments later Sir Christopher was leading them up the Steelyard steps. Moments later they were in Dowgate itself and the street led straight up into Thames Street which followed the course of the river six solid properties up from the north bank itself. Once in Thames Street, Sir Christopher turned right and, with Bacon at one shoulder and St Lawrence at the other, led them through the bustle of hawkers, shoppers and carters coming and going along the busy thoroughfare. Weaving in and out between the people, the herds of sheep going to slaughter on Newgate Street and market at Smithfield or Leadenhall, and the cart-horses pulling their heavy loads to and from the Cornmarket and the Haymarket. He strode past Cousin Lane and Windgoose until he turned right into Church Lane past the church that gave it its name. A few yards down, he pushed a narrow door open and they all followed him into a surprisingly roomy shop. Sir Christopher gestured at the man who stood behind the counter, nodding and smiling a welcome. 'This, Masters, is Herr Jacobus Merkel of Solingen, and he supplies some of the finest swords money can buy.'

There were no steps leading down to the river at the end of Church Street, so, half an hour later, Sir Christopher, with Bacon and St Lawrence at his shoulders, led the little group back up toward Thames Street. The blade which now lay in Poley's possession was by no means the finest Herr Merkel could supply but it was a reasonably priced, perfectly serviceable workaday weapon. Wearing it would not greatly enhance his reputation, but neither would it shame his aristocratic kinsmen. Poley was particularly pleased because the Master of Defence who had tutored him in swordplay had often told him that blades marked with the running wolf of Solingen were the best. Legge and Cuffe were immediately behind him and just in front of Nick Skeres, chattering excitedly about the German swords and how they could afford one of their own. The little group turned into Thames Street. Poley was paying scant attention to their conversation and his own surroundings as they joined the bustle once more, distracted by his new possession and calculations of how he could pay Sir Christopher back for it.

He was so preoccupied, in fact, that he did not hear the first cries of '*Ware! Ware runaway!*' It was only when the others crowding the street began to push themselves nervously against the walls and into recessed doorways that he sprang into full wakefulness. And not a moment too soon. The crowd in the road in front of him parted like the Red Sea at Moses' command to reveal a runaway horse dragging an empty wagon. Eyes rolling, nostrils gaping and steaming, mouth foaming round the bit it was chewing wildly, it thundered straight towards him. He had a heartbeat to assess the danger. This was one of the largest cart-horses he had ever seen. The wagon behind it was by no means a toy, and yet it was galloping forward as though its burden weighed nothing. Metal wheel-rims sparked off the cobbles of the street. The noise was so overwhelming that everything else seemed to fall silent. Sir Christopher, Sir Francis and St Lawrence leaped back, flattening themselves against the wall behind them. Poley froze for a fatal instant as it suddenly occurred to him that this might be another elaborate but extremely dangerous attempt to kill him. But then Sir Francis's hand closed on his shoulder and pulled him aside. The horse and the cart thundered past close enough to buffet him with the wind of their passage, spray him with foam and shower his toecaps with sparks. But as they did so, another sound suddenly overcame the overwhelming din. A series of sounds. A scream. A thump. A crackling.

Poley swung round. Cuffe and Skeres stood wide-eyed, flat against the wall of the nearest house. What was left of Legge after the hooves and the wheels had stamped him down, rolled over him and crushed the life out of him lay sprawled and bleeding in the gutter.

5

'It looks suspicious to me,' said Sir Anthony Bacon. He didn't need to elaborate.

But Sir Henry Wotton did. 'The fact that Poley here is the very man we need to replace poor Legge?'

'Indeed.'

'It's not so much of a coincidence, really,' argued Poley, his calm tone belying his racing pulse. 'As I have explained before, my travels on behalf of the Council, Walsingham and Cecil over the years - before I was betrayed and thrown out of their favour - have been so wide and so often repeated that I would be able to replace almost any man in the Secretariat. Had an accident robbed you of your German specialist, for example; or your Dutch or French, men, I could have stepped in. It goes without saying that any one of us could replace your Latin and Greek specialists.'

'If you tell me you could replace my code-master, then I'll have to cut your throat myself,' said Sir Anthony and there was no mistaking the threat in his tone as well as his words. Poley left his expression blank as he weighed the possible fundamentals behind the menace. Because he was almost certain that Sir Anthony was his own code-master.

'Anthony,' said Sir Francis. 'Surely that's enough. I was there. What happened to Legge was an accident. Had I not pulled him back, it would have been Poley who was trampled to death. But I did pull Poley back and so by chance, it was Legge who was killed. Nick Skeres tried to pull him aside as I pulled Poley but it was not to be. So, if fault there was, it was mine. Now Poley is in a position to help us. Is keen in fact to help us, if only to revenge himself against his erstwhile masters who have stabbed him in the back as a reward for long and diligent service. And how is his offer to help us answered? With threats of throat-cutting!'

Sir Anthony and Sir Henry exchanged a long look. 'Very well,' said Sir Anthony at last. 'Your help will be welcome, Master Poley.'

Sir Henry nodded silent agreement. 'But do not expect to be working on anything other than the dullest, everyday communications,' he warned.

'I expected nothing more,' said Poley.

And so it began. At first there was a quiet, sorrowful interim during which Sir Francis, apparently blaming himself for the boy's death as much as he congratulated himself for preserving Poley's life, attended Legge's post-mortem. He did so on behalf of Essex House, sympathising with the coroner who had several witnesses to the accident, Nick Skeres chief among them, but no-one able to identify the owner of the horse and wagon that had killed the victim. Legge's head had been so badly crushed that only the Queen's Counsellor Extraordinary or Skeres could have formally identified him, both having seen him fall. But no-one at all was able to say where the fatal vehicle had come from or gone to.

These were sinister facts which Sir Francis pointed out in private to Poley, for the Queen's Councillor still believed that only his quick thinking had saved him and doomed the young man. Poley might, therefore, have been the intended victim, had the whole 'accident' actually been staged as Sir Anthony suspected. But this was something that had already occurred to the cautious intelligencer. Meyrick and St. Lawrence stood high on the list of his suspects – unless they had persuaded the Earl of Southampton to take fatal action on behalf of his friend the Earl of Essex. Unless, of course, he had got the whole situation back-to-front and Legge had been the actual target after all. The youngster had detailed his experiences in Denmark at length and within the hearing of Lady Janet amongst others. A word to Cecil might have generated just this outcome – a place for a replacement Danish expert in Wotton's secretariat. The only element of that theory which unsettled him was the thought of Lady Janet passing on the fatal information. Perhaps it had been Southampton's doing after all…

Henry Wriothesley, Third Earl of Southampton remained an enigma, thought Poley. As Essex's General of Horse he had been the Earl's right hand in Ireland and clearly remained his most powerful supporter here in England. But, like Poley himself, Southampton obviously found his hands tied by his commander's incarceration in York House. Yet there still buzzed around the Earl and around Southampton House, a body of men like a swarm of bees in search of their queen. Many of them, like their companions in Essex House, soldiers by avocation and training, impatient by temperament and brutally ruthless by nature. No matter what was going on in circumspect secrecy in Essex House, Poley could not imagine that things were quite so calm and quiet in Southampton House. Or in Drury House in Wych Lane, which Southampton also leased, and which, apparently, was becoming a popular meeting-place.

*

It was also the guilt-stricken Sir Francis who had arranged for Legge's broken body to be returned to his home parish of Swyncombe in Oxfordshire after the coroner's ruling of 'accidental death', Poley discovered. Here, in the absence of the family and the aristocratic sponsors who had smoothed his way to Oxford – all dead of the plague – he had arranged for the young man's funeral to be held in St Botolph's church there. According to the parish records, it was where Legge had been baptised less than 30 years earlier. And finally Sir Francis arranged for him to be buried in the nearby churchyard beside the rest of his kith and kin – those who were not in the local plague pits.

Meanwhile, under the grudging protection of Sir Henry Wotton and Sir Anthony Bacon as well as of Lady Lettice and her husband, Poley was able to put aside any immediate fears that he might again be the victim of Meyrick and his bully-ruffians or the mysterious entity who had arranged for the horse and wagon to come charging down Thames Street. The bellicose element were in any case increasingly fully occupied as couriers taking the letters produced by the Secretariat to their destinations and returning with replies. It seemed that the Earl's steward Gelly Meyrick as well as his wife Lady Frances managed occasional visits to the Earl; visits which generated yet more correspondence.

Poley used the quiet time of household mourning to settle to work, with the Leicesters' blessing, next to Cuffe who appointed himself as mentor. It was Cuffe who explained the further sub-sections of the Secretariat. Letters that went out over Essex's signature and seal were destined not only for contacts abroad but also for the Court and the men and women who held most power therein. Essex himself wrote most regularly to the Queen and relied on the occasional visitor to take his missives out of his prison and into the royal presence – if not always into the Queen's hand. Poley, with his more limited remit, was able to replace Legge swiftly, painlessly and surprisingly easily, though Cuffe's last unthinking revelation made the intelligencer begin to wonder whether there was anyone in the Secretariat with the ability to copy the Earl's handwriting and style so closely that it might be mistaken for his own. That way the number of letters heading toward the Queen might be augmented and the Earl's case strengthened. He put the idea on one side to be discussed later with the younger Bacon brother.

In the aftermath of Legge's death, this section of the household went out less and less. Poley, keen to keep away from the sort of trouble that nearly hit him on Thames Street and, in any case, eager to become just another unremarkable face amongst the busy secretariat, stayed within the confines of the House as well. Not that there was much temptation to go abroad. For, had the Summer and Autumn been unseasonably wet and cold, the Winter closed its icy jaws upon them like those of a ravening wolf. The Thames froze and fairs were set up on it, easy for those in the houses on the Strand to visit – for they just had to step down off the steps at the end of their gardens. But for many, the forced excitement of the Frost Fairs was more than counteracted by the number of frozen corpses lying like statues in the ice-bound streets. By the faces of the helpless suicides staring up through the glass-clear ice at passers-by walking above. The only time they all ventured out was on the Sabbath when, registered in the Parish of St Clement Danes with its associations with Leicester, they all trooped across the Strand to services.

At first, Poley was surprised by the amount of Danish correspondence required of him. Regular letters sped away to young King Christian IV at Elsinore; to Councillor Holger Rosenkranz and several others of the powerful Rosenkranz family; and, indeed, to others on the Danish Council. To the youthful prodigy Caspar Bartholin at Copenhagen University who had caught the Earl's eye a couple of years earlier when he gave lengthy and impressive public orations in both Latin and Greek while still in his teens. And had, by all accounts, impressed the Danish Royal court by reading aloud to them at the age of four. The infantile Bartholin had read not only to them, but also the young Scottish King, visiting Denmark in pursuit if his princess bride.

Every now and then Poley also found himself writing to the princess bride herself: Anne, King Christian's elder sister, now Queen of Scotland. But there was little of importance in these missives speeding east and west across the North Sea or north and south along the length of England. Nothing of even the faintest political relevance to the current political situation, the Earl's incarceration or the ageing Queen's succession; not even in those destined for the Scottish court. They were all so bland and innocuous that he began to suspect a cypher hidden somewhere within the innocent observations. But, try as he might, he could find nothing. He further began to suspect that many of the most tedious missives were simply given to him to ensure he had something to do while his loyalty was verified yet again. The extension of that thought, of course, was that the letters were not only used to occupy the intelligencer but also to keep continued contact with a range of people who might, when the time was right, be relied upon to sway Queen Anne and, through her, her husband. Meanwhile the truth of his story was being tested, with the care and meticulousness that King James apparently applied to the testing of witches.

*

Poley found it strange to be at once at the centre of so much industry and yet so far away from the centre of power. It came as an absolute surprise to him – and one that he found deeply unsettling – when Sir Francis appeared during the last days of November and dashed straight through the house to talk to his brother. Poley had no idea at all what the emergency might be. He had not been this ignorant of momentous events since before the Great Armada sailed. He didn't have to wait long to find out what was going on, however. Sir Henry Wotton came grim-faced into the Secretariat, heavy with Sir Francis' news. 'My Lord the Earl is to be arraigned before the court of Star Chamber,' he announced. 'He is to admit in detail to his shortcomings both in Ireland and since. He will have to answer examination by the Lords of the Council who are the Star Chamber judges and Sir Francis fears he will have to do so without his legal support.'

Poley was so surprised, he nearly gave himself away. 'Has not Her Majesty demanded Sir Francis also attend?' he asked. 'Surely, as Queen's Counsel Extraordinary…'

'Ah,' said Cuffe, unconsciously turning suspicion away from the intelligencer, 'You know all about the Star Chamber do you not, Robert? The Star Chamber was the weapon Cecil the Toad used to destroy you!'

'To attempt my destruction indeed,' answered Poley. 'Though all he achieved was to drive me here into Essex House and make me his enemy and the Earl's friend 'til death.'

He was interested to learn, however, that whatever the Queen's desires in the matter, Sir Francis did not attend the procedure when it came to pass. For, a matter of days later, Essex's formal arraignment was cancelled. He remained sickly in York House with Lord Keeper Edgerton and nothing more was done to him. On the other hand, the Star Chamber was addressed by Edgerton and others who detailed the charges that would have been brought had the Earl been well enough to face them. Poley watched this shadow-play of judgement from a distance, feeling unsettlingly removed from the action. A sensation he was sure he was sharing with many other residents of Essex House, trapped in a kind of limbo or purgatory as they were. Until the Queen or her Council decided precisely what to do with Essex, whose continued imprisonment was becoming more and more of a problem.

Whoever had persuaded Her Majesty to move against Essex through the Star Chamber had clearly failed to convince her to follow the threat into any meaningful action. Try as he might, albeit in secret, Master Secretary Cecil and his associates had not convinced Her Majesty to continue with the destruction of her one-time favourite. If the instigator of the move had, in fact, been Cecil, he had learned once again, that he could not rely on the Queen to take the next, fatal, step. Poley remembered all too well how an identical situation had proceeded with Mary, the Queen of Scots, attracting deadly plots as a honey-pot attracts wasps. Until the Secret Service had caught her red handed, plotting Elizabeth's downfall with Babington and his associates. Only then – and only just – had the Queen been moved to take action. Which, by all accounts, she still bitterly regretted. Regicide was a dreadful sin in anyone guilty of it, she believed – but in another Sovereign it was especially damnable.

Furthermore, even the limited freedom presented by their visits to church made the keen-eared intelligencer increasingly vividly aware that the procedure at the Star Chamber had only served to complicate matters. The Earl's presence had been made impossible by his sickness. Allowing things to proceed in his absence had only managed to enhance the Earl's popularity and the hatred in which the Toad and the Council were held by the general populace. Sunday sermons began to address the matters of the Earl's sickness, how it was identical to the questionable ailment that had killed his father; how it was brought upon him through the evil of his enemies; and how were he to recover, he and he alone could mend the sickness in the Realm which so dangerously paralleled his own. Psalm 147 became a favourite text: '*He healeth the broken hearted and binds up their wounds...*' As did Proverbs Chapter 12 Verse 18: '*There is that speaketh like the piercings of a sword, but the tongue of the wise is health.*' And when the Queen retired to her palace at Richmond, it was to the sound of the bells in all the City churches being rung for her ailing victim.

Although nothing more was said or done as the year and century dragged to its icy end, and Lady Janet arranged no more secret assignations, Poley felt the lack of contact with her keenly. But pressure was growing on him, from outside the House as well as inside, to undertake some sort of action at the earliest possible moment. However, until the Earl of Essex came home, the intelligencer's hands were tied.

*

By the third week in December, everything had apparently returned to normal in the Secretariat. The Council tried to muzzle the recalcitrant priests with limited success, though their texts were soon dictated by the Advent and approaching Christmas seasons. The Queen went down to Richmond Palace for Christmas, as though fleeing from those accusing bells, taking the court and Lady Janet with her; Poley found her absence strangely compounded by distance. Sir Francis retired to

Twickenham Lodge for the festive season, once he had organised Her Majesty's Christmas Present of a beautifully embroidered petticoat. Twickenham Lodge was immediately across the river from Richmond palace. His present was particularly expensive because his failure to appear against the absent Essex before the Star Chamber had angered the Queen and he was close to becoming *persona non grata* at court. He invited his brother to go to Twickenham with him but Anthony was too unwell to be moved or, indeed, to bother with gifts. And besides, thought Poley, Anthony would never rely on Wotton to keep a close enough eye on him.

The Earl's sisters, Dorothy Percy, Countess of Northumberland and Penelope Rich, Countess of Warwick, came to pay their respects to their mother and sister-in-law; and to report on how their efforts to make the Queen look kindly on their wayward brother were progressing. One precious present after another, Poley calculated as he shook his head at the closeness of the families – as if there weren't enough Percys involved in the situation already. Or Blounts, come to that, for Lady Rich was widely known to be Charles Blount, Lord Mountjoy's, mistress.

But amid all this bustle, Poley found himself penning yet more tedious missives. He produced one after another in a seemingly endless stream of banality, hardly leavened by the Yuletide greetings they contained. Wearily cynical, Poley began to believe that they were never actually despatched. They were probably piled in a file somewhere, or used as kindling for the fires needed more and more often as the bitter winter continued to close its grip even inside Essex House and the century slowly died, lingering as doggedly as the old woman on the throne. *Like an ancient stepdame*, he thought half-remembering a line from a play he had seen in happier days, *long withering out a young man's revenue*. 'And the hopes of every powerful person in the kingdom,' he added under his breath.

Poley's protectors kept him safe, but still nobody trusted him. Which was not really a worry. The Earl's household continued to behave as though their master was in residence, even though he remained caged in York House. Poley was certain that Lady Frances had some way of communicating with her husband between those rarely-permitted visits but he could not find out precisely how this was done, any more than he could find out what really happened to his laboriously transcribed letters. The grieving wife continued to plead her husband's cause almost daily at court, however – as long as it was at Whitehall. And Poley knew better than most how effective a conduit the court was for the passage of messages all sorts to every conceivable destination. Even to those kept close in prison. But he was content to watch and wait until the Earl was granted his freedom.

Then word spread though the household that the Queen had run out of patience. None of Essex's supporters – wife, sisters, mother – was allowed to come to court, not even to see the New Year entertainment of Thomas Dekker's *The Shoemaker's Holiday*. The winter season became almost as bitter within Essex House as it was without. And the slowly-approaching Spring promised no better.

It was Francis Bacon who brought the news two bitter months later at the beginning of March, hurrying in out of a wet, near-freezing evening that, like most of the new year so far, prophesied so little for the new century. The Queen had stayed longer than usual at Richmond and Bacon had also been staying at Twickenham Lodge for an extra couple of weeks, to be only a ferry ride away from the court, still in the Queen's bad books, despite the petticoat and her constant need of his advice. And he remained as unpopular at court as he was in the streets – each faction pro- or anti-Essex suspecting him of working for the other side. But as the new year progressed, the Queen returned to Whitehall and Sir Francis moved back to his rooms in Greys Inn. From where he visited the court almost as often as Lady Frances had done before she was forbidden entry, slowly winning his way back into Royal favour.

So it was Sir Francis who brought the astonishing news: the Earl was now restored to full health. Lord Keeper Edgerton had confirmed the near-miracle. And therefore Her Majesty would allow the Earl to return home. Soon. The information galvanised every element of Essex House. Lady Frances stopped visiting Whitehall to beat upon the doors fast closed against her. She and Lady Lettice spent time with the Fitzherberts instead, ensuring that Earl Robert would be presented with Essex House at its most glittering, warm and welcoming when he returned to the safety of his home and the bosom of his family.

*

Then Essex's closest friend and associate, the Earl of

Southampton arrived with his recently married Lady Elizabeth and a small retinue from their London home Southampton House and set to work alongside Lady Frances and the Fitzherberts. To begin with, their arrival made little difference but after a while, Poley began to catch glimpses of Henry Wriothesley watching him in unguarded moments. The unease arising from that was compounded when he saw Southampton cloistered with Gelly Meyrick. It looked as though there were yet more enemies moving south out of Southampton House, via Drury House and congregating in Essex House. Lady Penelope and Lady Dorothy arrived to offer their aid and to join in the general excitement. Lady Janet also arrived in Lady Dorothy's train. She was much more closely related to Henry Percy the Earl of Northumberland after all than Poley was to Sir Christopher Blount. But she did not add to the excitement. Instead of plans for the future, she brought a warning. Warning of a danger that Poley was growing increasingly uneasy about; a warning presented in such a manner that it deflated all the excitement he had felt on seeing her after so long.

'There is a chance,' said Lady Janet as they met, apparently by accident, in the corridor leading to Sir Anthony's sick room. 'More than a chance, that you have been left unmolested only because you present no serious danger while the Earl is held in York House. But now that he is to be returned to Essex House, you may well present a very real threat. One that must be countered at all costs.'

'I am alive to the possibility, Lady Janet…' he explained.

'And what are you prepared to do about it?' she wondered softly, her tone and expression full of genuine concern.

In fact there was little Poley could do about it other than to keep the most careful watch. He got more of an opportunity to do this because his work began to tail off as everyone waited for the Earl to come and direct their efforts in person.

But his increasing idleness brought about more reason for him to keep a weather eye out. Fewer letters meant fewer reasons for Gelly Meyrick and his associates to be abroad. They gathered in Essex House generating an increasingly intense air of dangerous hilarity as they waited. Observing them, Poley cynically calculated that they were doing as much as they could to restore the Earl's fortune by drinking vast quantities of sweet wine. Had he held the monopoly on all wines instead of just the sweet ones, his men might have drunk him into a fortune. Except for the fact that it was all his wine they were consuming and only he was paying for it. Or, rather, promising to pay for it. Lady Frances, erring as ever on the side of her husband's fabled generosity, did nothing to stop them; nor did Lady Lettice, nor did the Southamptons, both of whom simply joined in the burgeoning overconsumption. After a while it became obvious that Fitzherbert and his men were encountering increasing difficulty in finding butchers, bakers and - especially - vintners willing to extend yet more credit. Fired by anticipation, alcohol and idleness, Meyrick and his men became increasingly dangerous to the servants, to each other and, finally to Poley.

Poley had seen to the strengthening of the bolt on his bedroom door but nevertheless returned to his original habit of sleeping almost fully dressed. And nowadays, a workmanlike rapier with its fine Solingen blade kept his daggers company on his bedside table. Even so, when they came for him just before dawn a week after Sir Francis had brought the news, they were able to take him relatively easily. It was a mixture of the soldiers, the secretaries, and, from the appearance of some unfamiliar faces, the Earl of Southampton's men as well. Their expressions were set and grim, their expressions clearly boding no good for their captive as they gagged him, bound him, bundled him out of his room and down the stairs. At least there was no sign of Cuffe amongst them, Poley observed, which was pleasing. Nor were Sir Henry Wotton, Sir Christopher Blount, Sir Francis Bacon or Southampton himself. It was another positive sign, thought Poley, that he was shoved past Sir Anthony's sickroom and into one of the store rooms overlooking the garden. It was a pokey, low-ceilinged place whose dirty leaded window gave little light as dawn was only just beginning to arrive. There was nothing remarkable about it other than the beams in it ceiling and the chair at its centre. Poley and his captors pushed in first. The rest of their companions crowded after them.

Then any positive aspects to the experience were soon overwhelmed by painfully negative ones. Meyrick was inquisitor in chief. Gerrard and St Lawrence played the part of Rackmaster Topcliffe's torturers. Instead of a rack, they dumped him in the chair and lashed him securely to it, tying his hands behind his back and running a rope round his waist before securing his ankles to the chair's front legs. The chair was solid. Once the ropes were tight, he had no chance of working them loose, let alone pulling them free. It was also quite heavy – so that no matter how hard they punched him, it did little more than rock back and forth.

*

They settled into a kind of rhythm so that one punch sent him rocking back and then he was met by the next as he came rocking forward once again. The only sounds in the crowded chamber were the smacks of fists hitting flesh and the grunts of impact; the squeak and tap of the chair legs lifting and settling rhythmically on the floorboards. There were no questions to begin with. Gerrard and St Lawrence simply started beating him while Meyrick leaned against the wall, arms crossed, watching in apparent boredom while the others clustered in the doorway behind him like the audience at a bear-baiting. The technique was well thought through, Poley admitted, and his torturers made up in enthusiasm for what they lacked in experience or expertise. But the intelligencer had been through this kind of thing before and knew a trick or two to help him survive. He tucked his chin hard down against his chest and met the rain of blows with his forehead and crown, preserving his eyes – if not his eyebrows – his nose and his teeth as much as possible. Fortunately, all the most recent damage to his skull had been at the back, well clear of his interrogators' fists.

As time passed, it began to dawn on the two inquisitors

that their fists were actually sustaining more damage than Poley's face. In their initial enthusiasm, neither had thought to wear gloves, which would have stopped the skin on their knuckles from splitting. Nor, it seemed, had it occurred to any of them that a club would be a useful addition to their equipment until long after the bones behind the split knuckles began to crack as their fingers started to swell. Meyrick, too, seemed to have little understanding of the true state of affairs. When he pulled Poley's battered face up to look at it in the grey dawn light, he seemed to have no idea that almost all of the blood spattered so impressively across it did not actually belong to Poley at all.

He undid the gag and pulled it free. 'Now,' he said. 'Where shall we begin?'

Poley forbore to point out that they had actually begun a good deal earlier, a fact to which his face bore mute witness. He had no desire at this stage to appear commanding, witty or clever; to appear anything other than beaten and suffering, indeed. He blinked dazedly, a glowering frown pulling his swollen brows low over his eyes, making the damage look more serious than it was. 'What is it?' he mumbled. 'What have I done?'

'Sold your soul to that spawn of Satan Master Secretary Cecil.' Meyrick answered.

'I have done no such thing! He cut me off, had me arrested, arraigned before the Star Chamber, ruined…'

'So you say…'sneered Meyrick.

'Master Cuffe…'

'Is as gullible as a virgin fresh up from the country. No.

Your time has come, Master Poley. Convince us now or go to warn the Devil that your Master Cecil the Toad will be joining you both soon.'

'I have nothing more to tell you,' mumbled Poley at his most abject and defeated. 'I have been wronged by Master Secretary, traduced before the Star Chamber and have come here seeking to aid the Earl in revenge for the hurts done to me. That is all!'

'Well then, as I said, let us proceed.' Meyrick straightened, clearly keen to get down to business.

Poley could see little of what happened next but he understood what was going on well enough. A second rope was tied to the wrists behind his back. A rope long enough to be thrown up to run through some kind of hook screwed into a beam in the low ceiling. All this went on behind him of course. Also of some interest was the stirring at the door in front of him as someone to the rear of the little crowd gathered there shouldered his way out. But then Poley's focus closed down onto more immediate matters. Gerrard's and St Lawrence's fists might have been damaged by their repeated contact with his head but they were strong enough to pull the rope taut. Poley was forced to lean forward as his wrists rose relentlessly towards the ceiling. The strain on his shoulders was enormous and agonising. The chair teetered on its fore legs as the rear ones rose an inch off the floor. 'Wait there for a moment,' ordered Meyrick.

*

The room fell silent. The creaking of the rope ceased. The scrabbling of the chair legs across the floorboards stilled. There was no sound except for Poley's heaving gasps. The pressure did not ease – but then, neither did it worsen.

'Now,' said the Welshman. 'We are mere heartbeats from tearing your arms out of your shoulders and crippling you for ever. If you have any *truth* to tell us in place of these lies and prevarications, you have until the count of five to vouchsafe it. *One...*'

When he reached *Five* and Poley still remained silent, Meyrick gestured at his torturers and they pulled the rope. Poley had not been frightened by the count-down because he saw it as another mistake in the interrogation process. He had simply invested the extra time and the warning, which proved how inexperienced Meyrick really was in such matters, in preparation to counter as best he could what must inevitably follow. He therefore used the countdown to tense the muscles of his shoulders, upper arms and back as tightly as he was able. Arms and shoulders mercifully strengthened by the hours of practise he put in with his rapier at the behest of the master of defence who was striving to perfect his technique. His racing mind promised that he might have a chance of getting through this less severely damaged than his overconfident torturers threatened. He had never suffered the strappado, but had seen men put through it, either standing - or seated, as he was now. And it seemed to Poley that someone with sufficient self-control and fortitude could survive the first elevation without too much harm. When he had seen it done in The Tower's torture chambers, he had noticed that the real damage was done when the victim was raised almost to the ceiling and dropped – then brought up short just before they hit the floor. It was the jerk of stopping the victim so suddenly that allowed his bodyweight to tear his arms out of the shoulder sockets. Just as, when the executioner at Tyburn got the drop exactly right, the hanged man's weight could snap his neck instantly and cleanly. There was a fair chance that Meyrick's men did not know this. And even if they did, this room was far too low to allow them to copy the technique, even though they had tied him into a chair.

Poley's theories were put to an agonising test at once. Gerrard and St Lawrence pulled the rope as soon as Meyrick gave the signal. Fortunately they did so smoothly, hand over hand, like sailors raising sail. Poley swayed clear of the floor, tilting further forward, the weight of his body swinging him and his chair like a pendulum back and forth. The strain on his shoulders was enormous but the joints seemed to stay secure while the pain was intense but bearable. Up he went, watching the stout boards of the floor recede beneath his toecaps. Sweat ran off his forehead. Rather than flowing into his eyes, it dripped off the swollen ridges of his eyebrows onto the edge of the seat between his thighs. He ground his teeth together, feeling his twisted muscles begin to judder and jump with the strain. He found to his surprise that he was continuing Meyrick's count – *six, seven, eight…*

He had reached *twenty* when the group at the door exploded inwards, pushed forward by the arrival of Nick Skeres, Henry Cuffe and Francis Bacon. He caught a glimpse of the Earl of Southampton in the shadows behind them and it occurred to him more forcefully than ever that Southampton might well have been the mysterious individual responsible for the murderous runaway cart. Especially if it really had been aimed at him but killed poor Legge instead. Unless, of course it was Cecil and it hit its intended target after all.

'What is going on here?' bellowed Bacon, his voice quivering with outrage. The surprise of his arrival made Gerrard and St Lawrence lose their grip. Poley's chair crashed to the floor and it was the joints in the wood rather than those of sinew and bone which yielded. The chair was simply smashed apart. Poley luckily fell sideways as it did so – hitting the floor with his shoulder rather than his already battered face. He rolled as clear of the wreckage as he could, the front legs still secured to his ankles, the rest in sticks and splinters all around. He was winded and his shoulders burned almost unbearably but he was otherwise unhurt. There was nothing he could do for the moment, however, other than lie there trying to catch his breath and control the pain, watching and listening as events continued to unfold.

'We have to establish once and for all where he stands,' snarled Meyrick.

'And this is the way to do it?' countered Bacon. 'Methods worthy of the Inquisition?'

'As used in the Tower itself, by Rackmaster Topcliffe and his men and you know it Sir Francis! Desperate times call for desperate measures.'

'And we have precious little time before the Earl comes home and we need to be certain do we not?' added St

Lawrence, ready to make a fight of it.

'Before…' Sir Francis looked around the room, his face set in an expression of shock. 'Have you not heard, man? Do you not yet know the truth of the matter?'

'Heard what?' demanded Meyrick. 'Is the Master not returning after all?'

'Returning?' echoed Sir Francis. 'Oh yes, the Master is returning. But to an empty house. Lady Francis, Lady Lettice, My Lord of Southampton and his Lady, you, me and all of the others must leave the place at once. Even Fitzherbert, his family and the other servants apparently must do so. The Earl will be accompanied by Sir Drue Drury and Sir Richard Barkely, who will bring specially selected retainers with them. It seemingly makes no difference where we go or how long we must go there for, but the Earl will not be allowed to return until Essex House is emptied of every single one of us!'

*

'And that means you had no call to torture my friend!' added Cuffe, his outrage giving him courage to stand against Meyrick and his bullies. 'He will be no nearer the Earl than he has been while the Earl was held at York House!'

Poley rolled over, shouting, his tone full of justified outrage, 'No more of a danger to him than I have been since I came here out of the Fleet, hoping his friendship would allow me to come to quits with Master Secretary in the matter of my revenge! And I would be grateful,' he added, 'if some one of you would loosen my bonds now that the matter is settled!

It was Cuffe who came forward to untie him and help him unsteadily to his feet. By the time he was upright, the room was all-but empty. Only Cuffe, Skeres and Bacon remained. Meyrick and his cohorts had slunk away. Poley began to wonder whether he had really seen Southampton in the outer shadows after all.

'No doubt they are all gone at once to pack their necessaries and plan where to seek refuge, sustenance and sweet wine now,' he said pensively as he straightened. The moment he did so, the rising sun came out and the brightness flooding the little room lit up his face. Sir Francis crossed to him in a couple of strides and took him gently by the chin, turning him further into the light. 'I will get Sir Anthony's physician to look to you once more,' he said. 'Your face clearly needs attention and I have no doubt your shoulders will need careful tending or you will end up looking like Master Secretary in the matter of a crooked back. I am taking Sir Anthony to Twickenham with me. Doctor Wendy will go there too. I shall arrange for you to accompany us and remain there until you are fully recovered. It is but a short voyage upriver after all.'

Then he continued, 'The Earl and Lady Southampton must sadly return with their retinue to Southampton House. Lady Lettice and Sir Christopher will return to Wanstead and Lady Frances will go to Barn Elms where her mother resides. How many of the Earl's … ah… *retainers*… will be welcome at either establishment – or at Southampton House - I cannot say. Sir Henry and the Secretariat will settle at Barn Elms with Lady Frances I'm sure, though Wanstead Hall and its associated property at

Stonehall is the larger of the two. Sir Gelly will go from place to place as his responsibilities as Steward dictate. As for the others…' He shrugged.

'I'll try my luck at Wanstead,' said Skeres. 'And maybe use your name as my petition for entry, Master Poley; if I could bear a message to your cousin Sir Christopher Blount about your situation and imminent arrival when you are healed.'

'By all means,' said Poley. 'But, friend Cuffe, I would suggest that you make no play on my name at all when you join Sir Henry Wotton and the others at Barn Elms.' Poley had been a frequent visitor there when Sir Francis Walsingham had been in residence, splitting his time to the north and the south of the river. There were too many amongst the household there who knew him of old – it would be back to square one, he thought.

'Nor would I,' agreed Cuffe. 'No more than if I sought to use the Persian King Xerexes' name to gain passage past Leonidas and his Spartans at Thermopylae.'

'I would hardly compare Wotton with Leonidas nor your companions with three hundred Spartans, but the point is well made,' said Poley. He went to shrug his burning shoulders, only to gasp with agony as he realised that Sir Francis' point about him needing the services of Dr Wendy for the immediate future was also well made. It soon struck Poley, however, that his sessions with Dr Wendy so far had focussed on the back of his head. Now that the attention was shifted to the front of his head, to wit, his face, it was as though he was meeting the good Doctor for the first time.

Dr Wendy, the son of King Henry's court physician, was a slim, middle-aged man with tinning white hair and a grey beard. He also had piercing blue eyes that seemed to look deep inside the intelligencer, apparently obviating the need for a lengthy consultation or a detailed examination. But in fact he gently stripped off Poley's doublet and shirt, cleaned and tended his battered face then carefully manipulated the damaged shoulders, tutting and shaking his head. 'Your face will mend swiftly enough, as the back of your skull seems to be doing. But these shoulders will take a time to heal,' he warned. 'And are likely to get worse before they get better. You will have to be careful how you use them or the damage might become permanent. In any case it will be painful. I have distillations of willow bark and poppy that will ease the discomfort…'

'Aye,' said Poley shortly. 'And cloud my mind into the bargain. I thank you, doctor, but I'll live with my hurt and keep my wits sharp for a while yet.'

Dr Wendy looked at his reluctant patient for a moment. Then he nodded. 'From what I have observed,' he said, 'that is likely to be the wisest decision. In the short run at least.'

So they agreed, and parted. For the time-being.

*

Sir Francis Bacon's interruption of Poley's torture succeeded in alienating him from most of the inmates of Essex House, who joined those at Court and those on London's streets in their unanimous dislike and distrust of him. Fortunately, the Queen's mood seemed to be becoming more forgiving, as far as Poley understood the situation. Sir Henry Wotton, Lady Lettice and Sir Christopher as well as Lady Frances all still trusted the Queen's Counsellor. Southampton remained inscrutable in the matter of who he trusted and who he did not. But, on the other hand, everyone associated with the Earl and his promised return held Sir Antony Bacon in such high regard that it bordered on fear. So, when Sir Francis began arranging for his sickly elder brother and his near-crippled associate to be moved upstream to Twickenham, nobody threw too many hurdles in his way, much to Poley's increasing relief as Dr Wendy's warning became prophetic and his shoulders almost entirely seized up.

During the next few days, Essex House steps became an unusually busy part of the establishment. Only the Earl of Southampton, his Lady and their retinue departed along the Strand, heading for Southampton House via Chancery Lane and Holborn, an easy journey of half an hour or so. They took with them a number of Essex's supporters who planned to return to the war in Ireland, where accommodation and food could be guaranteed, if not pay. Though even that had become more reliable under the efficient generalship of Mountjoy. This group included St Lawrence and Gerard noted Poley.

Barn Elms was upriver *Westward Ho* like Twickenham – and like Twickenham most easily accessed from the Thames. It was, in fact, half way between Essex House and Twickenham, on the south bank. Even the twin properties of Wanstead Hall and Stonegate were accessible via the Thames from two of its northern tributaries, the River Lea or the River Rodding, but to access those Lady Lettice and her party had to go eastward and shoot the Bridge downriver. Then they needed to pass the Isle of Dogs and Greenwich before turning north. The Lea, the nearer of the two convenient streams, would get them as far Hackney before it vanished into the marshes and they had to take to the road.

Both women, capable and used to commanding households, set everything in motion at once. Mistress Fitzgerald, with Tom in tow, was sent to Barn Elms to negotiate with the servants there and prepare the house for the influx while Fitzgerald oversaw the packing and physical movement of Lady Francis' necessities. Lady Lettice sent Sir Christopher himself to Wanstead and only the damage to his face and shoulders excused Poley from accompanying his aristocratic relative.

Almost everyone obeying the orders to vacate Essex House did so down the steps to the river, therefore, one group at a time, depending on leadership, destination and the state of the tide which reached upriver all the way to Teddington. The weather did little to support their efforts. The clouds stayed low, the rain persistent, the wind both forceful and northerly while the temperature rose only a degree or two above freezing.

Lady Lettice was hesitant to leave under these conditions, especially with the river running so high. She wanted to hear from Sir Christopher that everything at Wanstead was prepared and she further needed to be careful of the tide. Lady Lettice more than any of them needed to watch the water, because shooting the Bridge was a dangerous undertaking under perfect circumstances and the current ones were far from that. Lady Francis left first, therefore, the household overseen by Fitzgerald and the roisterers by Gelly Meyrick. It took several sizeable ferries to move them and everything they needed to take with them up to Barn Elms. It promised to be a slow and weary passage against the overfull stream, reckoned Poley, even though they waited for help from the incoming tide.

Once Lady Frances had gone and with Lady Lettice still hesitant, it was time to move the Bacon brothers. Henry Cuffe and Nick Skeres remained behind to help, planning to be dropped off at Barn Elms on the way to Twickenham. And their help was needed. Apart from Dr Wendy, there was no-one from the Bacon household here. The servants from Greys Inn had been sent straight to Twickenham with orders to open the house and Sir Francis had not thought to order any to attend on him here as they went. So Lady Lettice's servants aided by Cuffe and Skeres did most of the heavy work. And it was Cuffe and Skeres who finally supported the ailing Sir Anthony as circumstances forced him to walk the length of the garden and hobble down the steps into the boat, where Dr Wendy was waiting for him in a dry area under the waxed awning.

*

The river was running high and rough. The wooden steps were wet and slippery. Poley, who had only managed to get aboard with the utmost difficulty, watched as the three men approached. Sir Francis, beside him, was fussing over the trunk containing his books, fearing that the water would get in at them while Dr Wendy worked on making the small and shrinking dry area as comfortable for his approaching patient as possible. The boatman and his boy were working at holding their vessel still against the landing below the bottom step, their attention all on their mooring lines. So it was only the intelligencer who saw what happened next.

Sir Anthony slipped. He was wearing his nightgown and slippers, wrapped in blankets with a corner of one folded over his head like a hood to protect him against the sleety drizzle; a hooded cloak thrown over the whole ensemble and clutched as close to being closed as possible by one shaking hand. Sir Anthony's escorts were holding his arms but only through the thickness of the woollen cocoon he was swathed in. When he slipped off the bottom step, they lost their grip at once. The invalid pitched forward onto the landing, his slippers flying one way and another, leaving his cloak and blankets in the hands of his would-be helpers. He took one step across the wet boards and was lost. A wave caught the boat at that same moment and pulled it out into the river so that a black-throated gap opened in front of the falling man.

Without thinking, Poley was up and reaching for Sir Anthony. His muscles gave a warning twinge as he stood but the situation was moving forward too fast for him to pay any attention to the stiffness and the pain. It was only as their hands met and the full weight came onto his shoulders that Poley realised what he had done. He shouted with anguish, but held on grimly as their combined weight pulled the side of the vessel hard up against the landing once more while Essex's spymaster came tumbling aboard. Poley's bellow galvanised Sir Francis and Dr Wendy. A moment later Sir Anthony was safe, shaken but unhurt. A moment later still, Cuffe and Skeres were aboard as well, still carrying the blankets and the cloak. The elder Bacon brother was tucked in the dry space beneath the boat's awning, wrapped against wind in his blankets and against the spray by the cloak once again with his physician crouching protectively over him. Poley sat in the stern as they pulled away, shaking, pale and sick from the re-ignited agony blazing in his shoulders. The pain consumed him to such an extent that he remained oblivious to the increasing downpour and the intensifying cold. In fact it was only when Dr Wendy approached him that his mind returned to his current situation. 'Sir Anthony wishes to thank you for saving him,' said the doctor. 'Can you move closer to him?'

Poley tensed himself to get up once more and froze, his face pale with shock. 'Ah,' said Wendy sympathetically. 'I see the rescue has come at a price. Stay where you are. I will inform Sir Anthony. He will have ample opportunity to show his gratitude when we arrive at Twickenham. We are likely to be stranded there for some considerable time.'

The weather eased and the river settled so that by the time they reached the Barn Elms landing, Cuffe and Skeres were able to go ashore quite easily. Cuffe was at his planned destination, for Sir Henry Wotton and the rest of the secretariat were with Lady Frances at this house. Skeres still had some way to go – and in the opposite direction – if he was going to get to Wanstead as he planned. As Poley watched him leave, it occurred to the ever-suspicious intelligencer that Skeres would be alone and unobserved on his long journey. Much of it through London if he went by horse via the Horseferry or over the Bridge. So Skeres could easily contact a range of powers involved in this situation under the convenient cover of having come so far out of his way to help an old friend.

Poley was still turning such cynical thoughts over in his mind when the boat finally arrived at Twickenham. At Doctor Wendy's cheery, 'Here we are,' he looked up. Away to his right, standing magnificently on the north shore, was Richmond Palace – a favourite of the Queen's by all accounts, as Hampton Court had been a favourite of her father's. The south bank, towards which they were drawing, was lightly wooded. A park, thought Poley; and a pleasant one by the look of things. Though walking through it to reach the house would be a labour worthy of Hercules, with his shoulders the way they were.

But he need not have worried. There was a rivulet leading up towards the house itself that opened from the River's south bank. It was wide enough to allow the ferry easy access through the trees and between the lawns to a convenient landing only a matter of yards from the garden door. The exterior of the place was in very good order indeed and seemed recently decorated. As Dr Wendy helped Poley into the arms of a couple of stout servants, the intelligencer recalled that the Queen herself had come visiting here not long ago.

The inside of the house also betrayed touches added in expectation of a royal visitation; and that was all to the good. Every part of the place where the royal foot might have trod – or been expected to tread – was even more impressive and comfortable than Essex House itself. Certainly the servants' quarters through which Poley was half conducted, half supported, seemed to have no dark and sinister low-ceilinged chambers suitable for torturing suspected spies. Inevitably, the rooms were smaller than those in Essex House, but Poley found himself deposited in a homely chamber warmed by a fire and enlivened by a view of the tree-lined park, the river beyond and Richmond Palace in the distance. He was looking a little woefully down at his trappings and wondering how he would unpack without the use of his arms when Sir Francis arrived. 'I have given orders that the servants pay particular attention to you,' he said. 'Of course they will unpack your bags and put everything away. In the meantime, if it would not inconvenience you too much, Master Poley, my brother is settled in his usual room and is desirous of having a private conversation with you.'

6

'I have to thank you,' said Sir Anthony Bacon with little sign that he meant what he said. His manner was brusque and his expression almost petulant; his voice rough and a little breathless as though he was still shocked by the near-disaster. He appeared to the injured intelligencer to have been forced into this gesture against his will, immediately after having been bundled into the warm security of his sick bed in Twickenham Lodge. Probably either by his brother or his doctor. Which might explain the lack of attendants to hear his humiliation as he expressed his grudging gratitude to a man he neither liked nor trusted.

'It was nothing,' said Poley. 'Anyone would have done the same for anyone in your position'

'I am certainly not just *anyone*, Master Poley,' he observed icily. But then his tone thawed. 'And neither are you. Especially in the condition of your shoulders. Dr Wendy says he cannot conceive how you were able to act so swiftly and effectively under the circumstances.'

'Well…' Poley would have ventured a modest shrug but the movement was out of the question.

Sir Anthony held up a hand that commanded silence even though it trembled like a leaf in a gale. Even though, thought Poley, it was hard for a bed-ridden ghost of a creature peering out from beneath a pile of blankets to command anyone. Except, perhaps, for a man currently without the use of his arms.

The shaking hand gestured towards a chair that had been placed nearby. Poley sat, and was grateful to do so. The atmosphere was stultifying. The window, which overlooked the gardens down to the River, was tightly closed. A fire burned in a wide grate and a brazier glowed like the eye of a devil in the nearest corner. The topmost foot of air beneath the ceiling was clouded thickly with woodsmoke and the rest of the atmosphere was fragrant with it. 'Nor can the doctor calculate how much more suffering you will face because of what you did,' Sir Anthony wheezed. 'Nor, indeed, how much further into the future you have set the date of your eventual recovery.'

'He does not suspect, then, that I have been attempting to deceive you about the seriousness of my hurts only to be fooled into revealing the truth by my unthinking actions as you stumbled?' Poley leaned back in the chair as though able to take his ease.

The commanding hand fell. The expression changed; a flicker of wry amusement came and went. Sir Anthony regarded Poley for a heartbeat as though he was seeing him in a new light. That of a duellist, perhaps, measuring a surprisingly able opponent. 'I had indeed wondered,' Sir Antony admitted. 'But the doctor assures me that your hurts are real enough and you have made them worse by doing me good service.'

'And you trust him to make that judgement? It is crucial after all, is it not? As a test of my veracity if as nothing more.' Poley leaned further back, eyebrows raised, trying not to wince at the sudden stab of pain.

'And as a test of whatever is likely to transpire in the

relationship that circumstances and propriety have now forced upon us? Yes indeed. But consider. Dr Wendy is my personal physician and any man who cannot trust his own doctor is lost, is he not? Especially one as unwell as I am. Furthermore, Dr Wendy *is* only my personal doctor because he has an unrivalled reputation. I poached him from the Queen herself, an act she has yet to forgive. His father, after all, tended her father towards the end and she covets him in consequence. He would have spent the winter visiting my Lord of Essex with all her other doctors had I not spirited him away.'

'Though that might have been to your benefit...' Poley observed and then could have bitten his tongue. Just because Dr Wendy himself was not at Essex's bedside did not mean that he could not converse with colleagues who were; all of them were free to come and go as they pleased. A most potent conduit for information of all sorts heading one way and another, therefore. And one that Sir Anthony would be less than happy to find a man he did not yet trust suspected might exist. And, now it struck him, it might quite possibly be the manner in which letters had been smuggled into and out of York House – for he had little doubt that the convalescent Essex had been back in contact with Southampton amongst others of his friends and fellow plotters.

*

Sir Anthony apparently didn't register the slip of the tongue. 'Indeed,' he continued, a man who was not used to being interrupted, 'the good doctor informs me that had a man in my condition actually been pitched into the river, as I so nearly was, death would have followed almost immediately. Either in the water or soon after any rescue that was achieved.' He paused. Gave a sigh that rattled somewhere deep in his chest. 'In short, you have saved my life at considerable damage to yourself. And I thank you. You may call upon myself or Sir Francis my brother in any matter at any time and of course you must remain here under Dr Wendy's care until you are fully recovered.'

'You are most gracious, Sir Anthony,' Poley answered formally. 'I will try not to impose upon you and Sir Francis to any great degree. Indeed, if you agree, I will try to search out ways in which I can be of service to you both. Though I recognise of course that I have not yet earned your trust.'

'Well, we will see. Your offer is appreciated. As is your understanding.'

'My position and level of trust within the Secretariat at Essex House has been made plain to me both in the quantity and quality of correspondence I have been asked to undertake. But that aspect of my employment must stop, of course; for the time-being at least. A man who can hardly move his arms is not best suited to the writing of letters.'

'Indeed,' allowed Sir Anthony. 'But I would judge that you will be capable of carrying messages, if not of transcribing them, as soon as you are well enough to travel between here, Barn Elms, Gray's Inn and Wanstead. We must, sadly, leave Denmark aside for the moment.' The skin at the eye-corners crinkled in a fleeting smile at his little jest, though there was little movement of his lips.

'And as soon as you feel you can trust me with such messages.' *Which will probably be never*, added Poley mentally. *Though Sir Francis might be a different matter…*

'Indeed.' The tone of the word was a dismissal. The pallid face turned away. Sir Anthony was clearly exhausted. The breath seemed to rumble like a thunderstorm in that blanket-buried chest.

Poley rose a little unsteadily and crossed towards the door which he had left slightly ajar on entering to save his shoulders the painful work of raising his hands to the latch. He turned. 'But in fairness, Sir Antony, in the mean-time, you must consider me *armless*.'

There was a moment of silence as he stepped out and then as he walked down the corridor away from the sick room, he heard a sound he had never heard before. Sir Anthony Bacon was laughing. It was a small step along a long road that might lead to Sir Anthony's trust, thought Poley. A trifling step – but a beginning.

He had gone perhaps half a dozen paces when he bumped into Lawson, Sir Anthony's personal servant, companion in that position to Jacques Petit. Lawson had been sent on ahead to prepare the sickroom and was clearly shaken that a near-fatal accident had occurred while he was away from Sir Anthony's side. 'You have not tired him?' he asked with a worried frown.

'I amused him, as you can hear.' But even as Poley said this, the laughter turned into a hacking cough.

Sir Anthony's servant nodded grimly. 'I will go to him,' he said. 'Dr Wendy will be attending him soon as well, with potions to aid his rest.' He took a deep breath which seemed to shake a little. 'And I thank you for preserving him, Master Poley. That I was absent at his moment of need… You may call upon me at any time…' There was no doubting the man's shock and sincerity. Poley bowed and they parted.

Poley found the household at Twickenham fascinating to observe as the condition of his shoulders slowly began to improve under Dr Wendy's care. Sir Anthony never stirred from his bed except as neatness, cleanliness and bodily functions demanded. But he wrote and received copious letters, keeping a modest secretariat of his own, headed by Petit and Lawson – though it was nothing on the scale of the one Sir Henry Wotton headed for the Earl of Essex. Messengers carrying missives came and went, sometimes packing the sick-room, sometimes leaving it empty of everyone except Sir Anthony and Lawson. And the copious files of his correspondence stretching back, in all probability, over years past.

*

No doubt Sir Francis also corresponded but he kept no scribes or archives here. Poley calculated that if he had any number of both, they were probably housed at his lodgings in Gray's Inn. Whither, amongst countless other places, including the Queen's private audience chambers, the Queen's Counsel Extraordinary was in constant motion and attendance. It was Sir Francis, therefore, who brought back an unending stream of gossip, though little that could actually be called 'news'. He was as careful as might be expected of a leading lawyer, never to overstep legality in what he disclosed. What the Queen told him was discussed under legal privilege, of course, and could never be revealed. And were that not the case, there was still the Tower, housing Dick Topcliffe with his rack and Tom Derrick with his axe, waiting for anyone with loose lips or ill intentions towards the Her Majesty and her realm.

However, there was a strange air about Twickenham Lodge which exercised Poley's mind to quite a degree at first. He hardly slept, kept wakeful by pain despite Dr Wendy's distillations of poppy and willow bark. Nor did Sir Anthony, it transpired. The night was filled with scurrying and whispers. The messengers arrived at all hours, were greeted by Lawson or Petit, passed their messages to them or were escorted into the sick-room to deliver them to Sir Anthony in person. What these messages were, Poley was at pains to discover, but he could never do so – in the beginning at least.

Slowly at first but increasingly successfully, Poley began to follow these secret comings and goings. He learned the safest places to listen outside Sir Anthony's chamber, especially as a clement spring approached, opening the grounds to him day and night. Apparently casual strolls between the Lodge and the River and all around the margins of the increasingly unkempt and overgrown gardens, clearly reduced to order for the Queen's visit and left fallow now, allowed him to discover a convenient hiding place. This was in a bower well-hidden behind a cascade of ancient honeysuckle woven through an ill-tended trellis which did not quite grip the wall. This was hung above the top of a herb-green mount piled against the south-facing brickwork. The entire trellis was pushed further out by a modest buttress outside Sir Anthony's window. There was a gap behind it just large enough to contain Poley, even when he was wearing a cloak. One that was thick against the cold and damp, and dark to blend in with the shadows.

Even secreted here, Poley found it frustratingly difficult to overhear anything of critical importance beyond what Sir Francis had already brought home and made common knowledge, not least because the window itself was tightly closed against the last cold draughts of winter. And at least part of the point of Sir Anthony's correspondence, the long-experienced intelligencer knew, was that the recipient could read and write secret matters without an incriminating syllable ever escaping his lips. Until circumstances altered, and both actions and words began to speak loud.

As week succeeded week and he found the feeling of being constantly watched beginning to ease, Poley's less clandestine comings and goings were not without their little nuggets of intelligence. Even at the outset, when the spy felt himself under the closest scrutiny, the doctor often saw both his patients at once to make best use of his time. He would direct his helpers to massage Poley while he treated Sir Anthony under Lawson's watchful eye and discussed the day's news; or he might tend Poley himself with herbs and unguents while Lawson or Petit saw to Sir Anthony and chatted as they did so. On such occasions the gossip sailed close to secrecy with increasing regularity as the intelligencer slowly became just another familiar face around the Lodge.

During the early days, also, he took his meals with Sir Anthony, his companions, the doctor and the doctor's assistants. Sir Anthony needed feeding by hands much steadier than his own. Poley needed arms capable of moving between trencher and lip in the first place. It was as often as not Lawson's steady hand that gently fed Sir Anthony while Petit was also almost constantly there. Wine flowed, as did conversation and guards on tongues were lowered with each succeeding glass. Towards, but never quite into, the realm of dangerous revelation.

And then there was Sir Francis. He exercised Poley's mind in quite another manner. What was the outcome of those long conversations face to face with the Queen herself? he wondered. Was the younger Bacon brother most assiduously trying to protect Essex's interests or his own? Was he advising her Majesty to hesitate in the face of the continued negativity in London, where even the walls of the Palace were now being daubed with pro-Essex graffiti. Or was it he who suggested that the Earl's failures and shortcomings should be paraded in public as soon as this could be done without danger to the invalid's health? So that the men causing these waves of civil unrest would learn what it was had so offended their righteously outraged Monarch? Master Secretary Cecil wished to be seen to take no part in this – beyond what might be expected of a dutiful subject conscious of his duty to sovereign and state. And yet there seemed little doubt that the Earl's fortunes continued to wane and someone of enormous power was set on pulling him down in spite of the Queen's continued vacillation. If not the self-serving Sir Francis then who? And how could Cecil's secret intelligencer become most fruitfully involved?

*

It was, Poley realised, precisely as Sir Anthony had feared from the outset, but short of murder could find no way of controlling now. The armless intelligencer had been flung into the middle of a closed and very secret society like a cat amongst pigeons. A cat constrained by his hurts, but a cat nevertheless; and one that circumstances had made it impossible to eject. Everyone else at the Lodge had worked for the Bacon brothers or their family for years. They were absolutely trusted. Were, in fact, like the company aboard a well-crewed vessel; each knowing his place and his role, able to rely absolutely on all his companions to do the same. Twickenham Lodge was a kind of sounding-board for what the two brothers knew, suspected, believed or imagined. And, perhaps with the exception of the organisation run first by Sir Francis Walsingham and latterly by Master Secretary Cecil and Walsingham's nephew Sir Thomas, it was the most efficient intelligence gathering network in the country.

A network originally designed by Sir Anthony to find facts for the Earl of Essex. A network now, it seemed, becoming dedicated under Sir Francis to finding facts *about* the Earl of Essex. The historic unity was clearly coming under strain as the new mission pulled elements of the network in opposite directions. Poley's thoughts and observations kept returning to one question above all. Was the knowledge accrued by the Bacons' intelligence network designed to help Essex as it had been in the past – or to destroy him as Cecil wished to do in secret and as soon in the future as possible? So whether or not Poley could write was irrelevant. All he had to do was to listen carefully and remember accurately. Everyone in Twickenham Lodge knew that as well as he did.

Much more deeply and obviously than the case had been at Essex House, Lawson's attendance on Sir Anthony became almost that of a mother – or a wife. It was clear that they had been in the past – and were in the present as far as Sir Anthony's frail body allowed – lovers. Poley observed this with no surprise. In the days when he worked for Walsingham's secret service, he had heard rumours of Sir Anthony's proclivities and, indeed, the charge of Sodomy in France. He did not judge – and would never dream of condemning such a relationship. Catholic though he had been raised, from which religion he had lapsed, and Protestant as he pretended to be in hopes of a quiet life, despite all the beliefs surrounding him, he was too well aware of his own sins to rush to condemn others.

For he had himself uncovered the truth of the plot that caused Queen Mary of Scots' downfall by forging exactly the same relationship with the headstrong young Anthony Babington, who had died calling for his beloved Robert to be treated kindly. Unaware that Poley had been there in the crowd to watch him hung, drawn and quartered. Just as he was at Fotheringay to watch the laughable fiasco of Queen Mary's beheading. And the earliest methods he had used to worm his way into Babbington's confidence were almost the same as those he was employing now.

The first important fact that the legal and political gadfly Sir Francis was able to report was that Essex had been returned to his house with his jailer Sir Richard Barkely ten days after their exit from the place. He also disclosed that Sir Gelly and Lady Frances had been allowed to visit him there. Poley suspected that it was Sir Anthony, however, who was first apart from himself to link this information with the sudden departure of the Earl of Southampton for Ireland at the beginning of the next month – as soon as his passage could be arranged, in fact. Almost as though it dropped from the aether of the sickly spymaster's lodgings, the suspicion that Southampton was heading west at his friend's behest to discover whether Mountjoy was still willing to lend Essex the Irish army should circumstances demand it, seemed to appear, ghost-like. And Southampton's return suggested, again, like the dead king of Denmark in the ancient play of *Hamlet*, that Essex's request had been refused. Poley could all too well imagine the desperation that must be mounting not only in the erstwhile occupants of Essex House but in the Earl himself; and any hesitation on Mountjoy's part would only add to it. Lady Frances reported that he had been well recovered in body when she saw him. Well enough recovered, it was whispered, for him to have lain with her and made her with child again. But, some wondered, was he as well recovered in mind?

*

The increasing desperation of the Earl was emphasised within another month when Sir Charles Davers again headed west to see whether the start of the campaigning season in Ireland had done anything to change Mountjoy's earlier decision. Poley doubted that it had. The gossip from Ireland filtering into the Lodge was that Mountjoy had found a new vocation – he would conquer the island and reduce it to order in the name of his Queen. Thus positioning himself, calculated Poley, as a reliable military leader in the eyes of her successor – whoever that turned out to be. He had neither the troops nor the inclination therefore to indulge Essex and his plots. Especially, thought Poley, as he considered things from Mountjoy's point of view, that if the Queen was supposed to be the weakling Richard II in popular imagination, the only possible Bolingbroke in a position to succeed her was Essex. All the other contenders were as far removed from battlefield commanders as it was possible to imagine. Even the leading male contender, James VI of Scotland, was noted for his intellect and his hunting of witches rather than for his leadership qualities. So even King James would need a few experienced and successful generals close at hand. Thus it might well suit Mountjoy to support Essex in approaches to the Scottish king as success in that endeavour would obviously serve Mountjoy's ends as well; but only after he had kept the army tightly under his command and led it to a victory which would enhance his reputation almost beyond measure.

Amongst the more regular visitors to Sir Anthony's bedside during these months was Penelope Rich, Essex's wilful but brilliant younger sister, who was Mountjoy's mistress and, therefore, no doubt, the courier bringing his personal thoughts and plans directly to the spymaster's ears as direct access to her brother was impossible for her. Her repeated visits promised to give some strength to Poley's suspicions about Mountjoy's true position in the game. Poley would have given much to eavesdrop on their whispered conversations but she was always attended by a group of sharp-eyed retainers from her husband's household; men who made Gelly Meyrick look like a milksop and, unlike the grudgingly grateful Sir Anthony, would have no compunctions about slitting his throat.

But the spring and early summer did not pass entirely barren of solid intelligence – though Poley was at first uncertain how to use what he learned. As the Bacon brothers – from opposing points of view perhaps – both became concerned about Essex's increasing desperation, so Sir Anthony, Lawson and Petit began a new project. At first, Poley was only a witness to their actions – he did not become an auditor until part-way through.

One night, crouching beneath the trellis, surrounded by the fragrance of honeysuckle and wrapped against unseasonably late April showers in a heavy russet cloak, Poley peered through the tight-closed window into the sick-room. Sir Anthony and his two servants were sorting through the great mounds of paper and parchment which, Poley calculated, represented Sir Anthony's correspondence over many years. There was no great surprise that they should be reorganising it – it was a considerable body of work in volume as well as in variety. Poley had taken the rare opportunities when he was alone or unobserved in the sick-room to glance through as much of it as chance allowed.

It had a range of importance – from the philosophical correspondence with Michel de Montaigne, through legal correspondence with the courts of France, medical correspondence with doctors over half of Europe, family correspondence with his sickly mother whose letters in reply were increasingly incoherent, legal and commercial correspondence about the various properties he was being forced to sell as his finances crumbled alongside those of the Earl of Essex. There were probably copies of begging letters which the Queen failed to respond to; Sir Francis was much more successful in that department. And of course there must be – although he had never seen them - the secret and incriminating letters arising from Sir Anthony's work as Essex's spymaster. But what surprised Poley, night after night as he watched them working now, was the manner in which Lawson and Petit were sorting so relentlessly through one pile after another. They were glancing at the sheets of paper, then bringing them to Sir Anthony who studied them in more detail, discussed them briefly, then handed them back. A few were then re-filed. But the vast majority of the correspondence was simply thrown into the golden throat of the wide-mouthed sickroom fire.

Was he watching a conscientious record-keeper tidying up his archives, wondered Poley; or a nervous secret agent ridding himself of anything traitorous or treasonous? Motivated, perhaps, by fear that the master for whom he had written most of the burning correspondence was beginning to lose his grip on power as well as on his finances and, conceivably, his mind.

*

It was the wind that helped Poley come closer to answering those simple but vital questions. As full summer approached, the breeze swung round so that the weathercocks on the local church steeples all pointed to the South. And it so happened that a steady southerly had the unexpected effect of blowing the smoke back down the chimneys of Twickenham Lodge. Especially the chimney rising from the sick-room. Suddenly the foot or so of smoke that habitually hung as grey as spider-webs beneath the ceiling was joined by choking clouds of back-draught that came billowing unannounced out of the flue. The first time this happened Sir Anthony fell to coughing and choking at once. Lawson came running across the room and opened the window so quickly that he almost caught Poley peering over the sill. But once the window stood wide, it released more than smoke. It released the conversation.

'That's better,' wheezed Sir Anthony. 'At least I can breathe.'

'But you're not too cold?' asked Lawson. 'A chill will do as much damage as…'

'No. This is better. If I feel cold there are more blankets and Jacques can bring the brazier a little closer. Let's get on.'

'This one, Monseigneur?' asked Petit.

'Let me see… No it is from Montaigne. Put it with the others to be kept.'

'And this one?' asked Lawson.

'Ah,' said Sir Anthony. 'This one's from Spain,

confirming my suspicions about Cecil.'

'Keep it to use against the Toad should circumstances…' wondered Lawson.

'No. We are too late. See the date: it was written years ago. All the world nowadays knows he has a pension from the Spanish court. He says he takes it so the Dons suppose he is in their pocket while in fact the opposite is true. It's useless. Into the fire with it. But, in spite of the work we still have to do with my letters, I want you to go to Barn Elms tomorrow and ask Sir Henry to send over Henry Cuffe with any correspondence he wishes me to assess – and perhaps get rid of…'

Next afternoon, Poley was waiting as though by chance as Lawson returned from his mission with Cuffe in tow. Both men were laden with old correspondence for the spymaster to assess. Cuffe was enormously pleased to see that Poley was healing so well and, once the letters were delivered, he gossiped about doings at Barn Elms and Wanstead with that open-hearted innocence which made him such a valuable asset to the secret agent. As Cuffe settled into a routine of couriering Henry Wotton's archives over to Twickenham section by section, so he and Poley fell into a routine of sharing a glass of sack and an apparently inconsequential conversation before his return to Barn Elms and Lady Frances.

It was as though Poley's acuity returned in full strength as knowledge of the Lodge's secrets grew and information about the doings in Barn Elms and Wanstead came in one drip at a time with Cuffe. His shoulders began to ease and his orbit began to move outside Twickenham; but never in company with Lawson or Petit. Never with messages from Sir Anthony, though that was less of a frustration now. At first he accompanied Sir Francis or was accompanied by one of his most trusted attendants – by the river and then by horseback to Barn Elms, where he was careful to wait outside, avoiding the all-too familiar household as much as possible. But he was never sent to Wanstead. That was a blessing. He did not mind being a shade in the background of conversations with Lady Frances or Sir Henry Wotton or even Sir Gelly Meyrick – and there was always Henry Cuffe, buoyantly pleased to see him at Barn Elms. But he would have found it hard to stand ready during conversations with Lady Lettice or his cousin Sir Christopher Blount, to whose household in Wanstead he really ought to have returned. But of course, whatever he could have learned at Wanstead was as nothing compared to what he could discover by remaining at the Lodge.

This was especially true as, like Poley's shoulders, Essex's strictures began to ease. With the spring came freedom for the Earl to walk in the gardens or on the leads around the roof of Essex House. Lady Frances was permitted more visits, and longer ones. He was strong enough in body to play at tennis; something Poley particularly envied. He was strong enough in mind to read plays and poetry, to discuss art, philosophy and politics. Poley wondered whether he was alone in seeing the possibility of danger here. The caged sparrow – and a sickly one at that – had returned to his accustomed form of an eagle. The cage that would hold the former would by no means hold the latter for any length of time. In due course, also - perhaps because the improvement in Essex's situation made his supporters less wary of potential enemies - Poley was trusted by Sir Francis to carry letters and messages alone. But only as far as Gray's Inn and with communications so anodyne they might well have been filed alongside his earlier correspondence with Denmark. Or, like so much else passing through Sir Anthony's hands, thrown into the fire.

*

Then, as chance would have it, Gray's Inn was where the gossip circulating amongst all the lawyers there, every man agog with it, pushed Poley towards the next step. It was something he found out about on one of his unaccompanied journeys. He was actually carrying a message to Sir Francis's friend and colleague Nicholas Trott to be passed on to the men working on the Inn's gardens, which were in a notably better state than those at Twickenham Lodge. But what he overheard led Poley to see the inevitability of the next phase of Essex's destiny as it hurled towards the desperate Earl like some sort of massive wave towards a doomed ship. Sending Davers west to Mountjoy in Ireland had clearly been a step too far; particularly now that the Earl was fully recovered and fecund. It may even have been, speculated Poley, that his ability to do so had been yet another trap. Into which the Earl's restored vigour and mounting frustration led him with a kind of inevitability. His action had clearly been reported to the Queen along with commentary detailing precisely what Essex had sent Davers to ask of the reluctant Mountjoy. His action begat a reaction as surely as his lying with Lady Frances begat another child.

The news that Gray's Inn was bursting with was that the Earl was to face a Special Commission of seventeen judges in front of two hundred specially selected witnesses at York House in a hearing to be conducted by four Prosecutors. And this time Sir Francis would be major amongst them, friend to the Earl or not. At the Queen's direct order. Whether he was willing or not. He protested loudly that he was forced into it against his will.

Poley was not so sure.

'I *must*,' whispered Sir Francis.

'Because *she* orders it…' Sir Antony's tone verged on a sneer.

Someone tutted at the danger of the tone: Lawson, no doubt.

Poley stirred, moving a little closer to the window. This was the first time he had heard the brothers at odds like this. Perhaps these nocturnal visits to the garden and the trellis were an even better investment than he had supposed. Especially now that summer was drawing near and the nights were both dry and clement, allowing the casement to stand wide whether the fire was smoking or not.

'Because she believes you are a part of all that she wishes hurled at Essex's head!' snapped Sir Francis. 'You did have a hand in the *Aoplogia* that the Earl wrote and Cuffe passed to you in the year '96 for polishing, editing and publishing. Which has been so recently and mysteriously republished and now begins to look like an argument for his own succession. Or so it does according to Master

Secretary, Sir Walter Raleigh and their factions. But she also suspects you of knowing more than is safe about the banned book of *Henry IV* and the play of *Richard II* which she supposes are designed to show her as a weak monarch ripe to be replaced by a strong and decisive war-leader.'

'We lodged for a while amongst scribblers and actors in Bishopsgate,' Lawson reminded Sir Anthony.

'You did, did you not?' emphasised Sir Francis. 'Even that is turned against you, innocent coincidence though it might have been. And over everything hang two fatal phrases which seem to have sprung to a life of their own – a life she supposes you have helped to animate: *May not a monarch err*? And *Her conditions are as crooked as her carcase*.'

'And the upshot?' Sir Anthony's tone had changed.

'The upshot is a simple one. Either I go to York House tomorrow or you go to the Tower. Tomorrow.'

Poley knew as well as Lawson and Sir Francis that a move to the Tower would bring death as swiftly and surely as Tom Derrick the headsman's axe.

The next day dawned, bright and clear; the weather at striking odds with the increasingly thunderous atmosphere in Twickenham Lodge. Sir Francis rose before dawn and was gone before sunrise. But soon after he had departed, others concerned in the situation began to arrive – seeking news that no-one as yet possessed. First Dorothy, Countess of Northumberland and the elder of Essex's sisters appeared, closely followed by Lady Lettice his mother. Both, of course, well attended. Lady Frances arrived soon after midday and Lady Penelope early in the afternoon, with Lady Janet Percy; also attended by members of the Rich household but thankfully a less threatening group than those who normally attended her.

*

It was, thought Poley, just as well that the common rooms, unlike the gardens, were still as they had been when the Queen herself visited Sir Francis late last year. His intelligence, shared with Cecil at the time, suggested that the Queen had come with a purpose to meet Sir Anthony – were he in residence – and to discuss John Hayward's book of *Henry IV*, the reason the Earl had allowed Hayward to dedicate it to him, whether Sir Francis agreed that she was presented as Richard II therein with Essex as Bolingbroke – soon to become Henry IV – and how much longer the unfortunate author should languish in the Tower for having written such sedition in the first place.

Such a gathering of great ladies was a sight normally encountered only at court. But of course, today, the court was the last place on earth that the Earl's female relatives wished to visit. In any case, thought Poley, remembering the last piece of gossip Henry Cuffe had passed on over a glass of sack, most of the ladies here present stood at various stages of Her Majesty's sharp displeasure and were therefore banned from her presence.

Sir Anthony had no news to give them and directed that they be entertained with the best of food, drink and company that the Lodge could supply in the meantime. Lawson and Petit took over the running of the household – for a little while at least. It was not long before the bored and anxious women took over in turn and arranged things for themselves, tutting at a household run to ruin by having nothing but men in charge. The Devereux sisters snapped and bullied, treating everyone with thoughtless disdain. Lady Frances at least was courteous and Lady Lettice sought Poley out, expressed relief and satisfaction that he was so nearly whole again and promised to carry the happy news to Sir Christopher. But it was Lady Janet who sought and found an opportunity to be alone with him.

'Her Majesty is set upon his destruction; for the moment at least?' he asked as soon as he was certain they could not be overheard at the far end of the garden, down by the river bank. 'Does she give with one hand and take away with the other, permitting him a little more freedom only for that freedom to lead him straight into court?'

'Her current mood is that he still flies too high and she will bring him down to clip his wings.' Janet answered. 'So Master Secretary Cecil believes. And he also believes Sir Francis, while protesting his duty to the Earl, is actually serving himself and playing one side against the other. A dangerous game if so – he is as unpopular in London as is Cecil himself. But the commission at York House is not a court. It may censure the Earl of Essex but it may not condemn him as the Star Chamber could have done. As you have found out all too clearly yourself,' she answered.

'How so?'

'It is very much the construct we might expect from a gifted lawyer; a trial that is not a trial before a court that is not a court, which may issue any punishment except a criminal sentence. Master Secretary will take part, of

course, as he is directed, but it is not the outcome he hopes for in the fullness of time. At best it is but another step along the road.'

'And yet, Sir Anthony at least is worried about where the road will lead to and how soon the end will be reached. When Her Majesty will make up her mind on the matter and settle to one unchangeable course. He is methodically winnowing both his own correspondence and the Earl's – and burning any chaff that might prove dangerous should Essex and his associates actually face a full investigation and a real trial with their lives as well as their liberty at stake.'

'Burning his letters? That is interesting and perhaps instructive. I will pass that information directly to Master Secretary himself.'

'I believe that would be a wise move. Has he any specific instructions for me?'

Instead of answering, she changed the subject unexpectedly – prompted, Poley supposed, by earlier thoughts of Icarus and his waxen wings. 'Are your hurts healed yet, Master Poley?' Apparently without thought, she reached out to touch his shoulder. Both of them jumped. It was as though a tiny bolt of lightning had passed between them, flesh to fingertip, skin to skin, though the thickness of his clothes.

Lady Janet frowned. She had jerked her hand back from the intense sensation. Now she advanced it once more. Poley stood still, somehow robbed of breath and motion alike. This time her touch was firm, purposeful. The sensation was repeated but muted; almost a memory of the original. 'There is something between us, Master Poley,' she said, looking him full in the face from disturbingly close at hand. Her breath smelt sweetly of cloves, her person of a perfume he could not name. There were freckles across the bridge of her nose. Her eyes were moss green and the lashes framing them were thick and curling. Red, to match her hair which was styled after the queen's. But, thought Poley, Lady Janet's hair was all her own.

*

'I do not think she seeks to destroy him but she feels that she still must rein him in. She has been constant in that at least and it continues to be something he brings on himself through more and more desperate actions – even caged as he is. And as I say, there seems little doubt, certainly in Master Secretary's mind, that Sir Francis is advising Her Majesty to follow this path. They meet so often and talk for so long and all in private – what other explanation could there be?' Lady Janet continued after a moment, her voice low and throaty, as though her touch had made them lovers and they were now discussing country matters rather than courtly ones. 'Master Secretary is constant in his warnings against the Earl. But he hesitates to push matters further. Just like Sir Walter Raleigh. But Her Majesty is still unsettlingly skittish…' she glanced around, well aware that her words were very dangerous. But there were only the swans to hear them, Poley observed. And mute swans at that. 'They both fear that one wrong move will do *them* damage rather than *him* and prefer, therefore, to be as inactive as possible in the matter.'

'Other than bearing warnings and awaiting events,'

mused Poley. 'If inaction can be called an activity, then that is probably the best action they can take. As they wait in hopes that the Earl will somehow destroy himself.'

'Indeed. And if there are any instructions for you, they will be much the same. Stay where you are and continue to do what you are doing. Events may conspire to give you good reason to act. When they do so, then you might act; perhaps then you *must* act. But in the mean time we all must watch and wait.' She drew in a thoughtful breath. 'I don't know how much credence Her Majesty actually puts in the stories of the Irish army coming to his aid, or the mayor and citizens of London rising against her at his command, or that he is in constant communication with Scotland promising to secure the succession for King James in return for assurances that he and his friends will stand forever above Master Secretary and all the rest. But she sees that his current behaviour, even shackled as he is, could be a potent threat to peace at the very heart of her realm.'

'And so she has him dragged to York House and made to stand against a panel of his enemies so that everyone can see what dangers he presents?' growled Poley, his voice rough with desire.

'Not so,' she answered softly. 'Or rather not quite so. Hence Her Majesty's insistence that Sir Francis stand amongst the prosecutors, for Sir Francis is his friend. Or so he presents himself, though the people of London seem to doubt the truth of it. I reason that, rather, she wishes to make my Lord of Essex see as clearly as possible the wrongs he has done and the mistakes he has made nomatter how good his intentions. And the inevitable outcomes should the wrongs persist or be repeated. He is the beloved but wilful child in her eyes. And this day is the well-applied corrective birch.'

'Then surely Master Secretary Cecil reads him right and Her Majesty is wrong,' whispered Poley, well aware of how close to treason such thoughts were. As close, indeed, as his bearded cheek was to her red-freckled one. 'He is no spoilt brat but a man full grown and he sees no loving mother but an old crone set on thwarting him and ruining him. It is a race between his failing power and weakening finances and her failing health and withering body.'

'*Her conditions are as twisted as her carcase*? Did he not say as much? What woman – let alone a queen – could forgive such an insult?'

'And that is maybe the heart of the matter. Of her *skittishness* as you put it. There is a part of her, the spirit of her father, perhaps, which seeks full restitution for his insults, failures and disobediences. But another part, the spirit of her gentle mother you might say, which hesitates to rush upon his destruction. I have heard it said that she still on occasion weeps for Mary of Scots – who was at least seeking her dethronement and death as well as the return of her realms to the Catholic Church. Whatever Essex has done, it presents no danger comparable to this.'

'And, as we have discussed, perhaps that is what Master Secretary is waiting for, then,' she whispered.

'For him to take some action comparable with those of Mary of Scots.'

'If that is so, then he has chosen his watcher well has he

not? For it was you who spied out that last and greatest of the Scottish Queen Mary's plots.'

They both fell silent. He was thinking, not about Babbington but about the nature of womanhood. How a queen might react to her favourite subject seeing her not for the eternally youthful faery she wished to appear but as the withered old witch she had become. And how that injured Monarch might be led into seeing the man who insulted her as a potent and immediate threat to her throne, her religion and her life. At least, these considerations were where his thoughts began but they somehow ended with a lingering consideration of how full, warm and bonny the body so close beside him must be.

'And what does Master Secretary himself say to all this…?' he asked hoarsely before he said something utterly irrelevant to the real reason that they found themselves alone out here like a courting couple of lovers just escaped from their chaperones.

'Well,' she answered softly, 'further to what we have said of him so far…'

*

Poley and Lady Janet were still walking out in the garden, discussing secret and treasonous matters under the eyes of the silent swans, when the first of the messengers arrived. Each of the women, wise in the ways of both legal and royal courts, had left word that she should be informed as soon as the proceedings at York House were concluded. And by late evening all the messengers were in; each bearing nothing more than that one fact: the hearing was over and the Earl returned to Essex House under escort and incommunicado. It was only as the night drew on that the impatient visitors began to realise that their errant and unwilling host had no intention of returning home while they were there to greet him – and put him to the question every bit as brutally as Topcliffe might have done. So, one after another, starting with Lady Lettice who had farthest to travel, they assembled their retainers and departed. Lady Janet of course went with them, leaving Poley lingering pensively in the benighted garden.

Sir Francis arrived after midnight, his presence announced by a stirring that ran right through the Lodge. Put on their mettle by the ladies, the Bacon brothers' household sprang into action with food, drink, welcome and attention, but Lawson of course remained at Sir Anthony's bedside. It was well after one in the morning before everything began to settle. Sir Francis crept through to see Sir Anthony and Poley found himself crouching in his fragrant hiding place outside the sickroom window.

'The bare bones,' said Sir Anthony. 'I have been exhausted all day…'

'And the women haven't helped,' added Lawson.

'I'm sure they haven't. But the bare bones then, as you say. The whole procedure was held in the Great Hall at York House. Two hundred witnesses, seventeen judges including Cecil, of course. Three, perhaps four, favourable to the Earl. Four prosecutors including myself. Lord Keeper Edgerton in charge. All of us seated at one end of the great table there with the witnesses all around us. Sergeant at Law Yelverton led the Earl in and stood him at the far end of the table opposite us. He may be recovered but he did not look well. Archbishop Whitgift called for a stool so he could sit. Which was fortunate. Yelverton led him in at eight this morning and matters were not concluded until nearly ten tonight.'

'The bare bones,' begged Sir Anthony. 'This is too much flesh for my stomach.'

'Edgerton called for proceedings to begin and gave the opening address,' said Sir Francis. 'Then that foul creature Coke took over. If there is a murder done within the next few days it will be myself ridding the world of the bloated bag of spite.' Sir Francis paused.

Poley gave a wry smile. Coke had not only beaten the younger man to the coveted post of Attorney General, he had also stolen the beautiful young heiress Lady Elizabeth Hatton from under Sir Francis's nose. *No love lost there,* he thought.

'But he put the bones of the case,' Sir Francis hurried on as his brother stirred impatiently. 'These were that the Earl's actions showed disloyalty to the Queen as well as disobedience which verged on treason, especially his movement into Munster. That he disregarded the state of the army while knighting too many of his friends. And, most heinously, he treated with the enemy and made a treaty with O'Neil which gave great succour to the Papists and did great hurt to the Queen and the realm. Then Solicitor General Fleming spoke, repeating many of the accusations but in more moderate terms – this was not the Star Chamber after all. But he added the charges that the Earl had promoted the Earl of Southampton without permission and had been far too prodigal in his awarding of knighthoods to his friends. Then I spoke, and said that Her Majesty showed great wisdom and mercy in framing the proceedings as she had done. I quoted the letter My Lord of Essex wrote to Edgerton in the early days of his confinement saying the Queen's heart was obdurate against him – which I suggested the current proceedings proved to be untrue. Then, as instructed, I raised the question of Hayward's book of *Henry IV* and said that, although this was an ancient matter bearing no relevance to the current case, the Earl was at fault in allowing it to be dedicated to him and that he should have suppressed it at once in stead of referring it to Archbishop Whitgift as he did. Then the Earl, kneeling on a stool, gave a lengthy and detailed speech accepting guilt and responsibility…'

'As he might well do in a non-court capable of delivering only limited judgements, mostly non-custodial and none of them capital,' grunted Sir Anthony.

'… and begging that Her Majesty at last show him some mercy. Even so, the judgement passed down was that he be removed at once from the Council and that he be immediately dismissed from the post of Earl Marshal. And, although technically not a custodial sentence in that it simply reinstated the *status quo ante*, he was to be returned to Essex house, to languish there at Her Majesty's pleasure.'

Sir Francis straightened wearily and turned away from his bed-ridden brother. 'And, talking of Her Majesty's pleasure,' he said as he departed, 'I'm bound for Gray's Inn to begin preparing a full and detailed report of the entire event for the Queen's immediate attention.'

Poley sat silently, his mind racing. The Commission might have been a carefully constructed way to prove Essex's shortcomings and errors, but it also had the effect – purposed or not – of turning an anxious man into a despairing one. Whatever it was designed to do, it was simply likely to prove yet another step along the road leading the Earl to doing something desperate.

Something fatally desperate.

7

By the end of the month, Poley's responsibilities were extended. However, it seemed plain enough that Sir Anthony, having taken the measure of him anew, desired to keep him close-by. So there was never any talk of him returning to Lady Lettice's household currently at Wanstead. The spymaster wanted him where an eye could be kept on him, even though the situation did put the elder Bacon brother's doings and secrets at risk.

Poley saw the situation as something like a game of chess: Sir Anthony had his suspicions which he was making move after move towards proving. Poley's counter moves were working towards finding out whatever about Essex the Bacon brothers were trying to hide. And to do so before they discovered enough about him to move him on - either out of their house or out of this world. And then, of course, to use Essex's secrets against him in a manner that would ensure his destruction.

Sir Anthony's strategy seemed to the intelligencer to be one whose wisdom outweighed any risks it posed. If a man suspected he had an enemy keen to do him or his master harm, then it did not require the cunning of a Machiavelli to see that it was better to keep him close enough to watch rather than to let him wander away at will. And, of course, Sir Anthony could trust Poley to reappear after any unaccompanied mission because if Poley was the spy that Sir Anthony suspected, he could be relied upon to return like a bee to a flower-patch, always in the hope of more honey. An apt enough comparison he thought, considering his close association with the flower-laden trellis. But, he wondered with a shiver of apprehension, how did Sir Anthony keep watch on who he might contact as he was coming or going by river or horseback? Were even the watermen and the grooms in the Bacons' pockets? Could Lady Janet even be at risk?

In the meantime, Poley was moved out of his grotto beside Sir Anthony's window, not by any enemy action, but by the sudden arrival of a nest of particularly bellicose hornets. He had stayed away from the honeysuckle-sweet hiding place for the better part of a week as there was nothing to observe except for Lawson and Petit burning letters on an unseasonably large fire. Then, when he returned, there were the insects, nest and all – and the fact that they had taken up residence ensured that Sir Anthony's window was now firmly shut against them. Of course Poley considered demanding that the gardener remove them. But that would mean his hiding place would be exposed. He briefly considered trying to move them himself, but the initial attempt was painful enough to deter him, especially as the marks of their stings became a brief topic of conversation as Dr Wendy added them to his list of ailments needing medical attention. Sir Francis made a vague promise to deal with the situation but, as with so many of his dealings with the gardens here as opposed to those at Gray's Inn, nothing was done in the end. Coincidentally, however, Poley's banishment from the trellis happened at much the same time as the awarding of his new responsibilities as courier. It was at about this time too, he noticed, that a new destination was added to the rounds worked by the Bacon brothers' regular couriers. Drury House, on Wych Street, where the Earl of Southampton had taken to holding almost all of his clandestine meetings.

So it happened that Poley was at Barn Elms soon after midsummer when the next step toward the Earl of Essex's fate occurred, like lightning out of a clear blue sky. Cuffe had taken to reciprocating the glasses of sack Poley arranged for him during his visits to Twickenham with equal amounts from Lady Frances' cellar, or rather the cellar belonging to her mother Lady Walsingham in whose house she was living for the time-being. Barn Elms belonged to the Walsinghams, not the Devereuxs, which was why it was familiar to Poley and Poley was all-too familiar to the household there from his years as Walsingham's spy.

The two men were seated in a sunny spot of the stable yard, glass in hand, when Sir Francis arrived in such a hurry that he had winded his horse in getting here, though he had only ridden up from the stables by the Barnes landing place. 'Where's Sir Gelly,' gasped Sir Francis, almost as breathless as his horse. 'Is he here?'

'He was in the stables here a moment ago,' answered a groom.

'Find him. Bring him to me.'

Poley pulled himself to his feet. 'This sounds important,' he said. Cuffe nodded. 'Let's see what's toward,' decided Poley and the pair of them walked over to the stables. They arrived at the same moment as Sir Gelly appeared, stripping off his riding gauntlets as he came. The three of them closed on Sir Francis.

*

'What?' demanded the Welsh knight, a man of few words in a crisis.

'Do you have a list of the men the Earl knighted in Ireland?' demanded Sir Francis, clearly too concerned to be bothered that Cuffe and Poley were also here.

'I have. Why?'

'The Earl's right to award their knighthoods was questioned last month at the Commission in York House. Now it seems that Her Majesty has it in mind to strip them of the honours altogether.'

Sir Gelly stood for a moment, clearly fighting to come to terms with the news. Then, 'Strip them of their knighthoods? What will she gain by that?' he demanded.

'Two things,' answered Sir Francis. 'The first is that it will rob the Earl of the army of men beholden to him who continue to reside here and elsewhere in London, fomenting restlessness and putting the peace of the capital's streets at risk.'

'More likely she fears they will rise with him should he command them to,' snarled Sir Gelly. 'Or not so much Her Majesty as Cecil the Toad, yet again dropping his poison in her ear.'

'That's as it may be,' answered Sir Francis. 'But Her Majesty's second objective is to address that very problem. She believes that the knights, once stripped of rank and standing, will turn upon the man who gave them the honours that have now been taken away by her higher authority.'

'And why in God's name would they do that?'

'Because it will be plain that he had no right to award the honours in the first place.'

'And men who believe themselves so injured are more likely to turn on the Earl than to follow him in any schemes he had formulated during his imprisonment.' Sir Gelly's tone made the statement into a question.

'And she further believes, or has been led to believe,' continued Sir Francis, 'that the outrage of their wives, who will at the same time of course, lose their position as Ladies, will turn on their husbands and strengthen their motivation to turn upon the Earl.'

Poley could not contain himself. 'And has it occurred to no-one on the Council or in the court that the opposite may very likely result? That these men, already loyal to the Earl but wavering because they are staring starvation in the face as their fortunes fall away with his, will turn on him because they can no longer call themselves knights? When in fact he still represents their only hope of solvency, diminished though that hope may be? Surely, a fate such as destitution would be far more likely to disturb their wives and children than the threat of social disgrace. So the broken knights may simply find their faith and loyalty reaffirmed by the unfairness of such an action and the added desperation it would cause as debts would be called in and further loans refused. Butchers, bakers and vintners all closed against them. So that instead of blaming the Earl who raised them up, they will simply blame the Council and the Queen who have cast them down. A belief likely to lead to a great deal more disturbance and danger than simple graffiti on the walls of Salisbury House and Whitehall Palace?'

Sir Francis gaped at him. 'I don't believe anyone has put that interpretation to the Council or to the Queen. It is a potent danger that must be addressed. I will mention it myself when I hand over the list of names Sir Gelly will help me to compile. I thank you for your quick-thinking in this matter Master Poley.'

Sir Gelly grunted and nodded ungraciously. But there was no doubting that he too was thanking Poley for his quick-thinking.

'You have clear sight into matters such as these, friend Poley,' said Cuffe, punching Poley on the shoulder affectionately as the pair of them returned to their seats and the bottle of sack. 'I would never have dreamed that such a reversal of the Queen's logic could be discovered so swiftly. You have done Her Majesty and the Council great service there. But, I am pleased to observe, you have also done great service to the Earl and the men who have stood by him in Ireland and since his return. If Sir Francis carries your thoughts to the Council as forcefully as you expressed them, you will surely have saved the reputation of the Earl and his supporters at the same time as you have stopped the Council and Her Majesty from doing a great deal of damage to their own cause.'

He looked Poley straight in the eye and the intelligencer got a glimpse of the intellect that lay beneath the open-hearted bonhomie. It disturbed him a little, even as he gave an amenable smile and a nod of agreement. And it flashed into his mind that this is what Sir Anthony must have felt all those months ago when he reassessed Poley part way through the conversation just after they arrived at Twickenham Lodge. It was an unsettling feeling that made him wonder for an instant whether he needed to reassess his place in Essex's household, dispersed though it currently was. And whether, rather than the one doing the manipulating as he had believed, he was actually the one being manipulated.

*

'I wish,' continued Cuffe, 'that I had half your quickness of eye and mind. Instead I find I seek the *ataraxia* of Pyrro, the state of inner peace, as you may recall, where my efforts are bent upon understanding that neither our senses nor our beliefs can be trusted to tell us the truth. Any more than the lips and tongues of the men and women with whom we find ourselves surrounded. So we certainly should not rely on them. Rather, we should be without views, disinclined toward one side or the other in any situation and unwavering in our refusal to make a final choice.'

'This is surely a political or social dogma, if what I remember of it is true,' answered Poley. 'It cannot encompass religion.' But even as he said the words he felt an uneasy suspicion that the ancient philosopher had somehow defined his own relationship with the Church. Perhaps even with Heaven and Hell. It was deeply disquieting. He found himself wondering once again whether the man he thought he had been manipulating since their time in the Fleet together had really been manipulating him.

They finished the bottle of sack, then walked in silence down to the Barnes landing where Poley hailed a wherry and had himself sculled back to the Twickenham landing. Then, still wrapped in thought he strolled up to the Lodge. Sir Francis had beaten him home even though he had lingered until Sir Gelly completed the list of Essex's Irish knights. The place was buzzing with speculation, though its occupants except for the Brothers were a little way removed from the heart of the problem. 'So,' said Sir Anthony when Poley arrived in the sick-room for yet another treatment to ease his shoulders into full health. 'Sir Francis tells me you have out-thought Her Majesty and her Toad. The Earl will be beholden to you almost as much as I am myself if you have made this latest madness stop.'

'I had no thought who would be beholden or to whom. I spoke without any thought at all, in fact. The danger seemed so plain to me that it had to be stated.'

'And you are right. Sir Francis has gone back to Westminster and is even now detailing the dangers that you saw to the Council and – for all I know – to the Queen herself.'

'But,' said Dr Wendy, looking up from Sir Anthony's torso into which he was rubbing a particularly foul-smelling unguent, 'if the objective of the plan was to further unsettle the Earl, surely that task has been done, whether the men are stripped of their rank or not. The threat to do so was real and potent. The Earl must see that. It is just another way by which Her Majesty can emphasise her power and his helplessness. Many of the doctors attending him with whom I have regular contact, are increasingly worried that, as his body heals, his mind is beginning to lose its grip. He has no clear idea what to believe or who to trust. He sees enemies conspiring against him at every turn.'

'Her Majesty,' said Poley, 'and her Toad?'

'If not the one then certainly the other. Master Secretary Cecil, Sir Walter Raleigh and the rest.' The doctor turned back to his work and the room fell silent.

The wherry dropped Poley at the Middle Temple stairs one threatening afternoon a few weeks later and he ran up them into Middle Temple, then on up through the gateway, past the Temple Bar and into Chancery Lane. Here the press of people and the sticky heat they generated slowed his steps at once to little more than a snail's pace. He was headed for Gray's Inn with yet another message for the gardeners and Chancery Lane would lead him all the way up to Holborn which he would cross into Gray's Inn Lane which in turn would lead him directly to the Inn itself. It was a walk that should take no more than half an hour but he reckoned it would take at least twice that today; and he was by no means looking forward to the sweaty journey there or back.

Sir Francis' care with the Gray's Inn gardens so far exceeded his care for his own at the Lodge that Poley found some humour in it despite the hornets. But there was no denying that even this late in a disappointing Summer, Gray's Inn gardens still made a magnificent show, while most of the other public spaces around the city were overblown and beginning to wilt as August drew towards September and another sodden autumn threatened. But all the city sent thanks to Heaven that at least 1600 had not been yet another plague year.

*

The afternoon was hot and heavy. The clouds were low and thunder snarled occasionally in the distance. Chancery Lane was almost frantically busy, the jostling crowds forced ever-closer by the carts, wagons and carriages moving up and down the middle of the road. Poley kept an eye out even though he could not imagine any vehicle being able to force its way through the press of bodies with enough speed to threaten anyone. But the conveyance that stopped him in his tracks did so without posing any threat to his life at all. A private carriage moving north towards Holborn like him, slowed at his shoulder and a leather curtain was pulled back. 'Why, Master Poley,' said a familiar voice. 'Whither away?'

Poley looked up and found Lady Janet looking down at him with a quizzical smile. If he suspected anything beyond a fortunate coincidence in her arrival, the effect that smile had upon him distracted him from any misgivings he might have harboured. He stood gaping, like a hayseed up from the country. Almost as though he had been struck by one of the lightning bolts the lowering clouds threatened to unleash. 'Give you good day, Lady Janet,' he said breathlessly as soon as he found his voice. 'I'm bound for Gray's Inn. I have a message from Sir Francis for the gardeners there.'

The smile broadened. 'I fear Sir Francis does not value

you according to your true worth,' she said softly. 'A boy could have carried such a message. Men like yourself should be freighted with much more weighty matters.'

'Perhaps he has nothing more weighty to send,' suggested Poley foolishly.

'Oh, I doubt that!' Lady Janet was silent for a pensive heartbeat. 'I am bound most of the way to Gray's Inn and would be happy to carry you thither.' She reached out and opened the door. 'Climb aboard if you would care to share the journey with me.'

Poley climbed into the carriage which was in motion once more as soon as he was seated. Women of Lady Janet's consequence did not stir abroad alone, so Poley was not surprised to find Agnes Alnwick, her servant and chaperone, seated opposite her. Agnes was wearing the badges familiar from his time as a member of Lady Lettice's household. 'I had thought you were associated with Lady Rich, if with anyone, Lady Janet,' he said.

'Oh. Have you not heard?' wondered Lady Janet. 'Lady Rich approached Her Majesty on her brother's behalf late last week. Unfortunately she did so with such force, and used such intemperate language, that Her Majesty not only banished her from the court again but also placed her under what we might call 'house arrest' similar to her brother's. She is incarcerated with her entire household in her Holborn house whither I am bound at the moment, with a carefully-measured dram of sympathy.'

Poley stared at Lady Janet, his face a mask of surprise. 'She has done this to Lady Rich?' he asked at last. 'What has the Earl her brother to say to that, I wonder.'

'I fear he has little enough to say in the matter,' said Lady Janet. 'He is in like case himself and helpless even to plead for her as the Queen will not receive his letters. Lady Frances is likewise banned at the moment and her mother Lady Walsingham dare not tempt the Queen's anger. Even Lady Lettice is being circumspect and quiet, which speaks much of her wisdom. Though I have to say her husband Sir Christopher does not agree with her cautious approach which he insists is womanish and craven.'

'Lady Lettice is a woman,' said Poley. 'How could her actions be otherwise than womanish? Besides, the Queen has long held Lady Lettice in disapproval, ever since the Perrot affair. However, she is by no means craven, but rather she is extremely wise to stay away from this situation now, despite what her headstrong husband says.'

'So I believe also. But Sir Christopher compares her unfavourably with Lady Rich, Lady Frances and my cousin by marriage Lady Percy, Countess of Northumberland, who has managed to win her way back into the Queen's favour of late. But seeing Lady Rich's fate, even Lady Percy dare not go too far in begging for her brother's freedom.'

Poley shook his head. 'Every element,' he began. He paused. He met Lady Janet's green gaze with his most intense stare. His mind filled with the words Dr Wendy had spoken so recently. It was not the Earl's body that was at risk; it was his mind. He found himself speaking as though the chaperone was not there. 'Every element of this situation as it moves forward simply must add to the Earl's feelings of helplessness and frustration. It is bad enough that he is punished, continually punished, for his own misdeeds. This even after they have been freely admitted and with mercy and forgiveness begged by both spoken word and letter. Not only from himself but also from others on his behalf. But now his sisters are punished for putting his case. As are his mother and her husband. It is as though he was once a great statue, like a colossus, but little by little, lesser men are chipping away at him and he is helpless to stop them because they have the ear of the Queen and have made her heart obdurate against him.'

'You see his position and state it movingly,' said Lady Janet. '*Colossus*: it is a fancy worthy of a poem or a play. But you must also remember, must you not, that this colossus stands accused of plotting to use his Irish army to seize the throne, to put Her Majesty away – perhaps forever as she herself put away the Queen of Scots. Even to consider these things is high treason. To plot, plan and try to do them is to stand in the shadow of the headsman's axe.'

*

Lady Janet leaned forward, dropping her voice to a conspiratorial whisper. 'And he is still planning to act, if the rumours about messages running between Essex House and Drury House are true. Why, now that you have convinced Her Majesty to leave his knights alone, even though your message was sent via Sir Francis directly to her private audience chamber, the city is still full of desperate men whose only chance of avoiding ruin lies with him. Who will, therefore, do anything he might order them to do. Even rise up, if matters come to a sufficiently desperate pass. Rise up and join the army of citizens led by the men who scrawl their threats on the walls of Salisbury House and Whitehall Palace. And it would behove you also to remember that John Garrard the Mayor and the other leaders of the City like Sheriff Smythe are Essex supporters as well.'

'Not to mention a goodly number of the clerics hereabouts,' he nodded. 'Who preach his cause a'Sundays. Remember how the church bells rang out at the news of his near-fatal illness. And again at news of his recovery, peal after peal. But Her Majesty is refusing even to see his letters, you say?'

'Any addressed to her, certainly. Though I hear that on occasion she deigns to read a paragraph or two of letters he has written to other men and women around the court; or letters written by one courtier to another that say something of him as well.'

'Is that so?' Poley sat in silence for a moment, his mind racing. Then he said, 'If someone were able to construct such a letter in the hope that Her Majesty might read it, a case could be made on the Earl's behalf without seeming to address her directly at all.'

'Now that,' said Lady Janet, 'betrays in you, sirrah, a cunning that might out-Machiavel Machiavelli himself.'

As Lady Janet said this, the coach turned into the broad thoroughfare of Holborn and paused. Poley looked across toward the north-facing window. The breeze was strong enough to make the curtain flap and reveal the mouth of Gray's Inn Lane. 'I thank you for the ride,' he said formally and reached for the door beside him.

'Just before you leave us, Master Poley, you should know that my Agnes who is seated beside you is faithful to me, despite the livery that she is wearing at the moment. Faithful to death if need-be. If I need you, I will send her. If you need me, send a message to her at Wanstead and she will warn me of your need.'

On his return, Poley found Sir Francis in the study at the Lodge – a room which he hardly ever used. And he was writing a letter – something he hardly ever did here. 'You wished to see me?' snapped the Queen's Counsel with unaccustomed ill-humour. 'Be quick with whatever it is you wish to say. I am hard at work here composing a missive to the Earl.'

'Perhaps I should return at a more appropriate…'

'No. Now that you are here I will make use of you.' Sir Francis gestured to a nearby chair and Poley sat. 'Sir Anthony and I cannot agree on this course of action,' Sir Francis continued. 'So he and his familiars are of no use to me and I need to talk through what I wish to say to the Earl by way of apology, and the best way to frame it.'

'Apology, Sir Francis?'

'Indeed. Although I did my best to be supportive during the affair at York House nevertheless I was constrained to speak against him and that is something for which I am sorry. I have no wish to take a firm stand on one side or on the other in this affair. I can see nothing in it but sadness and ruin; perhaps even death. One death certain and close at hand through the inescapable workings of nature. The other all-too possible and brought about by impatience, frustration and the edge of the headsman's axe.'

'And you wish to achieve *ataraxia*, perhaps?'

'Hah!' Sir Francis looked up as he laughed. 'You have been talking to Cuffe about Pyrro and his philosophy, I see. Yes indeed, I had not thought of it in those terms but I do indeed find myself unwilling to believe much of what I see or hear and unwilling, therefore, to decide on one side or the other. It would be of great benefit to me if all this could bring me inner peace, but I fear it brings only confusion and concern.'

'But you are at the centre of things are you not, Sir Francis? How can you be distrustful of the events that are occurring so close beside you?'

*

'Well, well, Master Poley; simply have faith that it is so,' said Sir Francis, nimbly changing the subject. 'Now, as to the contents of my letter to the Earl. I plan roundly to state that I owe love and duty to Her Majesty above all, which he must allow, having said as much of himself in York House in front of judges and witnesses almost without number.'

'I understand that. It seems well enough,' nodded Poley. 'And should the letter through any ill-chance fall into Her Majesty's hands, or those of Master Secretary…'

'No great harm would be done!' Sir Francis smiled. 'But then, taking the other side as it were and applying *ataraxia* if such a thing can be done, I must stress that I am sorry to have been forced into the position of prosecutor. I owe the Earl my service and my friendship, which I am ever keen to exercise. He must be aware that he has risen like Icarus on waxen wings, and if I could supply better and more

214

reliable wings I would do so, but circumstances conspire against me.'

'And so the two sides would be balanced. I can see no flaws in your plans and have no doubt that you will exercise them perfectly when you come to put pen to paper,' said Poley.

'Even so – or at least that is my hope.' Sir Francis paused for a moment, thinking. 'I would conclude by asking his forgiveness and hoping for his continued good will.'

'You could do no better. And this letter will be smuggled into Essex House?'

'Not smuggled so much as simply carried. Just as the Earl is allowed a little more freedom of action and association, so of course he has a little more freedom of communication.'

'With everyone except Her Majesty, I understand,' said Poley easily. But he remembered what Lady Janet had said about messages between Essex House and Drury House – between the Earl and his bosom friend Southampton. 'My lord of Essex has written Her Majesty letters such as your proposed letter to the Earl himself but she refuses even to read them. So I have been told.'

'Aye. There's the rub. It is the old adage about taking a horse to water. He can write, but who can force Her Majesty to read?' Sir Francis sighed, then he asked, 'But you wished to consult me. What about?'

'About something that continues our conversation,' answered Poley. 'I believe Her Majesty in fact has read parts of letters that have not been written to her but which mention the Earl even though they were written from one courtier to another, and about matters apparently irrelevant to the Earl's situation.'

'I had heard the same.' Sir Francis sat up straight and focused on his guest frowning thoughtfully. 'What of it?'

'As I understand matters, such letters so far have been genuine missives from one person to another simply commenting upon the Earl in passing…'

'Ah,' said Sir Francis. 'I think I follow your drift. What if a letter could be written in such a manner that the news going from writer to recipient is just there in passing and the true purpose of the thing was a carefully presented case constructed in support of the Earl?'

'Her Majesty might well read such a letter just as she has read other, similar, ones. And, if so, then that might do My Lord of Essex a great deal more good than any damage that has been done by, let us say, offering an enforced speech of prosecution at York House.'

'It would be the act of a true friend, and all the while unsuspected by her Majesty! If such a letter could be constructed…' Sir Francis fell silent. 'But who would write such a letter? And to whom?'

'Someone constantly in attendance on Her Majesty, perhaps; and direct it to an ailing relative. A sickly brother, let us say…'

'You give me much to think on, Master Poley. And, perhaps, two letters to write…'

The conversation ended there and soon enough whether Sir Francis had in fact written such a letter and contrived to bring it to the Queen's attention was forced into the background by events. First, the Earl replied to the letter

Sir Francis had sent him having completed it along the lines he had discussed with Poley. The Earl's reply was courteous but non-committal. But Sir Francis was by no means downhearted by the cool response. He continued putting the Earl's case to the Queen, weathering the storms of her irritation as well as the calms of her approval. And, so far as Poley knew, he might even have shown her the carefully crafted letter Sir Francis pretended that someone had written to his brother.

*

The Earl at last was released from his incarceration. Before the month was out it seemed that Her Majesty was relenting towards him. He was no longer held under guard. He was released - free to go anywhere. Anywhere except where he most desired to go – to the court. He had had enough of Essex House for the time-being because it had been his prison for so long. And so rather than bringing his Secretariat and household back from Barn Elms, he joined them there. The Bacon brothers consequently remained at Twickenham and Poley continued to shuttle between the two establishments, eyes wide and ear to the ground, certain that there was more – and worse – to come.

And so there was; for although he was domiciled in Barn Elms, the Earl was free to go where he liked. And one of the places he most regularly visited was Drury House. Poley knew it and suspected that there was a good deal of plotting and planning undertaken there, but he could never contrive to be part of the privileged band who came and went between the two great houses.

But then even that frustration was forced into the

background.

Barn Elms was all a feverish bustle. It was just after Michaelmas, two years almost to the day since the Earl had returned from Ireland to invade the Queen's bedroom and, stirred by the anniversary perhaps, Essex had decided he was moving himself, his family, his household and his hangers-on all back to Essex House after all. There was hope hanging faintly in the air. Essex's one steady source of income, the tax on sweet wines, had not been stopped as many close to the Earl had feared it might be, when the agreement ran out at Michaelmas, on Saturday, 30th September.

'It is a sign of great hope,' Henry Cuffe told Poley as they observed the preparations. 'The Earl is certain that it is Her Majesty's way of telling him he is forgiven. We will return to Essex House and the Earl will live there quietly, keeping the great gate shut and seeing no-one. If he cannot go to court he will demonstrate his continuing penance by refusing to hold court himself. Only the oldest and most respected of his friends and supporters will be welcome. Modesty and rectitude will be the watch-words.'

Poley was careful not to look askance at his naive friend. The Earl might well plan to live quietly when he was in Essex House, but there were still those visits to Drury House to be taken into account. And the burgeoning number of desperate men finding shelter in one house or the other.

Poley and Sir Francis stepped up from the Essex House landing steps shoulder by shoulder as the wherry pulled away into mid-stream. The gardens stretched away in front of them, hardly better tended than those at Twickenham Lodge. Beyond the untended wilderness, the rear of the House itself was a blaze of light, quite dazzling even in the early evening at the end of a sunny October day. Even down here by the River it was possible to hear the din being made by the inmates.

'Modesty and rectitude…' said Sir Francis bitterly.

'I'm assured that the gates out onto the Strand are closed against all-comers, just as the Earl promised and Cuffe reported,' Poley told him. 'It may be that the Earl and his family are indeed living quietly in their wing of the house…'

'… while the knights who follow him celebrate the retention of their honours and their return to his house and his bounty with a raucousness that is near-riot.' Sir Francis completed Poley's wry observation. 'Both here and in Drury House so I'm told.'

'And in many of the streets in between, to the despair of citizens who live or seek to do business in them. If I was the Earl I would have Sir Gelly Meyrick clear them all out,' said Poley, raising his voice as they neared the House and the clamour that issued from it.

'Perhaps,' said Sir Francis, 'The Earl and Sir Gelly feel that it would be safer to keep such troublesome friends close at hand under some control rather than allow them to go rioting into the city any more than they do at present.'

'Possibly.' Poley was by no means convinced, though the words chimed disturbingly with what he believed Sir Anthony was doing to him. "Keep your enemies close" certainly seemed to be better watchwords than "Modesty and rectitude".

'Think of the damage that might do,' prompted Sir Francis. 'If they went out into The Strand in one great riotous mob, creating a hurly-burly such as this, it would give added weight to the Council's warnings that My Lord of Essex, his friends and acolytes cannot ever be controlled...'

'While at the same time offending the upright citizen upon whose support and good offices the Earl is still reliant. These are no apprentice-boys crying clubs or playing at foot ball with an inflated pig's bladder. These are well-armed ex-soldiers, proficient in the art of killing. The further damage they might do to businesses, premises and persons would be hard to calculate.'

*

Poley's summation was enough to take them onto the broad section of flag stones between the shaggy lawns and the back wall of the house. As they entered the nearest door, the intelligencer unconsciously drew nearer to his companion. His shoulders were fully healed now, but he had no desire to repeat the torture that had originally damaged them, and by the sound of things Gelly Meyrick and his companions would not think twice about putting him through it again; through the strappado - or worse. The noise grew louder as they hurried along the passageways leading out of the servants' quarters, past the rooms that had housed Sir Anthony before Essex House was cleared the better part of seven months earlier.

And so they came out into the entrance hall from which opened the Great Hall where the loudest noise was originating. The place was lined with tables and it looked as though there were more than fifty men seated at supper, the boards before them piled with platters of food and lined with bottles of drink. The majority there had clearly partaken of the drink rather than the meats, fishes and pastries steaming in front of them. The number of servants scurrying from kitchen and cellar to one table after another, young Tom Fitzherbert Essex's page joining his father and mother amongst them. The hubbub and confusion certainly explained why the knights' quarters had been so deserted and quiet, thought Poley, his mind filling with simple wonder at the almost Roman orgy of excess being enacted in front of him.

Poley looked in vain for a familiar face at the nearest tables and was by no means surprised to hear Sir Francis mutter, 'Who are these men?'

'I see some of the secretaries in the far corner by the fire,' he said. 'I see Sir Ferdiando Gorges, Lord Monteagle, Lord Cromwell and Sir John Davies. But these others are strangers…'

Then Cuffe appeared. He beamed as he recognised Poley and came pushing round the nearest table towards them. 'Robert!' he called, his voice slightly slurred. 'Well met! Have you supped?'

'What in Heaven's name is going on here? Supper for more than fifty? It is madness!' hissed Sir Francis as Cuffe came right up to them. 'How can the Earl possibly afford this?'

'Why this is nothing out of the ordinary…' The beaming face folded into a frown. 'We have dined and supped well ever since it became clear that the Earl would retain the tax on sweet wines. It is his primary source of income, the foundation of his credit. We seek to help him celebrate…'

'I see precious little of the promised modesty and rectitude here!' snapped Sir Francis. 'What is the Earl thinking of to let such behaviour run without let or hindrance?'

'The Earl and Lady Essex keep to their rooms with the children.' Cuffe explained. 'Sir Gelly is in charge of the House.'

'I am here to see the Earl,' said Sir Francis with a shake of his head which dismissed a situation he could not hope to mend for the moment. 'Can you take me to him?'

'Yes, of course.' Cuffe was as deflated as a child unexpectedly confronted by an angry parent.

The Earl's rooms were two flights up in the east wing of the sprawling building. The noise was by no means stilled up here but it was reduced to a distant rumble. Cuffe knocked on a door which was after a few moments opened. The three men were shown into the Earl's private rooms, though not yet into the Earl's presence. A small ante-room led through a door standing ajar into a private dining room where the family sat at supper. A door not only standing ajar but one guarded by Sir Gelly Meyrick. 'Sir Francis,' said the Welsh knight. 'What business do you have with My Lord of Essex?'

'I have a message. One of some urgency.'

'And Master Poley?'

'I am the man the message was passed to. I come with Sir Francis in case the Earl has any questions. And before you ask, Master Cuffe met us downstairs and is here as our guide.'

With no further word, Meyrick vanished into the larger room. After a few minutes, he returned with the Earl close behind. It was some time since Poley had seen Robert Devereux and he was struck at once by the changes that had overcome the man. He was leaner, almost starved in appearance. His clothing hung loose about him. He was very slightly stooped and his hands trembled a little. The right hand held a fine linen kerchief, lightly smeared with some sort of sauce. He looked a good deal older than his 35 years, particularly as his face was drawn, his eyes sunken and his forehead lined. But the spade of his beard and the tumble of his hair were both still full and brown. It was those sunken eyes, however, that claimed the intelligencer's fullest attention. They darted restlessly here and there, failing to meet his own steady gaze or, as far as he could see, that of Sir Francis either.

*

'Your message?' asked Sir Gelly.

'My Lord,' said Sir Francis. The Earl's gaze fastened on him as soon as he began to speak, but slid away again almost immediately. 'Master Poley here has been informed via a friend at court that you should not take it for granted that Her Majesty has decided firmly that you should retain the monopoly on sweet wines…'

'What?' He had the Earl's full attention now.

Until it slid over to Poley himself. 'Friend at court? What friend at court?'

'It was Lady Janet Percy My Lord,' Poley answered. 'As

you must know, she is one of Her Majesty's ladies in waiting and she let slip to me during a brief discussion of other matters that Her Majesty has been debating with her ladies whether or not to let the situation remain as it is at the moment with regard to the monopoly on sweet wines…'

'And…' demanded the Earl. 'The conclusion? Her Majesty's verdict?'

'She has not as yet come to a firm conclusion. Lady Janet gave me to understand that Her Majesty intended to await events before coming to a final decision…'

'Await events? What events?' Essex looked helplessly from one to the other, finally fastening on Poley once again.

'I gained the impression, My Lord, that Her Majesty was keen to delay her final ruling until she could see whether you would be able to stay faithful to her harsh strictures…'

Essex frowned, not quite understanding.

Almost inevitably, it was Cuffe who translated for his friend, speaking at his most professorial. 'Her Majesty is waiting to see whether you and your followers will bow to her wishes before she makes up her mind, My Lord. Whether you and your knights can be relied upon to behave moderately and keep the peace.'

That was as far as he had got before Sir Fernando Gorges pushed open the door. 'My Lord,' he gasped, seeing the Earl standing there. 'It is Sir John Heyden. He left Essex House just before we supped but he had taken a great deal of wine with his dinner. He has exchanged words with Sir Richard Mansell, whom he met immediately outside in

The Strand. They are old adversaries. Sir Richard has spoken in support of Master Secretary Cecil and against yourself on many occasions. And did so again just now. Sir John has declared himself insulted by this and has demanded satisfaction which Sir Richard has agreed to give him at once; he has chosen swords. They will go to a duel and fight to the death. Out there in the Strand immediately outside your gates. Neither man will listen to reason. You must stop them!'

The Earl looked utterly bewildered for an instant, then his gaze sharpened and his face folded into a frown as the true danger of the situation hit him with full force. 'I will come at once,' he said. He wiped the kerchief across his lips and then down his beard before throwing it aside. As he did this, he strode forward with such force and purpose that everyone else in the room was swept into his wake like skiffs behind a galleon. Poley followed them, his presence no longer a matter of concern, fading to nothing compared with the situation Gorges had reported. They thundered down the stairs together onto the ground floor and past the wide entrance to the Great Hall, which one swift glance revealed to be empty of Essex's knights - only the servants remaining.

They rushed out through the main door and down the steps into the courtyard in front of the house. The courtyard was also empty and the gates onto the Strand stood wide open, revealing where all the missing men had gone to. They were crowded into the great thoroughfare, jostling with excitement and shouting encouragement. Like a crowd of apprentices at a wrestling match, thought

Poley, or the audience at a bear-baiting. At first their backs presented an impenetrable wall, but a combination of Meyrick and Gorges soon made the excited soldiers realise that their general was trying to get through. Then it was only a matter of moments before Essex, Sir Francis, Cuffe and Poley, escorted by Sir Gelly and Sir Fernando, were standing at the edge of the makeshift battleground of the piste. A man stood at either end, each one stripping off his doublet and wrapping it round his forearm while a companion held his sword. A companion, Poley repeated in his mind – not a second. There was no formality here.

*

'Stop this madness!' thundered the Earl.

'Before someone calls *ware riot* and summons the watch,' added Sir Gelly, his voice as loud as his master's.

They need not have bothered. Their words were lost in the roaring of the crowd and it seemed to Poley that neither of the combatants would be willing to obey them in any case; they were clearly far beyond reason or any sort of control. It was unlike any duel that Poley had ever witnessed. There were no proper formalities, just two mad men out to kill each other. They were not preparing to wield rapiers such as the one with the Solingen blade that Sir Christopher had purchased for him at the Steelyard. These were poor men staring destitution in the face, with nothing left to them but their threadbare titles and their petty honour. They wielded short swords that would have been familiar to their forbears on Bosworth field; or indeed *their* forbears at Agincourt or Crecy. Their piste was roughly measured out along the gutter in the middle of the road and only existed because none of the excited audience was stupid enough to step into it.

As the Earl and his little group of followers stood helplessly, the two men threw themselves at each-other. They clearly owed nothing to the German, Spanish or Italian masters. If they followed the style of anyone it was that of George Silver but even that great English master would have been hard-put to see any of his short-sword techniques properly employed. They fought square-on, almost toe-to-toe. Their stance made Poley wonder for an instant whether they had daggers as well as swords. But no – each man had his left forearm wrapped in his doublet as a makeshift shield and his left fist empty. But, Poley observed, what they lacked in polish and technique, they made up for in speed and brutality. The blades rang against each other discordantly, like cracked bells. Unlike the Earl's orders, this sound had the ability to silence the shouting – for a time at least.

Poley was only able to tell one from the other because Sir John Heydon was vaguely familiar whereas Sir Richard Mansell was a complete stranger. But as the vicious contest proceeded, other differences became obvious to the intelligencer. It was not so much that Sir Richard Mansell was fair-haired while Sir John Heydon was dark; the Earl's supporter was as down-at-heel as the rest, his linen shirt thin, patched, elderly and none too clean whereas his opponent was more richly attired, his shirt silken and recently laundered. Sir John Heydon was also, Poley admitted to himself with some regret, the better swordsman. No matter how long or short the contest turned out to be, there was only one inevitable end in prospect.

'Shall I put an end to this my Lord?' Poley asked. 'It requires action rather than words. Someone must stand between them. If no one intervenes soon you will lose a passionate supporter at the very least.'

Essex looked at him, as Sir Anthony Bacon had, as though he was seeing him for the first time. 'I…' he said.

'The quicker your decision, the more effective it will be,' Poley insisted. 'I would suggest you need to stop this before someone dies or the watch arrives.'

'Yes!' said the Earl. 'Gelly, Fernando, help Sir Francis's man finish this.'

The three men moved forward but they were a fraction too late. Sir Richard Mansell feinted towards Sir John Heydon's head. A blow that started high and came sweeping downwards. Had it landed, would have split his skull. Sir John Heydon's reflex was to raise his arm, offering his padded forearm as a shield. But Sir Richard Mansell's blade turned at the last minute. The edge sliced past fingers and through palm almost to the wrist. It was done in a flash and a spray of blood. Almost all of Sir John Heydon's hand fell onto the ground, leaving only a section of the palm attached to his padded arm. Sir John Heydon's howl of agony and defeat was lost in the bloodlust roar of the audience. Which was in turn challenged by the shouts of the city watch as they arrived to clear the Strand and place the combatants under arrest.

The enemies spent a night in the Fleet, Sir John Heydon lucky to survive the basic doctoring he received on the way there. Then they retired in disgrace to their estates near Norwich - the crippled and the near-penniless Sir John Heydon to put his on the market in a hopeless attempt to repay his debts before he and his family fell into the hungry maw of destitution.

But the affair did not end there, for, a week later, as Poley was preparing to help move Sir Anthony back from Twickenham to the damp and chilly quarters in Essex House, Sir Francis came to see his brother, heavy with news. 'It is done,' he said grimly. 'The Queen has decided to take back the monopoly on sweet wines after all. The Earl is ruined. Utterly ruined.'

8

Poley had suspected as acutely as anyone what the results of the Queen's decision to take back the tax on sweet wines would be. He knew Essex House would be riven by incomprehension, anger, shock, a sense of outrage and unfairness. A sense of crisis – almost of impending doom - as the Earl's last source of income was cut off. The situation was made worse because the Queen's characteristic hesitation had allowed the Earl and his followers to deceive themselves that there was hope when in fact there was none. And now the full implications stared them all in the face, as horrifying as an approaching plague.

The bankrupt Earl ran out of control almost at once. Poley had hardly arrived with the Bacon brothers before he heard Essex ranting. 'If the Council are hag-ridden as I know they are, then I also know which is the hag in question!' 'May the devil take her, she has lived too long.' And, tellingly, the repetition of the old accusation with renewed vigour: 'Her conditions are as twisted as her carcase!' Casual visitors arrived, heard his ravings and hurriedly departed, never to return. But they took word of his behaviour to the Court and the Council.

Poley thought Essex's desperation was understandable. He owed a fabulous sum – more than £5000. And, as Poley observed, Essex was simply the leader of a growing army of debtors, many arriving from Wales, from Ireland and from the North. They now populated Essex House in numbers that challenged even the reliable Fitzherberts to accommodate and feed them all.

'The only thing keeping the Earl's creditors from coming to demand instant settlement of all outstanding debts,' Poley explained to Lady Janet at one of their meetings, 'is the presence of such numbers of equally destitute knights surrounding him. And not just knights. The Earls of Bedford, Rutland, Worcester and Sussex have all become regular visitors because they are in the same situation as Essex. And they've started attending the meetings with Southampton that are held at Drury House. William Parker, Lord Monteagle, has joined the new group as well, but he at least seems to be solvent.'

Lady Janet nodded. 'With the exception of Monteagle, most of the new men will be unable to afford accommodation elsewhere in any case,' she said. 'And I sorrow to say that amongst the latest arrivals are two distant relatives of mine, Charles and Jocelyn Percy.'

'They're all utterly desperate, fiercely loyal. Dangerously so,' Poley emphasised. 'Like a pack of starving hounds who have decided to protect the bear at a baiting instead of rending it to pieces. The knights are as frantic as their master – all of them with nothing left to lose. All of them deadly, therefore.' He paused. Shrugged; the ability to do so painlessly was in itself still a luxury. 'The Fleet, the Clink, the Borough Counter and the Marshalsea are all equally uncomfortable if you're being held chained in the cells. No matter whether it's for debt - or for murder. And, whatever your crime, they won't let you starve to death. Unlike the usual crop of unfortunates who have crawled up from the country to starve or freeze in the gutters hereabouts.'

'I will pass your observations on. If you need to see me again, send for Agnes as usual. You seem to have foreseen everything very clearly so far.'

'Except for the nature of the action it would be best for me to take.'

'Be patient Master Poley. Some chance will present itself. Something you have not foreseen, perhaps.'

Amongst the things Poley had not foreseen was the way in which financial ruin seemed to gather all the impoverished knights together as a desperate kind of brotherhood. And in numbers that grew and grew to Fitzherbert's mounting despair. Essex House. had been well filled before: soon it became over-stuffed, the lesser occupants sleeping two or three to a room – and that room in the servants' quarters as like as not, while the servants were packed into the garrets beneath the roof. It should have been obvious that this would happen as things progressed along their apparently immutable path, he thought. Individually, out on the streets or in their cheap, dilapidated lodgings in the city, Essex's men were at risk of being thrown in debtors' prison one by one. Or held without charge, simply on suspicion, like poor Heywood in The Tower being occasionally re-examined about his book on Henry IV and the downfall of Richard II. Gathered together, however, they were safe. There was simply no individual shopkeeper, no trade guild indeed, who was willing to come hammering on the great door on

The Strand requesting restitution from the Earl or from his house-guests.

Then again, the number of tradesmen willing to supply the Earl as his debts became ever more mountainous, grew fewer and fewer. Especially as word went round his erstwhile citizen supporters that he had lost Her Majesty's favour forever. They still blamed the Toad and the Council he controlled; but the truth of the matter was too obvious to be ignored. The dashing knight errant of happier days was wearing tarnished armour now and Gloriana the Faery Queene was no longer his to serve. The graffiti-writing tailed off. The sermons passed on to new texts. The only citizens who stood by him were those who shared the pauper-knights' dream - holding firm to the faint belief that whoever succeeded Elizabeth would raise Essex up again. And do so within months rather than years.

*

One other element Poley had not foreseen was that the air of crisis in Essex House would mount so swiftly, fed by the Earl's loud outrage and by each new arrival begging shelter from his creditors; with each new visitor bringing yet more bad news from court. With each group of desperate men going out into London in squads too large and too well-armed for the bailiffs to approach – who nevertheless always seemed to find trouble in one increasingly dangerous confrontation after another. Lady Lettice and Sir Christopher returned from Wanstead. Of course Lady Frances and the children came with the rest of them from Barn Elms, though her mother Lady Walsingham remained at home there.

The Bacons in fact had been the earliest arrivals coming downriver from Twickenham with Poley in their household the instant they were allowed to do so. And Poley began to observe matters at once, contacting Lady Janet through Agnes the moment he had anything worth discussing with her. Sir Anthony took up his previous residence. In one way his presence had added importance, for Sir Henry Wotton along with several of the Secretariat, had gone abroad and showed every sign of staying abroad – as St Lawrence and Thomas Gerard had decided to stay in Ireland with Mountjoy. Returning to the damp and dreary conditions of his rooms in Essex House made Sir Anthony relapse at once and so severely that what he could actually do became strictly limited. His doctor and his two close body-servants gathered round him, more than a little worried by his deteriorating condition.

Sir Francis came and went – carrying increasingly hopeless messages to the Queen and returning with no good news. Or rather, with the worst news possible – that Her Majesty was fit and well and had no intention of dying for a good long time yet. Or of forgiving her erstwhile favourite in the meantime. It was enough to make a man run mad - even one with a firmer grip on his sanity than the beleaguered Earl. Especially as the equally desperate men with whom he was surrounded were given license by his ravings to confront him with wilder and wilder schemes designed to mend all their fortunes at one desperate stroke, and repay the hag who had hurt them all.

Henry Cuffe challenged the Earl over his hesitation, telling his master in no uncertain terms that the time to act was ripe and he should grasp it before the overwhelming impetus arising from the Queen's cruel action was lost and yet more of his supporters in the City fell away. The irate Earl banished him for his trouble and moved a brace of newly-arrived knights into his accommodation. Sir Gelly, the wisest of the desperate councillors, circumspectly suggested that the Earl hide away in Wales, then slip across The Channel if the Queen continued to linger even further into bitter, unforgiving old age. Mountjoy, back from Ireland to report to the Council but a regular participant in Southampton's meetings at Drury House, joined with Fernando Gorges to push the old idea of promising to ease King James of Scotland onto the English throne as soon as Elizabeth's bony backside left it vacant. Sir Anthony designed a letter at their prompting, a hard task for the sick man. Sir Charles Davers took it north. One faction begged the Earl to befriend Lady Arbella Stuart, while others pleaded with him to approach the Spanish Infanta Isabella. The Queen was beginning to favour the Infanta, they said; Raleigh and the Toad were already in contact with her. The Toad, after all, was still in receipt of a pension from the Spanish Court – what could speak louder than that?

The one thing that Poley never considered, never saw coming at all, was the unexpected change that overcame his place in these schemes and in the Earl's reactions to them. But one evening soon after Cuffe's banishment, he found himself once more in front of the Earl, and the subject of his lordly consideration. For Sir Francis had suggested that Poley would make an excellent courier should Essex wish to contact the outer fringes of Court or Council, reliably and in secret.

'I don't trust him My Lord,' said Sir Gelly. 'Neither does Sir Anthony. He's the Toad's man. The Council's intelligencer, He always has been.'

'However,' said Sir Francis, 'he has served in Lady Lettice's household as well as ours and, indeed, yours, My Lord, with never a whiff of suspicion for the better part of two years. True, my brother does not trust him but, frankly, neither does he trust a number of your most vociferous supporters. Lady Lettice's husband Sir Christopher trusts him and vouches for him – they are related by blood after all. And indeed, both Poley and Sir Christopher worked for Walsingham when he was still alive. But that was long ago and circumstances have changed in the meantime. Master Cuffe would vouch for him were he back in your favour and present. They met in the Fleet and you know the story telling why this happened. Poley makes no secret of it. He was the Council's man when he unmasked Babbington's mad scheme to release the Queen of Scots and when Ingram Frizer killed Kit Marlowe in front of Poley at Mistress Bull's house in Deptford. Nick Skeres was there, and working for the Council too. Nick Skeres has also turned against Master Secretary and the Council and is currently part of your extended household, My Lord, and he will vouch for Poley as well. All the world knows Poley has been cast out. Traduced. Disgraced. He has been at the very least dismissed from the Council's service; and so he has changed from the Council's man to your man alone. And, were that not enough, he is, almost uniquely in this place, a man who has no debts to speak of. Who can come and go without the risk of a bailiff's hand on his shoulder. As has been demonstrated I believe by the fact that he has been able to meet and converse with Lady Jane Percy, close relative of some of your most powerful supporters in the North and the newly arrived brothers Charles and Jocelyn Percy.'

There was a short silence. Essex turned to Poley. 'Well, what have you to say?'

*

'It has all been said, My Lord. I have left the service of Master Secretary and the Council. I was thrust by them into the Fleet for some reason that I still do not understand. There I met both Master Cuffe and Sir Francis, through whose good offices alone I gained my freedom. And all the rest is as they have said. I speak simple, honest truth, and act upon it. And Sir Francis is correct. I owe nothing to any man outside these walls, except a matter of shillings to a man called Wolfall. And the debts I owe you and your household, Sir Francis and his, Lady Lettice and hers, are not the sort of debts that can be repaid with gold. But only with honest and truthful advice and service.'

'That's the nub of the matter, Gelly,' said the Earl with the slightest tremor in his voice. 'If we had acted sooner on the information Master Poley brought us. Directly from Lady Percy, who is related to the Earl of Northumberland, as he said… Taken his advice into account… If I had been just a heartbeat swifter to let him stand between those two fools duelling on The Strand and stop the matter before the watch arrived… He was right in both cases and acted to my benefit. If only we had listened… Acted… Sooner…'

'With that thought in mind,' prompted Sir Francis, 'Perhaps it is time to invite Cuffe back into the fold.'

'Perhaps,' allowed the Earl. 'I will think on it. Meanwhile, we have Master Poley to consider.'

Poley stood, his heart racing, trying not to look Essex full in the face. Trying to make sure he did nothing to put the desperate and unbalanced man off his latest superstition. Because it seemed to him that that the Earl now found himself surrounded by sycophants who did little more than agree with him. And in this they simply added the weight of responsibility to everything else he carried on his increasingly bowed shoulders. So he wanted someone at his side who made a decision, argued his case and stood by the outcome, taking his own responsibility. Someone from outside his usual circle, different to those men like Gelly Meyrick, Christopher Blount, Fernando Gorges and the rest who – whether they agreed with him or not – had allowed him to lead them to the brink of disaster and then straight on over the edge. Someone who might stand as a good-luck talisman, who could be relied upon to do precisely what Poley had done in his attempt to stop the duel in the Strand. He clearly regretted sending Cuffe away for arguing with him and advocating a course of action that even quite a short passage of time now made appear reasonable. Poley might even replace Cuffe in the meantime. And Poley saw as clearly as his friend Henry Cuffe had done, as, indeed Dr Wendy had done, that the Earl needed to take some action; almost any action – or he might indeed run mad.

'If you cannot talk to the Queen, and she will not listen to any of your friends or relatives any more than she will read your letters,' said Poley, 'then the next best is Master Secretary Cecil. Failing him, Captain of the Guard Raleigh. They both stand high in her regard and have her ear in all matters – for the moment at least. Which one of them fears you least and therefore wishes your destruction less?'

'They both conspire against me,' snarled Essex. 'They have done since long before I went to Ireland!'

There it was again, thought Poley. That tremor in his voice. Something that could often be heard, he had been told, in Bedlam.

'Then which of them would you trust more, My Lord, if he gave his word on some matter?' he enquired, keeping his voice soft and soothing.

'If I had to trust either, then it would be The Toad.' The Earl's tone was firmer now.

'Then, My Lord, allow me to suggest that you occupy your own mind and those of your closest advisors in seeking a way to build a bridge between yourself and Master Secretary. While, if you have not done so already, you send in secret to the King of Scotland. I know Sir Anthony has been in contact with King Christian, Queen Anne's brother in Denmark, asking for him to request her favour in talking to her lord the king on your behalf. And to do so especially while King James considers anything you have written to him so far. But I warn you, if you did not already know of it, that Sir Thomas Walsingham's wife Lady Audrey has been a frequent visitor to Edinburgh and Queen Ann's court, putting the case against you directly, woman to woman, on behalf of Sir Thomas and the Toad.'

'I sent Sir Charles Davers with a letter,' said Essex. 'Amongst other things it warns against Master Secretary, Thomas Walsingham and their creatures. It promises my aid in the matter of succession if he will move to support me now. But Davers is not yet returned with the king's answer.' He paused for a moment, then he added, 'And it is time I think that poor Cuffe returned. He has as much to fear from the bailiffs as any of us. Find him, Poley, and bring him back.'

'At once, My Lord,' said Poley, his mind racing. But as he and Sir Francis turned to leave the room, the Queen's Counsellor whispered, 'Fear not, Master Poley. I know where he can be found.'

*

A little more than an hour later, Sir Francis continued his explanation with a brief smile. 'I discovered him huddled in the gardens here, freezing and starving. He was there, he said, in hope that one of the benchers would be an Oxford man and remember him well enough to do him good service. Alas, his hopes were misplaced. The only men he had seen were actors from the Lord Chamberlain's Men preparing for the Christmas festivities. And actors as you know lack charity almost as completely as they lack morals and money.'

'Had he no friends? No coin?'

'He said he had approached Sir Thomas Sackville the Chancellor of Oxford in his London residence, hoping for succour and support from his old university. But Sir Thomas is also Her Majesty's Treasurer and a member of the Council. So he would not see him or help him in any way. Then he sold all his possessions except for what he stood up in and a cloak to save him from freezing but soon ran out of money nevertheless.'

'And you took him in?'

'What else could I do? Besides, I thought this would be the best place to hide a man standing in danger of being taken to court by bailiffs.' The pair of them walked out of the soggy, wintery gardens and into Bacon's rooms at Gray's Inn. 'At least if anything went wrong, he would not have to look far for someone to stand in his defence,' said Sir Francis.

'Surely you jest, Sir Francis,' answered Poley with a grim chuckle. 'I've yet to hear of any lawyer willing to defend a bankrupt. If a man cannot pay for food or lodgings, he's unlikely to be able to afford legal representation.'

Sir Francis grunted. 'You're in the right of it, Master Poley. I hope you do not speak from personal experience.' As Sir Francis said this the pair of them entered his rooms and discovered Henry Cuffe sitting at a desk, poring over a book by the light of a short candle-stub. A platter sat at his elbow that looked to Poley to have been licked clean. He glanced up in fright and it was only when they emerged from the shadows that his face relaxed, then was lit by a broad smile. Poley was struck at once by the way his friend had been reduced almost to skin and bone during his time of exile from Essex House.

'Sir Francis,' said the scholar. 'You have brought me a most welcome gift. How goes it with you, dear friend Robert?'

'Well enough, Henry. I am come to bring you home to the Earl. I believe he regrets having been so short with you.'

'Not straight to the Earl I beg you,' said Cuffe. 'Can we not stop at a tavern on the way? My belly flaps against my ribs. I am truly become a hollow man.'

Poley looked at Sir Francis. He might not stand in serious debt to anyone save the money-lender Wolfall but his purse was as empty as Henry Cuffe's belly. The lawyer nodded understandingly and crossed to a box in the corner.

Five minutes later the two men were back out in the wintery gardens with a silver crown to share between them, though Poley had no intention of eating or drinking. Just being out on the streets with Cuffe made him feel uneasy. Although clearly pleased and relieved to see his friend and to receive the news of his reinstatement in Essex's good graces, Cuffe was a bitter man. His view of his own importance, and his importance to the Earl, had been damaged - perhaps destroyed. But, happily or unhappily he was still Essex's follower. And Essex was famous throughout the city so his companions were well known to many, especially to their creditors. But it seemed clear that Henry Cuffe stood in urgent need of food and drink; so he had not been made free of the bench where those studying at the Inn could eat. Probably fearful, thought Poley, that one or more of the Cambridge men at dinner or supper there would recognise him and hand him in.

*

The nearest tavern was The Fighting Cocks just behind Barnard's Inn on the corner of Holborn and Fetter Lane so Poley took Cuffe there, calculating that Fetter Lane would lead them down to Fleet Street, parallel to Chancery Lane that led down to The Strand. Though it would also take them near the Fleet prison – a risk they would just have to accept. The tavern was dressed for Advent. There was holly above the bar, red berries gleaming in memory of Christ's blood as shed on the Cross and ivy wrapped round some of the tables symbolising Christ's fidelity and the evergreen promise of eternal life. Neither of which were likely to apply to me, thought Poley wryly as he glanced around. *See, see, Christ's blood streams in the firmament. One drop would save my soul.* It was a line from an old play that just popped unbidden into his mind; there for an instant and then, like the play, forgotten. The tavern was busy but not yet heaving. Poley was pleased to see no familiar faces. 'See anyone you know?' he asked Cuffe.

'No-one, friend Robert,' answered Cuffe, but his attention was on the prospect of food, not on the other customers.

They sat at a table positioned to allow Poley a clear view of the door and Cuffe a clear view of the great fire where the food was being prepared. They had no sooner entered than their noses told them that today's ordinary was fish - for today was a fish day. It was hardly any time before Cuffe was chewing his way through salmon in thick lavender, wine and onion sauce laid on a trencher deep enough to soak up all the juice while the serving woman went to get change from a silver crown for a meal that cost two fourpenny groats as it included a big pewter flagon of strong ale. At first Cuffe was too hungry for conversation. But time went on, the change came in the form of some shillings, more groats and some pennies, and the food disappeared. So Poley was able to describe the current situation at Essex House in the increasing certainty that Cuffe was paying attention. 'The Earl regrets the manner in which he treated you, Henry. I believe he sees now the strength of your suggestion.'

'Aye. Now that it is too late to act upon it,' said Cuffe bitterly pushing the empty platter to one side. 'And the City is not so supportive as it once was, I fear.' He licked his fingers, and reached for the big pewter flagon.

'I'm afraid you're right,' nodded Poley. 'Though the Earl can call upon more than one hundred knights as well as other friends and supporters and thus has little need of guildsmen or apprentices. Such an army might still convince the citizens of London to join in any endeavour he wishes to undertake. But he hesitates to act upon your suggestion – or any of the others presented to him.'

'Waiting for word from Scotland, perhaps.' Cuffe took a long swig of ale.

'Perhaps. Or perhaps he is hesitant to act because everything he has done since his return from Ireland has just made his situation worse. The latest setback in the matter of the wine tax has been the most dangerous so far. The next misstep could be fatal. And so he is fearful of taking it.'

That was as far as the conversation got before a familiar figure filled the doorway.

'Robert Poley,' sneered Wolfall, his voice carrying easily over the hubbub. 'Did you really think you could come this close to Fetter Lane without word coming down to me at the Fleet? And I see you have your light o' love Henry Cuffe with you. Hoping to rekindle your romance in the debtors' cells are we?'

'I have the change from a silver crown here, Wolfall. More than enough to satisfy the matter between us.' Poley stood, reaching down to the table top with his right hand, his left apparently casually on the hilt of his rapier.

Wolfall stepped forward and was succeeded in the doorway by the bulk of Ingram Frizer, Thomas Walsingham's man; enemy to Essex and everyone who worked for him. 'That might settle things for you, Poley,' said Frizer. 'But Cuffe there is another matter entirely. There's a good few bailiffs on the lookout for him. Willing to pay for information as to his whereabouts. It'll take more than Francis Bacon to get him out next time.'

'Debtor!' Blustered Cuffe, rising angrily. 'Do you take me for a man of no account that you threaten me with bailiffs?'

'I take you for nothing but a broken-down bankrupt who's wandered too far from the safety of Essex House,' answered Wolfall. 'And friend Frizer here will take you straight to whichever bailiff has promised the most coin for your worthless head.'

*

Poley understood the force of Wolfall and Frizer's

threats all too well. But Cuffe was his key back into Essex House and the tight-closed chambers of the Earl's trust, guarded by Gelly Meyrick and Sir Anthony Bacon though they were. He could not allow this to proceed. 'Come, Henry,' he said. 'While there are only two ranged against us. Be quick!'

As Poley spoke, he was in motion, striding towards the door as the crowd of customers parted in front of him. They parted faster and wider after he slid his Solingen blade out of its scabbard. The loud bully Wolfall stepped back into the safety of Frizer's shadow. But Frizer himself hesitated, knowing Poley and his prowess with the sword. He stepped back and the doorway was clear. Poley strode into Fetter Lane. Such bustle as there had been here also fell back at the sight of his naked blade. 'Get him!' Wolfall snarled at Frizer and the big man reluctantly stepped forward, pulling out his own short sword. A student of Silver rather than Capo Ferro, thought Poley with some satisfaction. But then which weapon and which master Frizer favoured became irrelevant. Cuffe's pewter flagon, weighted with a good half measure of ale, smashed into the middle of Frizer's face with all the power of a professional pugilist's fist and he went flat on his back in the gutter.

'I'm sorry Master Poley,' said Fitzherbert half an hour later. 'There is nowhere for Master Cuffe to be housed. My Lord of Essex insisted that his room be given to two other knights the day after his departure and the Percy brothers Charles and Jocelyn are in there now. Things have only worsened since they arrived.'

Poley paused for a moment, examining the alternatives. One of which was obvious. 'My room can accommodate more than one. Can you arrange things so that Master Cuffe could be comfortable there?'

'I can try, sir. But I make no promises.'

'Do the best that you can,' commanded Poley. Fitzherbert went off to try and find some bedding. He turned to his friend. 'Now, Henry, getting a place for you to bed down is only the beginning. Sir Francis told me you had been forced to sell almost everything you owned. Therefore at the very least we must find a way to replace your clothing so that what you are wearing now can be washed. What other necessaries do you need?'

Fortunately for Cuffe, the bath was due to be filled that evening and he took pride of place in its use. Mistress Fitzherbert searched the laundry for breechclouts and hose that had no obvious owners. The guilt-ridden Earl himself instituted a search for more clothing but there was very little to be had, and none of it either new or fashionable. When Cuffe, wrapped in a blanket, finally made his way up to Poley's bedroom, he discovered that young Tom Fitzherbert had delivered a threadbare ruff that had seen better days waiting for his throat, a patched shirt, a peascod doublet of the Earl's that had been fashionable a decade since, a codpiece that might have been used by a clown in a bawdy farce and various other bits and pieces. Poley himself supplied the rest. And Tom returned with a tabard bearing the Essex coat of arms to match all the others in the house.

But at least Cuffe was able to dress and descend to

supper without feeling himself to be an outright figure of fun. Or so he told Poley, who frankly did not believe him. And the spy suspected acutely that such rage and humiliation as the secretary felt was laid squarely at the door of his aristocratic master. Poley sat beside his angry friend but was soon distracted – not by the baked sturgeon, the mess of whiting or the eel pie which were the centrepiece of the supper but by the fact that sometime during his adventures at Gray's Inn and the tavern, Sir Charles Davers had arrived back from Edinburgh. He sat now beside the Earl, leaning sideways towards him almost constantly sharing a whispered conversation.

There was no entertainment after supper, even though Christmas was fast approaching, so Poley joined the diminished and leaderless Secretariat while Cuffe, exhausted and not a little embarrassed by his codpiece, went up to bed. Poley would have sought to join his old comrades in any case, for Sir Anthony was too busy to be visited and if anyone else in Essex House was likely to have information to impart about Davers's mission to Scotland and what had resulted from it, it was these men. Sure enough: Davers was the subject of their gossip. And, at long last, Wotton's absence and the Earl's new attitude towards Poley meant that he was trusted to share in the information.

'He brought a letter south with him,' Wotton's replacement Robert Prentiss was saying. 'It's in code, so Sir Anthony is to work upon it. But we might reason that the message is positive at least, for Sir Charles Davers has the bearing of a man who brings good news and whatever he is imparting to the Earl is making him cheerful rather than the opposite.'

*

It was all speculation, thought Poley. But if Prentiss was correct, it certainly explained the change in the Earl's mood. But what could King James promise under the circumstances? Or, indeed, do? Was there a suggestion of some sort of embassy from one court to the other? What else could James actually set in motion? The only alternative was yet more airy commitments– and the Earl had had a bellyful of those. These thoughts occupied his mind as he wearily climbed to his bedroom, holding a lamp high as he laboured up the stairs. The door to his room was ajar and he felt a shiver of apprehension that Gelly Meyrick and his cohorts might be up to their brutal tricks once more. He pushed the door gently and gingerly, then stepped in to find Henry Cuffe contentedly asleep on a makeshift bed on the floor. With a smile at his own foolishness, Poley closed the door silently, used the chamber pot, washed, stripped and climbed into bed. He blew out the lamp and was asleep almost instantly.

He awoke some time later from a dream about Lady Janet to find arms wrapped gently around him and a naked body pressed urgently against his. After a moment, he rolled over and returned Henry Cuffe's ardent embrace.

It was different to his affair with young Anthony Babbington. It was more measured; more occasional. Much more private – because circumstances had forced them to share one bedroom in any case. But it served the same ends. Poley was standing higher than ever in the

Earl's trust and regard. And now he had achieved a powerful hold over the man who was currently positioned to be one of his most influential advisors. Nor was that all. Because of his recent experiences and new responsibilities Cuffe never left Essex House and because of his maturity he was never jealous when Poley did so, usually as a courier for one or other of the inmates who dared not stir abroad for fear of bailiffs and bellicose members of Cecil's or Raleigh's households, their friends and allies. Though Cuffe might have been less accepting had he known who Poley was meeting alongside the recipients of the messages he was carrying. Despite – or perhaps even because of – his lingering anger and resentment, Cuffe no longer feared to advise Essex of the situation as he saw it and to suggest the most extreme remedies. Principal amongst them remained his idea of raising the City in revolt against the Toad and his lapdogs on the Council.

But, thought Poley, there were several elements that made the Earl hesitate to follow Cuffe's advice just at the moment, and he passed these thoughts to Lady Janet when they met – usually apparently by chance in her carriage now that midwinter seemed to be lingering and the weather was snow-filled and icy. Principal amongst these was the letter from King James. 'Precisely what it says, only the Earl, to whom it was addressed, Sir Anthony who deciphered it, and a very few of Essex's closest associates including Sir Charles Davers who carried it, know,' Poley explained, his breath smoking on the chilly air even in the carriage. 'But it's easy enough to guess what it contains. Its importance to the Earl is attested by the fact that he wears it in a black leather bag around his neck. It likely speaks of traitorous things, therefore, because the bag and its position, waking or sleeping, ensures it does not fall into the wrong hands. Though it is also a kind of talisman. A supernatural assurance that all will be well in the end. Almost, I suppose, a kind of witchcraft.'

'An apt thought,' said Lady Janet, 'as it comes from James, the witchfinder king.'

'But,' he continued, 'it clearly holds some great hope for the Earl – therefore King James must have promised to take some action at last. All I can think is that it must be the embassy to Queen Elizabeth that has been discussed more than once in the past. Certainly, that is the subject of speculation by the Secretariat now. But if we are correct, the king's promise may have an unexpected consequence. For the Earl to take any sort of action before King James's promises could bear fruit would indeed be utter madness.'

'I see. I would never have thought of that. You are indeed a wonder, Robert Poley.'

Poley actually blushed. He lowered his gaze to the carriage floor, looking at Agnes the chaperone's shoe-toes peeping out from beneath her dress. Fearful of meeting Lady Janet's ardent gaze. 'And for me to make any serious move to retrieve King James's letter to Essex, as I retrieved the fatal letter from his mother the Queen of Scots to young Anthony Babbington, would not guarantee a certain outcome. It likely proves the Earl has taken good long step down the primrose path of treason but it does not speak of any truly treasonous action. And in any case, it might well be open to interpretation and challenge. It is in code after all and codes can be tricky things.'

Lady Janet nodded and Agnes, privy to every word nodded also. Poley wondered for a moment whether both the women reported to the same spymaster; and, if not, whether each one of them knew who the other owed their true allegiance to. Which turned out to be his last waking thought about Lady Janet that year.

Because it was Christmas. London was choked with ice and snow – hardly conducive to raising an army of citizens, no matter what their objective might be or how passionately they wished to follow their leader. Moreover, the fact that it was Christmas meant that the Queen was at her palace at Richmond once more and the Council would be in attendance except for those who were scattered to their own estates and the bosoms of their families. Unless Essex wished to march his citizen army down the ice-bound River Thames, there was no point in raising them at all.

And so the seasons rolled round. There was precious little celebrating in Essex House and the hours spent in St Clement Danes over the holiest of days were bone-chillingly cold and deeply unsatisfactory because the vicar chose a Christmas homily that could not be twisted or interpreted into any kind of support for the Earl or his pretensions. And, thought Poley, if the Earl had lost St Clement Danes, then the other London Churches would be following suit – if they weren't already leading the way. After services on Christmas night, the Earl vanished into Sir Anthony's room. Poley observed this coldly and calculatingly. Another letter to King James, he suspected. Urging speedier action to fulfil any promises made in the letter the Earl wore round his neck.

*

The New Year was no better. As the Queen feasted and danced her way into 1601 with entertainments, masques and plays, there was lean fare in Essex House and no celebration of any sort. The only hope for the immediate future was brought by the visiting noblemen and there was very little of that. The Earl of Southampton, faithful as ever though almost as deep in debt as his friend was a constant visitor. Francis Manners, the Earl of Rutland, who was Lady Frances' son-in-law was there as well. The Earls of Worcester and Sussex were among the more regular visitors. As was Lord Monteagle, who at least could afford the presents he brought. Any of them who brought joy or provisions like Monteagle, thought Poley, also brought some faint hope of a brighter future. They brought hope through their numbers and their standing if through nothing else. But of course, the greater Essex's hope, the more dangerous his enemies became. The more dissatisfied nobles flocked to him, the more desperate his rivals became to ensure his downfall before he engineered theirs as the Queen still refused to stir against him in any meaningful way.

Sir Francis was near despair. 'The people still hate me because they believe I am *against* My Lord of Essex,' he said to Poley as the pair of them hurried towards Gray's Inn through the slush and mud of late January. 'And so I must rely on your good sword to guard me out here on the

253

streets. But the Queen has ceased to love me because she knows how strongly I have been arguing *for* him!'

'And that is why you are forbidden to talk to her about him, even when she consults you on other matters?'

'Even so. And of course no-one else at court dare be seen with me for fear that will arouse her suspicions and anger her further.'

'Perhaps it is time I consulted Lady Janet,' said Poley. 'I will put the matter in hand.'

Rain thundered onto the roof of Lady Janet's carriage, making her raise her voice – though Poley suspected acutely that she would rather have been whispering. 'It is a combination of things,' she said. 'Everyone at court can see how desperate and dangerous his situation has become – and therefore how dangerous the Earl himself has become. On top of that, there is the matter of King James's letter that we discussed at our last meeting. Its actual contents are irrelevant – the fact that it exists is a sufficient danger-signal to those who stand against Essex. And then there is the great and growing number of men who are flocking to him. Everyone, it seems, from Earls to common soldiers knighted by him in Ireland. Essex House has become a well-guarded fortress, from which may issue an army large enough to invade the City and overwhelm Her Majesty's court. Or so they fear.'

'And what do they plan to do about it?'

'Master Secretary urges caution and diplomacy. Sir Thomas Walsingham is sending Lady Audrey back north as soon as the roads are clear.'

'Well and good. And Raleigh?'

'Raleigh wants him dead. He is, indeed, looking at ways to kill him as soon as possible. Once the Earl is under ground, he says, the poison is drawn and the wound will no longer fester.'

'Dead?' asked Poley. 'Not imprisoned? Not banished?'

'He sees all too clearly how imprisoning the Queen of Scots only led to one deadly plot after another. As you of all people should know. No. He is for the direct approach and as soon as it can be done.'

'But Master Secretary…' Poley's voice trailed off. 'Were we Raleigh's followers, Lady Janet, you might well be passing me a vial of poison even now. But we are Cecil's and Cecil counsels caution. Or so you say and so I hope and pray.'

'Master Secretary is content for Raleigh to go his own way, for the risks of such an action might be very dangerous indeed. Her dreams, I think, of killing two birds with one stone as the saying goes…'

'That Raleigh might contrive Essex's murder and in so doing somehow cause his own downfall.'

'Even so, though he knows that this is little more than a dream. But more realistically, he is still hopeful that the Earl himself might follow the advice he seems to be getting most constantly and undertake some action himself that can only end in his death.'

'And he relies on me for that?' asked Poley. Though he knew the answer well enough.

'He does. Wait until you see your moment, and then…'

'So you do not need to pass me poison. I am the poison,' he said.

'You always have been and you know it,' she replied gently.

*

Poley was not the only source of information coming into Essex House and while he was mulling over the best way to warn Essex that Raleigh was seriously considering direct action against him, rumours to that effect started to circulate. The deadly threat came not only from Raleigh, of course, but from every man of the faction he commanded. And, the nervous gossips said, this was something much more organised and ruthless than the almost casual duels that might arise when men from each faction confronted each-other in the street. The duel that had brought calamity down on all of them was only the start, they whispered. Any one of them, out alone or even in a small group, had a great deal more than bailiffs to fear. Now Poley's reputation as a swordsman became an even more important asset. Sir Francis might have been the first to use him as a bodyguard but he was by no means the last. And the fact that both Francis Bacon and Henry Cuffe talked enthusiastically about Poley's prowess with a blade made him not just first choice for carrying messages but also for escorting anyone who had business outside the walls of Essex House.

Of course, Poley knew all too well that he was not the only swordsman amongst them. After all, Sir Gelly Meyrick led a contingent of battle-hardened soldiers. But they had gained their experience on the hills, valleys and bogs of Ireland or on the wide battlefields of the Low Countries. And, as often as not, on horseback. There the preferred weapons were short swords or broad swords; here the rapier ruled supreme both as fashion accessory and weapon of choice. Furthermore, they soon discovered that skirmishing on foot in the streets of London was a very different proposition to anything they had trained for or experienced.

Hardly surprisingly, therefore, Poley not only came to know all the alternative routes from Essex House to Gray's Inn very well indeed but also those from Essex House to Drury House, where the Earl of Southampton currently held court. The distance between these two was nowhere near as great as that between Essex House and Gray's Inn. The quickest way was to go across the Strand to St Clement Danes and then up Wych Street which was one of the thoroughfares that opened at the front of the ancient church. But the roads were crowded unless they were walked at night – in spite of the City's curfew. And in any case Wych Street was notoriously narrow, the overhanging buildings that lined it almost leaning against each-other at their highest points. If anywhere was designed for an ambuscade, then Wych Street certainly was. And yet, as winter began to ease its grip on London, increasing numbers of men went hurrying nervously from one great house to the other. The situation was becoming more desperate with each passing day. The Earl had given up all hope that the Queen would relent or that James would undertake whatever action he had promised in the secret letter he wore in the bag around his neck and was listening to wilder and wilder suggestions as he waited in growing despair to hear something positive from Scotland.

But each day brought disappointment and increasing desperation. Poley observed the situation dispassionately. Because all the talk in Essex House was of violent action, who it should be taken against and how soon, there was a general assumption that an equal measure of violence was being prepared against them. That Raleigh was gathering some sort of army to face the hundred and more desperate knights who had put themselves under the Earl's command. That there would soon be a kind of warfare on London's streets was almost taken for granted. The smithy near the stables in the courtyard was put to work almost day and night, mending armour, sharpening swords. Powder was smuggled in by boat. Barrels of it carried up from Essex House steps through the gardens and in past Sir Anthony's sick-room to prime both pistols and muskets. The groups of Essex men who ventured out began to carry guns as well as swords. It was the sort of situation, Poley told Lady Janet, that could be compared to a powder keg. It would only take one spark to set the whole thing off.

Gelly Meyrick caught up with Poley mid-morning one Tuesday early in February, an apparently casual encounter which in fact was nothing of the sort. 'My Lord wishes you to take this message to Drury House,' he said, holding up a carefully folded and heavily sealed letter. 'It's for the Earl of Southampton eyes alone. Do not surrender it into any hand but his.'

'Of course, Sir Gelly. I will go at once.'

As sparks went, it seemed little enough to have caused what followed.

*

Poley set out for Drury House with Sir Francis and Cuffe at either shoulder. They were each bound for a different destination, but their paths ran side by side to begin with. Although it was still winter, it was one of those days that sometimes appear in January and early February which give a foretaste of spring. The Strand was thick with slush and, at this, the narrower end, almost blocked with crowds of people. St Clement Danes was all agleam with drops and runnels of meltwater and many of the people out and about were heading there to hear early Evensong, the sacrament's approach proclaimed by all the church bells in the city. Wych Street seemed strangely clear of snow – the worst of it, thought Poley as he pulled his cloak tighter against the chill of the shadows – had been kept away by the closeness of the roofs whose eaves all-but touched high above them. This also added a strange element to the sounds coming from the street. They echoed, overlapped, grew louder and softer without apparent reason, as though this place was a cavern full of ghostly whispers. Even the church bells sounded strange.

'Make way there!' snarled an impatient voice immediately behind the three men. Poley looked back and up. There were several men on horseback trying to force their way along the busy road. They were wearing hats pulled low and cloaks muffled high towards their chins. But their leader's face was easy enough to recognise.

'Sir Thomas Grey,' mumbled Cuffe as Poley pulled him aside. 'The Toad's man. And an arrogant swine, I remember he pushed his way past us when we were on the way to Nonsuch on the day the Earl went into Her Majesty's chamber unannounced. Sir Christopher St Lawrence was all for striking him dead on the spot, as I recall.'

As if to emphasise Cuffe's bitter words, Grey's horse raised its tail and deposited a pile of steaming dung in the roadway immediately in front of them. Poley stepped aside, and as he did so, he got a clear view along the house-fronts towards his destination. He was just in time to see the great gate of Drury House open and a small group of horsemen come trotting out. They turned away, and started easing their passage through the crowds, heading down towards The Strand, Charing Cross, Whitehall Palace and the Council, the Court or the Queen. Whither, no doubt, Sir Thomas Grey was also heading. Poley recognised their leader at a glance. It was the man he had been ordered to give Essex's message to: the Earl of Southampton.

Avoiding the horse dung, Poley eased in close behind Thomas Grey and his escort, calculating that the horsemen would be moving through the crowd of people faster than a man on foot would be able to – especially given the riders' ruthless arrogance. Indeed, he thought, if he stuck close to Grey he would probably catch up to Southampton pretty quickly. The far end of Wych Street opened into Little Drury Lane, which ran down to The Strand not far from Sir Walter Raleigh's current home, Durham House. With the movement of the two groups of horsemen speeding up and slowing down as the density of the crowds dictated, Poley followed as close behind the horses as he could. Sir Francis and Cuffe stayed with him, each no doubt, intrigued to see what was going to happen next.

Although The Strand was even more crowded than Wych Street – explaining Sir Thomas's choice of the route - nevertheless, most of the traffic on this, the wider section of the thoroughfare as it led down to Charing Cross was horses and wagons. So Grey at last managed to draw level with Southampton while Poley was so close behind them that he witnessed in some detail what happened next. The clamour in the street – augmented not only by the bells but also by the action of the horsemen themselves - made it impossible for him to hear exactly what was said, but with breath-taking suddenness, Grey pulled out a broadsword that had been hanging from his saddle beneath his left thigh while the Southampton pulled out the rapier he carried at his left hip. Steel clashed against steel as Poley leaped back from the melee to avoid being trampled by the horses. Grey had the upper hand at once. Both he and Southampton were cavalrymen, indeed their enmity had arisen over Southampton's leadership of Grey in Ireland as Essex's Master of Horse. Their control of their mounts was good. They fought with their horses shoulder to shoulder, each facing the other. Their companions jostled around them, uncertain whether to part the combatants or join the battle. But, thought Poley grimly, Southampton would be lucky to survive this. His rapier was being wielded by a practised hand, almost as well-schooled as Poley's own. But Grey had the broadsword, which was designed to be an efficient mankiller in situations just like this. The double-edged blade flashed down. Southampton was lucky to turn it aside without damage to himself or his mount. He riposted, but Grey leaned sideways so the rapier's point passed harmlessly along his ribs.

'That's it,' said Poley, though his voice was lost in the hubbub. 'Southampton's dead.'

Grey swung his blade round and down with all the power of a headsman's axe. But just as he did so, one of Southampton's companions crashed his horse into the Earl's, knocking man and mount aside. It was too late for Grey to stop the blow or turn the blade. The power of it nearly toppled him out of his saddle and he pulled back so hard his horse reared. The group broke up, the combatants wrenching their horses away from one another. All except for Southampton's companion who sat stock-still in the saddle, stricken with disbelief, staring at his arm. Which now ended at the elbow. Except for the fountain of blood that was pumping out of it, spraying away across the road in great steaming arcs of red as bright as holly-berries. While the agitated horses trampled his severed hand and forearm into the gutter.

9

'He meant to kill you, My Lord,' said Poley. 'There can be no doubt.'

The Earl of Southampton looked at him, the long face pale, eyes wide, full of horror; not yet rage. That would come later, thought the spy. After all, Southampton had been a soldier in Ireland. Violent death was nothing new to him; though he would have been hard-put to rival the butchery enacted by his enemy Sir Walter Raleigh there. Working under orders of Sir Thomas Grey's father Baron Arthur Grey, Raleigh and Macworth were the captains who oversaw the brutal execution of more than six hundred prisoners after the castle at Smerwick surrendered to them. Still, to come so near death, so suddenly, at the hand of someone he knew so well. And in the middle of The Strand...

'If your page hadn't intervened...' added Cuffe, dragging Poley back to the present. He shook his head in horror that seemed almost as great as the Earl's; but there was growing outrage there too. Even though Cuffe had seen much less of the battlefields in Ireland than Southampton or Essex had – or Grey or Raleigh.

Southampton nodded vacantly. 'Poor Ben,' he whispered. He had plainly liked the boy, thought Poley. And the regard must have been mutual for the lad to give his life for his master's like that.

'Who drew his weapon first?' wondered Sir Francis,

ever the lawyer. 'I was in no position to see. But it may be a crucial question, My Lord. You know The Queen has strictly forbidden you and Sir Thomas Grey to fight under any circumstances. She will be outraged when word reaches her...'

'Grey,' answered Poley at once. 'I'd lay my life on it. Grey drew that mankilling broadsword he had hanging down by his left stirrup.'

'Left over no doubt from his time in Ireland,' observed Gelly Meyrick, joining in the discussion for the first time.

'A fearsome weapon to be carrying around the streets of London,' emphasised Cuffe. 'Did he think the Irish were about to attack the City?'

'No,' grated Sir Gelly. 'He thought he might come across some friends of the Earl of Essex. The very fact that he has been allowed to go about the streets armed, and with such a weapon to hand, is sinister in itself!'

Southampton nodded, face white, his eyes wide. 'As you say,' he said to Poley as though the Welshman hadn't even spoken. 'Grey drew first. I only drew in order to defend myself.'

'And what passed between you?' pursued Sir Francis. 'What did you say to so enrage him?' Sir Gelly glared at him icily and drew in breath to speak. 'The Queen will want to know,' added Sir Francis hurriedly cutting Essex's steward off.

'I? I said nothing!' Southampton was stirred to righteous anger. 'It was him! He sneered at our Irish campaign and noted how much more successfully it was progressing now that I am here in London instead of serving as General of

Horse and Lord Mountjoy has replaced My Lord of Essex…' He paused and looked round the room, finally locking his angry gaze with that of his friend and sometime general.

Essex sat behind a sizeable table, almost as pale as Southampton. His hands had closed to fists as they rested on the board, however. They at least spoke of Essex's outrage at the attack and the near-death of his closest friend. Gelly Meyrick stood at his left shoulder with Christopher Blount at his left beside William Parker, Lord Monteagle. Ironically, apart from Poley the only man in the room not yet buried under mountains of debt. The Percy brothers Charlcs and Jocelyn recently arrived from the North and sharing the room that had once been Cuffe's, stood behind the Welshman, their broad, ruddy faces, like his, folded into thunderous frowns. It was hard to see them as being related to Lady Janet, Poley thought. Fernando Gorges and Sir John Davis stood on either side of them, making the little chamber seem crowded.

*

In fact they were a random selection of Essex's supporters who had been nearby when Southampton on foot staggered in off the Strand with his naked rapier in one hand and his reins in the other. And with Poley close behind, leading a horse that carried the dead boy draped over it. Too late even for the attentions of Dr Wendy in whose chamber beside Sir Anthony's sickroom he was currently lying awaiting post mortem and funeral preparations. The immediate furore their entrance had crerated was quieter now, but the shock and concern it caused were, if anything, deeper. Silence settled on the room. And lingered. The entirety of Essex House seemed to be holding its breath.

'Grey is Master Secretary's man,' said Poley into the cavernous stillness. 'It seems that it is not only Sir Walter Raleigh who is keen to catch the nearest way of defeating you, My Lord. Though it could hardly be called coincidence that the attempt on the Earl's life was actually made outside Raleigh's London dwelling.'

'It is clearly inviting a violent death at the hands of one faction or the other for you or any of your friends to walk in the streets unguarded,' said Cuffe.

'I cannot believe that Master Secretary would countenance such bold-faced murder,' observed Sir Francis more calmly, in the face of the gathering outrage.

Everyone else in the room looked at him as though he was fit for Bedlam.

'I will go to Whitehall via Gray's Inn and look more deeply into this matter,' he said as their growing hostility registered with him. He hurried out of the door, their gazes following him. Like so many daggers in his back, thought Poley.

'He'll need to go further afield than that if he wants to find the court,' said Sir Ferdinando. 'The Queen is still at Richmond.'

'Well,' observed Gelly Meyrick grimly, 'he's certainly the only one of us who can walk the streets in absolute safety, no matter whose blades are thirsty for our blood.'

'It is clearly a matter of life and death now,' said Sir John Davis later still as they continued to chew over the implications of Grey's attack on Southampton over a supper of lamb and umble pie, eels in calves' foot jelly and a pig's head.

'What we must do,' said Fernando Gorges, 'is to formulate a plan of action. Something we can prepare and then enact flawlessly, all as agreed, when the moment is right. We are soldiers after all. It should be planned like a campaign.'

'Which cannot be undertaken immediately,' observed Poley, admitted to the top table now. 'Not if it involves The Queen, as you all must see that it will. For, no matter what else we plan, Her Majesty must be removed to a protective custody where she is incapable of taking action, or you may lay your lives that she *will* take action.'

'Whatever we do, it *must* involve The Queen's person,' emphasised Cuffe. 'But surely we are no Jesuitical murderers about some kind of regicide. She must be held for a time while whatever we agree on is enacted. She must be held apart. Inviolate. But, as Master Poley says, powerless to intervene. But if she comes to any harm then we are all lost.''

Lady Frances, Lady Lettice and Lady Rich all nodded, wide-eyed at the seriousness of the discussion, finding it hard to finish their meals. The combination of desperation, tension and shock at the young page's death robbing them of appetite. Not to mention the stark reality of what was being discussed. Though, thought Poley, Lady Lettice and Lady Rich would not be too greatly saddened to see the Queen taken down a peg or two. Not would Lady Walsingham were she here rather than in Barn Elms. All three had cause to be out of love with their irascible monarch.

'I see that,' said Essex, but he did not sound particularly sure of himself. He pushed his platter away, piled though it was with untouched food. The enormity of what Cuffe was discussing so calmly and logically seemed also to have winded him like a fist in the belly. The possibility – no matter how remote – that having survived so many years of plots to murder her in any manner that could be devised by her enemies abroad or their secret representatives in England, Elizabeth might finally face death at the hands of someone who had once been her closest and most loving friend and favourite.

But then again, thought the intelligencer, this entire situation had originated with Essex himself demonstrating the inconceivable truth: that it was possible for a determined individual, though armed and covered in mud, to access The Queen's person, even in her most private chambers, unguarded, unprepared and helpless.

It had been done once, almost by accident. It could be done again.

*

But the words, the thought, the memory and the possibility, calculated Poley, were what made the Earl's eyes dart all around the bustle of the great hall as servants and diners came and went. Looking as though Essex feared that Captain of the Queen's Guard Raleigh and all the equally ruthless soldiers at his command could come sweeping in through the walls themselves. Clearly Essex House was no place to be discussing such matters or making such plans if they wanted their leader to remain in firm command of his faculties.

'So, we can plot and we can plan,' said Poley. 'But we can take no actual action until the Queen returns from Richmond.'

'And when will that be?' wondered Cuffe round a mouthful of the savoury pie.

'Later in the month,' said Sir Christopher Blount, signalling for a further helping of pig's cheek.

'Then,' said Sir John Davis, 'that is how long we have to formulate and agree a plan; to realise what elements we will need to address to ensure success, then to assign every man a part in it and prepare to put it into action.'

'When?' asked Poley quietly. 'When should we put it into action?'

'During, shall we say, the first week of February,' answered Davis confidently. He lifted his cup as though toasting the enterprise and all associated with it, then drained it at one draught.

'But we should do none of this here in Essex House,' said Poley. 'Here there are too many men coming and going who have only the most casual acquaintance with any of us. Too many ears in the employ of Master Secretary, perhaps. Too many tongues willing to whisper to the Council almost certainly.'

'Indeed,' agreed Cuffe readily. 'History proves that such matters are best resolved by a small group of dedicated leaders working in absolute secret until the very last moment. I adduce as my proof the downfall of Julius Caesar.'

'A band of sure, selected men, therefore, meeting in secret at Drury House,' said Southampton.

'And, although we take Cuffe's example,' emphasised Poley, 'let us remember that The Queen is not Caesar; and that the conspirators' actions led to ultimate failure because they did not kill Marc Anthony or Octavian – a mistake pointed out by Marcus Tullius Cicero himself. And one we would be foolish to emulate. Especially as Antony and Octavian are the very men we wish to strike down.'

Talk of Caesar's deputy and his heir in place of Raleigh and Cecil seemed to settle Essex a little, though Davis's announcement of a possible date for action had clearly done yet more damage. Assigning the objects of their planning names from Classical times appeared somehow to reduce the mental turmoil that their plotting and planning engendered – in their leader at least. Then again, Southampton's offer of Drury House – where indeed most of the discontented men had met and plotted so far – seemed to give Essex yet another straw to grasp at. At least he no longer looked like a man who was drowning in this overwhelming flood of events.

'Let us agree on Drury House, then,' said Essex more firmly.

'And let us set our minds to drawing up a list of men we might trust to meet there and do this business,' added Sir Gelly. Did he emphasise the word *men*, wondered Poley; certainly he was uneasy about the involvement of so many women in such a range of roles, no matter how firm their commitment and how clear their allegiance. He would have been even more worried had he known about Lady Janet.

But even as Sir Gelly spoke, the man who was least likely to figure on his list was shown into the room. 'It is all over Gray's Inn already,' said Sir Francis. 'Sir Thomas Grey is taken up for the affray in the Strand and the death of the boy and is imprisoned in the Fleet at Her Majesty's pleasure. Surely that must prove that the action was neither instigated by Sir Walter or Master Secretary!'

*

Sir Francis' news convinced no-one and he was soon off once more, called to a conference with Her Majesty at Richmond. Meanwhile, the plotters moved to Drury House and began to formulate a plan, led by Sir John Davis and Sir Fernando Gorges. It was inevitable now, given everything that had happened, that Poley and Cuffe should be among their number.

Cuffe, indeed, took an early lead. 'Surely this is no matter for great armies,' he said. 'In spite of everything, My Lord of Essex is no Bolingbroke come to grasp the throne. Rather we are dealing with what might be called a *coup*. It is a method of transferring power popular in France and Scotland, so history informs us, as well as in our own island story. Allow me to adduce as my example the removal from her throne by certain Scottish lords of the Queen of Scots in 1567, replacing her by the infant James VI under the guardianship of her half-brother the Earl of Moray, and removing the friends, confidents and advisors who had guided the Queen of Scots so ill. All it took was a few powerful men overwhelming her palace and her guards and capturing her person. Able, therefore, to bend her to their will.'

'London is not Edinburgh,' said Sir John Davis. 'And Her Majesty is no unpopular French-loving Queen of Scots trying to force Popishness on her Protestant subjects.'

'Though,' countered Cuffe, 'as I observed on our ride to Nonsuch, Her Majesty's Poor Laws do little to relieve the poor; the local officers hardly have the wherewithal to replace the system of relief that the Queen's father broke down when he dissolved the monasteries. More and more come to die starving or freezing in the streets. Even London, once a jewel, is grown tawdry through the endless grasping greed of the men we seek to destroy. I am sure the citizens see all this as clearly as we do ourselves and are simply waiting for someone like the Earl to lead them towards a better place.'

'There is the kernel of an idea there,' said Fernando Gorges. 'We would need to stir the citizens…'

'They would follow the Earl, surely,' said Sir Christopher Blount, nodding his agreement to Cuffe. 'Especially if he voiced the fears we all have that the country is as good as sold into Spanish hands.'

'The court and the city, then,' said Cuffe. 'And where else?'

'The Tower,' said Poley. 'We would need to take the Tower.'

That stopped all conversation dead in its tracks for a good ten seconds. Then there was an overwhelming babble as everyone began to speak at once.

Gorges and Davis were still arguing over the best method of securing the Tower several days later, back in Essex House, when it became important in the situation in a way that not even Poley had anticipated. The author and pamphleteer John Heyward had been held there accused of treason since he had published his book of *Henry IV* and dedicated it to Essex. A fact that gave the Earl's enemies yet more ammunition to use against him. Now Sir Francis arrived with yet more news. Perhaps he had already calculated what its impact would be. Perhaps not.

'The Queen is preparing to return to Whitehall Palace,' he said a little breathlessly. No-one showed any surprise, least of all Poley. It had been clear that the Queen would return to her London palace sometime in January. She always did. But there was more: 'And, as part of her resumption of the reins of power, she has commanded that John Heyward be examined by the Council once again.' Sir Francis turned towards Essex. 'He stands accused of writing seditious and treasonous material at your behest, as you know, My Lord. And should he admit as much, it might give the Council further cause to demand that you are returned to prison yourself.'

'I wonder who prompted her to command such action,' said Poley.

'You know very well, friend Robert,' said Cuffe who missed the irony in Poley's tone. 'It must have been Master Secretary.'

'It is clearly the next step in their campaign against me,' said the Earl. 'The moment for action approaches apace.'

Sir Gelly actually *tutted* – that his master should voice

such an observation in front of the one man the Welshman was certain they could never trust, despite his repeated protestations that he only lived to serve the Earl. Poley saw the look the steward shot at the Queen's Counsel and wondered whether Sir Francis' elder brother the ailing Sir Anthony still trusted his sibling after all. He could well believe that Sir Francis could be added to the list that included himself, Nick Skeres and Christopher Blount, all of whom had worked for Walsingham and the Council in the past and, of course Fernando Gorges who was Sir Walter Raleigh's cousin. But for the moment, the head of the Earl's secret service was too ill to be disturbed.

*

But, thought the intelligencer, the Earl was right. It was time to stop all this plotting and prevaricating. For in fact Sir John Davis had completed his plan, though he was keeping it secret from all of them for the time being. He wanted to talk it through with the ailing Sir Anthony before opening it fully to the others. Sir Anthony's illness was the only thing holding matters up – and Poley knew it would not be allowed to do this for long. Unless Sir Anthony began to recover soon, Sir John Davis would find a substitute – probably Fernando Gorges. All they needed to do was examine it, agree it, assign the various roles and responsibilities and then put it into action.

Which put the secret agent into a dangerous position. He had to use this momentary delay to warn his masters on the Council that the plan was so close to being implemented. But his new position at the heart of things made it almost impossible to do anything unobserved and if he was discovered to be in communication with Lady Janet and the men she reported to, he would be dead in the blink of an eye. He was still based in Essex House in the room he had first occupied near those of Sir Christopher and Lady Lettice. This was the room he shared with Cuffe now, though as the end of the matter drew nearer there was less dalliance between them, especially as even when sharing their manly embraces, he found his head filling ever more powerfully with Lady Janet. In the beginning, his closeness to Cuffe had been a useful key to doors that would otherwise have remained closed to him. But now, Cuffe's clinging nature meant that they were always together – something he needed to escape from, if only for a few vital hours. And yet he was reluctant to take the obvious way and pretend a lovers' quarrel. There was something appealing in Cuffe's devotion as he clung like a spaniel to its master. In the mean-time, Poley main employment was as a courier between the Earl, who was being careful to remain aloof, and the plotters in Drury House. He went between Essex and Southampton alone only on the rarest of occasions. He was almost perpetually in company with Cuffe, and often also with Sir Christopher Blount, both of whom with Fernando Gorges, Sir John Davis, Southampton and a tight but varying group of others. The core of the plot currently seemed to involve an increasing number of Catholic sympathisers such as Pearce Edmonds, Francis Tresham and Robert Catesby along with Lords Monteagle, Cromwell and Sandys; as well as Sir Charles Danvers and the indefatigable Lady Rich. And, although he often saw Agnes apparently coming and going to services at St Clement Danes, he could never speak with her or pass any message via her to Lady Janet.

But then, as had been the case in the past, an outside agency came to his aid. He and Cuffe were hurrying past the front of the great old church. It was early February and the weather was closing in again. Poley and Cuffe were pushing through a crowd of citizens who were keen, like them, to reach their destination before the next sleety downpour. The pair of them were carrying a message for Southampton the most important element of which seemed to be that the time had come to dispense with Sir Anthony Bacon's services and move the helpless invalid out of Essex House and into his old lodgings in Bishopsgate.

As they crossed the open space in front of St Clement Dane's, Poley caught sight of Agnes lingering in the doorway of the church which, like the rest of London stood in need of refurbishment. No sooner had he locked eyes with Lady Janet's go-between than Nick Skeres appeared out of the crowd. 'Cuffe,' he gasped. 'Cuffe, come, go with me. I have urgent news for the Earl.' He grabbed Cuffe by the arm, pulling him away from Poley. 'At once, man! At once!'

Overpowered by Skeres' urgent demands, Cuffe allowed himself to be swirled away with only one helpless backward glance. Poley turned without a second thought, heading for St Clement Danes and Agnes. As soon as she saw he was approaching, she turned and vanished inside. The next time Poley saw her, she was standing at the side of an ancient pew. Most of the old pews had been ripped out with the other original popish artefacts by indignant Protestants who wished to address their God more directly rather than via priests and objects that brought them dangerously close to idolatory. But one or two of the original pews remained, with doors, high backs and private spaces so that the great and the good could perform their rites of worship out of the common gaze. As Poley approached, Agnes opened the door of one of these and Poley slid past her to find Lady Janet waiting for him. 'How near are they to acting on their plans?' she asked at once, her voice low.

*

'Close. All that has slowed them so far is the illness of Sir Anthony Bacon but he is in process of being removed to his old lodgings. Sir John Davis and Sir Fernando Gorges are supposed to agree the final details within the next few days but...'

'But?'

'There is a tension between them. They agree less and less. It seems likely to me that Sir Fernando will challenge Sir John's plans, in part at least. Furthermore, the nearer we come to action, the less confident the Earl seems to be.'

'Treason is a sufficiently weighty matter to give the most fearless or desperate men pause,' she nodded. 'And he must know that, no matter how well planned the action, there is always the chance that it will go wrong.'

'He has led armies and navies into battle. He knows that better than most.'

Lady Janet nodded her understanding.

'Then perhaps if Master Secretary wishes the Earl to

act,' Poley continued delicately after a moment, 'he should seek to apply just a little more pressure. A final push so to speak.'

She nodded again. 'I will report what you have said. We will see what can be done.'

That seemed to be all. Poley began to slide along the pew towards the door which was still guarded by Agnes.

But Lady Janet stopped him with a gentle hand on his arm. 'And, Robert,' she said softly.

He turned back. Even in the shadows of the private pew, her green eyes seemed to shine. 'Yes Lady Janet?'

'Take good care,' she whispered. 'We are, I think, approaching a truly dangerous time and I would be deeply saddened were anything to happen to you.'

Henry Cuffe was waiting at Drury House when Poley arrived and his news had caused enough of a stir to cover Poley's tardiness. The news, indeed, was enough to drive the thoughts of Lady Janet from his mind, which had occupied it to the exclusion of everything else all the way up Wych Street.

'Sir Thomas Grey has been released from the Fleet,' Cuffe was saying. 'Skeres swears it was by the Queen's own command as enacted by Sir Robert Cecil himself.'

'So,' said Southampton grimly. 'In Queen Elizabeth's realm, the life of a brave boy so casually slaughtered is worth little more than a month in jail!'

'Especially if the killer is a friend of the Toad's,' added Cuffe, all righteous outrage.

There was a murmur of agreement and concern which ran through the room at these bitter words. Poley paused in the doorway and looked around. There were nearly a dozen familiar faces present, their owners all seated round a large table at whose centre was spread a map of the city. Poley was pleased to see that Southampton, like Essex, liked company to share his concerns and support his views. But of course a circle as large as this one could never remain secure. Poley was almost certainly not the only spy amongst them. Wherever the finger of suspicion pointed, it could not point exclusively at him.

'It is as clear as day that they are all in league against the Earl, even Her Majesty,' said Poley at once as he came fully into the room. 'We needed no further proof, but they have furnished us with proof in any case. Surely it is time to act!'

Sir Gelly nodded grudgingly. He might have been forced to allow Poley this close to the heart of things but he still didn't trust him. Poley met his gaze. His was as cold and stony as Meyrick's; there was no love lost between them, nor ever would be.

'But we must wait!' snapped Sir John Davis. 'Sir Fernando has doubts about the plan. He agrees that we can place our men in and around the court with relative ease, as well as in certain areas of London itself, such as here in Durham House. The Toad has spies everywhere but even he does not know how widely we can cast our nets amongst apparently faithful courtiers, guards and the Royal Household. Or, indeed, amongst the watch and the constables of the City. These men could arrest the Toad and Raleigh when the word was given. And so allow the Earl direct access to Her Majesty. Thus permitting him to converse with her face to face. To warn her about the ill council she has been receiving and the men responsible for it. How she must remove them and summon a new parliament to address these vital matters before England becomes just another province of Spain.' He looked around the assembled faces, almost all of which were aglow with excitement and enthusiasm. In stark contrast, thought Poley, to the expression he had last seen on the face of the man who was supposed to be at the head of all this.

*

After a brief pause, Sir John Davis continued, 'And he agrees that we should be able to raise the city with relative ease, especially if we time our action carefully so that we can put our case before the greatest number of people all at once, as I have suggested.' He paused again. He sighed heavily, clearly irritated. Either with Fernando Gorges' intractability or with his own inability to address the problems his friend had seen.

Then he continued, 'But the Tower remains intractable. Sir Richard Berkeley commands it and he is the man who has, with Lord Keeper Edgerton, been put in charge of keeping the Earl under house arrest in both York House and Essex House. The Queen trusts him to stand by her no matter what the circumstance, and with good reason. He is hers, body and soul. We have no hope of turning him to our cause – nor of placing men within the Tower or of turning or even simply bribing any of the garrison already there.'

'Can we not act without the Tower?' demanded Charles

Percy truculently.

'It doubles the risks,' said Sir John Davis.

'More than doubles them,' said Poley. 'Unless the citizens of London can be roused in such numbers that they put a wall of flesh between the garrison in the Tower and the Palace, the Council and the Queen. A wall that will stand with us for long enough to allow the Earl to achieve what he wishes to achieve in those quarters. What does the Earl himself think?'

'We have not yet discussed this with the Earl,' admitted Sir John Davis. Fernando Gorges nodded agreement.

'Then perhaps it is time to do so.' Poley glanced at Cuffe then back at the rest. 'If what Skeres told Master Cuffe is correct, then the Council is preparing to take action against us. If we do not move, we will never outmanoeuvre them and we will all be destroyed.'

'But if we do move,' said Gelly Meyrick, 'and move too soon. What then?'

'Either way, it rests in the hands of Fortune,' said Cuffe. 'If the Fates are with us, we snatch great power in the land and become masters of the present and the future. If they are against us, then our heads will roll.'

'That's not very encouraging,' said Gelly Meyrick.

'But still,' said Poley, 'it's true. If we wish to progress, we must put the matter to the Earl himself and place ourselves in his hands as well as in Fate's.'

But the Earl was still hesitant. Nothing any of them could say would push him into making a decision and taking action. Skeres had brought the news to the meeting at Drury House on Monday, February 2nd, the day Poley had passed his information to Lady Janet for the ears of Master Secretary and the Council. But, like The Earl himself, they seemed hesitant to act. As the week passed, more and more discontented knights, penniless minor aristocrats and disaffected Catholic recusants flocked to Essex House. By the end of the week Poley calculated that there must be approaching two hundred of them. Their swords were sharp. Their pistols and firelocks were loaded. Their patience was running out. And still nothing. Nothing from either side.

Until the Percy brothers came up with an idea. Poley got wind of it when they approached Sir Christopher Blount for a loan of one hundred shillings and he offered to join in whatever enterprise they were planning. Whither he went, thither went Cuffe. They ended up talking to the least destitute of the recusants who came and went through Essex House, William Parker, Baron Monteagle, who advanced them one hundred shillings on condition that he too went with them to see how they proposed to spend such a sizeable sum.

And so, early the next morning, they all wrapped themselves in their warmest cloaks and walked through the slush of the garden down to Essex House steps where they hailed a wherry. The river had not frozen, despite the cold, and within a matter of fifteen minutes, they were climbing up the Falcon Stairs onto Bankside. As they slogged through the freezing mud, Poley for a wild moment thought they must be heading for the Bear Baiting or the Bull Baiting pits. 'We cannot claim all the credit,' Jocelyn Percy was saying. 'Our cousin Lady Janet suggested that we might see whether doing what we propose might move matters forward.'

*

Poley's ears pricked up at this and his mind began to race at once. If Lady Janet had made the suggestion, then it might as well have been proposed by Master Secretary Cecil.

Charles and Jocelyn Percy suddenly turned aside and the secret intelligence realised they were heading, of all places, for the Globe Theatre. Despite keeping company with some of the most avid playgoers among the aristocracy, Poley had seen nothing staged in a year or more and had no idea what was playing at the Globe now. But this early in the day, the flag was down and the takings booth at the entry was unmanned. Nothing daunted, the Percys strode through the pit where the groundlings stood during performances and ran up the steps that led onto the stage, thrusting past some stage hands and carpenters no doubt preparing things for the next performance. They pushed through backstage as though they owned the place and here they found a small office where a man was seated, a ledger in front of him and a box of takings at his elbow.

He looked up in surprise at the invasion, but before he could speak, Jocelyn Percy said, 'Master Phillips?'

'Aye,' said the stranger. 'Augustine Phillips, at your service.' He tried to make the closing of the takings box casual and unremarkable. He failed, thought Poley with some amusement; not much of an actor, then. 'How can I be of service, gentles?'

'Our cousin Lady Janet Percy, one of Her Majesty's

Ladies in Waiting, suggested we talk to you. We wish to commission a performance of an old play by your company,' said Charles Percy. 'Just one performance. This afternoon. Here, at the Globe. Open to all comers.'

'An old play? What old play, masters?'

'I believe it is properly called *The Life and Death of King Richard the Second.*'

Poley gasped. The scales fell from his eyes. He realised what was afoot here; what Lady Janet was up to. It took his breath away.

'It is so called. But we have not enacted it in several years,' said Phillips.

'Could you do so? Today?' insisted Charles Percy. 'Perhaps in place of your play as proposed this afternoon after dinner?'

'Well, we are due to play *Twelfth Night* as we played so recently before Her Majesty…'

'How much?' snapped Percy. 'How much to replace *Twelfth Night* with *Richard the Second* for one performance?'

'Well,' Phillips's eyes narrowed. He glanced down at his ledger then up again. 'Our usual fee for a private performance would be twenty shillings. I suppose we could…'

'We'll double it,' snapped Percy. 'Your usual fee plus forty shillings and you keep whatever you take at the gate.'

Augustine Phillips gaped at the red-headed northerner. 'Usual fee plus forty shillings,' he said. 'Done!'

Poley could hardly contain himself on the way back. 'Have you discussed this with The Earl?' he asked. 'No matter what audience comes or what they see within the play itself, Hayward is still under close questioning in The Tower for his book about the same matter. The Queen herself has admitted that she is seen as Richard II, ripe to be toppled by the Earl as Bolingbroke.'

'Aye,' agreed Jocelyn Percy without the shadow of any regret. 'Lady Janet said as much. But there's no guarantee it will do more than stir the cauldron of events a little. There's no need as yet to warn the Earl, Sir John Davis and Sir Fernando Gorges.'

'I agree,' said Poley at once. 'Take my advice and let matters rest for a little time at least. It is an old play as Master Phillips said. One licensed long ago and played to great effect if I remember rightly. But because of changing circumstance it has gained a hitherto unsuspected relevance. Mayhap it will come to the Council's notice. But then again maybe not. Think on it, Jocelyn. You and Charles would look foolish to put it mildly if you warned everyone that some great danger threatened and nothing happened at all.'

'True enough,' said Jocelyn, not a bit dashed. 'But I'd hazard that something will come of it!'

And I'd hazard the same, thought Poley.

*

Poley would have liked to attend the performance. Quite apart from anything else, he reckoned that Lady Janet, having originated the idea, would almost certainly be there herself. But things at Essex House called him away. Sir John Davis and Sir Fernando Gorges had almost come to blows over the plan and had managed to split the group of the Earl's closest advisors into two camps. As supper proceeded that evening, some middle ground was established as everyone agreed that taking The Tower was out of the question. Poley listened, distracted – as were some others – by the thought that the flag on the Globe was being raised and the trumpet blown to summon in the audience to the unexpected performance of a suddenly dangerous drama.

But when his full attention returned to what was being said, he realised that half of the counsellors maintained that the first action should be the overwhelming of Whitehall Palace, the securing of the Queen and the arrest of Cecil and Raleigh. The rest argued that it would be better to rouse the City. 'You are still the hero of Rouen, Cadiz, the Azores campaign. You defeated an Armada with the aid of Heaven and only failed in Ireland because you were betrayed by the men you are seeking to depose. The people worship you,' insisted Sir Christopher Blount.

'Very well,' capitulated the Earl. 'Let us retire to discuss the detail of how such a thing could be done – and when would be the best time to do it. Gelly, Sir John, Sir Fernando and Sir Christopher may all attend me in my private chamber.'

The Earl rose and everyone rose with him. The majority, however, sat down once more when he and his named friends had left the room. Only the ladies remained standing and then, led by Lady Frances, they too left. The remaining men fell to eating, drinking and discussing what the immediate future might bring. But, as it turned out, not even Poley, who knew most about the truth of the current situation, could have foreseen what was actually to happen next.

There came a great banging on the outer gate as though some giant stood in the Strand demanding entry. Fitzherbert ran to answer it, followed by half a dozen sizeable servants. Poley heard the commotion even over the chatter in the Great Hall and saw the major domo hurry past the open door. He was up and out at once, following Fitzherbert and his men out of the front door, down the steps and across the chilly courtyard. As he did so, he became aware of a considerable press of bodies behind him. Fitzherbert opened the small postern in the great gate and stepped back. A group of men wrapped in cloaks with hats pulled low, entered. 'I am here to see the Earl,' said the leader of the group.

'Of course. May I tell my master who is requesting an audience with him?'

The stranger looked up, little more than eyes and nose visible in the flickering light of the blazing torches. 'Tell him Sir John Herbert, Secretary to the Council, has been sent to summon him to appear before them. At once.'

Herbert strode forward. The major domo walked at his side, the house servants forming up beside Herbert's guards. Poley stepped back as they came up the steps towards him and he felt the press of men at his back falling away as well. They all crowded into the entrance hall as Fitzherbert led the Council's emissary into a side room where there was a fire and sufficient seating for the unexpected, most unwelcome arrivals. Then, leaving the door ajar with his men standing guard outside it, he hurried off to warn the Earl what was happening.

It had to be the play, thought Poley. The performance of *Richard II* at the Globe had indeed stirred the Council. Like a stick thrust into a hornets' nest. He looked around, seeking amongst the assembled faces for the Percy brothers but he couldn't see them. What he could see, however, was a combination of outrage and suspicion. Both of these emotions grew so swiftly and so widely amongst the assembled knights that he abruptly began to wonder whether the canny Fitzherbert had left his men there not to make sure that none of the visitors got out but that none of the Earl's outraged friends got in.

*

Fitzherbert returned, not with the Earl but with his steward. He showed Sir Gelly into the room and once again he left the door ajar. 'Well, Sir John?' said the Welshman. 'You have a message for the Earl?'

'Not a message,' snapped Herbert. 'A summons. The Council has noted several things of late that have disturbed them. The meetings at Drury House. The arrival of increasing numbers of armed man here in Essex House which seems to us to be in process of being fortified. Perhaps as the base for some sort of military action.'

He stopped to draw breath and Poley glanced around at his companions. To a man, they were frowning angrily. The short silence before Herbert began to speak again was underpinned by a sort of communal growl which began to build as he resumed, 'The continuing communications between Essex House and Edinburgh which in our opinion have led directly to certain movements by the Earl of Marr on behalf of King James. And, lately, the privately financed performance by the Lord Chamberlain's Men of the play of *Richard the Second* at the Globe Theatre. A play which chimes all too closely with the book for which Thomas Hayward is currently close confined in the Tower.'

He paused again. The atmosphere in the hall was growing dangerous and Poley began to wonder whether the arrogant John Herbert was going to make it out of Essex House alive. Or, indeed, any of his cloaked companions. But, seemingly unaware of the growing danger, Herbert concluded, 'The Council is assembled at the house of the Lord Treasurer Lord Buckhurst and we require the Earl to present himself there forthwith to explain himself and his doings.'

'But, Sir John,' answered Sir Gelly coldly, and the growl in the hall quietened as the men strained to hear his soft Welsh tones, 'the Earl knows the truth you are refusing to reveal. Namely that you and other members of your Council are conspiring with Sir Walter Raleigh and his friends in the matter of a planned assassination. My Lord of Essex knows that the moment he sets foot outside this house, especially were he escorted by you and your men instead of me and mine, he would be dead in a matter of yards. How the deed would be done, by dagger or by gun or by garrotte he does not know. But he does know that it would be done.' The atmosphere around Poley became almost feral.

'You do realise, Sir Gelly, that such suspicions, leave aside the aspersions they cast upon the Council, Master

Secretary and the Captain of the Guard, are very close to madness?'

'I fear not, Sir John. I suspect that they are all too well-founded. I have heard reports, and repeated them to the Earl, that Sir Walter has personally suggested murder as the swiftest and surest way to solve the Council's problems with the Earl. And I understand he has even offered to undertake the task himself. Something he is more than qualified to do, judging from the reputation he left behind in Ireland. Specifically in a place called Smerwick. Along with six hundred headless corpses.'

'That's as it may be, sir. But you are wasting my time. I am here for the Earl. I must see the Earl. And I must take the Earl. I speak with the voice of the Council and Her Majesty. I may not be denied.'

'You will be denied should the Earl choose to deny you. You and your men will also die here and now should the Earl choose to call for it to be so.'

'Then my death would only be a pre-cursor to the Earl's. Nor would the Earl die alone. A finger laid upon me or my men is an act of outright treason. As though violent hands had been laid upon the Queen herself. The man or men who acted so are guilty. The man who ordered it so is guilty. Every man who saw it and did not intervene is guilty. Even the men who knew it might happen and did nothing to prevent it are guilty. Hardly a man in this house, indeed, would escape the noose or the axe. Now go and fetch My Lord of Essex before I run out of patience.'

But before Sir Gelly could say or do anything, Essex appeared. Poley sensed his arrival first in the sudden stirring of the angry crowd around him. In the change in timbre of the noise that they were making. A path parted and the Earl strode forward. His doublet and waistcoat were gone. His shirt clung to him like a second skin, so wet with sweat it was possible to see the pale flesh it clothed. He reached the door. Fitzherbert's guards stood back, wide-eyed. The Earl tore the door wide and stood framed in the doorway, large enough to hide all the other occupants of the room. All hesitation gone, thought Poley. All uncertainty put aside. Here at last was the hero of Cadiz reborn. 'I am sick!' he bellowed. 'Feverish, sweating, as you see and on my way to bed while my men summon the physician to me. I cannot see the Council! I am too sick even to see the Queen! Get you gone Sir John. You and your lackeys. Get you back to the Council and tell them I will see them when I am recovered. I will see them when I am good and ready. And by God, when I am ready, the Council will certainly see *me*!'

10

Poley followed Fernando Gorges down the length of the Essex House gardens. Both men were wrapped in cloaks against the early-morning chill and had hats pulled low. They seemed to be little more than animated versions of the pollarded trees and tall bushes through which they were moving so carefully and silently. Poley was keeping as far back as he dared, given that he didn't want to lose track of his man in the icy fog that hung over the river and the banks beside it. And also because he had a disturbing feeling that he and Sir Fernando were not alone.

Gorges was being careful too. He was clearly a little nervous about what he was doing; and Poley could hardly be surprised at that. He was certain that Gorges was going to secretly meet someone – someone on the water therefore, brought to the meeting-place by boat. And the likeliest candidate to be Gorges' contact was his cousin Walter Raleigh. They had been close friends as well as kin and the only thing that had ever come between them was Robert Devereux, the Earl of Essex and their opposing views of the man. Poley was very much of Sir Anthony Bacon's opinion regarding the likelihood of Sir Fernando being Sir Walter's spy – much as Poley himself was Cecil's. But if the pair were ever to risk a face-to-face meeting, then this was the time to do it. For, Sabbath Day or not, this day, Sunday 8th February, was the day that the Essex had to take decisive action or offer ignominious submission. Sir John Herbert's visit last night had simply left him no other options.

The Earl had dropped his pretence of sickness the moment Sir John Herbert and his men had left and, instead of retiring to bed, had thrown himself into preparations for the morning, guaranteeing everyone in Essex House a sleepless night. But, despite Sir John Davis's meticulous planning, confident in his own standing with London's citizenry and his friends in the Palace alike, the Earl could settle on nothing concrete. Like his advisors, the only thing he was certain of was that the Tower of London was beyond their grasp. But the City was his for the taking. Then again, Whitehall and the Court were little more than a mile distant. And could effectively be invaded either by land from Whitehall and the Court Gate into which it led, or by water from the River, up the Court Stairs or the Privy Stairs just beside them. The Earl had friends and allies in place who would smooth his passage to the Royal Chambers as surely as the Fates had done at Nonsuch.

All through the hours of darkness, as yet more men came secretly in through the postern gate from the Strand, he strode around the rooms that seethed with impatient allies, muttering to himself, rehearsing what he would say to the Queen when he confronted her. The fawning tenor of his words interspersed with his best commanding tones as he practised what he would say to the adoring citizenry if he chose to go into the City instead of the Palace.

It all made sense to the Earl, thought Poley. But it must look distressingly like the ravings of a man who was losing his grip to some of the more recent arrivals. Lady Frances begged and begged him to think again. Lady Lettice advised him to pay close attention to her husband Sir Christopher Blount's advice, which added further complications to the plans outlined by Sir John Davis and Sir Fernando Gorges. But Penelope Rich simply took Sir Charles Davers aside and Poley overheard her ordering the knight to go out in the first dim light of dawn and bring back an assessment of how things stood at Whitehall Palace.

In amongst all this bustle, Poley also observed Sir Christopher Blount and Sir Fernando in close conference. Something – a piece of paper perhaps – passed between them and Poley was suddenly struck by just how close Sir Christopher had got to Sir John Herbert's escort on their way out. The intelligencer understood it all in a heartbeat. He glanced at Cuffe standing beside him, gazing around with a slightly puzzled frown, and was certain that his constant companion had not noticed what had gone on between Gorges and Blount. A message passed from outside Essex House via Sir John Herbert's man to those inside. Via Sir Christopher to Sir Fernando. From that moment on, Poley had managed to keep close watch on Sir Fernando. So, soon after Davers was despatched to Whitehall, Poley had managed to detach himself from Cuffe in the crowd. Now he found himself, unsuspected, following Gorges down the garden path through the early-morning fog, unsettlingly aware that there was someone else out there, hidden by the bushes, trees and swirling mist, following him in turn.

*

Gorges came to the Essex House stairs and Poley heard the sound his boots made on the wooden steps as he descended. Then there was silence. A little breeze sprang up, making the fog swirl and dance. If it gets much stronger than this, thought Poley, it will likely blow the fog away. And so it did. Not completely, but enough to show the surface of the water and the boat coming up towards the steps with a rhythmic creak of oars. The little vessel loomed out of the clouds, almost monstrous, misshapen, with the tall figure of a man standing in the bows. 'Wind's shifting, Fernando,' called the stranger in a broad west-country accent. 'The tide's turning. In more ways than one.'

'I'm here, Walter,' answered Gorges. 'And I hear you. What is it that you want?'

'You know what I want, Fernando. I want all this madness to end. I want that fool Essex to settle down and take his punishment like a man instead of a wilful child. If I can't achieve that, then I'd like you and anyone else I care about well away from Essex House before the Mattins bells start ringing. I warn you, it's a lost cause. A *long* lost cause…'

'And I warn you, cousin! You should scurry back to court and cower there for you are likely to have a bloody day of it!'

No sooner had Gorges finished speaking than there was a sound as loud as a clap of thunder close enough to make Poley flinch. It was only when he smelt the powder that he realised – someone was shooting at Sir Walter. The Captain of the Queen's Guard seemed unhurt and unshaken, however. He simply sat down, making himself a smaller target and called on the waterman to row him away as fast as possible. But whoever was shooting had time for two more shots before Poley found him, guided by the shower of sparks that accompanied the third bullet out of the musket's muzzle. The would-be assassin had hidden himself behind a tall bush, which he used at a rest for his weapon and as an efficient method of concealment. When Poley reached the place the shots had been fired from, the man was gone and only his musket remained, leaning against a branch. On the one hand Poley could see a clear view down to the water at the steps; on the other, he saw the fleeing figure vanishing into the foggy shadows. But before he could even begin to give chase, Sir Fernando arrived. 'Poley!' he bellowed. 'Was that you?' He gestured at the gun which was now resting suspiciously close to Poley's right hand.

'No, Sir Fernando. I don't know who it was. He vanished before I got here.'

'Well, if do you find out who it was, tell him he missed!'

Poley picked up the gun and followed Gorges back up the garden, in through the rear entrance, past the vacant rooms that had housed Sir Anthony Bacon and his physician as well as the room in which Gelly Meyrick had him strung up in the strappado and so into the great hall. Poley leaned the gun against a convenient wall shrugged off his cloak and followed Gorges into the main part of Essex House. Here he discovered Essex and his army standing in a restless crowd, partaking of a meagre soldiers' breakfast of bread and small beer. 'It is what

Caesar himself favoured,' Cuffe was saying to anyone who might be listening. 'Though he preferred to drink vinegar, not beer'

Essex seemed to swell a little, being compared with Julius Caesar on the morning he had decided to go to battle. But, thought Poley, looking around the assembled faces, this is hardly a Roman legion, let alone a Caesarian army. Gorges crossed to his leader and whispered to him, no doubt about Sir Walter. Essex frowned and shook his head, clearly too preoccupied to think Gorges' news through in any detail. The atmosphere was well beyond impatience now, more like desperation; and Essex knew it. He had to take action and soon. But what? Poley could almost see it running out of control through his dizzy head. Whither should he lead his eager army? Against the Court or into the City?

Court or City?

Court or City?

*

But the question was answered almost at once, for Sir Charles Davers returned, his desire to report so urgent that he had not even paused to remove his hat or his cloak. He glanced, frowning, at Essex, then crossed to Lady Rich, who had sent him on the mission from which he was clearly just returning. The pair of them approached Essex, who was talking to a group comprised of Gelly Meyrick, of course, as well as the Earl of Southampton; Lord Monteagle and the Percy brothers with whom he had arranged yesterday's performance at the Globe. Edward, the third Baron Cromwell, great grandson of Thomas

Cromwell who had been responsible for the destruction of the monasteries, as Cuffe had pointed out. Edward Cromwell was a newer arrival but he stood with, Sir John Davies, Sir Fernando and Sir Christopher Blount. Poley came close enough to overhear Sir Charles Davers's report – though as things turned out he need hardly have bothered. 'They've doubled the guards at the palace,' said Lady Penelope Rich, her voice carrying over the surrounding hubbub. 'Every entrance to the palace and at the door to every room has double guards. Sir Charles says there are triple guards at the entrance to the Queen's apartments. And they've closed off access from the River via the Court Steps and the Privy Stairs.'

'Doubled the guards!' said Essex, stunned. 'How did they know to do that?'

'Sir John Herbert gave you a list of reasons they might think to do so last night,' said Lady Rich tartly. 'The secret meetings at Drury House that clearly weren't so secret after all. The arrival of hundreds of your supporters in Essex House. The Strand has been heaving with them lately, day and night. The preparations you have been making in the nature of sharp swords, guns, bullets and powder. Surely you must have realised that the Council would have suspected something, even before your intentions were even more loudly announced by the playing of *Richard the Second* at the Globe yesterday. Or have you been so wrapped up in your plotting and planning that you have been blind and deaf to the real world around you?'

'However that may be, my Lord,' said Cuffe as he

appeared unexpectedly behind Poley's shoulder, 'it settles matters does it not? If the Court is closed against us and the Tower is beyond our grasp, then the decision is made for us. We must raise the City!'

Essex stared at Cuffe as though the academic had predicted some dreadful fate. But then his look of horror became one of resolution. 'The City,' he said. 'I will raise every man, woman, child, master and apprentice. I will raise the starving beggars in the gutters. I will raise the frozen dead if I have to! The City loves me and they will follow where I lead!'

'We will need to organise our troops for an orderly march through the streets, though,' observed Fernando. 'You must be at the head of an impressive force, My Lord; not of a simple mob.'

'You are right, Fernando,' said Essex. He turned to the men immediately surrounding him. 'See to it,' he snapped. Then he was off, walking through the assembled crowd, both indoors, and outdoors – down the crowded steps and into the courtyard. Poley followed, fascinated and not a little moved. 'They seek my life, boys,' Essex was saying over and over. 'Raleigh and Master Secretary Cecil. You are all that stand between me and death; my stout body – guard…' Poley lingered on the top step, watching as Essex rallied his men while, behind him in the great hall Sir Christopher, Sir Fernando, Sir Gelly and the rest tried to get them organised.

But before anything concrete was achieved, there came another loud knocking on the postern gate. Fitzherbert came pushing past and Poley followed him. Essex's major

domo opened the postern to reveal not one figure surrounded by guards but four. Poley recognised them all. There was Lord Chief Justice Popham, Essex's uncle Sir William Knollys, his old jailer Lord Keeper Edgerton and finally the Earl of Worcester. Worcester's presence surprised the intelligencer. This was clearly a deputation from the Queen and her Council. But Worcester had been a regular visitor to Drury house and one of Essex's staunchest supporters. An interesting mix of messengers, he thought. Mostly men who were at least partially on the Earl's side. Able to understand his point of view. The better to argue against it, perhaps. But then the time for speculation was past. The Earl was at the gate himself. 'So, he bellowed, 'The Council sends my friends and relatives to slaughter me! I am become Julius Caesar in all truth!'

The men around him began to echo his shouts so that it became impossible to hear anything further. But within moments, the Earl and Fitzherbert were escorting the four messengers through the mob and up the steps. As they passed Poley, he fell in behind them. There was far too much noise and excitement for anyone to pay particular attention to him so he was able to follow them up to the Earl's library while Gelly Meyrick, Fernando Gorges, Southampton and Baron Cromwell joined them. And while the assembled supporters waved their swords and shouted, 'Kill them! Kill them all!'

*

Poley pushed through the door with several others before Fitzherbert managed to close it. The Earl was locked in lively discussion with one messenger after another.

'You accuse me of writing seditious letters to many men and the King of Scotland and I tell you such letters have been forged and I am innocent of them. Moreover, my life is at risk! There is more than Walter Raleigh who seek my immediate death...'

'That is nonsense,' answered Popham at once.

'Tell that to my page whose arm was cut off when Thomas Grey tried to kill me,' snarled Southampton.

'An act for which he has been jailed!' said the Lord Chief Justice.

'A sentence of less than a month!' answered Southampton. 'He is out on the streets once more. With the same mankilling sword, I'll wager, on the hunt for My Lord of Essex, for myself, for any of us!'

'That's enough,' snapped Essex. 'My Lords, I leave you here for your own safety. As you can hear, your lives would be lost on the instant were you to venture out of the room. I will have the door guarded and release you as soon as it is safe to do so.' Then he led all the others out, closed the door behind them and locked it. 'Gelly,' he said. 'Fetch Sir John Davis to stand guard and any one of your own men who can be relied upon to stand with him.'

'Sir John Davis and Owen Salisbury then,' nodded Gelly and went off in search of them.

'Right...' Essex stood with his back to the locked library door, surrounded by men awaiting his orders, the wind utterly taken out of his sails. 'To the City, My Lord,' Poley prompted, like the devil in Marlowe's play of *Faustus*. 'To make the citizens rise in revolt.'

Southampton emphasised Poley's words as he advised,

'Think, My Lord, the bells for morning prayer have sounded. If we organise our time as well as our forces, we will arrive in the City just as the congregations are all coming out. All of London will be on the streets and able to hear our message.'

'Especially somewhere like Paul's Cross,' added Cuffe, 'where great crowds gather on Sundays in any case to hear the preachers. Today, they will hear you instead.'

'And rise at your word as you plan,' added Poley once more.

'Not to mention that Paul's Cross is but a stone's throw from Sheriff Smythe's house and he has often sworn to support you,' concluded Southampton. Somewhat hopefully, thought Poley. Sheriff Smythe lived on Gracechurch Street, a goodly number of stone throws from St Paul's. But who was he to argue? Especially as the Earl seemed to be stiffening his sinews and summoning up his blood at last, as Burbage had put it, playing *Henry The Fifth* at the Globe, just as Essex was leaving for Ireland; the last time Poley had seen a performance at the theatre.

The Earl swept forward, clattering down the stairs as the crowd parted to let him past then closed ranks to follow him. Down the stairs, across the entrance hall and out onto the top step. 'Open the great gates!' he ordered. Then he realised he was not yet armed. But Fitzherbert once more rose to his rescue. 'Your sword, My Lord,' he said and Essex raised his arms as the faithful servant buckled his belt in place. 'And your standard.' Fitzherbert's son Tom pushed to the Earl's side, holding a banner with the distinctively complicated Essex coat of arms high and proud.

The Earl ran down the steps and into the yard with Tom his page hard on his heels. The excited mob of his supporters, still not quite organised, parted before him and he strode towards the slowly opening gates. Beyond them lay the Strand, which as far as Poley could see was utterly deserted. Even the guards who had escorted Council's messengers had vanished. At the threshold, Essex hesitated once more. As he looked back it must have been obvious to him that his senior officers had not yet organised his army of followers. But he had opened the great gates and could not wait any longer now. He glanced across at the stable beside the smithy. His thoughts were clear as day. Should he ride into the city? To do so would elevate him, make his position more powerful, establish him as the leader. But that had already been done by Tom Fitzherbert and his banner. Riding would also make his plan of addressing crowds and congregations more difficult. A moving and convincing speech could all too easily be ruined by a restless mount.

*

As he stood there, characteristically hesitant, Sir Christopher Blount strode past him, taking a contingent with him to form a vanguard. He pulled out his sword, and began shouting. Such was the clamour in the yard that Poley couldn't really hear what Sir Christopher was saying; but it sounded to him like, 'Saw, saw, saw. Trey, trey, trey!'

As Sir Christopher's men moved out into The Strand, the Earl at last committed himself. He pulled out his sword and turned to the men behind him. 'For the Queen!' he shouted. 'For the Queen!' And he too strode out into the Strand young Tom Fitzherbert staunchly at his side, the Essex coat of arms high and bright on the dull, misty morning. Poley stood and watched. For once, the intelligencer was hesitant himself. Every fibre of his being demanded that he follow and see this madness through to its end. But his mission was complete. There was no more for him to do. In spite of what he was shouting, the Earl of Essex was leading an army out into the City in direct contravention of the will of Queen and Council. It was High Treason and there was no going back from that. Not now. Not ever. Master Secretary had won. Without having been involved in the situation at all, except as the Earl's apparent friend and wise councillor, he had pulled off his deadly trick just as planned. He had caused the Earl destroy himself. Absolutely and utterly. Whatever happened this day, Essex had nothing left to look forward to but the Tower, the block and the axe.

But then Cuffe was at Poley's shoulder, fizzing with excitement. 'Come, dear Robert,' he said. 'We stand at the dawn of a brave new day! Let us go and see history being made! Perhaps even make a little history ourselves, what say you?' And before he knew it, Poley was down the steps, across the yard and out into the Strand with the rest. He and Cuffe joined what looked in truth very much like the mob that Southampton, Gelly Meyrick and the others had been ordered to organise into some semblance of order. The fact that their leader had set off before they could do so and they had simply given up was soon made clear when Southampton pushed past Poley astride a horse. Baron Cromwell followed him, also mounted. The Strand was now packed with Essex's supporters, many waving their swords, most of them shouting. The horses slowed, unable to push any further through the press of people, but Southampton yelled, 'Make way there!'. He and Cromwell walked their horses more quickly and Poley pulled Cuffe into the space they left behind them so that the two of them could also make faster progress. Also, noted Poley, the road widened as they came to St Clement Danes. But it was here that the first whisper of trouble appeared. The two horses and the two men behind them caught up with the Earl, who was standing, frowning as he looked towards the great old church. 'What is it?' asked Southampton.

'I was expecting the congregation to come out and join us, the first of all the churches that we pass by. But they haven't and Sir Christopher tells me they've even shut their doors against us.'

'No doubt the fearsome spectacle we present has frighted them,' said Southampton bracingly. 'Let us go on. I'm sure the people will join in behind us when they realise what's a'foot. And you still have your great speech to make at St Paul's Cross.'

But Essex still hesitated; which was fortunate in one way at least, thought Poley, for it allowed Monteagle, the Percys, Gelly Meyrick and Fernando Gorges to catch up with him. They were also all on foot and were quick to form a protective ring around him, as though he was in fact leading his two-hundred man army into battle, banner flying bravely.

'I'll go on ahead,' announced Baron Cromwell as they closed ranks. 'Sheriff Smythe should be at his home in Gracechurch Street as soon as he has returned from church. I'll tell him what's going on so that he can start organising his people. It was the apprentices, was it not, and the City Watch that he had promised?'

'Very well,' said Essex. 'I will be there in person soon after noon. Tell him…' But Cromwell had already eased his horse through the men following Sir Christopher who was now marching towards Temple Bar and Fleet Street. The Earl looked around at the houses lining the roadway here. All their doors were closed but their upstairs windows were open. As far as the eye could see, stony faces were gazing down on him and his men. 'For the Queen!' he shouted up at them. 'We march for the Queen. Her Council have sold us all to Spain. We must rescue the Queen from them or we will soon have the Infanta upon her throne!'

*

He had just started to march forward once again when Sir Charles Davers pushed through, also on horseback. 'The Council have closed off Whitehall at Charing Cross to our rear,' he said grimly. 'They have mobilised their troops and barricaded the road.'

'What does that matter to us if they close that door after we have already left?' demanded Essex a little wildly. 'We are marching on the City, not on Charing Cross! What is the next church we pass?'

'St Dunstan's in the West,' answered Cuffe. 'I'm sure

that congregation will join us, despite St Clement Danes' reluctance.'

Reassured, Essex nodded and set off, sword high, shouting, 'For the Queen!'

But no supportive crowds came boiling out of Bell Yard or Chancery Lane as Essex led his army past them. And, noted Poley, the doors of St Dunstan's in the West remained as resolutely closed as did those of St Clement Danes. The windows all along Fleet Street stood wide but the doors beneath them also remained shut. Even Fetter Lane, also to their left, was utterly empty and when he looked up it in passing, and, had it not been for the wild cries of Essex and his followers, it would have been eerily silent, especially for a Sabbath. Nevertheless, they pushed on, past Hanging Sword Court on their right, past the Fleet Street conduit which stood in the little square at the end of Shoe Lane on their left with Salisbury Court on their right. Salisbury Court led down to Salisbury House where the hated Cecil might be squatting even now. It was short enough to tempt Essex to attack the house it led to, thought Poley. But it was so narrow the army would have to go in single-file along it and even in this mood, Essex had to see how dangerous that would be. So, on they strode over the Fleet Bridge and onto Ludgate Hill. Then on down the hill, past the end of Old Bailey to the Lud Gate. 'Named for an ancient king of Britain,' Cuffe explained. 'It is said that King Lud built London even before the Romans came and that he is buried hereabouts.'

Poley nodded. Whoever it was named after, Lud Gate was impressive. He found it odd that he had never really thought of it as a fortification before. Never really considered the walls that stretched away on either side of it as possessing any military significance. But then, he thought, he had never before been part of an army invading the City beyond. It stood nearly five stories high, more than forty feet by his reckoning, extended in its centre to fifty feet or so by a tower. At street level, it followed the traditional pattern of many other gates. There were two smaller openings for pedestrians, ten feet high and four feet wide. These stood on either side of a wider, taller opening some twenty feet high and more than fifteen feet wide designed to accommodate the road and any traffic passing up and down it. As he and Cuffe followed Essex, his gaudy banner, and his immediate supporters along the roadway beneath the central arch, Poley glanced up. There was even a portcullis there, held in its fully elevated position. He idly wondered whether it could be lowered or whether, like the entire fortification, its primary function was little more than decorative these days. But then his attention switched from looking upward to looking forward, for there at the bottom of Ludgate Hill stood St Paul's Cathedral.

It seemed to Poley that the ancient cathedral might well have stood as a symbol for much that Essex was fighting against. The shell of the great old building had fallen on hard times in so many ways. Farmers drove their sheep to market through it. Starving beggars sought refuge against the elements within it – shelter but scant relief. And, depending where such wretches chose to shiver, scant shelter in any case. The great steeple had been struck by lightning three years after the Queen ascended her throne, and collapsed, tearing a great hole in the roof. The damage had been lauded by her enemies as an act of God against the heretic queen, bastard spawn of a heretic king. But whether or not that had been the case, nothing had been done – or even attempted – by way of repair. Poley knew many a foreign visitor who had been shocked into simple disbelief that nothing had been done to restore such a holy site. It had once been the jewel of London. Now, like much of the rest of the city, it stood in dire need of love and money. Money that all too easily found it way into the coffers of the Council and their acolytes instead of into the welfare of the city and its citizens.

The churchyard itself was a vast market where, on an average day, a man might purchase everything from a book to a bawd; a slim volume of odes to a goodly basket of oranges. But today was clearly no average day, thought Poley grimly. St Paul's churchyard was all-but deserted. The Cross Yard in the far section of the cathedral grounds was usually packed with men and women eager to hear whoever was preaching from the open-air pulpit that stood there. It was this pulpit from which the Earl planned to deliver his rousing speech. But it seemed to Poley that the only people there to hear it were the men already following Essex, Southampton and the rest. Well over a hundred spilled into the churchyard, joining Sir Christopher's vanguard who were waiting, hesitant, around the empty pulpit. More than two hundred armed men thronged the place, waiting for their leaders to reveal the next section of their plan to rouse the city and take control of the council, court and country.

*

Because he had planned to do so, the Earl climbed into the pulpit and looked down on his assembled troops. Because he had planned to give a speech and could think of nothing else to do, he began to speak. 'We are the last hope for our beloved Queen and our country. Look around. You can see that the men her Majesty is surrounded by have nothing in their minds but the acquisition of money and power. Money and power which they simply pass to their offspring never thinking about their country and its citizens. Her Majesty must one day yield to time and nature, the same as any mortal being. They know that, and their desire to cling to power has led them to look to Spain for the succession. They will put the Infanta on our throne so that their grasp on power will never be loosened. And they know too well that we are the only men to stop them. Only we can thwart their plans and...'

The crowd stirred. Monteagle and the Percy brothers forced their way through. 'My Lord!' called Monteagle. 'The Council have closed the churches. Every one has been ordered to keep their doors closed and their congregations must remain inside until we have passed them by. It is not that no-one wishes to follow you. No-one *can*!'

'And, worse than that, My Lord,' called one of the Percy brothers, though Poley could not see which. 'Lord Burghley is out with a squad of heralds...'

'I shot at him,' said the other brother. 'But I missed...'

'You are declared traitor My Lord,' concluded

Monteagle. 'You and all we who follow you. Traitors.'

Amid the angry outcry that greeted this announcement, the Earl climbed down from the pulpit, but stopped half way when his head was on the same level as those of his mounted followers. Poley and Cuffe were close enough to hear his muttered conversation with Southampton. 'It is Sheriff Smythe we must rely on now,' said Essex. 'He must help us or all is lost. And I must reach him before this word that we are called traitors does.' He looked around desperately and Poley shook his head as Southampton realised that Gracechurch Street was much more than a stone's throw away. Sir Charles Danvers provided an answer. 'Baron Cromwell has gone on ahead, My Lord, and will have warned the Sheriff of your approach. Take my horse and you will be in Gracechurch Street all the sooner.'

He dismounted and stood beside young Tom Fitzherbert, ruffling his hair. 'Your page, your colours and I will lead your footsoldiers on behind you, fear not!'

Poley frowned. He might have joined this rag-tag army at Cuffe's request, but now that he was here he wanted to stay as close to Essex as possible. Something he would find it hard to do if the Earl galloped off on Danvers' horse.

'But My Lord!' he said, the urgency in his tone freezing Essex in the act of mounting. 'To go on ahead alone. And mounted! You would present such a perfect target! Lord Burghley has been shot at. So I believe has been Sir Walter Raleigh. You could all too easily be gunned down were you to go on horseback. We have gained not one gesture of support from the men and women looking down from their windows on either side of the streets. Who's to say some of them might not be working for the Council, or friends of Sir Walter Raleigh, seeking revenge?'

Essex stepped back down. 'A fair point,' he allowed. He raised his voice. 'Come then, my brave companions, let us march to Gracechurch street together. Let my banner lead the way. FOR THE QUEEN!' he bellowed and was off, with Tom Fitzherbert at his side.

They followed him, flooding into the streets behind him and spreading from side to side until the walls and doors of the houses on either hand contained them like a river in spate. The mass of bodies was so tight-packed, that those on horseback, led by the Earl of Southampton, observed Poley, soon left to find alternative routes. Those on foot quick-marched behind the Earl along Watling Street, then straight on into Budge Row and London Stone before turning left into Abchurch Lane which led to Lombard Street and so along to the right turn that took them down into Gracechurch. 'It is like the German legend of the Pied Piper,' said Cuffe excitedly, his eyes shining. Poley, who knew the ancient story from his travels in Saxony, cynically wondered whether that made them all spellbound rats – or doomed children.

*

Gracechurch Street was home to the Leadenhall Market. It was closed for the Sabbath. But, reckoned Poley, even had it been open it would have been empty – just like the streets they had been following to get here. Just like, indeed, the Cross Keys tavern where he and Joan Yeomans had been accosted by Wolfall, Frizer and Skeres on the day his downfall began.

Sheriff Smythe's house was doubly easy to find because it was opposite the tavern and Baron Cromwell's horse was standing tethered outside it. The Earl went in. Poley and Cuffe crowded close behind. There was no room for them in the house itself and no question of actually entering. But they could see in through the ground floor windows that the Sheriff was greeting the Earl with all due form and courtesy. But the expression on his face was hard to read. Which, thought Poley, was sinister in itself. The conversation became so animated that those, like Cuffe and Poley, who could see into the room started to become restless. Baron Cromwell came out with a report as to what was going on in the hope that it would ease the tension. 'Sheriff Smythe says that his hands are tied,' he shouted. 'He cannot lift a finger until he gets permission from the Lord Mayor William Ryder. The Earl has given him permission to go and see the mayor at once. We will await his return.'

That was all.

As they stood there thronging Gracechurch Street, it started to rain; an icy, sleety rain. Those who had thought to bring cloaks as well as swords in that first fine frenzy when they streamed out into the Strand, pulled then tight. Those who had not, stood and shivered. Cuffe and Poley were amongst the latter group. The chill gripping their bones made worsened by what they could see inside the Sheriff's house. The Earl was apparently so hot, his shirt was soaked with sweat. He took off his doublet and, with

Sir Christopher's assistance, pulled his shirt off altogether, scrubbing his chest and armpits with the bunched-up linen. Then he threw it aside and called for a clean one. The Sheriff's household hurried to obey but no sooner was the Earl fully dressed again than he was calling for service once more.

It was early afternoon now and, like his shivering army outside, the Earl had consumed nothing but bread and small beer so far today. A fat capon obviously destined to be the Sheriff's Sunday dinner appeared in front of the Earl who tucked in apparently without a second thought, pausing only to offer a leg to Cromwell and a wing to Sir Christopher. He was certainly paying scant attention to the hungry men standing shivering outside. He had just eaten his fill, when the mounted contingent arrived, led by Southampton and Fernando Gorges. It was clear that they had taken time to get cloaks and hats; and, from the look of them, thought Poley, they had also dined. They dismounted and crowded into the room with their leader. Several bottles of wine appeared. But as their leaders ate and drank, a whisper seemed to percolate through the assembled troops. 'Sheriff Smythe will not return. There is no army of apprentices ready to aid us. Lord Mayor Rider will not help. He has declared the Earl a traitor and has had the news heralded through the City, just as Lord Burghley has. Anyone who leaves now will not be charged. Anyone who stays, dies.'

'Can this be true?' Cuffe was aghast.

'It seems likely enough,' said Poley grimly.

'Then we are lost!'

'There was always a chance it might come to this,' observed Poley gently, with genuine sympathy. He was simply torn between his duty as he saw it to the Council, Cecil and the Queen and the friendship and duty his undercover self owed the men and women who had taken him in and befriended him. Who, in short, he had betrayed in return. In all his long experience in this dark game he was playing, he had never felt so conflicted. Not even when young Thomas Babbington, in the midst of the most horrible and agonising death imaginable called, 'Do not hurt my poor Robert…' because the poor deluded lad was still in love with the man who had betrayed him, his associates and the captive queen he worshipped.

As much to get away from Cuffe's uncomprehending, pleading eyes, Poley took action. He crossed to the Sheriff's door and pushed it open. He strode in past Cromwell before the surprised young Baron could stop him. And he entered the room that Essex occupied with his aristocratic friends. 'My Lords,' he said to the men grouped round the table. 'Neither the Sheriff nor the Mayor will aid you. You are called traitors all throughout the City and for all I know all throughout the land. Your cause is lost.' He turned on his heel and left.

*

Striding out through the door once more, Poley was struck by the manner in which the Earl's army had shrunk. For the last hour and more they had been behind him as he looked in through the window into the sheriff's house. Now he was looking directly at them and it was plain to see that more than half of them had slunk away. The men and women living on Gracechurch Street, including the Smythe family, were still watching events from their upper windows, as though this was some pageant being enacted for their benefit. A pageant that had started out as a History, but was descending into Tragedy. And, soon enough into Farce, he suspected.

Southampton and Fernando Gorges led the Earl's inner circle out into the icy drizzle of the afternoon. The Earl followed them, cloaked, hatted and nearing the end of his tether. 'We do this for the Queen!' he bellowed up at his audience, whose stony faces showed how completely they were unmoved either by his appeals or by his predicament. 'It is the Council who are the traitors! They do not seek the Queen's good or the country's! They only seek to enrich themselves and their offspring. They only seek to be certain of clinging to power once Her Majesty finally yields to the dictates of time and mortality. They do not care who succeeds to the throne as long as they can control the new monarch, make sure of their powers and privileges and let the rest of us all go hang or burn! They have sucked the wealth out of the city and the country like the leeches and lampreys that they are!'

In the echoing silence that greeted his agonised pronouncement, a lone, anonymous, voice called. 'You and your fucking Irish army! That's what leeched the good out of me and mine! And much good has it done any or all of us.'

The Earl span wildly around. 'Who… Who… Who…' He choked on his rage and fell into gasping and coughing. Poley was almost sorry for the man.

Almost.

'Come away, Robert,' said Southampton gently. 'Let us return to Essex House and review the situation. The place is well fortified and easy enough to defend if the Queen will have it so. And we will still be able to send her messages directly.'

'And we have four hostages, remember,' added Fernando Gorges. 'Important men, friends to the Council…'

'Very well then,' said Essex. 'Back to Essex House. Come, my brave lads. Follow me home!'

''Tis always darkest before the dawn,' said Poley quietly as though plucking the platitudes from the Earl's own lips, his tone dripping with bitter irony. 'Stand by me shoulder to shoulder and we can win through yet!'

'Well said, dear Robert,' said Cuffe. 'That is the spirit which will help us to victory!'

Poley could not bring himself to answer. Instead he fell in beside his all-too-gullible friend and turned to follow their leader. Someone had managed to get a spare horse and the Earl was helped into the saddle. Then, with a glance around, he set off, with Tom Fitzherbert at the mount's right shoulder, thew Essex coat of arms held high and proud. The mounted contingent walked their horses; Essex's and Southampton's experiences in Ireland teaching them the dangers of letting cavalry get too far ahead of infantry in a potentially dangerous situation. The infantry that followed close behind the horses now, however, was a mere shadow of its former self. If Essex realised that his troops had melted away – as so many had done in Ireland – he gave no sign. Fernando Gorges, however, kept glancing pensively over his shoulder, as did Cromwell and Sir Christopher. The weather moderated swiftly so that the mid-afternoon was dry with watery sunshine giving a little almost illusory warmth. The improved weather did not lead to any improvement in the atmosphere, however, thought Poley. The audience had grown bored with the pageant and the upper windows were as tight closed as the lower windows and the doors. The streets they followed, Gracechurch, Lombard, Abchurch and Watling Street with its easterly extensions, back to Paul's Churchyard remained eerily silent and deserted.

Until they reached Lud Gate.

*

Poley had been struck by the gate's military potential on the way in when he considered it as part of the city's fortification for the first time. Those thoughts returned in force as the Earl led his modest army out of the north side of Paul's Churchyard and into the wide space by Bowyer Row. Ave Maria Lane ran north between the house fronts on their right, hardly wide enough to accommodate two men walking side by side; and Creed Lane, even narrower, ran south between those on their left. Other than those, the approach to Lud Gate was literally walled in with tall buildings, all shuttered, barred and bolted. It was as though the Earl and his men were moving into a funnel with brick and plaster sides, Poley thought, a funnel whose only possible exit was Lud Gate itself.

It was a situation made immediately worse by two things, Poley realised, his mind racing. The first was that the army behind them, modest though it was, was pressing relentlessly forward, all heading for Essex House. The second was that Lud Gate was closed. They had not lowered the portcullis but they had stretched a chain across it at waist height. Behind the chain, using it as a rest for their weapons, knelt a line of musketeers, their firelocks primed, smoking and ready to fire. Behind them, their barrels steady on the forks of their musket rests, stood another line. Behind them, it was just possible to see rank upon rank of soldiers, waiting, like their friends in the artillery, for the order to engage the enemy.

The horsemen in the lead reined to a stop. The first ranks of foot soldiers, including Cuffe, Poley and Tom Fitzherbert, were thrust past them, and were soon positioned between their commanders and the gate. Not a very safe position to be in, Poley realised. He glanced down at Tom Fitzherbert and saw only a look of shining confidence on the young standard bearer's face. He looked across at Cuffe; whose face shone, if anything, even more brightly. The same look as transfigured the countenances of Christian martyrs in the Roman Coliseum, he thought. Until the lions came.

There was a moment of silence then a tall, square-shouldered man of middle years stepped into the one space left at the right-hand end of the musket line. He paused, waiting for everyone's attention to focus on him. He wore a steel breastplate and a crested helmet, both of which glittered coldly in the light of the westering sun. There was a broadsword at his side. One gauntleted fist rested on its pommel. 'I am Sir John Leveson, my Lords,' he said, his voice filling the space despite the restlessness of Essex's men. 'I command this unit of soldiery here at the behest of the Earl of Cumberland and the Lord Bishop of London, under orders of the Queen and Council. I request you, my Lords to surrender yourselves to me. No harm will come to you and you will be held pending trial for high treason against the Crown and State.'

Poley turned back just in time to see Essex lean towards Sir Ferdinando. 'Go and tell him we are merely seeking to make a peaceful return to Essex house. That and no more. Tell him.'

Sit Fernando spurred forward and delivered the message just as though Leveson could not have heard the Earl's words himself.

But the old soldier answered formally, playing the game. 'Sadly I must refuse the Earl's request. Please inform him that my orders are to hold this gate until the Earl and his accomplices surrender or retreat.'

It was strangely theatrical, almost biblical, thought Poley, watching as the ritual was repeated time after time. Three more times to be exact, as tension grew and patience diminished on either side. Then someone in the ranks of Essex's army fired a gun. The bullet sang past Poley's head and, by his calculation, must have buzzed past Leveson's ear as well.

The front rank of musketeers opened fire in return, even as Leveson bellowed, 'Hold your fire. Hold fire dam you!' Poley had leaped back as the first shot whizzed by and he had pushed Cuffe out of the line of fire as well. Acrid gun smoke rolled into the circumscribed space. The sound was overwhelming. The horses reared and curvetted, terrified but unhurt. Several leading foot soldiers collapsed and several more started screaming with pain as the musket bullets took their toll. But Poley was paying no attention to any of this. He was looking at Tom Fitzherbert. The lad was standing, staring down in simple horror. There was a huge red stain spreading rapidly across the breast of his doublet. He looked up at Poley, his face ashen and his eyes huge. 'What?' he asked. The Earl's banner fell out of his hand and clattered into the gutter, all that gaudy brightness dulled and soiled in an instant. He coughed. A fountain of blood gushed out of his mouth. He collapsed and crashed to the ground, stone dead at Poley's feet.

*

'Forward!' bellowed Essex and led his force forward in a wild charge.

'Fire,' called Leveson.

The Earl led his troops straight into the barrage of musket balls. A man-high wall of smoke rolled forward. It was thick enough to choke the men nearest to the chain – those who hadn't been cut down by the bullets. The horses reared and turned aside, screaming. Surely to God, thought Poley as he dashed a hand down his face to clear his streaming eyes, Southampton as an ex-General of Horse should have known the poor beasts were useless in this situation. What did he expect – that they would jump over Leveson's troops like a hedge during a hunt? At least the mounted earls, lords and assorted knights had the sense to pull their horses back, preparing to dismount. The foot soldiers charged on through, swords drawn and thirsting for a fight. And this was the best moment for a direct assault. The musketeers, having discharged their guns were moving aside to reload. The ranks of infantry behind them were moving up towards the chain barrier, still drawing their swords and disposing their pikes, getting ready to engage Essex's men. As Sir Christopher led the charge, Poley pulled Tom's corpse out from under foot. But when he straightened from doing this, he realised that Cuffe had gone. A glance at the narrow battle-front showed him that Cuffe had joined the others, hacking and stabbing wildly, hard up against the chain. The noise, intensified by the walls confining the battle, was incredible.

The whole thing was pointless, thought Poley bitterly. There was no way for the Earl's army to overcome Leveson's disciplined soldiers. No way for them to win through, take down the chain and open the way to Essex House. Someone had to point this out to their general before the killing got really serious. And Poley once again was just the man to do so. The Earl and Fernando Gorges were the last men still mounted, and as Poley approached them, he heard Essex order. '… by water back to Essex House. Set Popham free. Let him take the message to the Queen and Council. But only Popham. We will need the others as bargaining counters should things grow any worse. Tell Sir John Davis and Owen Salisbury. Remember: only Popham. Hurry!'

Gorges wrenched the head of his mount round and disappeared into Paul's Churchyard. Poley moved forward once again but the Earl also wrenched his horse's head round. To face the opposite way to Gorges. 'Once more, lads,' he yelled, and charged the gate once more. Moved by memories of Rouen and Cadiz, no doubt. Or seeing himself perhaps as Henry V at Harfleur charging for the breach in the French walls. And, miraculously, his men surged forward with him. Poley ran forward at the Earl's side, looking for Cuffe, trying to work out whether – how – he could extricate him from the battle and the fatal charge of treason.

'Well; done my gallant soldier! Onwards. Onwards.' called Essex. Poley glanced up and gasped. The Earl was talking to him, mistaking his wild attempt to get Cuffe clear of this murderous debacle as the bravery of a trooper, loyal unto death.

And the need to reach Cuffe suddenly became even more urgent. The infantry fighting hand to hand suddenly stepped aside and the first rank of musketeers reappeared. Just as they did so, Poley at last caught sight of Cuffe, right in the heart of it all, fighting at Sir Christopher's side. Poley did not hesitate. He dived forward and managed to catch Cuffe round the waist, his shoulder driving into the small of Cuffe's back. The pair of them toppled sideways and crashed to the ground. The momentum of Poley's charge rolled them beneath the chain, against the feet of the musketeers just at the very moment that they fired. With his back to the enemy's shins, half on top of Cuffe, Poley got an odd but vivid view of what happened next. Essex's hat flew off. His head snapped back and he rolled backwards off his horse as it reared in panic. For a moment, Poley thought Essex was dead. But no. He picked himself up, looking around in confusion. And he saw what Poley only felt. The first rank of musketeers was being replaced by the second.

'Back!' cried Essex. 'Retreat! Withdraw my brave lads! Withdraw!'

By the time the Earl had babbled the final word of this order, Poley had managed to pull himself to his feet, still with his back to Leveson's men.

'Hold your fire!' ordered the old commander, unwilling to have retreating soldiers shot in the back; especially as some of them had, in all probability, served with him in the past, thought Poley. Not to mention the fact that, treasonous or not, the flower of English aristocracy was among them. But then he realised, with a stab of pure horror, that there was a group of men, led by Sir Christopher supported by Lady Janet's relatives the Percys, whose blood was up; who had no intention of disengaging or retreating.

'Charge!' roared Sir Christopher and hurled himself forward.

'Fire,' ordered Leveson.

The noise was so great that Poley was disoriented by it. He stepped forward into yet another wall of smoke, dreamily aware that there were burning motes of powder and packing all around him, floating on the choking air, landing on the bare flesh of his neck, face and hands like wasp-stings. He thought perhaps his hair and beard would catch fire. Only the fact that he had been so close to the musketeers and posing no threat to them had saved him. But what had that final fusillade done to Sir Christopher and his men?

*

The answer came staggering out of the smoke immediately in front of him, given motion only by the power of his original charge. It was Sir Christopher. But half his face was missing. His left cheek, from cheekbone to jawline, from nostril to ear had been blown away. Poley could see the tight-clenched teeth, the gums in which they were bedded, the bones that held the gums in place. Muscles and tendons like an anatomist's drawing all awash with blood. The horrific gargoyle crashed into Poley with surprising force, knocking him back one step after another. The terrible wound seemed to have given the fainting Sir Christopher great weight, added to the power of his last full charge. Poley was driven yet further back. He tripped over Cuffe and felt himself falling. The chain hit him across his hips, below his sword belt, just above his buttocks. He toppled helplessly backwards over it and crashed to the ground at the feet of the musketeers, with Sir Christopher sill on top of him. The back of his skull smacked into the cobbles of the road beneath the gate, Sir Christopher's forehead crashed into Poley's forehead like a cannon ball made of bone, smashing consciousness into unconsciousness with a single blow.

Poley woke up instantly. Or at least so it seemed at first. His head hurt fiercely, both at the back and at the front. He opened his eyes and realised he could not have woken immediately after he was knocked unconscious, though the sight of Sir Christopher's face was still vivid in his memory. He looked around. He was in a stone-walled cell, lying on a makeshift bed. A couple of candles on a low table gave sufficient illumination for him to see. He supposed at once that he was back where this mission had begun – in the Fleet prison. But no. The stench of gunpowder lingered on the air. Unless the smell was coming from his own clothes, he must still be quite near the battlefield, though he could no longer hear the sounds of battle. Still close to Lud Gate, therefore. A room in the gate house maybe. He tried to sit up. His head swam. He felt sick. Perhaps it was as well that his belly was empty. He persisted grimly, determined to find out what was going on. He had just managed to swing his legs out of bed and sit on the edge when the door opened and Nick Skeres swaggered in. 'Awake at last,' he said. 'Good.'

Poley said nothing.

'You're lucky to be alive,' continued Skeres. 'Word is you've been playing both sides against the middle.'

'What? How?' Poley demanded.

'Was it you not who fired at poor old Leveson?' queried Skeres. 'Nearly frightened him to death!'

'What? No.' Poley went to shake his head. He stopped at once; the room seemed to rock as though Lud Gate were afloat..

'And Master Secretary's big brother Lord Burghley,' Skeres continued. 'Someone took a shot at him too, I'm told…'

'Who has been saying…' Poley stopped half way through the question.

'Well, it was certainly you who shot at Sir Walter Raleigh this morning,' Skeres continued, regardless of

Poley's interruption. 'We have Fernando Gorges' word on that. No. Don't deny it. He came and reported to Master Secretary as soon as he had released the Earl's hostages. Wise man. Might just have saved his neck. You'll need to be careful yourself if you want to save yours.'

'What? Why?' Poley suspected all too well what the answer to that would be.

'Master Secretary Cecil wants to see you.' Confirmed Skeres. 'He wants to see you at once.'

11

Robert Cecil, Chief Secretary to the Council, looked up at the scaffold, then around the green at the heart of the Tower. The chilly rain of a late-February morning caused him to shiver, even though he was wrapped in a thick cloak and had his hat pulled low. Was it only the cold, wondered Poley, or was it the tension that seemed to be mounting with every heartbeat? 'It is as though the Earl and I have been duelling for so long,' said Cecil quietly, 'that our wounds have all begun to fester. I rely on you to draw out the poison from mine so that I can deal with his legacy equably and with no residual malice.'

Poley knew what Cecil meant, and what he had to do. Convention demanded that Cecil take his place with the other witnesses to Robert Devereux's execution. There must be a hundred of them arranged around Tower Green. They were placed far enough back from the scaffold to see justice being done. But too far away to experience the procedure in any depth. The Queen's desire for the same level of detail explained why Francis Bacon was standing nearby. But, thought Poley, Her Majesty could also have demanded the same thing from her Captain of the Guard. For Sir Walter Raleigh was standing as close on Poley's left as Bacon stood on his right.

'Remember,' said Cecil. 'Every element, no matter how trivial.' He paused, oddly hesitant. This was his moment of victory, thought Poley. And yet he simply wasn't enjoying it. Cecil went to take his place amongst the other more distant dignitaries, shaking his head sadly, as though he was the loser in this long dark game after all. Poley himself had nodded agreement to Cecil's orders only to catch his breath at the sudden stab of agony. He had forgotten how much it could still hurt when he moved his head suddenly, though the bruise at the front and the lump at the back were both well healed now. Without thinking, he probed beneath his hair and winced. Well healed but still tender, he thought.

Poley and Bacon stood silently as the tension continued to mount. But Raleigh's way of handling the growing suspense was the opposite of theirs. He talked non-stop to his lieutenant in a low voice that nevertheless carried to Poley quite clearly. And Poley was happy enough to listen, for he too felt the quickening of heart and fluttering in his throat that betrayed in him the tension of someone who had come within an inch of sharing the same fate. Not a formal, almost private execution, such as the Earl had been granted, but hanging before the baying mob at Tyburn. Hanging - and perhaps drawing and quartering. The fate that Gelly Meyrick and Henry Cuffe were doomed to. He had seen that done and just the thought of it happening to him made his scrotum clench.

Master Secretary was still of the opinion that it could well have been Poley who shot at his brother Lord Burghley and Sir John Leveson as they deployed town criers and armed troops over the City announcing that Essex was a traitor and arranging to defeat him by force of arms. And, three times, at Sir Walter – as the turncoat

Fernando Gorges testified. Not to mention the fact that the Earl himself had singled out Cuffe and Poley as the men who had prompted him most forcefully to rise in revolt and lead an army into the City in the end. Coupling them with his sister Penelope Rich as the individuals most responsible for what he had done. Cecil was still deciding whether Poley's name should be expunged from the records or whether he should simply share Cuffe's fate and close the matter for ever. In the meantime Poley had his freedom – on condition that he obeyed Cecil's orders in every detail, no matter how distasteful they were.

But the intelligencer's thoughts were tempted out of this dark tunnel by Sir Walter's broad west-country tones. 'Leveson closed off London and went about trapping the Earl and his army within it while troops from the Tower began to scour the streets. Leveson's men did well. They covered everything from Lud Gate, moving eastwards: closed all the gates to the north and also the stairs and wharves to the south along the River. Blackfriars Stairs, Paul's Wharf and Broken Wharf were all in loyal hands by the time Essex called retreat. So he had to run as far as Queenshythe before he could actually get to the water and hail a wherry. Then, when he got back to Essex House the first thing he discovered was that Fernando had released all the prisoners and come over to our side. Sir John Davis and Owen Salisbury had simply cut and run.'

'But Essex still set up some kind of resistance? Even then?' The lieutenant, like Captain Raleigh, had been guarding the Queen's person – especially as she showed every intention of taking herself into the City and challenging her errant favourite face to face, secure in her belief that her people loved her and would stand by her no matter what. But the young lieutenant lacked Sir Walter's wide circle of contacts and so what the older man had discovered was news to him.

'He did,' continued Raleigh. 'But it was as well organised as his attack on the City. Which is to say, not at all.'

*

'The Strand was filled with our troops,' Raleigh continued. 'Essex House steps were seized and closed. He and Southampton blockaded the doors and windows as best they could, then went up onto the leads of the roof and called down that they would bring up their own musketeers to destroy any force attempting entry through the main gates. There was a short stand off which led to a truce while the women and children were released. Lady Lettice was long gone to her house in Drayton Bassett. I doubt she'll ever see Sir Christopher again. And that's all to the good, considering the state of his face. Lady Penelope Rich was arrested on the spot. I hear Rich is considering a divorce and you can hardly blame him for that, given her activities. And, of course, her time as Mountjoy's mistress.'

Raleigh paused. Took a deep breath that seemed to Poley to shudder a little. Then he continued, 'But Lady Frances and the children were treated well. Once the women were clear, Leveson simply informed those men still in the house that he was bringing the cannons down from the Tower here and he was quite willing to pound Essex House to rubble with them inside it. At last Essex capitulated. Came out. Surrendered his sword. Cried. Begged to send a message to the Queen asking for mercy. He and Southampton were taken to Lambeth Palace immediately and brought here later, when their accommodation had been prepared. Southampton's in the White Tower. Essex was in the Devil's Tower. He was there until this morning, that is. It has a secret passageway directly to the Church of St Peter ad Vincula, where Essex is now, surrounded by clergymen and praying that God forgives him as the Queen hasn't. There was never any doubt that he would need to use the tunnel or the chapel. And the church of Saint Peter in Chains is where he'll be buried. Just beside Her Majesty's mother Queen Anne, I'm told.'

Raleigh fell silent. But after a few more agonising moments, he glanced away from the scaffold and the block, turned on his heel and marched off. He paused after a few steps and turned back to look at his lieutenant. 'Master Secretary Cecil is not the only one of us sorely scarred by years of duelling with the Earl,' he said. 'I will observe matters from a distance. If you need me I will be up in the Armoury.' He gestured at the great keep of the White Tower and strode off towards it, head bowed; looking almost as defeated as Cecil.

Silence flowed back, except for the restlessness of the waiting witnesses and the blustering of the wintery wind. 'You know how many we arrested?' asked Bacon quietly.

'More than a hundred, I heard,' answered Poley.

'That's right.' Bacon nodded.

'But not so many charged and fewer still condemned,'

continued Poley.

'You'll understand the reasoning behind that.' Bacon's tone let the words hang between a statement and a question. A lawyer's trick, thought Poley.

'Aye,' said the intelligencer. 'The more men charged, especially noble men, the greater weight Essex's argument becomes that they were a band of well-meaning knights and lords, like knights of the Round Table, looking to save the Faery Queen from grasping commoners like Master Secretary. Who may have a title and whose brother may have a title but it goes back one mere generation.'

'So does Essex's.' Bacon countered.

'True. But of course Essex is the Queen's cousin.'

'Twice removed, if I understand genealogy,' Bacon's tone made it clear that he did. 'But yes, descended from the Bolyens and the Howards who trace their lines back and back.'

'So, fines for the others, Monteagle, Cromwell and so-forth. Nooses for the commoners of course. Even petty knights count for little more than common folk, especially if Essex dubbed them. And Southampton?'

Bacon glanced up at the White Tower just as Raleigh vanished through the door. 'Will be kept here at Her Majesty's pleasure. The longer her life, the longer his confinement.'

'So he doesn't share Essex's fate. Even though Thomas Grey who killed his page, and spent less than a month in the Fleet for it, was one of the judges.' Poley was relieved. There was a great weight of guilt on his soul already. The doomed men would die because of him. The others, ruined by punitive fines or locked away for lifetimes, were suffering because of him. Their families destitute because of him.

*

It seemed that Bacon, witch-like, could read his very thoughts. 'If there is any blame, it falls to the men who broke the most important laws in the lad – those of fealty owed by a subject to his monarch. The head of the Church, divinely appointed. Treason and blasphemy are kissing cousins. Essex and Southampton acknowledged their guilt at their trial, and have repeated the same since. The Queen has taken the path of leniency with Southampton because he is young, impressionable and too willing to follow Essex's commands. It is the men who understood the full import of what they were doing who will suffer the full weight of the law.

As Bacon said this, there was a stirring amongst the assembled observers. Poley and Bacon both swung round to look towards the church. The tall, black-clad figure of Robert Devereux emerged, surrounded by three spiritual advisors who were still fighting to save his soul now that his body was forfeit. 'Is he still Essex?' Poley asked Bacon. 'Or have all his titles and honours been removed. Like his right to take the tax on sweet wines was?'

'That is still for the Queen to decide,' said Bacon. 'And I have not heard that she has made the decision yet. There is the son, young Robert. If the titles are removed, the innocent child cannot succeed to them. And of course there is the guiltless Lady Frances in the mean time.' He paused, then returned to the list of lesser punishments arising from the Earl's actions. 'And then there were those who were simply banished. The Percy brothers may never come to court again, for instance, though Lord Henry Percy, the Earl of Northumberland, seems to have escaped all suspicion despite his Catholic leanings and his marriage to Lady Dorothy, Essex's elder sister. Lady Janet Percy has been ordered to accompany the brothers back to their estates in the North. There is nothing left to hold her here, according to Master Secretary and she remains a possible risk to the Queen's safety. It is highly unlikely that we will ever see her again.'

The wind backed. Poley's face filled with the dust and stable-smell of the rushes and the straw that had been laid on the top of the scaffold. His eyes filled and he was forced to wipe the tears away with one hand. 'It is a tragic scene,' said Bacon understandingly. 'I am nearly unmanned myself.'

The pair of them fell silent as the four black-clad men walked slowly to the scaffold. As they approached the low wooden stage, the witnesses stirred once more and the square, muscular figure of the executioner stepped forward, his axe with its massive blade carried almost reverently across his breast. He mounted the straw-covered platform first, and stood by the block, waiting for his victim to arrive, head bowed. Bacon leaned towards Poley. 'It is Thomas Derrick,' he whispered, recognising the man despite his executioner's mask. 'Two executioners were detailed for the task in case one of them found he could not bring himself to do the deed.'

'I'm surprised Derrick agreed to it,' answered Poley. 'I

hear the Earl refused to let him hang when he was charged with rape and so he became an executioner instead.'

'That is so.' Bacon nodded. 'The life spared will take the life of the man who spared it. A situation fit for a tragedy by Sophocles.'

'Or one by Christopher Marlowe,' concluded Poley.

Essex stopped beside the block, spread his arms and called, 'God be merciful unto me the most wretched creature on the earth!' As Essex continued with his short speech, the intelligencer who had done so much to bring him to this place and time, wondered whether there was any truth in Bacon's supposition that his tears arose from emotion rather than from dust and chaff. Or from the news about Lady Janet, who he would never see again. A fact that seemed to claw at his heart with unexpected force. He shook his head, winced at the sharp pain, and looked up again as Essex declaimed 'The Lord grant Her Majesty a long and prosperous reign...' A hope that was at least pious and perhaps barbed. It caused a stir amongst the witnesses. 'I never meant any harm to Her Majesty,' the condemned man persisted, and once again repeated that his one objective, as a knight who was loyal to both his monarch and his religion, was to save the Queen from the machinations of men who were advising her badly, were the root cause of the destitution of the common people and who were in the pay of the Spanish government, planning to hand the country back to the Pope as long as they could retain their affluence, influence and power.

*

A dangerous proposition to air in public, thought Poley.

But, to be fair, it was too late to punish him further for it.

Essex knelt and silence fell, undermined perhaps by continuing mutters of shock and outrage from the witnesses. Particularly those, like Master Secretary Cecil, who were in receipt of Spanish pensions, he suspected. After a few moments, the Earl stood up again. He took off his black hat and handed it to the nearest of his spiritual companions. Then he paused, the cold wind stirring his long brown hair. He swung the black cloak off his broad shoulders and handed it to the same man. He paused again and began to unbutton his black coat, something he found challenging, Poley noted, because his fingers were trembling slightly.

'You need not fear, my son,' said one of the divines.

Essex smiled. 'I have faced death often enough on the battlefield not to fear it now,' he said. 'The Lord will give me strength now as he did then.' He slipped off the coat, revealing a long-sleeved black doublet. He paused again, then he turned to Thomas Derrick. The executioner sank onto one knee. 'I beg forgiveness, My Lord, for the act I am about to commit.'

'Of course I forgive you, Thomas,' said Essex gently. He reached down and placed his hands on the kneeling man's shoulders. 'You are the minister of the Queen's justice.'

Essex turned back and briskly unbuttoned his black doublet. One of his companions helped him pull it off and there was a gasp from the witnesses. Poley smiled and shook his head in admiration. Under the black doublet was a shirt of the brightest, blood-red scarlet.

Like a burning flame, Essex knelt before the block once

more and loudly began to pray. Poley looked around, finally meeting Bacon's gaze. They both shook their heads in something only a little less than wonder at the Earl's final performance. 'Lead us not into temptation but deliver us from evil,' the Earl concluded. But then he repeated, 'Lead us not into temptation but deliver us from evil. Amen.'

He turned towards the block but one of the three priests called, 'My Lord, you must also forgive your enemies.'

'Ah, yes,' said Essex. 'My enemies.' Still on his knees he looked around the assembled witnesses; probably just a wall of pallid eyes and noses belonging to anonymous figures heavily cloaked and hatted to him. Therefore his gaze finally settled on the two enemies whose faces he could see clearly: Francis Bacon and Robert Poley. 'Let the Lord forgive my sins as I forgive every man who has trespassed against me,' he said. It seemed to Poley that he looked long and hard at Bacon and himself. Almost as though he was excluding them from the prayer.

Essex turned to Thomas Derrick, still on his knees. 'I wish to die reciting the fifty-first psalm,' he said. 'When I reach the line which says *cleanse me from my sin*, I will spread my arms as a signal for you to strike.' He spread his arms to illustrate what he meant. And looked to Poley, like a man hanging on a cross. Probably just as he had intended.

'Oh God, I prostrate myself before your deserved punishment,' he said. And did so.

The block was a solid piece of wood little more than a foot in height. It was hollowed on one side, the indentation designed to accommodate the condemned man's chin. The other side was flat and the victim's collar bones would be pressed hard-up against it. A ridge separating the square side and the hollow was designed to make the victim's neck stretch out, lie still and present a clear target for the headsman's axe. In order to place himself upon it, Essex had to lie face-down on the damp rushes. As he did so, and took a moment to settle himself as comfortably as possible moving both hair and beard out of the way, another minor squall brought a gusty, drizzle-laden wind blowing across the green. A flock of black ravens lifted off from their perches on the battlements, and hovered screaming, as though Master Secretary Cecil and his companions had somehow taken wing.

'Have mercy upon me oh God,' called Essex, his voice ringing. 'According to thy loving kindness, according to the multitude of thy compassions, put away my iniquities. Wash me thoroughly from my iniquity and cleanse me from my sin. *Executioner strike home*!' He spread his arms, fingers grasping the straw as though he could grip the earth and somehow hold himself to it. 'For I know my iniquities…'

Thomas Derrick had raised the axe on Essex's signal and now he brought it down with all his might. He was a strong man, capable of exerting great force. He was well practised. He had chosen to do this himself in order to see it done right. He had chosen the heaviest-looking headsman's axe Poley had ever seen and honed it to the greatest sharpness its edge could hold. It thudded unerringly onto Essex's neck, cutting into skin and muscle; burying itself in the wood on the condemned man's left. It crushed the bones in the Earl's neck, clearly severing the spinal cord, and the raised edge of the block standing between chin and collarbones, crushed his windpipe. There was a brittle *crunch*; to Poley's ear, the sound of a hasty footfall on a gravel path. The red-clad body convulsed. The head hung at a strange angle and Poly knew the man was dead. Derrick jerked the great blade free of the scarred wood. The axe rose and fell again. This time it cut through almost everything. Blood flowed copiously, but did not spurt. The heart had stopped at that first unerring blow – there was nothing to pump it. The third blow finished the grisly task, severing the few last threads of muscle, sinew and skin. Derrick stooped, picked up the head by the hair and held it high.

'Behold the head of a traitor!' he shouted.

Poley was no longer sure he believed that.

*

'I never thought he'd do it,' said Nick Skeres. 'The mob nearly killed him after he took off Essex's head. He was lucky to get away in *one* piece. Now he's going to oversee Meyrick and Cuffe cut into *four* pieces each. Five counting their heads. Even the Fates must be laughing at that.'

'Essex's beheading was three weeks ago,' said Poley absently. 'Memories hereabouts can be surprisingly short.' He looked around. The royal hunting ground of Hyde Park contained one side of the excited crowd because it was bounded by a strong fence. The cross roads and the Ty Burn stream seemed to contain the rest, though Tyburn Road itself was packed as far as the eye could see. There were men and women hawking winter apples, Spanish oranges, and roasted chestnuts. The smoke from the chestnut sellers' stoves mixed unsettlingly with the smoke from the executioner's brazier which stood beneath the gibbet. Beside the blazing iron basket stood a great cauldron of boiling water kept bubbling by a fire beneath it. Beside both stood a sizeable table at one end of which the executioner had arranged all the tools he was going to need. These looked more like those a butcher would want, rather than what an executioner might require. Hooked knives, straight knives, saws and cleavers. But there were pokers and tongs there as well, needed to keep the brazier bright.

The three-legged gibbet of the Tyburn Mare stood at the centre of everything. Thomas Derrick and his helpers were up on long ladders at the moment – except for the burly lads guarding their table full of equipment. The executioner and his men were stringing the ropes they planned to use on the two condemned men who were being drawn here on sledges. Poley reckoned their journey from Newgate of nearly three miles sway would already have started. Slow going through packed streets full of people out to see the grim show.

The words of the sentence still rang in Poley's memory because that sentence had so nearly been his: 'You will be drawn on a hurdle to the place of execution where you shall be hanged by the neck and being alive brought down, your privy members shall be cut off and your bowels taken out and burned before you, your head severed from your body and your body divided into four quarters to be disposed of at the Queen's pleasure.' He knew every detail of the reality those words described. Why he was waiting here to see the terrible sentence carried out on poor Henry Cuffe was something he could not quite fathom. Was it the same obscure motivation which had driven him to attend Anthony Babbington's death fifteen years ago?

'That's good,' enthused Skeres, cutting into Poley's dark thoughts. 'They're greasing the channels that the ropes will sit in. A nice smooth pull. That's what we want. No fatal accidents to spoil the show, eh, friend Poley?'

Poley grunted by way of reply. His mind was a whirl of conflicting emotions. Uppermost, if he was brutally honest with himself, was relief. That he was not making the pair of condemned men a trio after all. It had come so close...

'Lucky you made the Toad see reason,' Skeres continued. 'Though how you convinced him that joining the Earl's invasion of London was part of your mission I do not know. Your job was done when he led his army out of Essex House and you know it. He was always going to lose his head for doing that. But then you had to go and spoil a perfectly elegant mission by going out there with him.'

'To make assurance double sure,' said Poley automatically, still not really a part of the conversation.

'Which is why you took shots at Burghley, Leveson and Raleigh, no doubt...'

'I didn't. And you know it.'

'Well, the Toad seems to know it and that's really all that counts, isn't it? Mind you, I still think he punished you in other ways, just so you'd know he wasn't happy. Getting

Her Majesty to banish that Percy woman, your light o' love Lady Janet. That must have stung. Especially as Master Yeomans has closed his doors to you and Mistress Yeomans has closed her legs.'

Poley grunted again.

'Broken hearted Lady Janet was, by all accounts. Mind I only have her woman Agnes's word for it...'

'Leave it, Nick or we'll come to blows.' Poley's fist closed on the pommel of the Solingen steel rapier Sir Christopher Blount had purchased for him in the Steelyard. The disfigured gargoyle of a man was due to lose his head on the public execution block atop Tower Hill in five days' time. That too added to Poley's feelings of guilt and anger.

Skeres saw that he was serious and let the matter of Lady Janet drop. Instead, he began to shoulder through the crowd, pushing his way ruthlessly to the front row. Poley followed him, willy-nilly, as though he was his brutal colleague's shadow. Once at the front, they stopped. The guardians of the butchers' equipment were prowling in a circle, keeping everyone well back, slapping nasty-looking cudgels into broad, callused palms. Because of this, Poley found himself part of a large circle of onlookers at the centre of which stood the gibbet, the brazier, the cauldron and the table. There was nothing between him and the executioner's equipment other than a few yards of open ground, floored with cobble stones. Thomas Derrick and his other assistants were climbing down the ladders, careful to ensure the ropes did not slip out of the greased channels. Once on the ground, they began a simple but disturbing ritual. Derrick himself took hold of the first noose. One of his men pulled the far end of the rope, testing how freely the rope ran through its channel high on the cross-beam. Satisfied, Derrick extended his arms until the noose was as high above his head as he could reach. The assistant tied the rope to a solid peg on one of the uprights. Derrick pulled himself up off the ground and swung there kicking and jerking. The peg held firm. 'That'll do,' he called and lowered himself back onto the cobble-stones. Then he and the assistants went through the same ritual with the other rope.

'Why'd they need two ropes?' mused Skeres. 'They'll take them one at a time. One traitor at a time, one neck at a time, one rope would do for both.'

'Tradition,' said Poley.

'And profit,' said a new voice. 'Rope that's hanged a man is powerful magic. Sell it off for a pound a foot.' Poley turned to find John Wolfall standing at his left shoulder. 'A foot of rope from a drawing and quartering's worth a great deal more, I can tell you!'

'G'd day John,' said Skeres companionably. 'Here to collect the money you lent to Poley in the Fleet?'

'That's long settled, Nick,' said Wolfall. 'I'm just here to enjoy the show. Better than a bear-baiting, I'm told. Especially if you know the man who's about to meet his maker the hard way. And you know them both, eh, Poley?'

Poley was saved from making any reply by a sudden explosion of sound from the mouth of Tyburn Road. The hurdles had arrived and suddenly everyone nearby was shouting. Some were cheering, some were hurling insults.

Two horses emerged from Tyburn Road in single file. Each horse was pulling a hurdle like a simple wooden sledge on which lay a man. The men were trussed like capons ready for roasting. They each lay on their side, curled like new born babies, trying to protect themselves from the rain of spittle, night soil and rotten vegetables that was pouring relentlessly down upon them. But each of the condemned was escorted by a pair of guards to ensure that nothing was thrown at them which could knock them unconscious or kill them. They needed to be wide awake and in good repair for the terrible sentence to be carried out. Cuffe would have been able to explain the origins of the punishment and the relevance of each element as likely as not, thought Poley. Were it not being done to him.

When they reached the three legged mare of the gallows, the horses stopped, the condemned men were pulled to their feet and supported while the animals were led away. Lord Chief Justice Popham was far too important to mix with the common creatures here to see this grisly spectacle, so it was his representative who stepped forward and read once again the familiar words of the terrible sentence. At least it wasn't Francis Bacon, thought Poley with a kind of relief. But once that final formality was done, the actual procedure got under way.

Gelly Meyrick went first. The two men supporting him moved forward until he was standing beneath the gibbet. If the Welsh swashbuckler had any last words, he kept them to himself. Derrick placed the noose over his head, slowly and carefully, settling it round his neck and tightening it by hand. Meyrick did his best to stand tall and invest his death with the dignity that everyone now knew the Earl had achieved on Tower Green. But that was hard to achieve when you're covered in rotten vegetables, spit and shit, thought Poley grimly. At least he didn't whimper or beg. Once the noose was settled to his satisfaction, Derrick gestured to his assistants and they pulled the far end. The rope tightened, then continued to slide smoothly through the greased channel high above. Meyrick was pulled into the air. He began to wrestle with the rope binding his wrists behind him at once, but he stayed as still as possible for a moment or two. When his feet were level with Derrick's belt-buckle, the executioner's assistants tied it off. Meyrick hung there, slowly choking. After a few minutes he lost control and his body took over, fighting for the breath that the noose denied him. His legs and body began to convulse.

'Now that,' said Skeres, impressed, 'is what I *call* a Tyburn Jig.'

Meyrick's approach seemed to change then. Whatever shred of self-control he still possessed went into an increasingly frantic attempt to end it all by breaking his own neck. But he simply couldn't summon the weight or force to achieve his desperate objective. Five minutes passed. Then ten. Fifteen. The struggles grew weaker as consciousness began to slip away. Judging his moment with expert care, Derrick gestured to his helpers. Meyrick was lowered until his toes were mere inches above the cobbles. Derrick turned, reached for a knife with a viciously hooked blade, turned back. He reached for Meyrick's cod-piece and pulled it aside. Poley closed his eyes.

The crowd roared. The sound seemed to Poley to be a strange mixture of horror and lust. Meyrick almost achieved speech after all – a high, shrill scream. There was a loud hiss from the brazier and an errant breeze brought the stench of burning flesh. Poley opened his eyes for a moment. Meyrick's thighs were covered with blood, which was pumping out of him with surprising rapidity. Derrick swiftly pulled the hanging man's shirt front wide. The tip of the curved knife went into his chest at the lower point of his breast bone and sliced swiftly downwards. Meyrick's final word was an animal bellow compounded of agony and horror. The sides of the huge wound gaped. Derrick reached in and helped Meyrick's intestines out, drawing him like a goose being prepared for the oven. Rope after rope of intestine tumbled free. Derrick did his best to control it all but some of it ended up on the ground. As the serpentine cascade slowed, Derrick gave a few more deft cuts and, with the help of an assistant, the intestines were free to join Meyrick's genitals on the fire.

Derrick swung back, like an actor animated by the applause of his audience. He pushed his hand through the massive gape in Meyrick's belly and up into his chest. He tore something out. Held it high.

'His heart!' said Skeres, simply awed. 'I've never seen the like!'

'And still beating!' added Wolfall. 'I swear it was still beating. But not for long, eh?'

The heart went onto the brazier with the rest, then Derrick was turning, gesturing. The corpse was lowered and Derrick guided it onto the clear section of the table, face down. He took the largest cleaver and hacked the head off with half a dozen brutal blows. He did not hold it up, and some of the crowd booed as he tossed it into the cauldron of boiling water while the bloodied noose swung free. As Meyrick's head bobbed and seethed there, the executioner's assistants tore off Meyrick's clothes and spread the body, chest down. The cleaver chopped into the white flesh, cutting a line across the top of the hips until the torso and the legs could be pulled apart. Then another line was chopped up between the buttocks until the legs were free of each other. As the assistants added these to the cauldron, Derrick chopped the torso in half, following the hollow of the spine. The arm sections with the ribs still attached joined all the rest in the cauldron, boiling to preserve them for display at the Queen's direction. The head would likely be dipped in tar and spiked at the Southwark end of London Bridge alongside all the others there.

'That was as neatly done as I have ever seen it!' said Skeres approvingly.

'And your friend's next, eh Poley?' said Wolfall.

Even as Wolfall said this, Cuffe was brought forward and positioned beneath the second noose. His face was white. His eyes were tight shut but tears of terror still glistened on his cheeks. Like Meyrick, he was too wise to attempt any final words and too proud to whimper or beg. Poley was glad about that at least. Even so, the assistants still held his arms, keeping him erect despite his shaking legs. Derrick settled the noose around his neck and tightened it. He gestured to his assistants at the far end of the rope and it tautened, holding Cuffe upright as the men holding his arms released them and stepped back. The rope stretched a little but even so, Cuffe was pulled slowly up into the air. When his boots were level with Derrick's belt buckle, the executioner made a gesture and the rope was secured to the peg in the upright.

Cuffe's poor attempt at dignity failed then. Where Meyrick had achieved several minutes of control, Cuffe went straight into the Tyburn Jig. His bound arms flapped like clipped wings behind him, as though he was in the strappado Meyrick had arranged for Poley all that time ago. His legs pumped as though he could find a stairway in the air and leap up it to safely. Even though he was choking, he achieved a kind of animal bellow compounded of rage, terror and despair.

The sound called to Poley in a way he had never dreamed anything could. Before he knew it, he was in motion. He ran wildly into the circle, taking Derrick's assistants by surprise. He shouldered past the nearest before he could even raise his club. Then he was pounding across the clear circle, his boots skidding on the cobbles. Derrick looked up as Poley approached the gory table with its terrible, blood-covered instruments. There was an instant in which the executioner could have stopped the intelligencer, but he hesitated, recognising him, no doubt, from Essex's execution, as a man he had seen standing between Sir Walter Raleigh and Sir Francis Bacon. Likely to be a man of consequence, therefore. In that instant of hesitation, Poley was round the end of the table, skidding in the lake of blood that soiled the ground beneath the gibbet.

'Stop him,' bellowed Derrick.

His assistants jerked out of the shock that had held them like statues and began to run forward. But they were too late. Poley leaped up with all the power at his command. His shoulder smashed into Cuffe's convulsing thigh. His face slammed into his hip, bruising and skinning his cheekbone. He bit his tongue and tasted blood. His arms reached up and closed around Cuffe's waist. The pair of bodies swung like a pendulum, both sets of boots well clear of the ground. And Poley pulled downwards. The combination of weight, power and desperation did the trick. There was the sound of a wet branch breaking. Poley felt himself fall by several inches as the broken neck parted and stretched. Cuffe stopped dancing.

Poley let go and dropped to the ground. His forward motion hardly slowed. He pounded out from beneath the gallows and hurled toward the crowd on the opposite side to where he, Skeres and Wolfall had been standing. Something about his actions or the desperate look of him made the bloodthirsty audience fall back and he plunged into the middle of them, forcing his way through. But this was not something that could go on for long. At last he staggered to a stop, looking around, dazed. Confused. Like a man just that second stepped ashore in new-discovered America finding nothing familiar in front of him.

Poley stood there, surrounded, the centre of a circle walled with angry people: a bull in the baiting pit. He stared at them, helplessly, every emotion drained out of him: joy, despair, terror, rage. It was as though he was hollow; in a strange way, like Gelly Meyrick after Derrick disembowelled him. Well, he thought dully, at least he had saved poor Cuffe from that.

Someone shouted something. A cobble stone flew out of the crowd and smashed into his forehead, in the centre of the place the faceless Christopher Blount's skull had knocked him unconscious at Lud Gate. He went down like a stunned ox. More missiles came but he hardly registered them, curled up just as Meyrick and Cuffe being drawn here on the hurdles to die had done. Then a pair of boots arrived to stand astride his head, one boot each side.

The last thing he heard before the darkness came was Nick Skeres saying, 'Mother of Christ, Poley, how in God's name are we going to get you out of this in one piece?'

AFTERWARD

The only characters in this story who are not historical figures are Lady Janet Percy, Agnes, her maid, and the Fitzherbert family. Everyone named in the Essex faction is part of the historical record and acted in the manner described, as did the various members of the Council, Sir Thomas Grey, the Bacon Brothers, Cecil and Raleigh. Sir John Heyden and Sir Richard Mansell/Robert Mansfield (authorities differ) had the duel as described but they had it just outside Norwich and Sir John's hand is in the Norfolk Museum. Poley, Skeres, Frizer and Wolfall not only lived but also served as secret agents; however, making them witnesses to and/or participants in the Earl of Essex's downfall is where the fiction begins.

SOURCES & AUTHORITIES

The Reckoning Charles Nicholl

Elizabeth and Essex Steven Veerapen

Elizabeth and Essex Lytton Strachey

Robert Devereux, Earl of Essex Sidney Lee

Essex Tudor Rebel Tony Riches

Golden Lads Daphne DuMaurier

The Winding Stair Daphne DuMaurier

The A – Z of Elizabethan London Adrian Procter and Robert Taylor

Shakespeare's England R E Pritchard

Elizabeth's London Liza Picard

The Time Traveller's Guide to Elizabethan England Ian

Mortimer

The Elizabethan Underworld Gamini Salgado

Hung, Drawn and Quartered Jonathan J Moore

Virgin Queen Christopher Hibbert

The Reign of Elizabeth J B Black

Elizabeth I Anne Somerset

Elizabeth, A study in Power and Intellect Paul Johnson

The Elizabethan Secret Service Alan Haynes

Elizabeth's Spymaster Robert Hutchinson

The Thames Peter Ackroyd

Shakespeare The Biography Peter Ackroyd.

Several internet sites were consulted and may be of interest, primarily the SAT Conference 2019 which deals with the Essex uprising and which is available on You Tube.

I must also thank my wife Charmaine who is prime editrix on all my manuscripts, Dr Jonathan Botting for his advice on the medical aspects of beheading, Angela, Librarian at Castletown library on the Isle of Man, and Dr Steven Veerapen for his excellent book, his help and advice.

Peter Tonkin, Castletown and Tunbridge Wells, 2021